Becky ♡

FREE TO DREAM

TRACEY JERALD

Always
Believe in dreams
of love
xoxo
Tracey
Jerald

Book
Splash
2019

Free to Dream

ISBN: 978-1-7324461-0-6 (eBook)

ISBN: 978-1-7324461-1-3 (Paperback)

Editor: Trifecta Editing Services (https://www.trifectaedit.com/)

Copy Editing: Holly Malgeri - Holly's Red Hot Reviews (http://hollysredhotreviews.com)

Cover Design: Amy Queau – QDesign (https://www.qcoverdesign.com)

To my husband for believing in us enough to try, to wait,
and to show me love every day.
My heart.
My soul.
My beloved.

THE LEGEND OF AMARYLLIS

There are variations regarding the legend of how amaryllis flowers came to be. Generally, the tale is told like this:

Amaryllis, a shy nymph, fell deeply in love with Alteo, a shepherd with great strength and beauty, but her love was not returned. He was too obsessed with his gardens to pay much attention to her.

Amaryllis hoped to win Alteo over by giving him the one thing he wanted most, a flower so unique it had never existed in the world before. She sought advice from the oracle Delphi, and carefully followed his instructions. She dressed in white, and for thirty nights, appeared on Alteo's doorstep, piercing her heart with a golden arrow.

When Alteo finally opened his eyes to what was before him, he saw only a striking crimson flower that sprung from the blood of Amaryllis's heart.

It's not surprising the amaryllis has come to be the symbol of pride, determination, and radiant beauty. What's also not surprising is somehow, someway, we all bleed a little bit while we're falling in love.

PROLOGUE

CASSIDY

I am haunted by my dreams, particularly when the glory days of summer start to feed into the longer days of fall. As the sun comes up later each day, casting its shadows deeper across my bed, I feel imprisoned by nightmares that torture my psyche.

In my sleep, I have no sense of reality versus imagination. All of this occurs in the narrow void of time between sleep and awake, where all I see are my impressions of Heaven and Hell.

I often wonder if Morpheus hovers in the shadows of my bedroom in his long, black and white coat, fighting with his brothers Phobetor, Phantasos, and Ikelos over who gets to play pinball with my dreams on any given night.

Seeking to rid myself of my nightly trauma, I've read every book about control dreams. I've talked to doctors. I resolutely stay away from known triggers. I've documented my daily habits to such a degree and kept a regimented order over my life, I could tell you what I ate last year on this same exact day for breakfast.

I'd like to think I could exert some control over my damn dreams rather than letting them control me.

Control is apparently an illusion.

I was forced to give up control long ago.

Control over my life.

Control of my emotions.

Never again.

IN THE HOURS just before dawn, my head tosses restlessly on the pillow and my lips part, feeling dry.

I look at the door with no handles, just a keyhole.

No one can get in and I can't get out.

There's nowhere for me to go.

So I sit, day after day, in this tiny room.

After he had to kick in the door the last time, he removed the bathroom door as well, making the smell of the air bad all the time.

I pull my knees up to my chest in the corner.

The air is too hot. My skin sticks together where it touches, even between my fingers and toes. I wiggle them just to get the sweaty feeling away and let out a small breath.

I don't dare touch the air. I remember what happened the last time I did and my stomach churns.

He made me pay for it all right.

I look longingly at the faucet, missing the water. He said it was my fault. If I had just done a better job, we would have had enough money to pay for it.

I won't complain, I don't dare. He made it hurt so much worse the last time I did.

I rub my hand over my legs, noticing that they're more tender than usual. I pull up my shirt and find fresh bruises from last night. My little finger runs over the indentations, picking out the individual teeth marks.

Maybe he won't come back, the almost dead part of me whispers in my head. Maybe he's finally done.

Maybe you can go home.

Time passes. The heat is so unbearable, I'm panting. Like...what's that phrase? A bitch in heat? That's what I am now, right? What he made me?

My stomach rumbles. Food is a privilege, one I have to earn. It could be hours or days before I get anything that might resemble food. Maybe it won't have worms crawling in it if I'm really good. Though, if not, I have gotten used to them.

The shadows start to cross the floor. No! As much as I dislike the hopelessness I feel in the heat of the day, it's the wicked night I dread with everything I am.

Maybe the sun will burn through so hot, it will burn me to ash.

Maybe I can suffocate under the smell.

I'd rather die than face the night again.

If there's little hope in the day, there's no hope in the night.

None.

I don't know how I ended up here in this place called Jacks. I don't know if there are others. I don't know how to escape. I don't know how to die. I don't know... I don't know... I don't know...

When the night falls, I remember what I do know.

I do know how to fear. I do know how to cry. I do know pain.

I know how to scream.

My bloodcurdling scream wakes me from my dreams.

Breathing heavily, I pull my knees up to my chest and begin to rock, the motion instinctively comforting as I try to ignore the torrent of tears dripping down my face.

What did I do that was so wrong? Isn't it enough that I'll always be alone because no one will ever understand what happened to me?

My arms slide away from my knees and clutch around my neck as bile begins to churn in my stomach.

Is this my punishment for wanting to be "normal" and finding comfort in someone's arms? To not be alone anymore?

I start taking deep breaths, just as my therapist had taught me.

One...Two...Three...Four...Five...Six...Seven... Eight...

As the panic starts to recede, I reach for the water on my nightstand. My hand is shaking so bad, I'm afraid the water in the glass is going spill on my bed.

I'm marked by what happened to me forever.

I have no escape.

I throw my legs over the side of my bed and stand on shaky legs. Walking to the bathroom, I flip on the light and shuffle to the vanity to stare at myself in the mirror. The memories from my dream leave me wondering if I've truly been living since I survived the storm of my past.

1

CASSIDY

More days pass with night after night of lost sleep and more dreams.

Clutching my pillow to my chest, I watch from my bed as the midnight sky slowly lightens by indiscernible increments. A combination of purple and rose colors spread over the lake outside my bedroom window as I curl into myself for warmth and comfort.

Listening to Ray LaMontagne sing an old favorite of mine, I stare blankly at the pearlescent sky, knowing that there is nothing I can do to save myself from my thoughts.

Having no one, I always feel alone, even when I'm surrounded by people.

Rolling over, I turn on my bedside lamp and glance at the clock—it's only a few minutes before six. While it's not much earlier than I normally get up, Sundays are reserved for sleeping in. Since I don't sleep, the luxury of lounging around on a Sunday morning lacks any excitement for me.

In the sanctuary I've created here in my home, I sit up in bed, pulling my pillow tighter for a moment longer, giving myself time to push away those indulgent feelings I so rarely allow.

Swinging my legs over the side of the bed, I shiver in the early morning air as I step into my fleece-lined slippers. Rather than turn on the heat to ward off the chill inside my house—resulting from the crisp fall weather outside—I quickly grab my sweatshirt lying on the foot of my chaise and throw it on before heading downstairs to make coffee.

As I make my way down the stairs, I pass family photos I'd carefully arranged on the stairwell walls. Each one is in black and white, meticulously framed. The earliest photo dates as far back to the day that Em and I won our rights to be declared legally emancipated minors. My eyes land on the photo that was taken the day Ali, Corinna, and Holly all graduated from their schools, and then to the one of us closing on the formerly dilapidated mansion on Main Street which, for a long time, served as not only our office, but our home.

Phillip, Emily, Alison, Corinna, Holly, and I aren't what you would call a conventional family. We adopted one another as we found each other, gradually becoming a cohesive unit. You'd never know that it all started when a thirteen-year-old boy ran into a room one night and rescued a nine-year-old girl from the kind of torture people keep hidden from their children in polite households. Until we found each other and believed that the promises we made to one another were steadfast and true, none of us believed in the concept of anything.

Not pride, not beauty, and sure as hell not love.

Which is what makes the fact that the six of us own and operate Amaryllis Events, a wildly successful wedding and event service in New England, astounding.

Every single one of my family members are brilliant. From Phil and the way seasonal hues are embraced in his floral arrangements, to Em's magical skills in finding just the right design for every bride and groom. Corinna's sinfully decadent cakes, Holly's stunning memories captured on film, and Ali's deft capability to keep all of us out of every possible legal and financial mishap there could be, my pride in my family knows no bounds, even when I want to strangle them for being dramatic and overbearing. Even when I'm being driven to the edge of insanity because every one of them are lunatics in their own right. Their goal in life is to break me of my obsessive habit of organizing everything. Yet nobody minds when we're on schedule for the weddings we plan and coordinate. My OCD isn't going to change anytime soon.

I plop my chin in my hand and look at the list I left on the counter last night of things I have to complete today. Working out is the first item on the list. I figure that joyous task can wait until the sun starts to rise over the Berkshire Mountains. Items like reviewing my work calendar and grocery shopping, as well as laundry, are also listed. The final reminder for today is our family dinner.

I thump my head on the counter. While I normally love spending time with my brother Phillip, his husband Jason, and my sisters, they're observant as hell. Phillip will take one look at me and determine that I've had less than six hours of sleep. He will undoubtedly ask about it, and that will spark my entire family into the fray.

It's not the questions I mind. To be honest, I'm just weary of answering them again. The nightmares are always more frequent this time of the year. Probably because it was around this time, almost twenty years ago, that Phillip picked me up and saved me from a life worse than death.

I have no memory of my life before Phillip found me in that rancid little room. I had been bound and beaten, and so defeated. My wrists and legs were so bruised from the tape, from trying to pull away. My body was shaking from the repeated sodomy I'd endured that particular night and from the energy I expelled kicking the thin wall, praying for a miracle. Phillip picked me up gently and carried me away, having to soothe me like I was a wild animal. Twenty years later, there's a part of me that still can't wrap my mind around why he did what he did. I'll just forever be grateful he did.

We're free, but we weren't supposed to be. No one would have believed that six individuals, children at best, surviving together under the circumstances would be safe. It's a good thing we weren't a bet. We never would have made the odds board.

Mentally berating myself for thinking of the past, I decide it's time to stop reminiscing and check off another item on my list for today, starting with the laundry.

Rinsing out my coffee cup, I place it in the dishwasher before going upstairs. After starting a new load of laundry, I change into my running gear and head back to the kitchen.

Before I step outside of my home, I check the towels with a red pen.

HOURS LATER, I've long since cooled off. I'm inside my office in leggings and a sweatshirt. After I returned from my torturous three-mile run and cleaning up, I quickly made my way into our office located in a converted mansion off Main Street in Collyer.

Collyer, Connecticut, population 21,522, is the sleepy little town the six of us had been looking for our entire lives. In our wildest dreams, as kids trying to survive, we never could have imagined the beauty of this town. Collyer is close enough to New York City when we need some excitement, or to celebrate some milestone in our lives. Gorgeous oak-lined streets boast several hundred-year-old trees whose colors are already turning a gorgeous bouquet of gold, red, and orange to celebrate the coming of fall.

After Phil—at age twenty, Em and I at age eighteen—finally helped Ali, Corinna, and Holly become emancipated, we started talking about where we would move to get out of the South. As someone who used to help him study to get his GED, I think it was the longest amount of time Phil had ever spent in a library before or since. Since we lived on such low overhead and with all of us working (including Ali, Corinna, and Holly, per their emancipation requirements), we had amassed a fairly substantial amount of money to put down on the start of our dream.

Now, sitting at my desk with my planners in front of me and my iPhone synchronizing with my Outlook calendar, I take a moment to look out my window, admiring the view I rarely get a moment to enjoy.

I admit it, I'm freakishly organized. It also makes me feel in control knowing company meetings are marked in blue, unmovable events are marked in pink, phone calls in green, and family events in purple. I find my spirit calms when my lists have items marked off and are not rolled over to the next day. I like knowing events are completed, on time, and under budget. My Erin Condren planner and iPhone calendar play off each other, making me highly effective. Adding an "rsvpBOOK" entry makes me one happy little Chief Executive Officer for our company. I lead my siblings, whose talents are many, though they lack the organization gene that is directly related to how our business flourishes.

Take Phillip for instance. I mean, what's so hard about using the family calendar feature on our iPhones to indicate when Jason's parents will arrive in town for your wedding so we can have the guest room at the farm ready for them? Leaving a sticky note under the windshield of my car during a summer storm so it's blurred to resemble a Rorschach test is not an effective way of communicating important information. Hello? We're a wedding planning service! Call and leave a message on our work line! He's often an absent-minded artist, but for all that is holy, there are days I'm amazed our business has stayed afloat.

Taking a final look at my planner and phone to make sure the calendar events are synchronized, I quickly scan back and forth, paging through the week before, letting out a slow, relieved breath. The scheduling is in place with enough time for contingencies.

Our family business has quite a few events taking place this week. Running a business the size of Amaryllis Events takes not only long hours, hard work, and talent, but quite a lot of planning and organization. Hence, why I'm CEO.

I suddenly realize it's after ten and I haven't eaten. I grab a protein bar, and as I munch my way through it, I jump in surprise when my office phone rings. I wait for the second ring before answering.

"Amaryllis Events, this is Cassidy Freeman. How can I help you?" I tuck the phone against my chin as I make my way to the other side of my desk.

"Yes. You can stop showing up for work when we have no events planned and making us look like complete assholes," my sister Emily complains.

Out of all my sisters, Em, who is my complete opposite physically, is most like me from a comedic standpoint. Laughing, I sit down in my desk chair for a quick bitch session. I have plenty of time. "I'm not the only one here, Em," I say mildly. "Phil is here as well."

"That's because Phil's husband gets up at the ass crack of dawn to leave for work in the city," Emily smarts back. "Phil just wants to blow out of work early some night this week, I'll bet." We both crack up, knowing Em speaks nothing but the truth about our brother.

"Seriously, Cass, you know if it wasn't for Jason, Phil's ass would still be gracing his gazillion thread count sheets. He would be bitching and moaning for one of his precious little sisters to bring him his coffee made to his liking. And like the little worshiping morons we are, we know one of us would succumb to his dumbass demands."

My lips tip up before I laugh. "Em, I've said it before and I'll say it again—thank God he married Jason."

"Seriously, Cass, why are you at work on your day off, *again*?" Em questions, sounding concerned. "Is something bothering you? Is it the dreams? Are they back again?"

"No," I lie. "Nothing is wrong. Some of us just like things done in an orderly fashion without rushing around on a Monday or meeting clients unprepared."

"One time, Cass. It was one time. And you'll never let me forget it." Em's annoyance with me is clear.

"Would you let me if I walked into a meeting and didn't know the name of the client, sister dear?" I kick back and get comfortable in my chair.

"Fuck no." And she wouldn't.

Em loves to provoke me. She would no sooner give up the chance to taunt me than I would her. It's just our way. After close to twenty years of knowing each other and living together, I consider it part of our sisterly privilege.

"Okay, fine. Keep being a bitch about something that happened eons ago," Em huffs. But she's in no way offended.

"Always will."

There's a pregnant pause before Em continues. "Cassidy? I just want you to know I—we—are all here. We always have been."

I look at the framed photo of my family on the wall. It's a new photo, with Jason included. He joined our family after he married Phil over the summer.

I murmur quietly into the phone, "Not always, Em. But always when it counted. I know that. I'll see you tonight?" Hopefully I can pull off this charade a little longer—aided by a lot of eye makeup to camouflage the evidence of not sleeping. And maybe a nap.

"Actually, that's why I'm calling. Phil just called and dinner's off tonight. He has to meet Jason in the city. Do you want to go shopping with me instead?"

Phil is in the building. Why didn't he tell me this himself?

I'm not one to look a gift horse in the mouth when it comes to shopping, so I relent. "Let me get home and change." I run my hand down my leggings and think maybe I need more time to compose myself from last night's nocturnal events.

"No worries. Just call me when you're ready. Love you."

"Love you too."

Checking our work schedule once more to make sure everything is set for Monday, I make my way out of my office. I know I'll be walking around the mall for hours with Em.

As I'm pulling up my gravel driveway a few minutes later, I vaguely wonder why I didn't see Phil's car when I left the office.

It's about 8:30 when my phone rings. I'm exhausted and running on fumes.

I'm sorting the bags filled with things Em and I purchased at the Danbury Fair Mall. It might be September, but most of mine are for Christmas, so I've pulled storage bins from my walk-in attic to store them. Yes, I'm one of those people. I always have most of my Christmas shopping done by Halloween. Sue me.

Carefully placing the dangling silver and amethyst stars for Alison aside, my phone display lights up with a call—it's Phil.

"You lived up to your nickname of the human whirlpool today, brother. Just needed to get a dose of spinning all our worlds out of order? You and I were both at the office, and even cancelling dinner, you still managed to stir us all into a tither talking about you. Don't worry though, it was the delicate cycle," I tease, reaching for another shopping bag. There's silence on the other end of the line. "Phil? Honey? Are you okay? Is Jason okay?"

"Sorry, Cass, you cut out there for a moment." Phil's tone is light-hearted, but even over the phone I can tell something is off with him.

"Everything all right, Phillip? It's not like you to schedule dinner and bail out," I probe gently.

"It's—" He sighs into the phone. "Fine for now. Don't worry about it." There's static on the line, and I realize he's muffling the phone with his hand to say something to Jason. I'm barely paying attention until I hear my name. "You're in the office at your normal time tomorrow, right?"

Um, when am I not? Deciding Phil doesn't need my dry wit right now, I reply, "Yes."

Still distracted, he asks, "Do you have your planner in front of you? I need you to squeeze a new appointment in tomorrow."

I laugh at this point. Whatever it is on Phil's mind has him completely rattled. After all the years we've lived together, he should know me better. I typically have my schedule memorized by Sunday evenings for the entire week.

I want to hear what he's proposing before I accept and add a new meeting to our schedule. I have a clear conscience as I lie, prompting him to continue. "Okay, I have it. What do you need?"

"Do you have time in the morning, or would you have to bump a client?" He sounds nervous.

"My morning is free, Phillip. I didn't have to look at our schedule, or lack thereof, for tomorrow morning to tell you that."

"Can you put down an appointment with a potential new client for 8:45? His name is Caleb Lockwood. Later, you'll be meeting with his brother."

"Lockwood. Why does that name sound so familiar?" I muse out loud.

Phil's deep voice has a snarky edge. "Oh, I don't know. Maybe because their name is on the side of almost every shipping container you see. At least that's what one of the brothers does. And both are in the society pages. You know, the Greenwich Lockwoods."

I let out a low whistle. No wonder Phil is nervous. The Lockwood family isn't just a name, it's *the* name in Connecticut society. If they are looking for our assistance with any event—big or small—this would be a huge account.

My stomach starts churning slightly.

"Of course. How much time should I block?"

"I would reserve until lunch. I'll try to explain more in the morning." He pauses. "I have to go, but you're the face of this company, Cass. There's no one we trust to do this more than you."

On those parting words, and without saying goodbye (typical Phil), he hangs up the phone. I remain standing beside my bed, absorbing the bomb he'd just dropped. The Lockwoods. They would want and receive VIP treatment, of course. Was the kitchen stocked? I shoot a quick message to our cleaning service to ensure it was restocked last Friday. One ping later and I have confirmation.

After programming the appointment in my calendar with a reminder set for 7:30 tomorrow morning, I put my phone down.

The Lockwoods. I wonder what type of event they're throwing. A fundraiser? A garden party? With a family of their stature, the possibilities are endless. My mind starts wandering into varying scenarios, cost estimates, and vendors. I yawn sleepily.

Nothing to do now but finish putting away these bins and mentally run through one of a hundred checklists and contingencies.

And try not to think about how agitated Phil seemed so I can get some sleep tonight.

2

CALEB

My brother is damned lucky I love him as much as I do. Otherwise, I might toss his newly engaged ass off the rooftop deck where we're sitting.

The cool snap of fall came quickly, so the deck opposite ours is empty. It's like these people who live year after year in this climate don't appreciate the fact that this will be one of the last times they'll have to use their magnificent spaces before winter comes, bringing snow and frigid temperatures.

The streets of Tribeca are alive below us, but we're high enough up that the noise and bustling crowd doesn't feel like it's closing in. I still want to pitch my baby brother over the safety rail, but I have to give him credit. This condo he scored for us in the historic Powell Building is amazing. City living wasn't what I'd expected when I came home from years overseas. But Ryan made the argument with both of us working in New York, putting in insane hours, it made sense to have a place to crash while we were here. At least we'd be able to catch more than just a few hours of sleep a night.

It's been more home here than the mausoleum we had grown up in. I'm going to miss it here. When he gets married in a few months, I'll be moving out.

It was easy to make the decision to move to New York once I knew Ryan didn't intend on making the family home he inherited his home base. I had no real emotional ties to the place since my father died before I joined the Army, and Ryan moved out shortly thereafter. Lord knows, my mother is as frigid as the glacier that sank the Titanic. How Ryan could bear to let her live there is a whole different matter.

I halfheartedly scowl into a face that's almost an angelic, younger version of my own. Christ, did I ever look that innocent? Maybe back in the early days of college, which is about how old Ryan looks this morning in his T-shirt and lounge pants. With our matching dark hair and eyes, our family resemblance is striking.

A woman I once slept with said she'd planned to seduce Ry into her bed because at least he had a heart. As I rolled out of her bed and pulled my pants back on, I told her she was welcome to give it a try, but that my brother didn't go for my seconds. He never had. I smirk at the memory.

The irony there is that two weeks ago, Ryan ecstatically got engaged to Jared.

Picking up the coffee in front of me, I take a large drink. "So, let me get this straight. Because of media problems in the past with large events, you want me to go to the office, on a Sunday no less, to do a background check on a wedding planning firm you and Jared are thinking of dropping a shit ton of money on for your wedding? You do realize that's five minutes of my time and way below what I actually do, right?"

Ry smiles at me. "I didn't think it would be such a big deal. I actually figured you could do it from here."

Normally, he'd be right. But the investigations my firm runs and the systems we access are either cleared at levels I can't discuss or not always legally obtained. I refuse, for both legal and security reasons, to use our home computers for work. "It's in the shop." I wait for his laughter because he knows I feel helpless without my laptop.

"Why do you have to have it today?" I argue as I stretch out my legs to get comfortable. I had planned to go to the gym to work out.

When I was in the Army, following traditions that could be traced back to the Revolutionary War, I worked out daily. I'd tried to maintain the habit, but I manage instead with four hard workouts a week.

"Because I'm meeting with one of the owners over dinner tonight." He reclines in his chair, doing some relaxing of his own. He knows I would do anything for him, including this.

"Way to wait until the last minute, brother," I grumble, kissing my long workout goodbye.

Sitting up, I start to stand when Ry motions me back down. "Relax. This shouldn't take you all afternoon. I wanted to talk with you about the wedding anyway."

"Uh, Ry. You realize you should be talking with Jared, right? I mean, I know I have pretty decent taste, but it's his wedding too," I tease.

He rolls his eyes at me and mutters "asshole" under his breath before taking another drink of coffee. Setting down his mug, he looks me in the eyes. "Stand up for me, Caleb. Be my best man." He smiles and my mind goes blank. I'm unable to answer him. "You're already the best man I know. But stand with me when I marry the man I plan to be with for the rest of my life." His complete trust and faith in me is overwhelming.

I swallow hard. Jesus. This is like a sniper attack—one shot and I'm down.

Rolling myself into a standing position, I walk around the table and pull my brother to his feet. Since he had his mug of coffee in his hands, it predictably went sloshing everywhere. As he's sputtering about the mess, pulling his wet T-shirt away from his stomach, I nab him for a one-armed hug. "Nothing would make me prouder." My voice is barely a whisper because I can't swallow over the knot lodged in my throat. "I love you, Ry. And I love Jared for you."

"Thanks, Caleb." Looking into eyes that mirror my own, there's something there. I've seen it for the last few years—a secret he can't or won't share. I know he's hiding something because the same look reflects back in the mirror every morning when I shave.

My thoughts and memories are wrapped up in government clearances that can never be shared.

"And as my first act as best man, I will forsake my workout," I joke to lighten the mood. "I'll go to the office on a sacred day off to research this firm you want to hire."

Ry laughs. "Right. Like if your laptop was working, you wouldn't be on it today."

Busted.

Ignoring the comment, I ask, "What's the name of the firm?" Now, I'm actually curious. I knew Ry had planned on proposing to Jared for some time, so I figured he'd been giving this some thought. Our family is wealthy and well-known, but I could not imagine a wedding planning firm requiring a deep level background check unless it was on an employee.

"An event planning company in Collyer, Connecticut. Amaryllis Events," Jared, Ry's fiancé, says from behind me as he makes his way over to Ry. The two of them share a kiss, murmuring their good mornings to each other while I lose myself in thought.

Amaryllis Events. It conjures up ideas of elegant tea cups with pinkies out, not the psychological warfare combined with lion taming required for events like this wedding is going to need...wait. Did he say Connecticut?

"Connecticut? Fucking Connecticut? Are you serious? You're going to have the wedding there?"

Ry turns from his fiancé to face me with steel and determination in his eyes. And if I'm reading my brother right, vengeance. "I refuse to let her keep me from doing what I want. And if Mommy Dearest doesn't like it, she can get her ass the fuck off my property. Despite the fact I've never wanted to live there, I do own and pay to upkeep the place."

"And you're hiring a company called Amaryllis Events? You should be hiring armed guards, Ry," I fire back.

He sits back in his chair, where Jared wraps his arm around his shoulders. "Everything I've heard about this company tells me this is the way to go. The CEO and event planner apparently could negotiate a truce in the Holy Lands and make them think it was their idea."

Humored by his response, I ask, "How'd you hear about them?"

"Remember Austin's wedding? Right after his dad married his personal admin?"

Austin is one of our friends from high school. I nod as a snort escapes me. "You're kidding. They organized his wedding?"

I remember how stressed Austin had been about that wedding. There was talk of sex tapes being released to the media by Austin's vengeful mother. Board members threatened to vote his father out as chairman of their company, and the press circled like vultures. About a month before the wedding, it was like someone had given Austin a Xanax salt lick. "Hell, why do you need the background investigation? Hire them. That wedding was a catastrophe waiting to happen and you would never have known it." Literally, I attended with multiple pairs of handcuffs, thinking I might need them to keep the peace. But it went as smooth as honey.

Ry and Jared exchange a look.

"Wait, *was* someone drugged?" I demand.

Jared laughs, while Ry says, "Nothing like that. I just happen to have an indirect connection to the owners. Before we sink twenty-five percent of the cost of the wedding with the potential for acrimony, I'd like to know more about the business."

Twenty-five percent? I'm thinking even I don't charge my clients enough when the rest of his sentence penetrates. "What acrimony?" My eyes narrow on my brother, trying to siphon the things out of him that he's not telling me.

"I'll let you know after tonight's dinner, if there's one at all," Ry waves off my concern. "So, could you run the background check?"

I sit for a moment and think it over. "Yes. I'll head downtown in a while. It shouldn't take too long. What time is your dinner?"

"It's at five."

"I'll call you if it's a no-go."

～

I MANAGE to get in a run and a boxing workout before hitting the showers to head into the office.

Standing beneath the warm spray, I brace my thick legs apart as the suds slide down my body, over my abs, and around my cock. Letting out a low hum at the sensation, I realize it's been way too long since I've gotten laid. To be honest, a woman didn't seem worth the effort when I could rub one out a hell of a lot quicker.

To me, women came with one of three problems—they want my money, my body, or my face, and pretty much in that order. I need one who not only has her own success, but is a challenge. Beautiful, but doesn't live or die by the need to look into every reflective surface she passes. A woman who wants to be held as much as she wants to be fucked.

In other words, I want a fucking unicorn.

Slipping on a pair of well-worn Levi's, a thin cashmere sweater over a T-shirt, and my steel-toe boots, I quickly toss my dopp kit into my gym locker. Shrugging on my leather jacket, I walk the mile-and-a-half to my office near Rockefeller Center.

Sundays in New York are unlike any other day of the week. If you want to know why a person would live in the city, explore it on a Sunday. Sure, there are tourists. I mean, it's New York, when are there not? But there are also random people finding what little green space there is for a nap, lines for people waiting to eat brunch wrapping around a city block, and random street fairs fucking up traffic. I stop at one of the street fair booths and order a Gyro to eat as I make my way toward Rockefeller Center.

Thirty minutes later, I'm behind my desk at Hudson Investigations, having tossed my assistant a quick wave on my way in. I shake my head as I pass. Time and again, I let my assistant know Sundays are not required as part of the job. I've given up trying and just caution now against burning out.

When I left the Army, I knew I could live the rest of my life on my inheritance, but that's not my style. I knew I would be bored within two-point-five seconds if all I was doing was playing golf. I knew I would need something in my life to give me a challenge. I wasn't like the pampered society darlings my mother kept tossing at me, who wanted to fuck and produce Lockwood heirs. Seriously, the idea of settling for one of those dumb bimbos bored me. If I had to go through life as a bachelor, buying lube so I didn't chafe while taking care of business, I didn't care. I refuse to settle.

Instead of what would amount to buying a relationship, I put my time, effort, and soul into the investigative agency I bought out three years ago. The former owner, Laskey, had a solid business, but he was ready to retire. To me, compiling competitive intelligence and digging into companies to look for things like fraud was better than a woman scraping her false nails up the inside of my thighs. Protection details with the occasional high-level missing persons case could send a chill up my spine more than hips swaying in the right dress. Helping fend off corporate espionage was better than a night of hot sex.

I want the things in my life to require some effort. I want my life to have meaning. I was born with the proverbial silver spoon in my mouth. I think I spit it out within minutes of it being shoved there.

I like puzzles. I love a challenge. I crave the high I get from figuring out a mystery. It's probably why I excelled when I was in Army Intel for eight years. Give me a good case to dig into and I'm like a dog with a meaty bone. I don't rest until I own all the answers.

While I'm waiting on the basic financial report and background check I requested on Amaryllis Events from one of our new analysts —mostly to disclaim my suspicion the business didn't drug anyone— I receive a knock on my office door from my head of missing persons and protection services. He's carrying a thick file under his arm, a file I don't recognize.

First, it's paper. Second, I would recall authorizing its creation.

"Charlie, what are you doing here on a Sunday?" I stand, my eyes dropping to the folder now in his hands.

"You requested the Freeman file, Caleb. I need to know why." No nonsense and to the point, Charlie Henderson shakes my hand before sitting down in one of my guest chairs. He places the thick file on his lap, his hand absentmindedly tapping it.

Dragging my eyes away from the file, I find him looking at me with his head tilted. His expression is serious. "The Freeman file? The only thing I've asked for today is a business check on an event planner for my brother's wedding, Charlie. A company called Amaryllis Events."

His eyes don't leave mine. He doesn't say a word, just continues to stare me down.

I say slowly, nodding to the file, "And I take it the file you're holding has something to do with that request?"

Nodding his head, his hands stop tapping Morse code on the hard copy. He shifts in his chair, but doesn't speak immediately. I wait patiently, because I know Charlie. He's not deciding on whether or not to tell me, he just needs to organize his thoughts.

When I purchased the investigation firm, I inherited Charlie. He's a rare, raw, tell-it-like-it-is, pain in the ass that needs the right hand holding. He had turned in his resignation when I first met him. Now, he's one of my best assets.

I trust his instincts.

Giving him the minute he needs, I stand and walk over to the wet bar in my office. Grabbing two bottles of water, I place one in front of him before I sit at my desk again. Twisting off the cap, I wait.

"About eight years ago, a group of kids came to the office. Unusual case. They wanted a background investigation run."

I'm not sure what's odd about that. Parent who left them? Parents, plural, who left them? I tip my head as I take another drink. His next words do surprise me.

"The Freeman children wanted us to investigate them. There are six of them. They wanted to know how hard it would be for anyone to find them, and they wanted to know if the people in their previous lives were alive or dead. They were all hoping for dead. By the end of it, so were we." He shudders.

Charlie Henderson has seen a lot over the years, but I've never watched him visibly shudder.

"Those kids, the Freemans..." Charlie takes a deep breath. "They own Amaryllis Events."

Slowly putting down the bottle, I sit up straighter. Ry, you ass. What the hell did you get us involved with?

"It's all in there?" He nods. I reach my hand out for the file, and just as I'm about to touch the thick folder, Charlie puts his hand on top of mine. "Caleb." My eyes lock onto his. What now?

"Ryan came up as part of the investigation. There might be things; you know...things you don't know. I have no idea. But from the look on your face, I'm guessing the second." He releases the file as I sink in my chair. The file is easily six inches thick.

"I put the flags on the family so I could let them know if someone was trying to hunt them." He gives me a hard look that tells me if it was, I would easily be facing an aging ex-SEAL in a grudge match. "But based on what you just said, I'm assuming your check has nothing to do with that."

I'm left holding what may be the equivalent of a paper bomb. I can't take my eyes off of it.

I know instinctively if I handle what's inside wrong, my whole world is going to implode.

Charlie turns and walks to the door. With his hand on the knob, he turns and says something odd. "If I lived through what the people in that file lived through, it would be hard for me to choose dedicating my life to 'happily ever after' day after day." He takes a deep breath and slowly lets it out. "That's the only copy. Nothing's digital. I want it back in my hands by the end of the day."

Nodding at me, he leaves my office, closing the door behind him.

I set the file down in the center of my desk. Bracing myself, I flip past the initial confidentiality pages and get to the table of contents. Scanning it, there are names I am sure I'll become very acquainted with: Phillip Freeman-Ross, 32, Cassidy Freeman, 29, Emily Freeman, 29, Alison Freeman, 27, Holly Freeman, 27, Corinna Freeman, 27, and Jason Ross, 35 (with a notation that he is Phillip's husband).

Then, names that make my gut churn.

Ryan Lockwood, 29.

Mildred Lockwood, 62.

What the fuck does my brother and mother have to do with the Freeman's request?

Pressing a button on my iPad, I engage the locks on my office door and begin to read.

HOURS LATER, my world has shifted on its axis and I know two things.

One, that cunt will never again be called my mother.

Two, I need to meet the Freemans.

I pick up the phone, call Ryan, and tell him he's a go for the meeting with Amaryllis Events, setting their plans in motion. There's just one caveat. I want to meet the Freemans. As soon as possible.

Ryan is outraged. Especially when I won't share the reason why I feel this need to do so. We argue on the issue back and forth the entire time he and Jared are in transit to the restaurant in Westchester, resulting in Ryan hanging up on me.

Hours pass. After trying to clear up some issues I'll need off my plate for a trip out to Connecticut in the morning, I find myself unable to think about anything but the contents of that file. I stand in front of my office window, long after the sun sets, not seeing the beauty of the Manhattan skyline. The sky transitioned from a deep color that can only be found over the Hudson in the fall to a deep murky ink color when my phone rings. After a terse call from Ryan confirming I'll be meeting with the Freemans in the morning, he hangs up.

I let out my slow breath. I have my time to meet them. What I'll do with that meeting, I have no idea.

I'll use my instincts and figure it out in the morning.

3

CASSIDY

It took me forever to figure out what to wear this morning.

I wanted to dress to give the impression I wasn't nervous about the Lockwood meeting, but I wanted to carefully showcase the success our company has attained.

Looking down at my outfit, I'm satisfied with my decision—casual elegance with power thrown in. I figured my mulberry colored cashmere sweater dress, ending right above my knee, paired with high heeled black leather boots conveyed that. Hanging behind the door was a matching cashmere jacket in black that would graze the bottom hem of the dress if I needed to toss it on.

I can hear Phillip's words from last night. *"But you're the face of this company, Cass. There's no one we trust to do this more than you."* I can't imagine how he could think that.

My gaze travels over to Phillip and Jason's wedding photo. Both of them are beaming at the camera, with the rest of our family clustered around them. I hardly spare myself a glance, bypassing my image for those far more important in the photo.

When Holly showed me the photo after she developed it, she asked me what I saw. I told her immediately, "Golden beauty. I mean, just look at all of you." My compliment was sincere.

Holly had cocked her head and said rather enigmatically, "You don't see it at all, do you?"

"See what?" I had asked her, confused.

She patted my hand, took the picture from me and hung it on the wall where it resides today. "One day you will. I just hope I'm around when you do."

I shake my head and glance at the clock—it's 7:50. Perfect. I have enough time to run down the street for a cup of coffee and make it back in time to review the Lockwood notes Phil had tossed on my desk earlier. Phil generates event profiles before clients come in for their consultation.

After yelling at Phil's needy ass that I would get him a large, extra skinny latte with whipped cream, I grab my phone and wristlet, and duck out the side door into the crisp morning air, mentally wishing I had grabbed my coat. Fall is going to hit early in our little southern Connecticut town.

Other than my dreams, my life has become monotonous. My greatest stress comes from what I'll wear to the office. My complacency hasn't escaped me.

Pausing on the street, I take in the former gingerbread mansion on Collyer's Main Street, which now houses Amaryllis Events. I let out a wry chuckle. Who would have thought that six of the most cynical people—when it came to love and relationships—would become some of the best wedding and event planners in the Northeast? Not this woman, that's for damn sure. Each of us use our individual strengths for each event, providing unique moments crafted with elegance, considering everyone's wishes. We even incorporate input from the spinster aunt that no one wants to listen to. We all know feelings matter. Feelings count. Feelings can destroy souls, and an event as important as a wedding. We work to show people that, and people pay us damn well for our attention to the details.

Strolling down the street of the closest thing to a hometown I have ever known, I nod at several store owners unlocking their front doors minutes before their eight o'clock store openings. I shake my head, not knowing how people can stand to be rushed in the morning. The feeling of never having enough time to take a deep breath, let alone get coffee, before dealing with the good citizens of Collyer, it would be akin to a terrorist attack to my stability.

Passing by the dance studio and candy store, which I know will be filled with high school students later in the afternoon, I duck down the alley between the Colonial-era buildings to head toward The Coffee Shop.

Ava and Matt, the owners and my trusted confidants, look up as I enter. Matt frowns while Ava scurries over with her arms outstretched.

"Cassidy, darling. Why don't you let us bring you your morning coffee?"

"Ava, if you did, I would never leave the office," I reply, leaning down to give her cheek a quick kiss. "Besides, it would give Phil a reason to say we never do a damn thing for him."

"Mouth, Cassidy!" Ava scolds me, gently thumping my arm. Ava is a little bit motherly toward me. Toward all of us.

"Should have heard him this morning while he was whining about not having his extra skinny latte already, Ava. And how can one suck more skinny out of the already skim milk? I told him to stop lying around on his ass and use the treadmill he made Jason buy him, and maybe he wouldn't be worrying about those washboard abs of his." Ava tries to hold in her laughter. She finally gives in, and by the time she stops, she's wiping the tears of laughter from her eyes. "Besides, he wants whipped cream. You should have heard what I said about that." I smile and wink at Ava because Phil is beyond ridiculous about his coffee demands and we both know it.

Ava lets out one last bellow of laughter, throws a smile at me, and begins making coffee while talking to other customers.

Matt ambles out of the heat of the miniscule kitchen, resting his arms on top of the counter in front of me. "Not sleeping again?"

A former VA psychologist, I found I was more comfortable talking to Matt about my past than any other doctor before. Maybe it's because he'd gladly take one of his viciously sharp meat cleavers to anyone who would try to hurt me. I think it's because he understands I feel I'm at the end of my rope.

My childhood was stolen, and that made my future feel bleak. I feel like I'm alone and always will be.

Matt can sense my isolation and reaches forward for my hand. "You're not alone, Cassidy."

I laugh derisively as I try to pull my hand away from his large paw.

"You're not," he insists, holding onto my hand.

I lean forward, my braid falling over my shoulder. "Then why does it feel that way when I wake up crying and alone, Matt? No one wants someone that's ruined or damaged." I pull my hand away as Ava comes bustling over with my drinks. I stand up and smile at Matt. "I'll always be alone."

I drop a ten-dollar bill on the counter and tip my lips at Ava. Matt can't hide his concern, which I choose to ignore as I head out the door.

Holding our coffee slightly away from my body, I meander down the tree lined streets, back toward the office.

Em wasn't wrong. Something was going on with me. What I felt, I couldn't put into words to help my siblings understand.

I always recognize when something is losing its course in my perfectly organized life.

"HERE'S YOUR EXTRA SKINNY, practically water latte, with fat-laden whipped cream." I hand the coffee over to Phil.

"Don't you start with that mouth today, Cass," Phil warns, like I'm nine years old again and not twenty-nine. "I'm in no mood. My abs are just as washboard as the day you met me."

"It's not me who has to see them every night. That would be Jason. And I have no idea why you're freaking out over this, since you look the same as the day I met you. Most days, you act the same way too," I quip, sipping my cappuccino.

Phil stares at me for a minute before he puts the coffee down and places his hands on his hips. "I swear to God, that mouth of yours is going to be the death of you one of these days."

"What did you say to set him off this time, Cass?" Ali calls as she passes us, walking into my office.

"Phil, if you took after Ali and worked for those abs, you wouldn't be worrying about ways to filter out the 0.01% of fat out of skim milk," I taunt.

"Ohhhh," my sister drawls out as she pauses, her Southern accent making it a five-syllable word. "Should have run with me. I got up when y'all did and put in five miles. Maybe I'll go get a mocha with some extra whip from The Coffee Shop."

"Keep out of it, Ali," Phil huffs. He raises a perfectly sculpted eyebrow, challenging her to step into our argument more than she already has.

"Seriously, Phillip, what's wrong with you?" I ask. "We're actually here for a reason this morning. You know, a quick briefing before a potentially lucrative client walks through the door in about fifteen minutes."

Phil looks at us for a moment before speaking. His eyes, which are so incredibly blue and filled with a raging regret, begin to soften. "If I said nothing, would either of you believe me?"

In unison, Ali and I both say, "No."

Sighing, Phil follows Ali and sits in one of the chairs across from my desk. I join them, crossing my legs and folding my hands over my stomach as I lean back. "Okay, out with it. Why have you been a douche this morning? More so than normal? We have our first appointment coming in"—I check the clock—"in seventeen minutes. Out with it, and do it quickly."

"So, about that first appointment," Phil starts. I slowly uncross my legs and sit forward.

"Yes?"

"There's something you should know."

I'm going to throttle my brother. After all our years of working together, if he left out telling me any minute detail about this appointment, I'm going to lose it.

Knowing Phil, this could be anything from the appointment was supposed to be at the Lockwood company headquarters in Manhattan or their family compound in Greenwich. If Phil suddenly springs on me that he forgot to tell me the client's expecting to have a champagne catered breakfast ready, I'm going to give up on keeping my legendary control, take my scissors and straddle him while I cut off all his hair in massive chunks. He won't be able to stop me because he'll be too busy choking on the extra-skinny, watered down latte he just made me pick up.

In my calmest voice, I ask, "What about it?"

Ali whispers "Uh-oh" under her breath.

Phil looks at his hands, then at the clock. Another minute ticks by. Sixteen minutes until this appointment. He looks at Ali, who just stares back at him with a mean look. He looks back down at his hands. Silence. Fifteen minutes.

From the doorway, Holly pipes in with "Did you fuck the groom or something?"

Ali starts to laugh as I gasp. Standing in the door, Corinna, Em and Holly are standing in varying states of arms crossed, waiting for Phil's answer. Em just mean mugs Phil. I check the clock again. Fourteen minutes.

Phil sighs and looks at me with guilt on his face. That was my only warning.

"No, but Jason was engaged to him about ten years ago and broke it off to be with me. Or so the story goes."

Chaos erupts in my office. In my disbelief, I make a few mental notes. First, Phil is prohibited from doing any further client event profile forms. I also give myself a mental reminder to review all his other forms for new clients for the rest of the week. How could he not think this information was important for me to know, especially now, having more than mere minutes before the Lockwoods come through my door?

As I sit back, listening to my siblings yell among each other, I try to regroup. I have no time to call Jason to discreetly find out what occurred.

I now have five minutes to get this under control.

Forget who fucked who or who fucked whom over. This is not how we built this business.

Phil. Might. Die.

Slowly.

Blunt force trauma caused by my planner. That's a delicious thought.

But later.

I'll enjoy planning it in detail, after I deal with damage control.

"All of you, get out of my office. RIGHT NOW!" I yell at my siblings. "I have exactly four minutes to figure this out. I think you all might be depraved lunatics, and how I know this and continue to work with you all on a daily basis is eluding me. This is not the impression this company will give under any circumstances, short of the building catching fire. Find your offices and have your meltdowns in there."

Then I hear it. That fucking bitch Fate. Three goddamn minutes early. Of course.

"I happen to agree with Ms. Freeman. She and I have an appointment on behalf of my family."

I find myself staring briefly into a set of the most gorgeous, chocolate brown eyes I have ever seen, before they drift away, looking around the room.

My stomach turns. My skin tingles. My heart flips in my chest.

Holy Shit. Is this the groom?

Of course, it is.

Fate, throwing the first man at me that I find remotely desirable and absolutely can't have.

4

CALEB

I stare at the ensemble, every one of them frozen in front of me. I decide if the Freemans entered a mannequin challenge, they would likely take first place. Not just for standing completely still, but for the shock and awe on all their faces. Internally smiling at the humor of catching the notorious family in one of their battles, I let my eyes roam around the room.

Since I'd done my homework on them—frankly, I'd read everything about them—before I walked into the door, I'm way more amused than shocked at the scene unfolding before me. While my original intent was to make sure my brother didn't get swindled by these people to create his dream wedding, I was compelled to meet this family after what I read yesterday. I ran the background check for Ry, then carefully manipulated him and Jared into letting me handle the preliminary meeting today on their behalf. They're convinced the Freemans will create the perfect wedding and reception based on recommendations from friends and colleagues.

I think I just saw the reason why.

It's not the youngest, Corinna, whose cat eyes and curves likely have most men fainting before they ever took a bite of the cakes she baked. It's not Allison, whose devastating blue eyes and severe mouth could slice you in half. It's no surprise to me that she's the corporate financial officer and attorney, and didn't deal with the day-to-day wedding events.

Emily and Holly are both knockouts as well. Emily has her blonde hair pinned up, dark blue eyes flashing behind her dark glasses, and her red lips pursed, ready to spring to the family's defense. Her sharp style matches her sharp gaze. I could easily see Emily dressing Ry and Jared in appropriate wedding attire and not taking any bullshit in the process. No one was going down the aisle in gold brocade if she has anything to say about it. Holly, well, she's the dreamer. I nabbed her checking me out, as if she had her camera in her hand, trying to find the best angle to take one of her illuminating shots. I can practically see the wheels in her head spinning as she gnaws on her full lower lip.

Then there's Phillip, the older brother. Jason Ross' husband. The one who had fallen into Jason's life, breaking up my brother's sham of an engagement, the results of which left Ry reeling for a while. The Golden Boy, as Ry used to derisively describe him over Skype while I was overseas, and according to the file I read. He's probably afraid I'm here to upset his happy world order and ready to beat the shit out of me if I do.

The man standing in front of me took in five girls when he was barely a teenager himself, none of whom were related to him, and helped raise them to be the highly successful women standing in front of me. Regardless of what had happened in his or my brother's love lives, he has my respect for that alone.

I ignore the occupant of the room, the one I'm dying to look at, and reach my hand out to Phillip first. "Caleb Lockwood. A pleasure."

"Phillip Freeman-Ross. I apologize for..."

Now I let the smile cross my face. "No need. You should have heard the battles that would happen in our house as kids. And there were far fewer of us."

A bark of laughter leaves Phillip's mouth. He glances over my shoulder like he's been distracted by movement. I imagine daggers are shooting from the gem-colored eyes of the oldest Freeman sister.

"As my sister stated appropriately, at Amaryllis Events, this isn't the impression we like to provide to prospective clients. We like to save the crazy for meeting three, at least."

"Phillip." His name is said in a calm voice. She's too calm if I go by the number of choked sounds, accompanied by phones and hands raised in front of the mouths of the four sisters to muffle their snickers.

"Right," Phillip says. "I'll be leaving now. Say, Caleb, can I grab you a cup of coffee before you meet with my sister?"

"Phillip," the voice behind me says again. Calm. In control. "Get out. Now. If Mr. Lockwood would like coffee, I am more than capable of obtaining it for him. However, you may choke to death on yours and it will be the last extra skinny latte you ever taste. Now, do you want to press your luck and continue to speak in front of me another minute more?"

The sisters can't control their laughter any longer. They all offer their welcome, quickly introduce themselves, and leave Cassidy's office. Phillip doesn't say anything else, but shakes my hand firmly, his eyes meeting mine directly. His expression clearly says, have an issue with me, fine. Don't fuck with my family.

It's an expression I'm familiar with, as I wear it often.

As the door closes softly behind him, I turn to face Cassidy Freeman, CEO, event planner and distraction extraordinaire. Fuck, if I don't like what I see. I let out a soft breath. From the moment I walked in the room, I deliberately ignored her. I now get the full impact. From the top of her head to her booted feet, everything about her intrigues me.

Sweet Jesus, she's a knockout.

Easily the shortest member of the Freeman family, Cassidy's petite size doesn't take away from her presence. Fuck no. A face that is bewitching more than classically beautiful, with long curly hair pulled back in a braid, and the brightest blue-green eyes framed by the longest lashes. Her lower lip, painted a deep burgundy, is thrust forward, and her hands are on her hips, stretching the fabric of her sweater dress across her breasts. Shit, she's tiny. Even wearing boots with a three to four-inch heel, she only comes up to my chin.

During my discreet perusal of her, she takes a deep breath and turns her head toward the window, clearly regrouping. I glimpse the side of her neck where her amaryllis tattoo, the Freeman family logo, peeks out from beneath her heavy mane of hair. Damned if I needed yet another reason to be turned on by her.

She's a brilliant, badass puzzle in a package built for every fantasy I've ever had about a woman.

I don't know if I let an incontrollable sound escape, or if her self-preservation instinct kicked in, but suddenly her gem-colored eyes turn and lock on mine.

I'm standing at least four feet from her, and the delicate pulse in her neck is fluttering visibly. Mine starts to synchronize with hers—a little fast-paced and agitated. I'm not the only one affected, but I might be the only one who understands why.

Nothing I read about her yesterday, no picture I saw, could have prepared me for the impact of her on my senses. She's an enigma.

"Mr. Lockwood, I'm Cassidy Freeman. Again, I would like to offer my apologies for the circus you walked in on when you first came in. As I'm sure you likely overheard, my brother failed to provide me with the details of your appointment in enough time for me to fully prepare for our meeting. It's our preferred approach to be prepared well in advance in order to anticipate your needs."

"I don't think there's any way you could have anticipated what your brother had planned on telling you, Cassidy. It's fine. The most important thing is making sure Ryan has the wedding he's always dreamt of with no flaws."

The professional she is, she squares her shoulders, gesturing to the chair Phil had vacated earlier. "May I take your coat?" I gesture to her I'm fine. "Please take a seat then. Can I offer you that coffee Phillip mentioned earlier? Tea?" I shudder in revulsion. "I'll take it that is a no. For both?" A light laugh trickles out. "A Coke?"

"Please."

She reaches into a refrigerator nestled in the cabinetry in front of her. When she turns, she's holding a familiar red and white can and makes her way back to me on those fantasy-inspiring boots. Handing me the can and a coaster, she sits elegantly behind her desk.

It appears my girl's a bit obsessive about neatness. My girl? Whoa, boy. You just met her. Just because you know everything about her, doesn't mean she would be interested.

In fact, if I read her file correctly, she would never be interested.

Damn, if that isn't a deflating thought.

"So, tell me more about the groom," she inquires, picking up a cup from The Coffee Shop. Taking a sip, she scrunches her nose and puts it aside. Pulling her wireless keyboard closer to her, I glance around for the screen and realize she has it submerged beneath the profile of the desk. Efficient. Cassidy can take notes and not lose line of sight with her clients. I may need that setup for my office.

"Ry's fantastic." I can't help but laugh. "He's probably the most romantic bastard there is in the world. When he proposed, I know for a fact he bought out three nurseries of primroses to make the rooftop deck of our house a virtual Garden of Eden. You know the meaning of primroses is, 'I can't live without you,' right?" Waiting for her nod, I continue. "He took the day off work, got everyone we know involved in arranging them just right. We have a condo in the Powell Building with an outdoor roof deck in the city. Ry spends all day stringing lights all over the place, moves the speakers outside, and what happens? It starts raining! Not like it mattered, of course. Everything ended up just perfect for Ry."

Cassidy says nothing, but offers a polite smile I don't quite get. She looks down and begins typing. Did I miss something? Didn't she ask about Ry?

"Have you discussed what kind of wedding you two are thinking of? Something large, or small and intimate?"

Wait. What the fuck did she say? Ry and I? Married?

From the moment I walked in the door of Amaryllis Events and heard the husband of my brother's ex being ripped a new asshole by his five sisters, and having my dick turn semi-hard from my first glance at Cassidy Freeman, to now being asked what I would like at the wedding she thinks I'm having by marrying my brother, this morning has been nothing but a comedy of errors.

I toss my head back and laugh from the depths of my soul. I can't wait to replay this entire morning later in bed, while thinking of blue-green eyes and dark hair. I lean back in my chair and cross my legs at the ankles, putting my arms behind my head. I notice Cassidy's eyes do a quick bit of wandering themselves. So, the pixie at least likes what she sees. That's a good start.

"No, Cassidy. Ry and I have not talked about the wedding at all. However, I know he and Jared discussed it in detail the other night without me before I got home from a business trip. Since they have since shared their decisions with me, I have a fair idea of what's needed."

I think Cassidy gets whiplash, her head comes up so fast. Her left arm flings out, knocking her coffee cup off her desk and right onto the floor. As she jumps up, her office chair flies back and slams into the wall.

"Shit!" she yells, before her face turns to me in horror. Racing over to the cabinet where she got my Coke, she grabs paper towels from another one of those hidden cabinets, muttering under her breath, "Phil...Won't live to his first anniversary... Scissors...Hair" as she cleans up the coffee spill from the hardwood floor and her desk.

I make no move to assist her, because frankly, I'm enjoying the tight pull of her dress over her ass too damn much.

She stands, throws out the mess of towels and washes her hands at the wet bar. She appears to be doing some sort of deep breathing exercise that shows off her magnificent breasts.

Jesus. A woman like her needs to come with a warning label.

After the eighth or so breath, she has herself back under control and is apparently ready to deal with what she thinks will be my marriage to two men, one of whom is my brother.

I sit back with a shit-eating grin, ready to enjoy the hell out of this appointment with the fantasy-inspiring Cassidy Freeman.

"Again, I apologize, Mr. Lockwood—"

"Please, call me Caleb, Cassidy," I say with a huge smile. "After all, we're going to be working very closely together for the next few months. By the end of this, I imagine we'll know each other so well, we'll be exchanging holiday cards every year, at the very least." I toss in the last part for good measure.

Her eyes widen slightly. "Well, Mr. Lock—I mean, Caleb. In all my years in the business, I have never met a family member with as much...enthusiasm as you have. I'm sure we'll enjoy our relationship quite a bit."

Oh, Pixie, if you only knew.

Biting the inside of my cheek, I train my expression to be as deadpan as possible. "As much as I want to talk about Ry and Jared, and could do for hours, I do have a limited amount of time today, Cassidy. Let's get down to the nitty gritty. What do you need to know so we can get this under contract?"

Straightening, Cassidy gives me her professional smile and begins firing questions at me. Do I want to use all services offered in-house? Of course. Amaryllis Events has an enormous reputation for being the best at everything. Even if they didn't, I want it to be Cassidy's job to corral my mother's ass. I don't mention that point to Cassidy just yet. Do I have a preferred location? Our family home in Greenwich. I can't get Ry to budge on that. What is the date of the wedding? I ask if Thanksgiving weekend is too soon since the location is a private residence.

Back and forth on the questions. I think the only two items that even mildly threw her for a loop was when I dropped that there would be well over 500 guests in attendance, Thanksgiving weekend or not, and that we wanted unfettered access to her anytime, day or night, due to the scale and significance of the wedding.

Cassidy quickly sorted many details with an efficiency that, had I actually been planning my own wedding, would have impressed the shit out of me. Mentally shaking my head in wonder over how her brain works, there's a knock at the door.

Oh shit. Ryan and Jared are here.

"One moment, please," Cassidy calls out. "Caleb, I do believe we have about seventy-five percent of the major decisions made. You appear to know what Ryan and Jared are looking for with the wedding. I may make a few suggestions and recommendations for enhancements along the way, but nothing to detract from the vision coming together."

"Cassidy, there's one more thing." I look directly into her eyes. I want that physical connection between us before that door swings open. There's something between this woman and me, and I need more time to figure out what it is. I stand and hand her my business card. "I'd like to continue this conversation later, but I need to get going. That's my number on the card to reach me any time."

"Of course. And here's mine. Let me write my cell phone on the back for anything you might need. After all, once the contracts are signed, you'll need this if any of you have questions that arise in the middle of the night."

As she hands me her card, I feel my body already yearning for the connection to hers, which I know is about to be severed in just a few short moments. I continue to stare into her amazing eyes. I figure I have less than thirty seconds before my brother and his fiancé come in to wrap up this appointment, sign the contract, and the stunning pixie before me starts making a list of who to kill first—her brother or me.

"Cassidy? There's something I need to tell you," I say, as the door swings open, revealing Phillip, Ry, and Jared. Right on time.

"Yes, Caleb?"

"I'm not one of the grooms. I'm Ryan's brother."

5

CASSIDY

After Caleb introduced me to his brother Ryan and Ryan's fiancé Jared Dalton, the actual grooms, Caleb escaped with one of those man-hug things to both men and a wink at me with a reminder that he'll be using my number to talk with me soon, and that I should, of course, feel free to use his sooner if I don't hear from him. As if I would after he'd just spent the better part of an hour posing as a groom. I was mortified.

Thinking about everything that transpired, I wonder if my face might be turning as red as Holly's hair. If my body temperature is anything to go by, it might be close. As I sit at the conference table watching the final contract negotiations occur, I look over at a rare picture of my sister on the wall.

For the following hour after Caleb strolled out of my office, I pull every emotion in after the lingering embarrassment I feel over the behavior in my office this morning. We're a bunch of professionals trying to run a business. This is potentially our largest client ever. And between my brother's antics, my abnormal reactions to the presumed groom, and Caleb himself, I was better off not feeling anything. So, nothing was getting through. If Phil showed up with a trio of his exes who were a naked troupe of pole dancers for a ceremony the next day requiring latex wedding attire, I think I would still have been as cool as a cucumber. There wasn't a single emotion that crossed my face that I didn't have one hundred percent control over. My smiles were friendly, my laughter light. I was warm without being too invasive.

I've perfected the professional mask.

Under it all sat a simmering irritation that Caleb knew his brother so well, that Ryan and Jared loved everything Caleb had picked out for their wedding the previous hour.

Maybe I was just being a bitch, but I wanted them to dislike or hate something— anything, so I could be a little uncontrolled, and maybe completely stupid.

Like use that card Caleb left me to call him.

I don't know what's wrong with me. I want an excuse to pick up that phone, because despite the fact that up to an hour earlier he played me into thinking he was about to marry two other men, I still think he's the most intriguing man to cross my path in...forever.

Something about him called to me on some elemental level I didn't understand. I'd never experienced the feeling before. I felt sensitized to his presence in my office. I felt his dark eyes burn through me as I moved around my office. His hand when it touched mine, rough and strong, caused an immediate reaction. His broad shoulders begging to allow me to rest my head on them, leaving my burden with him.

Shit, where the hell had that thought come from? Shaking my head, I try to refocus on the room and its occupants.

The conference room seemed to glow. The former ballroom in the mansion where we worked was something we spent long, hard hours to restore. Jewel tones played off the rich mahogany. Diamond panes of the leaded glass windows offered privacy without diluting too much of the sunlight streaming in. The seating areas scattered around the room were warm and inviting with tufted velvet. We had also designed the more formal table we were presently sitting at.

Because of the size of the Lockwood-Dalton wedding, all the siblings, as well as the grooms, were gathered around the conference table. Truthfully, if Ryan and Jared had smaller wedding expectations that required fewer negotiations, it would have been just Ali and me finishing up this part. But a five-hundred-person wedding in a little over two months for the Greenwich elite? I knew that everyone present wanted to make sure each detail was captured in this preliminary document.

Apparently, I was the biggest chip in the negotiations. Unfettered access to me for two months. Completely non-negotiable by the grooms. Damn Caleb for being right about that.

Ugh. I needed to get him out of my thoughts and fast.

My thoughts drift again to the older Lockwood brother, and I don't hear my name being called. I feel the kick to my shin under the table from my sister, Emily.

"Cass," Em hisses at me.

"I'm sorry," I interject smoothly. "I was envisioning the wedding plan for the next week, mentally writing it out. As my family can tell you, I start daydreaming when lists are involved." I deliberately keep my chin held high, allowing my blush to show.

Ryan and Jared laugh outright.

Em lets out a breath and mouths, "Good save."

Crap, I never blank out at the negotiation table. I'm going to have to explain that one later.

"Do you have anything else to add before we lock everything in, Cassidy?"

I lean forward, clasping my hands in front of me on the table. This is my element, my stage, where I have the most control.

I look at Ryan first, hold his eyes for a count of two, and do the same with Jared. "Because of the compressed timeline, which let me reiterate again, we can completely handle, we will be unable to accommodate last minute changes on most of the major items. Since we handle so many services in-house, we're not concerned about consultations with hiring a photographer, ordering flowers, or your garment selections. However, when a caterer says we must be there for a tasting, one of you has to be there unless you're willing to compromise on potential quality. If you send a proxy and they love something and you hate it, Amaryllis Events will not tolerate less than favorable evaluation. We appreciate your work schedules and will try to do as much as possible to work around them. Sometimes, that will not be possible. We're professionals. We'll not trouble you with the small concerns. If we do call and we indicate we need a call back within a certain timeframe, please know it's urgent and something that will impact the vision you have for your big day." Sitting back, I smile, cross my legs and wait.

"Is there ever a time you're unavailable?" Ryan asks calmly. Jared tips his head in agreement with Ryan's question.

"Not for the two of you. From this minute, until the moment you leave on your honeymoon, you will always know my availability. As elite clients, you will know my exact schedule. You will have access to my out of the office times. I will provide you with a hard copy before you leave today and email you a copy for you to download to both your iPhones and Outlook calendars by close of business. Please note, all the data in those deliverables are covered by the language in our two-way non-disclosure agreement, which we will be signing in a few moments."

"A two-way NDA?" Jared says with some surprise, the lawyer in him perking up.

"Yes," I state firmly. "It protects both of us. However, for you to have the kind of access to me you are demanding with this schedule, our business and my personal privacy are both at stake. You will not just have access to my meetings with other clients, you will have access to every entry on my calendar, including my next physical and personal events, like my involvement in Collyer's homecoming weekend. Short of putting an electronic leash on me, you will know where I plan to be every moment of the day for the next two months."

Ali speaks up at this point. "This negotiation includes unfettered access to Cassidy."

Jared reaches over and takes Ryan's hand, giving it a quick squeeze. They speak quietly for the next few moments. Ryan nods, then smiles first at Jared, then around the table before saying, "Let's do this."

"First," Ali interjects in her most professional voice. "Let's discuss the pricing schedule. Please turn to Table A of the document in front of you. For a wedding of this size and on this timetable, you're typically looking at cost plus thirty percent to cover the services of Amaryllis Events. That includes all procured items as well as outside vendors."

"Alison, please reduce the amount by twenty percent." Phil speaks softly from his seat at the table.

"Excuse me?" Ali questions, with a more than a touch of asperity in her tone. "Can I speak with you outside, Phillip?"

"After the contracts are signed. Twenty percent, please. Use the discount code Delphi."

Fucking Phil. He'd invoked a family code word, referencing the oracle who told Amaryllis how to win the heart of her love. My hand immediately goes to my neck, and my sisters shift in their seats. Ali nods slowly and takes a breath.

I'd almost forgotten that Phil was still in the room, he'd been so quiet. No one was forgetting him after this bomb. The reasons for chopping off his precious hair are increasing by the minute today. I'm not alone now, I think with a private smile.

Ryan and Jared can only smile, displaying their delight. Of course, they're delighted. They just saved at least two-hundred thousand dollars.

I hear Em, who is sitting the closest to Phil, murmur to him, "Payback for this is going to be hell."

Phil pales and swallows hard.

About two hours later, after briefly stepping out to reschedule a conference call with a vendor for later in the day, the contracts, NDAs, and deposits are signed and paid. The only thing open is the NDA to be signed by Caleb Lockwood. Oh, that's right. Because of Ryan and Jared's schedules, and because Ryan's brother is trusted implicitly, they want him to have the same status they have to reach me.

Fabulous.

I feel my embarrassment from earlier start to climb back up my neck. Phil's list of transgressions keeps growing. I'll figure out a way to blame Caleb having unlimited access to me and my schedule on Phil. At the rate he's going, he'll be lucky I don't switch out his Gucci shampoo for Nair.

What I found interesting was that Ryan and Jared wanted it documented that Ryan's mother was to have no say in the wedding, other than the location, no matter the circumstance or reason. She wouldn't be privy to any of the decision-making. Any concerns were to be handled by me, with issues collected and passed along to the grooms as necessary.

Unshakeable trepidation has me thinking I would have earned that extra twenty percent personally on that request alone.

After printing out a hard copy of my schedule for the week, I sealed it in an envelope and promised the grooms I would have the electronic versions to them in a few short hours. I shook hands with both men and escorted them to the mansion doors.

After closing the door behind them, I whirl around. Before I can figure out what's happening, I'm being dragged back into the conference room, where Imagine Dragons is blaring from our sound system speakers. Shoes have been kicked off and my sisters and brother are dancing on the tables, pretending to grind with imaginary partners or pole dance.

I can't help but laugh at their craziness, and I love every one of them. Even Phil. Because while I might plot his death later, for now, we're celebrating.

Suddenly, Phil jumps off the table and starts dancing with me around the room. I let my laughter ring out as my sisters whoop it up from varying parts of the old grand ballroom.

I'd figure out how to pull off the biggest wedding of my career later.

I'd figure out how I'm going to work with the hottest man I've ever met later.

I'd figure out how to survive the next two months.

I'd conquer these nightmares and regain my control.

At this moment, I'm on top of the world.

6

CASSIDY

"So, what the hell did you do?" Ali demands later that night as we sit around our communal family room, drinking a bottle of wine. We might be on bottle number two. I don't care. I didn't want to be alone with my thoughts, so I sought out my sisters.

I managed to give Em the highlights earlier today when we both had a break after the Lockwood-Dalton wedding contract was signed —between Ryan Lockwood and Jared Dalton. Not Caleb Lockwood.

Right now, it's just me, Ali, and Em at the Farm. About ten years ago, we pooled our money to buy a 10-acre property with no inhabitable buildings. We got the land for a fraction of what it would have cost in Collyer. Five years ago, we started renovating the structures on the property, bringing in architects to preserve as much of the old charm of the property possible. What we ended up with was six homes made up from the smaller barns, carriage houses, and servant quarters. We each needed our own spaces, knowing we would likely kill one another if we continued to live under the same roof. We turned each of the out buildings into cottages, which are now our private residences.

The main barn, known to us as "The Farm," was converted into a spectacular space. It's a monstrosity of a building that overlooks a lake and includes a gourmet kitchen, gym, game room, and a living room that can easily hold thirty. The original stone fireplace dominates the space. In the old days, the main barn would have been the communal hall and our homes made up the village. It gave us space, and at the same time, it gave us security, something we all realized we needed.

I roll my wine glass in my hand and purse my lips in thought. Absentmindedly, I run a hand over the restored antique trunk. The symbolism of the way we continually surround ourselves with items we restored is not lost on me. Taking the beaten and the broken, and giving them life again.

Sighing, I reach back and unbraid my hair, shaking the thick, curly mass loose. My fingertips graze over my tattoo, which fills me with pride.

"After I politely escorted Caleb from my office, I finished my meeting with his brother Ryan—who, by the way, is Jason's former fiancé—and Jared." I raise my eyebrows in response to Ali's incredulous look. "Then I proceeded to escort Ryan and Jared over to you to sign the contract on the largest wedding we'll ever do in a two-month period. You were there for everything after that. With any luck, our sanity will remain intact through the crazy-ass schedule, because we'll need to keep it so our vendors won't want to kill us. I have a feeling the Lockwood name will help smooth some of that over though."

Ali's not mollified. "I don't get it, Cass. How are you thinking about schedules, timelines, and vendors? Did you find out more about Ryan and Jason? And who the hell are you right now? Is all you care about is the damn money? None of us ever sold ourselves willingly."

"Watch yourself." My jaw clenches, my teeth grinding in the back of my mouth.

"Just listen to me, Cass." Ali leans forward in her seat. "You need to put this Caleb Lockwood in his place. No one has the right to play you like that. I don't care if you did give them unfettered access in that agreement. There are limits."

"Ali," Em snaps, trying to get her attention.

I snatch up my wine, finish it in a single swallow and hold my glass out blindly to Em while I tear into Ali. "What the fuck do you think I should do, Alison? Tell me. Should I throw another temper tantrum in front of Caleb Lockwood to add to the one that started this fiasco in my damn office this morning? Should I have lost his brother as a client for us or sucked it up? Or maybe I should have done exactly what I did and acted with some dignity and class by maintaining a measure of my control by not telling Caleb to fuck off. Maybe I was cautious after finding out his brother is connected to Jason? Maybe I thought that, I don't know, we should hear the whole story first."

Ali had the good grace to blush. "Sorry, Cass. I'm sorry. It's just...I mean..."

"I was doing what I was supposed to do as the CEO and as your fucking sister. So, don't ever accuse me of doing anything for money. You could burn my share of the proceeds from this wedding for all I fucking care."

I stand with my wine and stalk over to the windows overlooking the lake, shaking in my anger at Phil for hiding information that wouldn't have changed the outcome of today, but it certainly would have changed how I handled it. I'm furious at Ali for her stupid ass comments, at myself for not having any control over my emotions, and at Caleb for taking what was an innocent assumption and turning it into a game.

Caleb is the only frustration from today I don't understand. Was it payback for something that happened before we'd ever met my brother-in-law Jason? Or for something Jason and Phil did? Now that the emotional high of winning the contract has faded, my embarrassment from earlier has returned full force. I rest my head against the cool glass and sigh.

Minutes pass in silence. Lifting my head, I take a sip of my wine, when I hear the front door open and close.

Not turning around, I stare into the reflection of the glass as I watch Phil and Jason walk into the room. Great. Just what I need to cap off the day. Brotherly love.

"Whirlpool," I mock, raising my glass to Phil with my back still to him. "You certainly put my day on a spin cycle, didn't you?" I tip the glass to my mouth as I watch Jason glare at Phil in the glass.

"Cass." Phil walks over, his hand outreached.

"No." The leash on my emotions is gone.

I whirl around. My stomach churns the wine I've drank, making me feel nauseated as my eyes meet the apologetic ones of my brother's.

Something in my expression must stun him because he's keeping his distance. "The time to explain to me was before this family insinuated I was only in it for the money. Rather like selling myself." I send a scathing look at Alison, who has the intelligence to look ashamed. "Not now. So, if none of you mind, I've had enough drinks and family drama for today. I'm heading back to my place."

The first tear of frustration falls down my cheek, which feels warmed from too much wine and anger. I refuse to let a second tear fall in front of them.

Putting my wine glass down on a nearby table, I walk out the side door and into the darkness as Holly and Corinna arrive at the front door. As I exit through the back, I hear the eruption begin behind me.

I don't have a Freeman-level family fight in me tonight. Not after the one-two punch from Phil and Ali.

I head down the path toward the lake before I walk to my cottage, needing to get what Ali said out of my head—caring only about money, selling myself for the family.

Nothing but a whore for Daddy. But you like it, don't you baby...

My stomach can't hold on and I promptly throw up all over the grass.

As I'm retching, all the thoughts I try to keep locked out of my head come flooding in. *Smack. Oh God, they're tying me down to the bed. Smack. The feel of a dirty gag in my mouth. Smack. Twisting my head. No,*

*I can't see. The feel of their bodies on me. Biting, grunting, sweaty smells.
Smack. Pain. Stop, stop, stop! I can't take it anymore!*

I'm so lost in my nightmare that when a soothing hand lands on
my back, I let out a blood-curdling scream.

"Cassidy." My handsome brother-in-law, Jason. He's holding out
his handkerchief and my coat.

I look at him with my eyes burning, feral. They gleam like a wild
animal. "She had no right to say that, Jason. I'm not a whore. I was
never a whore."

He faces me directly, not moving. "I know, Cassidy."

"Is that what they think of me? What you think of me? What you
all say when I'm not around?" The dam that's been holding back the
tears since Ali's words were spoken bursts, and the tears flow down
my cheeks.

"You know that's not true, Cassidy," Jason whispers, sadly.

Do I?

I stumble down the path and sit at the lake's edge, pulling my
knees to my chest. I'm not sure how long I sit there before I hear
behind me, "Cassidy, can I sit? I don't want to scare you." Jason's voice
is soothing.

I can't fucking speak, but I must make some sort of assenting
sound because Jason moves closer.

"Here, you're going to get cold. I didn't think you'd want to go
back in there." Jason wraps my coat around my shoulders before
sitting.

We don't speak. I'm pretty sure Jason is just out here to make sure
I'm calm and warm, but he surprises me with his next words. "It was
a night like this when I first met Ryan. He was in the alley outside of a
bar, sobbing." Jason looks over to see if I'm listening and holds out
the handkerchief. Warily, I take it, wondering where he's going with
this. "Caleb is older by a few years. Five maybe? I don't remember.
When Ryan told him he was gay, Caleb was right there, had his back.
But he was deployed shortly thereafter. He was overseas for years, but
he was in constant contact with Ryan. Every opportunity he had, he

told Ryan how proud he was of him. He's a good guy, Cassidy, despite whatever happened today in your office."

I nod. I still can't speak, but I want him to continue. Somehow, I know there's a reason he's sharing this story.

"Ryan's father died around that time." Jason's voice is sad. "He looked up to his father for so many things." His voice hardens significantly. In my current state where I've just returned from my childhood memory of enraged voices, it makes me more than a little uncomfortable. "Then there was their bitch of a mother, Mildred. The night I met Ryan, he was crying in the rain, wearing nothing but boxers and a T-shirt soaked in blood. He didn't have on shoes. I worried about internal injuries, but he refused to go to a hospital. I carried him to my car, called Dr. Harris, and brought them both to my place. I was an intern, so I was way outside my area of expertise. I asked if he had family to call and he said he had none. The only family he would trust was in the military overseas." Jason takes a deep breath. "It became obvious fairly quickly that keeping Ry at my place was tantamount to his safety."

What? Why? My head is spinning with wanting to ask, but I'm still trapped in my memories.

"Ryan was on the verge of being killed or committing suicide. His life was a different version of the hell I imagine you lived through before finding Phillip." He raises a dark eyebrow and turns back to face the lake. "Only in this case, because of who Ryan was, the only way I could think of to keep him protected was to be engaged to him."

Pausing, Jason turns to fully face me. "Phil, Ryan, and now you, Cass, are the only ones in the world that know I was never engaged to Ryan. I can only assume he's told his fiancé. I have no idea if he ever told his brother." Jason takes a deep breath. "At the time, it was the only way I could think of to protect a beautiful young man by getting him out of the house he was living in, short of pressing charges, which he refused to let us do. Ryan's mother was beating him senseless over being gay." I hear the fury in his voice when he says, "Twenty-two, Cass. Barely home from college, he told us at night he would get so sleepy, he'd have to go lie down. When he would wake later, he would be strapped down to his bed with someone in a mask beating him to a pulp. Not that he could put up much of a fight. Sometimes it was a ski mask, sometimes a clown mask, sometimes hockey mask; anything to cover their face. Later when Ry was off the drugs and he could think clearly, he reasoned it was someone on his mother's staff he'd be able to recognize. They had him on so much stuff there was no way he'd be able to fight back. It was the only reason he could figure. They would lay him on his back, spread apart his legs and whip him with a belt. He was too drugged to fight them off. If it wasn't for the bruising he'd find the next day, and the hangover from the drugs in his system, he swore he would have thought it was a dream. It was more like a perpetual nightmare, day and night."

I gasp, but I don't think Jason even hears me.

"Ryan lived with me for two years. We were friends until I met your brother. Best friends, actually. Remember the day I met you all? At Candlewood Lake? What's it been, eight years?"

I nod.

"I talked with you guys for hours after Phil landed on me. It was like a punch to the gut, what I felt when I met Phil. It still is." Jason looks at me. "Don't tell him, though. He doesn't need his ego stroked any more than it already is."

I manage a feeble smile as Jason continues. "Ryan freaked out that night. We got back to the apartment and he lost it," he says sadly. "To be honest, I was so wrapped up in that first meeting with Phil, so absorbed, I didn't think about Ryan or how he would feel, until I went to get my stuff and Ryan was waiting for me. I told him to stop acting like an idiot, that we were friends. He screamed at me that I was his fiancé and tried to kiss me. I pushed him away. I couldn't figure out what was going on with him, and I can only imagine the things I said. But as he stood there with tears in his eyes, I realized his feelings had changed."

He takes a deep breath, his eyes fixed on the farm where his husband is still arguing.

"I loved Ryan as a friend. He was the closest thing to a brother I had. But I had no intention of ever taking it any further. That night, I told him to go to bed, and that we would talk in the morning. He left, leaving only a note for me."

Jason turned to face me fully. "How could I experience such happiness when I never knew if Ryan was alive or dead after he left? After meeting Phil, you, and the girls, and seeing what you'd built with each other, it made it in some ways harder to bear. Here you were, a family, and I let a brother down."

My heart is breaking in my chest for Ryan, Jason, and my brother who never shared these struggles. The tears begin to slide down my face and Jason reaches out his hand, but pauses. I know he won't touch me in my current state unless I say it's okay, so I give him an small nod. He brushes the tears away, wiping away traces of vomit along with them, I'm sure.

"I can't tell you Ryan's side of the story because that's his story to share. I felt so damn guilty that I'd inadvertently hurt someone I knew was in a place of pain already. Phil told me what happened earlier today and I want you to know that I asked him to give Ryan the family discount. I expected Phil to have given you some warning, but he's so accustomed to protecting your secrets. I shouldn't be surprised he held mine so closely. You have to understand, to me, Ryan is and always will be my family, despite our not speaking. When Ryan contacted Phil to put out feelers about the possibility of using Amaryllis Events, I figured he might be reaching out. It's not like he doesn't know who Phil is." Jason lets out a derisive snort. "Hell, with the Lockwood money, there are a million places he could have gone. All I knew was that Ryan had asked for dinner last night and the meetings today. I thought Phil would have at least given you some kind of background, but not fifteen minutes before the meeting. I never imagined it would have led to this. You know I never would have forced you to go back there," he whispers fiercely.

Jason takes a deep breath. "You see, Cass, it wasn't entirely Phil's fault your day went to shit. I never meant for this to bring you to *that* place."

"Why didn't anyone tell me this before? Didn't you think I would understand?" I plead, still hearing Ali's words, and the memories of long ago in my own head. *Smack! Whore. Smack!*

"Of course, I knew you would. But when we talked over dinner last night, Ryan indicated Caleb wanted to meet you first. I have no idea why. But I will say you need to be at the top of your game with this wedding, Cass. Caleb's methods may have been asinine, but if he knows by now, he has reasons, and damn good ones."

"Caleb may have reasons, but no one gets one of our weddings caught up in the middle of their issues, Jason. Just like no one will ever imply I'm a whore again, family or not," I respond coldly. My body is rigid with tension, and not from the cold fall night permeating my bones.

Jason lets out a low sound. "I'm sure you'll find a suitable punishment only you can think of, Cassidy. I'm not even going to warn Ali or my husband because he deserves it for being a clueless dick and not warning you before that meeting. He stripped you of the one thing you crave—your control."

It's amazing how insightful Jason is.

He stands and reaches for my hand to help me up. Pulling me in for a quick, hard hug, he whispers, "As for Phil, I'd start with getting him breve lattes for the next month with extra whip." After holding me tightly for a moment, Jason winks before walking away, leaving me alone with my thoughts.

I stand still, listening to my brother-in-law's footsteps crunching on the gravel path, back up the trail. When he opens the door to step back into the barn, I can hear the screaming still going strong.

Knowing that battle could take a while, I decide to walk around the lake to my house. My emotional state has been all over the place and I need some space. What a fucking day.

7

CALEB

I kick back in the rooftop deck chair, wondering how things went with Amaryllis Events. "What happened after I left today?"

Internally, I'm still reeling from the contents of the file. Angry. Boiling over with rage over what had been done to six young children. Although, I think Phil might argue he wasn't a child when the abuse stopped.

I was fucking infuriated by multiple systems which failed those children repeatedly. And after meeting the family that made themselves into a wild success from nothing, I was more impressed than I've likely ever been in my life. Including with the man who married into them, Jason Ross.

When I gave up my commission three years ago and came home to find Ry, he was no longer a wreck and I was grateful. For years over Skype, he'd been shaken to the core over a breakup he'd described as his first real relationship. Until he met Jared about five years ago, he refused to talk about why. Turns out, it was his embarrassment over how he walked out on Jason, leaving only a note when the relationship ended. Now, having read the file, I know he walked away from a friendship that saved him from our cunt of a birth vessel.

My hands tighten and almost crush the Baccarat tumbler of Bowmore I hold in my hand.

I'm brought back from my own thoughts, realizing I had zoned out.

"Caleb? You okay?" Ryan asks, perplexed.

"Sorry, brother." I will myself to relax and lift my drink to my lips. "I keep thinking about a file dropped on my desk a few days ago. Can't get my mind off it."

"I know you can't talk about your cases," Ry starts, the concern he feels written all over his face. I watch as he shifts subtly toward Jared, and they communicate silently for a moment. A smile threatens my lips as I watch their interaction. "We're here for you. For anything."

"Thanks." I shrug my shoulders to release the tension residing there and push the contents of the Freeman file from my mind. "I'm interested in what happened with the wedding planners. I was under the impression there might have been a small explosion after I left."

Ryan sits back. "What makes you say that?" he asks curiously.

As I begin to recount the hour before Ryan and Jared walked through the door, I lose myself in the story. I'm not going to lie, thinking about Cassidy Freeman is detrimental to my sanity. The little pixie is a knockout with an incredible brain and a smart mouth. I close my eyes, replaying the hour spent with her. My heart kicks up a few beats thinking of her eyes, with swirls of blue and green framed by long dark lashes. So expressive when her passion kicks in like it did when she was in her element, planning Ry's wedding.

I wonder what color they'd turn if I slid my lips over hers, or while I cupped my hands over her luscious ass? I'm getting hard just thinking about it, and I know I shouldn't want to touch her. She'll likely never want to be touched by any man.

Fuck.

I recount the horror on Cassidy's face when I didn't disagree to being one of the grooms. The hilarity of how she threatened to chop off all of Phillip Freeman-Ross' hair. Being impressed with how efficiently she runs their business.

I know I'm smiling. I'm waiting for Ry and Jared to burst out into laughter.

What I get is a shrieking that would rival a twelve-year-old girl meeting Justin Bieber.

"Are you out of your damn mind, Caleb? What in the hell were you thinking? No wait, I can answer that. You weren't. Not with the brain on your fucking shoulders," Ry rails at me.

What the hell?

My brother is stalking around the coffee table, waving his hands in the air. I risk a glance at Jared, but he merely shakes his head. Shit, no help there.

"What's your problem, Ry? You wanted me to find out if she was professional enough. I did. Admirably, if I do say so myself." I mentally congratulate myself.

"You were there to find out if she could take you on and what? Give in like every other insipid woman you meet does? So, you decided to humiliate her, Caleb? Because that's damn well what you did. You humiliated a woman for nothing more than what? Revenge for what you think happened between me, her brother, and her brother-in-law?" Ryan snaps.

Leaning forward, I put the tumbler on the table. "What if I did, Ry? Reading between the lines over multiple Skype calls, one of which almost got me shot, Jason humiliated you." Ryan's face pales and he rears back at my verbal attack. Jason didn't humiliate Ry, but it was time my brother manned up and told me that. "You two"— pointing at Ry and Jared—"are about to drop a whack to him indirectly. Why in the fuck would you do that?"

Ryan's shoulders slump. "I told you—"

I hold up my hand, cutting him off. "I know what you said about the company, and now that I've met with them, I agree with you. I still don't get it though. Why them? We can afford anyone, and you turn over several million dollars to plan your wedding to the family of your ex-fiancé? Are you trying to make him jealous? Don't you think that deserves more than the average push on a new employee interview?"

Ryan starts trembling and turns to look at Jared who holds out his hand. Ryan walks away from me and resumes his seat next to his fiancé, his chest heaving.

I reach for the Scotch and hold it up to the two men in front of me before relaxing back in my chair. After receiving nods and topping off their glasses, I lean back and say one word. "Explain."

Silence.

"Now!" I bark out.

Ry takes a deep breath and says, "I was never engaged to Jason Ross, Caleb."

I raise an eyebrow, but don't say anything. I tip my glass at him to continue.

"Jason was my savior, my protector, and my best friend. God, I was so lost, so hurt, so alone. He found me one night after...and well, he saved me. During the time we lived together, he gave me so much." Ry looks at Jared, his cheeks flushing. "I don't know when my feelings for him started to change, but they did. Call it gratitude or hero worship. I'm sure there are a half a dozen names for it."

I don't let my facial expression change, willing him to get to the point where I can ask questions.

"It was long after we were living together when Jason and I went to Candlewood Lake one day. The Freemans were there. I don't know how we'd never ran into them before. As you know, they're all beautiful," he muses, lost in his own memories. "Together, they're absolutely stunning."

While I agree, I need him to move on to what I want to hear.

"Jason had jumped into the water to cool off and was near the docks. I was sitting on the beach, people watching, when I heard a round of laughter from their group, and saw Phil pick up a voluptuous brunette, Corinna, and toss her in the lake. She was able to pull him in with her, where he practically landed on top of Jason. And that's how they met. A completely random act."

Ryan takes a pull from his Scotch. "After Phil offered Jason a hand out of the water and apologized, Jason followed them back over to their blanket. He'd forgotten about me completely. He was immediately enraptured, and now, I know how he felt."

I lean forward and reach for the bottle, but Ryan shakes his head for me not to fill his cup. As I start to move back, Ryan grabs my wrist.

"I blew up at Jason that night, Caleb. I was a raging lunatic. I can't even fully remember what I screamed at him. I know I kissed him, and he pushed me away. I felt so hurt, so rejected. In my head, I had built up the engagement for my safety to be real, and my fiancé had just turned me away." Ryan flushes, ashamed at his behavior that day so long ago.

And there's the opening I need, but just as I'm about to ask a question, Ry continues. "I left in the middle of the night with my clothes, journals, and not much else. I was certain by doing it that way, I would hurt Jason the way he had hurt me. I'm sure I did. Fuck, I know I did. He was my best friend. He found me at my worst, bloody in an alley, alone." At this point, I know my brother doesn't know what he's telling me. Jared does, and his eyes cut to me, warning me not to interrupt. This needs to come out. It's been festering way too long. "Jason gave me a second chance at life. He gave me the chance to find true love, and I did." Ryan now has tears trickling down his face. Jared leans forward and kisses him softly, obviously knowing the story I'm hearing for the first time, but read about a few days ago courtesy of the file Charlie kept up to date with.

My jaw tics as I bite back the questions I need his answers to.

"I repaid that by being a shit, Caleb. A bratty, self-entitled shit. So, Jared and I attended a few events where I knew my name would end up in the paper. I wanted Jason to know I hadn't offed myself in a back alley somewhere—a very real possibility when he first met me, and that I had moved on. After we got engaged, I discussed the possibility of reaching out to Jason with Jared. He already knew everything else."

At this point, I stand and start to prowl around. Ryan shifts anxiously before continuing.

"I already knew Amaryllis Events' reputation. I figured that if we hired them, I could atone for what I did to Jason. It was so wrong of me, Caleb. God, he never deserved that. I also thought I would have a chance to apologize…" Ry trails off, staring out across the city lights.

"Several of our friends used them for other events. Cassidy Freeman is reputed to be able shut to down the devil and to talk him into her bidding at the same time. The rest of the Freeman family are amazing artists, true, but she could take over corporations. I knew she could handle our—"

"Don't say the word. If you call that cunt our mother one more time, I don't know what kind of reaction I'll have," I caution with pure ice in my voice.

One second passes. Two…

Ry's head snaps toward me.

"You fucking knew before I said a word?" he breathes.

"Only since Sunday." There's no bullshit in my tone. "I ran a standard background check on Amaryllis Events the way you asked me to."

Ry is about to breathe fire of his own as he stalks over to me. "There's no way the story I just shared comes up in a standard check, Caleb. What the fuck were you doing?" Ryan is shouting now. "You had no right!"

"I didn't."

"Then how did you know all of this? There is no way you would have known everything." Suddenly, Ryan's face pales. He looks at me. "You. Know." He stops and swallows audibly. "Everything?"

I smile grimly at him. "Oh yeah, brother. Every-fucking-thing. And we'll get to what you never told me in just a minute. But as for how I knew? When I bought Hudson, it turns out the Freemans were clients before I acquired the company. I asked my analyst for a standard business background. The information I got made me ready to kill on several levels, starting and ending with the fucking birth vessel who pushed us out."

"Oh my god," Ryan breathes, stumbling to the couch. "That's why you demanded a preliminary meeting. You wanted to meet them."

"You're damn right I did. And as for the apology you owe Jason Ross, money doesn't cover that, you stupid shit. You man up and call him! You give it to him face-to-face. He saved your fucking life," I roar. "And you never told me?" I end on a whisper, lost at the pain-filled younger version of myself before turning away and walking over to the railing, breathing hard.

Silence. Well, as much silence as Tribeca on a Thursday offers. You could hear a pin drop on the roof, but below us, there was the typical hustle and bustle of the cabs.

I'm just about to turn around to head downstairs, leaving Ryan and Jared, when I hear, "You're right."

What?

I turn, leaning my hips against the railing, not saying a word.

"Before you ask me any of the millions of questions going through your head, brother, please try to understand this from my point of view," he says wearily. He stands, walks over next to me and rests his arms on the railing, facing the city. I hate the look of defeat that has come over him. "You understand what it's like to be hit, maybe even beaten, but not to be beaten to the core where your very soul lives. You know what it means to be bullied, but not humiliated where your skin is being used as a canvas and blood is the ink. You've seen the images of torture, but until you've been tortured and left to die for being nothing more than what you are, you don't know what you'll do to protect yourself where you're cornered. You don't know how often I wished I could just rewind and be someone else. You don't know how many times I imagined taking my own life," he whispers.

He's silent for a few minutes, but what he says next guts me. "I always thought you blamed me for killing Dad the way she did."

"Never, Ryan. Is that the kind of crap she said to you?" My skin is crawling from the knowledge that my brother was so close to death. By his own hand or by our mother's. All for being who he was born to be.

"Yes. After the beatings would begin, I'd hear her voice say all kinds of things, like Dad had a weak heart and my revelation pushed him over the edge. You joined the Army because you wanted to be around real men. Dad never wanted a second son. Things like that."

His head remains turned toward the city. "Since I was hopped up on God knows what, I believed her. And then she gave me an almost lethal dose of GHB and dropped me in an alley in New Haven, probably with the intent of being raped and left for dead. I'm guessing you read the rest." I'm clenching my jaw and Ryan nods. "Once Jason and his doctor got me off the drugs, I never wanted you to know. I knew you loved me, Caleb. You always had. And you've always been my biggest supporter. You're absolutely right about one thing, I should have called Jason years ago to apologize. There isn't any excuse, and it's time."

Ry stands up straight and claps me on the shoulder. I do the same. We lock eyes, our father's eyes, and don't say a word. A million thoughts pass between us. Recriminations, apologies, acceptance, and most of all, love.

Just when I'm about to pull him close, he surprises me with a question. "What about you?"

"What about me?" I reply, confused.

"When are you planning on apologizing to the Freemans, Cassidy in particular, for your appalling behavior? I mean, seriously? I'm certain you know things they likely don't want you to know. The contents of the file you read, they must want what's in it buried for a reason."

That, little brother, is the understatement of the century. But I keep those words hidden and my face impassive. Or so I think.

"Right. So, with that in mind, do you really think tricking and embarrassing Cassidy was the appropriate move? Could you have gone there to meet her without being a dick?"

"I wasn't a dick!" I exclaim. "I had a little fun with her, but we got a lot accomplished for your wedding." Shit, was I a dick? I do a quick mental replay when Jared chimes in.

"If you had done that to me, you would be lucky if I took you on as a client afterward." Jared, the well-respected attorney, wouldn't tarnish his name by those means or any other.

Shit. All the things I found cute, Cassidy probably took mortal offense to. And knowing what I do about her history, it's going to take a nuclear bomb to get me in the door again.

Fuck.

"Can you give me her schedule for the next few days? I need to figure out when I can get out to Collyer to talk to her." Maybe I'll take her out for coffee to replace the one that went cold on her today. And I'll apologize.

My baby brother, the fucker, has the nerve to laugh in my face. "No can do, Caleb. Both Jared and I signed NDAs to get Cassidy's personal schedule. In fact, that reminds me, you need to sign one to get your hands on her schedule for the wedding. It's a two-way NDA. She won't provide you any details about the wedding until you sign it." Ryan and Jared both laugh.

No shit? Seriously? I would say good for the little darling, but this isn't helping me out right now.

"No offense or anything but, Jared, aren't you a damn lawyer?"

"I am, Caleb. And all I can say is that I was highly surprised by the degree taken to ensure everyone's privacy. But given the nature of the information we have in the file Cassidy provided, I now fully understand why Amaryllis Events insisted on having us sign it. If we were a competitor, we could do some serious damage with what she turned over for your brother and I to have unfettered access to her."

Again, not helping. I growl at Jared before I start pacing. Both are laughing, which I suppose is better than the crisis mode we were in not thirty minutes earlier. I reach for my glass of Scotch and turn my head to Ryan. "When are you calling Jason?"

"Oh no. There's no way he rolls on his sister-in-law, Caleb," Ryan warns me with a hardness in his eye.

"Actually, I want to meet with Jason as well. I need to offer my thanks, Ry." My brother slowly nods his head, understanding my need to atone. It isn't easy to comprehend that I wasn't around to protect my baby brother. "I'm hoping he'll be in the city over the next few days. I'll deal with Cassidy on my own."

They know I'm going to get eaten alive by a five-foot-four jewel-eyed, pixie-sized pit viper. Ry and Jared start laughing while choking on their Scotch.

I think I know how the praying mantis feels right before he has sex for the last time.

Eager and petrified at the same time.

8

CASSIDY

"My damn brother wouldn't give me your schedule. Do you know that?"

I close my eyes before opening them to a gorgeous face linked to the frustrated, yet amused voice at my office door two days later. I figured Caleb would show up sooner or later. Later worked for me. Much, much later.

Work was moving at the speed of light on the Lockwood-Dalton wedding. After the contract was signed, I'd spoken to Ryan and Jared three times. We'd solidified significant blocks of rooms with the Old Greenwich Ritz-Carlton and the Delamar Greenwich Harbor, locked in the caterer, and had a conference call to discuss the floral arrangements so Phil could start estimating the flowers—primroses would be spotlighted. Em and Corinna were already on Ryan and Jared's calendars with locked in dates for tailoring, menu selection, and cake tastings. Holly was meeting the guys in the city tomorrow to take their engagement photos.

As for me? I had already sent at least fifty emails pertaining to narrowing down options about save the dates (which had to be sent out by next week), the invitations, signature drinks, gift bags for the hotel guests, charitable donations in lieu of wedding gifts, and about one hundred reminders, including one for Ryan and Jared to buy their rings.

I warned them, this was just the beginning.

Things were progressing fast. I didn't have time for my heart to skip a beat at the husky sound of Caleb's voice, but my body is a traitorous bitch. I can feel myself squirm slightly under his gaze. As my nipples start to harden, I'm grateful I had decided to wear a military-style jacket over formfitting jeans.

Damn the man for being so gorgeous with his thick brown hair and inky dark eyes. I realize I don't need to give him any more ammunition against me. Hadn't I humiliated myself enough with him for three lifetimes?

Meeting his gaze head-on, I say coolly, "I don't believe you've signed the required non-disclosure agreement in order to have that information, Mr. Lockwood. It's a damn good thing your brother didn't share that information or I would have been well within my rights to terminate his contract and sue him." I pause for effect. "While keeping the retainer, of course." I reach for a folder sitting on my desk. "I'm fairly certain we're past the point where we would solely be keeping just the retainer. In fact," I snap open the folder, "I know it."

"You wouldn't do that," Caleb says with the charming smile.

The fuck I wouldn't. "No?" I raise an eyebrow while ignoring my traitorous body. "You want to push us that far to find out?"

"You gave me your personal cell phone number, Cassidy. I would think a good lawyer and a reasonable judge would reason an implied consent."

"And any reasonable judge would understand it was provided under complete misrepresentation of yourself, Mr. Lockwood. As you remember, you represented yourself as one of the grooms." I uncross my legs and stand to my full height, fully ready to do battle.

"Calm down there, warrior princess. I see you're dressed for battle." He gives my outfit a quick but obvious once-over. Arrogant, cocky ass. He slowly pulls his arm from behind his back and tosses the flowers he's been hiding onto the desk. Purple hyacinth. Shit. Apology flowers.

"I know," he says as he saunters into the room, closing the door behind him. "I was a complete asshole." He read my mind.

"You think?" I huff as I slowly sit back down. I don't make a move to touch the flowers. "And you could've left the door open. You won't be staying long." My voice is pure ice, not giving an inch.

"We have things to talk about, Cassidy," he cajoles.

"No, we don't." My mask slips a bit, and I'm suddenly drained. "I'm your brother's wedding planner. You got what you came for, Caleb. I understand you were pushing my buttons as a kind of test to make sure I could handle the stress of an event this size. I passed, obviously, since the contracts are signed. There's no need for you to be here."

"I disagree," he counters.

"Why does that not surprise me?" I mutter.

"Tsk, tsk, Cassidy. Not nice," Caleb mocks.

"Should I be?"

"What, nice?" Caleb smirks. I'm about to put him back into the asshole category, flowers or not.

"Yes," I bite out between gritted teeth.

"God, no." He throws back his head and laughs, just as I'm in the process of snipping at him again.

"Fine, I will—wait. What?"

"I said, no, don't be nice. I would hate our relationship to be on that level." His dark eyes are dancing.

"We don't have a relationship outside of this wedding, Mr. Lockwood. Remember, you were acting as if you were the one getting married to your brother and his lover, apparently." I tsk. "That reminds me, I'll have to make certain which one of you is actually marrying Jared. For the license, of course. Oh, that's right. You're not one of the grooms. Since that little stunt got cleared up, your participation in this wedding was relegated to emergency situations only. Since I handle those quite well, you can be assured you won't need to be called in for backup." Ah, let him deal with that bit of revived bitchiness.

He laughs hysterically. Damn him. His handsome head tosses back, exposing a strong neck. So sexy on a man...calm it down, girl! Remember, asshole. Client.

After his laughter recedes, he turns serious. "I'd like to explain."

"Why bother? Things are progressing perfectly with the timetable I established for the wedding, so I don't feel the need." I know I'm coming off as a bitch. It's a persona I've established to keep men away. Inside, though, I'm not sure how much of this is my residual anger at the way Caleb played me, the way Phil left me swinging out in the wind, or hurt from Ali's comment that's triggered my guard to be so relentless. But right now, I don't care. After more nights of no sleep, nightmares, and the energy I'm using to keep Amaryllis Events running, I really don't have the time or inclination to deal with this. Maybe in a few months. Maybe in a few years.

Maybe never.

Caleb Lockwood is just too damn potent.

Suddenly, he stands up.

"Do you have anything going on right now?"

I snicker and gesture around me. My desk is lined with plans for his brother's wedding. My planner is out and I have the contract spread out with a million notes in the columns. Sticky-note arrows are pointing to sections of the contract I need to highlight on the electronic version for reference later. The Lockwood wedding binder has about twenty separate lists already being created.

I raise an eyebrow and look down at the mess before me.

He reaches across the desk and picks up my cup from The Coffee Shop. Jiggling it a bit, he remarks, "This is empty. How about a quick walk and a coffee?"

"WHOA, there's no need to race there, Cassidy," I hear Caleb call from behind me.

I feel the heat climb up my cheeks as I pause and wait for him to catch up to me. With my back still facing the direction we're walking in, I wrap my arms around myself. My head drops forward a bit in embarrassment.

I don't know how to do this, be alone with a guy. There's always been someone else with me to act as a buffer to prevent my panic from overwhelming me.

What was I thinking agreeing to this?

How in the hell am I supposed to have coffee with this guy?

Footsteps land right behind me and I let out a startled yelp. Jumping back, I stumble, and Caleb's strong arms grab mine to catch me.

"Are you okay, Pixie?" Caleb asks with concern.

No. I'm absolutely not okay. "Yes," I lie convincingly. I start to move out of his arms, but he lightly tightens them.

My panic level increases.

"Since you led us off Main Street, I'm not certain where to go from here?" he says with a smile.

I blink up at him.

He continues to smile down at me.

I look around at where I am and let out a puff of air. "Oh, I walked through the shortcut. This way." I move out of his arms and pick up my pace, when I'm slowed almost to a stop.

My hand is in his. How did I not feel this?

My eyes snap up to meet his, even as they're narrowing.

"This way, I won't lose you if you walk too fast," Caleb explains smoothly. "Or you could slow down and walk to The Coffee Shop with me."

"The town is not grotesquely large, Caleb. Even if we were separated for a moment, we would still be able to find one another there," I patiently explain, as if I'm talking to a two-year-old. All the while, trying to pull my hand from his with no success.

"It's not such a hardship for me to escort a beautiful woman to have a cup of coffee when I owe her an apology," he retorts. "If you stop trying to get loose, I'll make you a deal."

I pause, my panic slightly receding. No one had offered me a deal when I'd been restrained before. My hand stills in his.

"If you let me escort you to The Coffee Shop, buy you a cup of whatever you normally drink, and we can talk for a few minutes, I'll let your hand go. I will, however, likely place my hand on the small of your back where your jacket meets your jeans to help you balance in those shoes, guide you there, and overall, be a gentleman." He pauses, searching my face. "Are we agreed?"

"Are we agreed," I parrot back, buying some time while processing all he said.

"Yes." Caleb stands tall, rugged, masculine.

The part of me that still fears the past wants to run away with my hands in my hair, screaming. The other part of me wants to leave my past behind, and curl into him like a purring cat and enjoy it.

I have to decide.

"Okay," I whisper.

He smiles and squeezes my hand before dropping it and gesturing for me to walk in front of him.

Instinctively, my pace slows. I feel him come up along my right side, matching his steps to mine.

And there it is.

His hand lands on the small of my back.

In that one gesture, I feel the warmth of his body heat mine, which has been cold for so long. I feel the courtly manners he was brought up with being extended to me, of all people.

And if I was completely honest, the little girl who lives inside me cries, looking at him for the first time without tears.

As we reach The Coffee Shop, he reaches forward with his right arm to hold open the door. As I walk past him into the store, ignoring the stares I'm receiving, I smile openly up at him before sliding into an open booth in the back.

I'm oblivious to the effect it has on him.

❧

AFTER WE PLACE our orders with a gleeful Ava, Matt watches us from behind the counter.

Leaning back in his seat, Caleb scrutinizes me closely before throwing out something that should surprise me, but doesn't. "I don't want to sign the NDA."

"Guess you'll never need to speak with me," I sass back.

But he continues, as if I hadn't just taken another swipe at him. "I want you to trust me enough to give me your schedule, to let me know when you're available."

Is he crazy? Probably so. He likely has so many women dropping to their knees to blow him, his brain has been sucked out through his dick.

I laugh at his arrogance until I'm in hysterics.

Wiping my eyes, I ask, "Are you crazy?"

Shit, I didn't mean to say that out loud. Regardless of what I think of him right now, he is still technically a client.

Caleb looks at me like he's accomplished something amazing, grinning like a fool. A hot fool.

With that smile, the last vestige of my control is destroyed. The professional mask I pride myself on wearing is shredded. I feel like the brunt of a bad joke everyone's playing on me and they expect me to get over. For once, I forget who I am and what my responsibilities are. For once, I'm just a woman. A woman whose hurt isn't fading, isn't being pushed aside. A woman who didn't do anything wrong to get played. I dare him to step up and show me who he really is on the war that has been waging in my head.

Fuck it.

"Maybe too much whisky last night? Someone slip something extra into the cigars at the Havana Room? Maybe someone was a little too enthusiastic doing the reverse cowgirl, broke your dick, and the pain meds have kicked you into the realm of insane? Should you be driving to Collyer under those circumstances? Our police force can be pretty stringent on DUI." I lean forward. "If none of those things happened, I'd love to know what explanation you have for the delusion you're living under right now to think I'd hand over the keys to my private life to you."

He wipes his hand across his sculptured mouth. When he takes it away, his mouth is set in a serious line.

"No drinking last night. Haven't been to the Havana Room in quite some time. As for the crazy hot sex, well, we can get into those details now, if you'd like. I was trying to keep this somewhat circumspect." I can't see his eyes through the lowered dark lashes. My pulse spikes when he raises them to look directly at me. "For now."

Suddenly, I'm mortified with myself. The line of business ethics and professionalism is gone. And this time, I was the one to obliterate the line. Not only did I just talk to Caleb Lockwood like I would my family, I basically insinuated to his face he was nothing more than a pretty face with nothing better to do than get tore up and laid. What the hell just happened with my brain?

I wonder, fleetingly, if I can excuse myself, go to the restroom and ask Matt if I can claim a temporary psychotic break to save my reputation. Picking at the threads of my jacket nervously, I take a deep breath and prepare to have my unprofessional behavior thrown back at me.

Sitting up straighter, I ask "Is there anything else I can help you with, Mr. Lockwood?" I flick up the fingers of my hand to pause him as he opens his mouth to speak. "Business related."

"No. Nothing for now. I wanted to apologize."

We size each other up. I begin to tap my foot. He crosses his arms. I click my nails on the table. His fingers tap on his bicep. "Well," I finally demand.

"Well, what?" the singularly obtuse man in front of me repeats.

"Where is the apology?" I grind out.

"I brought flowers," he says cheekily.

Ah, the glorious purple blooms waiting for me back on my desk. "Saying it with flowers isn't going to cut it, Lockwood. You have no idea what—" I catch myself in time before I verbally vomit my family's business all over this man.

It's suddenly so quiet between us, it's like someone pressed the mute button on our conversation. All the humor has left his eyes. "Tell me."

"No." I sound like a petulant three-year-old, but I don't care.

"You will." He's back to sounding like an arrogant ass. I can deal with that. I can handle that.

I lean back in the booth and stare out the window of The Coffee Shop. Turning back to him, he gives me a quizzical look. "Just checking to see if Hell froze over since we walked in. I'd say no. It's not that cold out."

A bark of reluctant laughter leaves his lips. "God, that mouth."

Caleb leans forward, elbows resting on the table. "Somehow, I didn't get the impression you were a woman where a simple, 'I'm sorry' would work. I've been thinking of you, reading up on you."

There's no way I'm about to allow that one to pass. I'm about to snark out some obnoxious comment when he holds up his hand. "You make men work for it. The flowers are just the beginning. I'm just starting to make my case. I'd get on my knees and beg, but I'm saving that for special occasions."

His eyes collide with mine. Stupid, stupid move, Cass. Despite his innuendo-laced words, part of me expected his eyes to reflect his apology.

Sweet baby Jesus, that is so not what I see.

There's heat. I feel the blaze reach out, starting to thaw the coldest parts of me. I'm going to incinerate if I keep looking at him. I might have been able to have held out against that, but it's the other things revealed there that start to suck me in.

Admiration.

Estimation.

Appreciation.

"What do you want from me?" I whisper, suddenly aware of the closed off environment of our booth. The relative privacy within a very public space. The thickening tension between us. Air so filled with want I could choke on it.

He gives me a slow curve of his mouth.

"To start with, the right to use your phone number, Cassidy, and not just because of this wedding." His voice is quiet, almost a growl. He never loses eye contact with me. "Despite what Ry and Jared put in that contract, I'm not your damn client. They are. I'm only on there in the event of...problems they can't handle without some intervention."

My eyes briefly flit to the left as I think back to my conversation with Jason. Caleb notices and reads my face immediately. "You've talked with Jason, then."

I nod.

He sighs, and suddenly there's something deeper in his eyes. All traces of flirtation are replaced with regret. True regret. "I wasn't planning on taking the misunderstanding that far, Cassidy. To be honest, when you assumed I was the groom..." He pauses, the silence flowing between us.

"One of three," I correct him, breaking the silence. For some reason, I'm trying to make this easier, to ease his burden. To make him smile.

"One of three." His lips quirk before he lifts his mug to them. "I thought I would let it go for a second and explain. Then you started cussing at your brother. Then the next thing I knew, you snapped into this professional and we had most of the wedding planned in one hour. I was caught between being impressed and in shock. I never had a chance to correct you before Ryan and Jared showed up."

I notice we've both moved, unconsciously, leaning toward each other in the booth.

I frankly don't know what to think. My head is spinning.

I gnaw on my lower lip. Caleb has no idea the storm he set off in the Freeman family with that little stunt. I nod slowly, and my concession seems to release him. Leaning back, he relaxes into his seat as I remain thoughtful, unable to break our détente to leave.

The silence starts to stretch out uncomfortably when Caleb admits wryly, "If it helps any, I think that little stunt might have saved my brother's relationship with his best friend."

With Jared? Had something else happened?

"What do you mean?" I ask cautiously. I hadn't felt any discord between the grooms.

"I mean, Ryan ripped into me so hard for being a dumb shit, I think I'm still bleeding from the shots he took." Caleb feigns being affronted. "As Ry tends to think that about me quite a bit, it was really Jared agreeing with him that drove home the point that I was a shit the first time I met with you."

I knew I liked this particular set of grooms for more than their taste and decisiveness.

"Oh?" I smirk, feeling more in control again.

Caleb appears thoughtful, choosing his next words carefully. "After the yelling died down that night, Ry called Jason and apologized for his big brother being a douchebag. He used me to open the door for a much more difficult conversation that needed to happen years ago between him and Jason."

My lips part as I let out a little puff of air.

Caleb chuckles softly. "I told him I could apologize for my own poor behavior, but Ry used it as an opportunity to apologize to Jason and Phil. Things didn't end well with them despite their initial business discussions, and Ry hadn't figured out a way to make it right."

Caleb's gaze drifts out the window. "Jason's a good man. A terrific one, in fact. Ry was so confused back then and didn't realize what he was feeling, or what Jason felt, until he met Jared. Hell, when I spoke with Jason yesterday—"

"You spoke with Jason?"

"Yes. He and your brother were generous enough to meet me in the city for lunch. I told Jason he could pretty much ask me for my life and I would give it to him. He took care of Ry while I was overseas in the Army."

His jaw tics as I watch him become lost in his memories. I don't interrupt. I give him a moment with his thoughts while I think back to what Jason told me last Monday evening.

"I'm glad they talked." My words bring Caleb back to the here and now. His fathomless dark eyes bore into mine. Mine don't break away. I'm captured, pulled under, and drowning.

"Have dinner with me," he says abruptly. Before I can answer, he blurts, "No, I take that back."

I feel the eruption of righteous indignation coming. Gee, that was quick. My brows, which had been rising, lower, but my eyes narrow at the man across the table. He merely grins.

"We'll have dinner, and afterward, I want you to join Ry, Jared, and I at a wedding."

I laugh outright. Because...a wedding?

"Seriously? You want to take a wedding planner to someone else's wedding?" I raise my cappuccino to my lips. Caleb's eyes dance over the cup.

"It's not really the wedding as much as it is the party. The person who got married is someone Ry went to school with and our family knows very well. He used to date her." Caleb winks and I shake my head. The irony is not lost on me. "It's a destination wedding, and the bride and groom are throwing a country party at the Molly Darcy's in Danbury. They rented the place out for the night, and we're doing dinner before that."

"Country night in an Irish bar?"

"Groom's from the South and she's Irish. They thought it was funny."

Makes about as much sense as this conversation. "Sounds like you guys will have a good time," I remark casually.

He leans forward and grabs my hand before I can react. I don't even have time to shift, to move from my deceptively relaxed position. God, his touch is like a bolt of lightning through my system. My nipples stand at attention again, just from touching my hand.

Have I ever felt anything like this around a man? Ever?

But it's his words that leave me breathless.

"How am I supposed to apologize properly if I can't get you away from work to do so? I can't apologize appropriately in your office or in a coffee shop."

Holy. Fucking. Shit. Thoughts fly through my over-tired brain. This man looks like he wants to devour me like I'm quite possibly a steak, or maybe the whisky I accused him of drinking last night. His long fingers caress the inside of my wrist. My nipples are so tight, they ache. I feel the nagging throbbing between my legs that I've only read about. What is Caleb Lockwood doing to me?

"Cassidy?"

"Yes." Wait. What? Did I just agree to go to a post-wedding party of all things with Caleb Lockwood?

"Good. I'll pick you up on Friday at six. Ry and Jared want to eat at Rosy Tomorrows. They have great burgers. Getting a seat in there after seven is a bitch."

I'm floundering. Did I just agree to a date with Caleb Lockwood?

I must be out of my mind.

I swirl the dredges of my coffee with suspicion.

"What is it? Is there something wrong with your coffee?" Caleb asks, immediately concerned.

"No, it's not that. I'm just wondering if there are drugs in there that made me say yes?" I admit with one-hundred percent honesty.

He barks out a laugh.

"Dislike me that much?" His voice is filled with humor at my candor, but I'm still undecided on what it is I'm feeling.

"No. I've never dated a client before." I'll give him that much for now.

He pulls my hand to his mouth and kisses the back of my knuckles. "And I told you, I'm not your client."

While I'm still reeling from the slick and very sweet maneuver, Caleb starts asking me personal questions. "Do you like to read?"

Without hesitating, I answer, "Absolutely."

"What kind of books?"

I open my mouth to tell him, but instead say, "You first."

"Nope, I asked first."

"At the same time," I offer.

"Deal."

I call out to Ava. "Hey, Ava! Can we get a pen and two pieces of paper?"

As she's swinging through with a tray of food, a pen and pad land on our table. I rip off two pieces of paper.

"Can you answer more than one?" I needle him playfully.

He gives me an extraordinarily patronizing scoff before picking up his own pen and quickly scribbling off a few lines.

I quickly write my answer, fold the paper in half, and half again. Caleb has done the same, holding it between two fingers.

"Deal time," he declares with a wink.

My heart flutters and my cheeks warm. "I'll hear the terms first."

Two glasses of water appear at our elbows while we were talking. I grab one and start sipping.

"One. Whatever's in these is for us to know only. It doesn't get shared with any family or friends." The witty charmer seems to have disappeared. Caleb's face is all solemn and pensive. It touches something in me.

"Deal."

"Two. You agree to go to the party with me." At my hesitance, which he can't begin to understand, he cajoles softly, "You'll have fun, Cassidy. I promise. And if you don't, we can always leave." His eyes bore into mine, willing the answer he wants.

Without giving my fears a voice, I say softly, "Yes."

The smile that breaks out across his face pushes back the demons for a while longer.

"Now, hand it over, Lockwood. I want to know if your reading level extends to more than *Captain Underpants*," I taunt.

"I've also read *Dog Man* as well, Cassidy. Let's not limit me to a particular series," he replies mildly as he hands over his list.

I take his, but can't seem to let go of mine. In fact, I'm crushing it tighter in my hand.

This list reveals so much about me. I feel exposed, and he hasn't even touched it yet.

"Cassidy?" Caleb reaches over and gently brushes his fingers across the hand holding my list. Involuntarily, the paper falls from my hand and onto the table. He doesn't reach for it. Instead, his eyes meet mine. "You have to hand it to me. I'm not going to take anything you're not ready to give."

That tells me so much about him.

Shakily, I reach down for my list and hand it to him.

I open his and immediately burst out laughing. Mystery, True Crime, Biographies.

"Predictable much, Caleb?" I laugh.

"Wait, let me add to that." He snags the list out of my hand and scrawls *Captain Underpants* at the bottom.

My reaction is fits of giggles that bubble out of me, unrestrained.

"That's probably the most beautiful thing I've ever seen," he murmurs.

As Caleb is facing the back of The Coffee Shop, I swirl around in confusion. He just shakes his head and reads the list in his hands and his eyebrows skyrocket.

I fiddle with my coffee spoon. I know what's written there. Romance, Self-Help, Humor.

He looks at me, down at the list, and at me again.

"Obsessed with work, are we?"

"Pardon me?"

"Research for work much?" Caleb asks, with a smile tugging at his lips. He lifts my list and turns it toward me. "I mean, I'm by no means an expert, but it's like a survival guide on how to get through the stress of wedding planning 101."

That was not the reaction I was expecting. Relaxing a bit, I smile, then I chuckle.

This feels good. Normal. I'm about to open my mouth to say something when I'm interrupted by Ava breezing by, asking me, "Cassidy, Phillip just called in the lunch order. Do you want to take it back with you, hon?"

Lunch?

I look down at my watch and gasp. We've been having coffee for that long? I jump up out of the booth and berate myself for the time I've lost that I'll have to make up.

"I have work to do...I need to get back." My voice is shaky, and I have to work to control it. "Ava, charge everything to our account, please, including Mr. Lockwood's coffee," I call out.

"You got it, hon," Ava replies cheerily. A large brown bag waits on the counter near the cash register.

Caleb is still sitting in the booth, his dark eyes boring into mine as he stands slowly. Even in my heeled boots, Caleb is still a good eight inches taller than me.

I try to control my flinch as he raises his hand to my face, brushing back a curl.

"So, instead of the date, can I call you?" he asks softly.

Unable to speak, I nod.

"Okay. And we'll talk more about Friday?" Caleb's mouth crooks up before he trails his finger down my cheek.

I feel that single touch scorch through my body like a burning flame. I teeter on my heels and end up pressing my hands against his warm chest. Gasping, I move to step away, but find his hands are locked onto my elbows.

I say the only thing I can. "Yes."

Caleb leans down to press a soft kiss to my forehead. "I will never make you do anything you don't want to do, Cassidy. We can talk later about Friday when you're less in a hurry."

I tilt my head back. "Thank you." Such simple words to convey such a depth of feeling. But I'm thankful he seems to understand I need to process this.

"Cassidy! Phillip's called twice. Apparently, the boy is starving," Ava yells from the front of the shop.

Disconcerted, I glance back up at Caleb who's mildly annoyed at my brother's interruption. However, his voice is nothing but warm when he speaks.

"I'll give you a call later," he promises.

With mixed feelings of excitement and dread, I flee, snagging the bag of food on my way out.

I already miss the man with the crossed arms standing behind me as I leave.

9

CALEB

I'm standing beside the booth where Cassidy and I were sitting when I hear a rough male voice behind me say, "Son, I hope you're not playing games with that girl. I'd really hate to have to take one of my cleavers to you."

The voice belongs to the weathered face of the older man who had been standing at the counter the entire time I was speaking with Cassidy with his arms crossed. He looks like he'd like nothing more than to carry out the threat.

"Matt," Ava snaps, walking up with her fists on her plump hips. "Leave him alone. Cassidy is a big girl and can take care of herself."

I choose my words carefully. "Actually, it's nice Cassidy has so many people who care for her. I suspect she doesn't let many in." I sit back down in the booth, leaving the older man in a position of power.

Deliberately.

During my time with the Army, I was an intelligence officer. It was my job to be able to ferret out information from difficult sources. I was trained to blend into a crowd and to eavesdrop on conversations. I was taught to pick up social cues in conversation to determine how best approach a wary target.

I was also taught when to stand down.

"Ava, she's fragile," Matt growls.

"No, she's not," Ava snaps back. They start bickering, forgetting about me for a moment. I listen with one ear while thinking of the woman in question.

Cassidy Freeman went through a metamorphosis, forged of the strongest steel after being shattered into a million pieces. It isn't the beauty of her dark curls or ocean blue eyes that have me captivated. Her courage to carry on when there was nothing is what's drawing me in. She could have broken at any time, fallen on her shield and given in. No one who knew the truth of what she lived through as a child would have faulted her for it. But each day, she wakes up and dedicates her life to her family, to her business, to her community, with wit and humble grace.

Like the people who uncovered the atrocity that was her life before she turned nine, I hope every one of the motherfuckers who caused her such trauma are dead.

"He's not even listening." I tune back in to hear Matt berating me. Ava's shaking her head at his antics.

"I'm not standing around while you talk about our girl," Ava announces. Giving me a once-over, she mutters, "You'll do, Mr. Lockwood."

I'm surprised because we were never introduced. I stand out of ingrained manners and respect. "Madam, a pleasure as well. I hope our paths cross again."

"If you take care of our girl, I'm sure they will," Ava tosses over her shoulder as a customer walks in.

Matt's eyes narrow on Ava before he slides into Cassidy's seat. He's not done saying what he feels he needs to say, so I slide back into mine to listen. Neither of us speak for a moment.

"Lockwood. Do you have a first name, son" he grumbles.

I hold out my hand. "It's Caleb."

"Matt." He sighs and gives me a firm shake. "We're both right, Ava and I...about Cassidy."

I decide to stop him. She doesn't need everyone betraying her. "Matt, can I ask a question before you continue?"

He nods.

"Would Cassidy want you to tell me what you're about to tell me?" I ask cautiously.

Matt's face tightens before letting out another sigh. "No."

"Then would it help you for me to tell you about me?" I offer unexpectedly.

He blinks. "Well, damn. I wasn't expecting that. Go ahead, Caleb. Hit me with telling me about you. Why should I give a damn?"

I pick up the remainder of my coffee. Swirling it around, I lift the cup to my lips and drink it. I make a snap decision to reveal what I'm about to as I put it down. "Because I'm a private investigator. The company I own used to be Laskey Investigations."

Matt's face freezes with complete shock.

He's not just the short order cook at The Coffee Shop, but he co-owns it with his wife, Ava. He's also a former psychologist. I know from the file I read, he helped Cassidy as much as he could to get her through her nightmares, to pull out the details of what happened in her past.

I know he and his wife, Ava, consider themselves surrogate parents to the Freeman family.

Matt is regarding me with a mixture of shock and anger. "Does she know?" he hisses.

I know he means Cassidy and not his wife. "I shouldn't know, Matt." Still disturbed by what I read in that file, I slowly shake my head. "And yet, if I didn't, I would keep making more mistakes when it comes to her. Does that make sense?" I seek guidance.

Absolution.

"How long have you known?" His voice still holds a note of fury, but it's tempered.

"Since Sunday," I answer immediately. "My brother asked me to run a background check on the company. He's using them for his wedding."

"Lockwood, Lockwood..." Matt mutters to himself. "Ryan's your brother?"

I nod.

"So, you also found out..." My expression gives him his answer. "I'm sorry, son. Jason used to bring Ryan in to talk to me. I hope it helped some."

I swallow hard. Here's another person I have to thank for saving my brother while I was off saving the world. "No, Matt. I have you to thank. I had no idea...I never would have left..." My voice trails off.

Matt reaches over and claps my shoulder, bringing my eyes back to his. "You have nothing to feel guilt over when it comes to Ryan, Caleb."

I shrug. I'm still working through that.

"When it comes to my girl though, you'd best be sharing that shit soon. She won't tolerate a betrayal like that," Matt concludes.

"How" I demand. "How do you bring this up in a conversation without destroying something so new, it hasn't even been defined yet? I haven't even gotten her to agree to go out on a date with me. I had to bargain with her for a phone call."

Matt smiles and shakes his head at me. He reaches into his apron before grabbing a note pad and pen. He scribbles something quickly on it. So quickly, that if I didn't know his former profession was being a doctor, I would be able to tell just by the way he's writing. I just hope I can read whatever it is.

Matt tears off the sheet and hands it to me. Then he stands and holds out his hand.

Standing, I shake his automatically. "Try that. I have faith in my girl. A pleasure to meet you, Caleb. Drop by any time."

He ambles away, back to the kitchen, before I read what he wrote.

I recognize it's a quote from Thomas Paine.

"The real man smiles in trouble, gathers strength from distress, and grows brave by reflection."

On the other side of the paper, he wrote, "You'll figure it out."

I fold the scrap and put it with the one Cassidy wrote earlier in my wallet before walking out of the coffee shop.

10

CASSIDY

C aleb, as promised, called me that night.

It was the first time a man outside of my family called me for any reason other than work.

When the phone first rang, I stared at it like it was a snake. It almost went to voicemail before I picked it up.

After a few minutes of stilted conversation, Caleb decided to let me know he was going to download a romance novel to his Kindle.

I laughed at him.

"What? I need to be able to get inside your mind, Cassidy. I need a playbook of sorts. Don't these things help a guy out?" he teased.

I think I might have crushed him when I told him that the real reason we read them was because of the hot guys on the cover.

We spent the next few minutes debating whether or not Caleb would get disowned if he decided to take up cover modeling as a profession.

By the end, I was laughing and recommending a few romantic suspense books I didn't think would traumatize him for life.

They also didn't have models on the cover.

"So, Cassidy, given any more thought to what I asked earlier?"

Caleb tries to sound nonchalant, but I can hear the cautious optimism in his voice.

Friday night. A date. Any more thought? How about all my thoughts?

I hear a low chuckle.

"Crap, did I say that out loud?" I can feel the blood rushing to my face, I'm so mortified.

Caleb laughs harder.

I desperately search the room, trying to find anything to extract myself from this humiliation, and find the clock. "Oh, look at the time. I have to get some sleep. I guess I better go."

Still chuckling, Caleb says, "Wait, Pixie. Hold on a second. I'm not laughing at you. I'm laughing because it's all I've thought about all day too."

I pull the phone away from my ear and stare at it. Seriously?

"Oookay." I have no comeback to that.

"Seriously, Cassidy." His husky voice fills my ear and leaves me feeling like I just drank a glass of wine too fast. "I'm still in my office because I barely got any work done today, wondering if…"

"Wondering if what, Caleb?" I ask quietly.

"Wondering if you'd say yes?" he replies, just as quietly.

I curl up in the middle of my bed into a ball, my arm wrapped around my knees because I'm petrified.

Do I have the courage to try to reach through time and space for the one star I never thought I would ever get to make a wish on? I look around my room. I've tried to build dreams in here. It's time I tried to live one.

"Okay," I whisper.

I hear a rush of air come from Caleb on the other end of the line before he says huskily, "Great. I'll pick you up at six on Friday."

Hearing the rustle of clothing, I picture him walking on plush carpeting, muffling the sound of his boots.

"What are you doing?"

"Fist pumping the air," he says seriously.

I blink a few times, then I burst out laughing.

Smart. Funny. Arrogant. Gorgeous.

What the hell did I just agree to?

"I love that sound, Pixie," Caleb murmurs. "Perfect way to end a call.

"Wait, Lockwood. What the hell am I supposed to wear? How will you know where to pick me up?"

"I'll call you tomorrow, but you should be ready by six." He hangs up the phone before the thoughts of possibly backing out can even formulate.

Told you—arrogant. But maybe not quite the asshole I thought he was on Monday.

Plugging my phone into my bedside charger, I wrap myself in my blankets with a smile on my face.

And for the first time in weeks, my dreams don't end in nightmares.

They end with Caleb.

~

IT ISN'T until the next morning at the office I realize I never thought to check my planner to see if we have an event on Friday night. This man has me so off-kilter, that I, the freaking obsessive compulsive wedding planner, never looked at any calendar the day before while I was contemplating accepting Caleb's invitation.

I snatch up my calendar and grab my iPhone, comparing both for Friday at six. I groan and put my head in my hands. I never do this. I double booked appointments.

I never double book appointments.

Never.

This is what Caleb Lockwood does to me. He throws me off my stride. He makes it so I can't think. I come up with all kinds of preposterous thoughts to downplay these feelings for him. This is why going out with him is a bad, bad idea.

Reaching for the phone, I call Em. She'll help me get my head on straight. Jabbing my finger on the extension, I call her office phone.

"What's up?" she answers distractedly.

"Can I come down? I need to talk to you," I ask, sounding desperate to my own ears. I pray she doesn't notice.

"Sure." Her voice now sounds calm and tranquil. "I'm just going over the Lockwood-Dalton designs. I could use a second eye."

Of course she is. I can't get away from the Lockwoods.

"Be right there."

Taking calming deep breaths, I grab my phone and planner and walk out the door to my sister's office. My heels make sharp tapping noises on the refinished hardwood stairs as I make my way to what I hope will be a sanity check.

Walking into Em's office a few minutes later, I'm enveloped in her creative wonderland. I chose to convert two of the upstairs bedrooms to be the model of efficiency and organization while still maintaining charm through hidden organizational compartments in cabinetry leaving me with a gigantic office. Em chose to keep two separate areas only allowing one as her client space by taking over the old drawing room and the front parlor.

The drawing room where Em entertained clients grabbed your eye because the upscale elegance didn't cater to one sex or another, one generation or another. It didn't throw bridal in your face. The gray palate plays off the restored mahogany wood. As Em once explained to me, color popped more off gray than any other color, including white. So, to truly get whether something (including white) was a correct shade, hold it up to gray. Fortunately, this wasn't where Em spent most of her time. It would have driven us all insane.

Connected to it is the front parlor area, which she uses as her design space because of the natural sunlight that streams through the bay window. It's filled with jewel-toned colors, pillows made of every color and texture imaginable. Beautiful stained-glass dream catchers catch the fall sun and throw translucent shapes around the room as you walk in. Framed, antique art deco posters decorate the walls.

This space is Em's soul put on display, which is why very few are ever invited here.

Em could be found here most of the time sketching in the window seat, lying on the antique rug, or on a chaise lounge, as she is today. She has music playing softly as she works.

I drop into one of the overstuffed chairs facing her chaise. Hooking a leg over it, I wait for her to finish what she's doing. I learned early on with Em's art to never interrupt. If I didn't have the time to wait, then what I have could wait until she had time.

Being as organized as I am, some might think I would spiral in a panic spending this much time in Em's space, but to be honest, I always feel myself relaxing here. There's a warm comfort here, rather like her. It's like a continuous embrace of her arms wrapped around me. Already I could feel some of the panic that had been building inside me receding.

Mugsy, Em's elderly rescue dog, gets up from where he's been lying next to Em's chaise. After licking my hand, he proceeds to scoot his butt up against my legs. Taking that for the signal it's meant to be, I start stroking his silky ears as Em's pencils scratch on the sketchpad she's holding. I begin to replay both meetings and my phone call with Caleb in my head.

Putting down my phone and planner, the hand not petting Mugsy combs through my hair. My fingertips graze where I know my amaryllis tattoo sits at the base of my hairline. Not for the first time, I think we were so lucky to have found one another.

Mugsy puts all of his weight on me, bringing me back from my wandering mind. Em has changed the music, a clear indication she's finished her drawing and is waiting on me with one eyebrow raised.

I lean back in my chair, away from Em's penetrating gaze, staring at the coffered ceiling. "I fucked up."

"I doubt that," Em says calmly.

"I double booked an appointment."

"That wouldn't have you down in my workroom, Cass. You would just adjust one or the other. Now"—she puts on her patronizing face —"what happened?"

"I booked a date over the Collyer Homecoming Dress Extravaganza."

That knocks the look off her face. She starts sputtering, "Wait, what? A date? You? Over the dress extravaganza? That's your baby and you forgot about it?"

I groan. "I know. I have no idea how either happened, Em." I lean forward and put my head in my hands, partially covering my ears.

I think I hear her ask "With whom," but I deliberately ignore her until she reaches over and snags my hand, ripping it away from my head. Not for nothing, she takes a few pieces of my hair along with it. Bitch.

"With who?" Framing my face with her hands, I know there's no avoiding the question this time.

I breathe in and out while glaring at my sister. I know my reaction isn't helping this situation. I mean, it's not a big deal, right? But even I know I'm lying to myself as my heart picks up speed when I say, "Caleb Lockwood."

She looks at me. I stare back.

A moment passes. Then two.

I'm expecting an explosion. The howling laughter as her hands drop is not the one I anticipated.

"Are you kidding me?" she gets out, gasping for air. "The 'former groom' asked you out on a date? When?" She falls back on her chaise, clutching her stomach as she laughs, her long legs draped on either side.

I debate picking up one of her gorgeous throw pillows and smothering her with it.

"Are you done yet?" I sneer, all my earlier calm rapidly disappearing.

"Not even close. This beats anything I've ever done by a mile, sister. You will never again be able to hold anything against me. This is my perma get out of jail free card."

Just wait until she realizes I have photo evidence I've been holding onto. Forget about it. I'm a big girl. I'll figure this out on my own.

Em is still laughing when I stand up to stomp out of her office. "No! Wait Cass, hold on," she pleads, still chuckling. My hands are holding my phone and planner so tightly, my knuckles are turning white. "Please, Cassy, sit with me."

Pausing, because Em pulled out a name only she ever gets away with calling me, I plop back down next to her, setting my stuff to my side on the chaise.

Em takes one of my hands and gives it a squeeze. "What are you more upset about, Cass? The schedule snafu, a date in general, or with Caleb specifically?"

"I have to choose?" I ask her in return. My voice is rich with derision.

"No, but it helps to have a place to start."

Sighing, I squeeze our joined hands. "I think it's because he throws me so off balance, I can't quite catch myself. I mean, a few days ago, I thought he was getting married to two other men! He came to see me, took me out for coffee, and the next thing I know, I'm agreeing to a date." I catch Em's grin. I release one of her hands and start to pick at an imaginary piece of lint on my jeans. "I didn't even think at what might be on deck. It was like I knew we didn't have anything important going on for his brother, so it was okay to accept. What if we had another wedding that night? It's bad enough it's the dress extravaganza."

She's quiet for a few minutes. "What's your heart telling you?"

"About Caleb?"

"No, about Santa Claus." She rolls her eyes.

I narrow my eyes at her through my lashes.

"I know you, darling. The nightmares have come back, haven't they?"

My head flies around. It's a good thing she's so damn tall or I would have clocked her.

"Just because you're older, doesn't mean we don't *see* you. It doesn't mean we don't know when you're hurting. What happened here and at the farm...let's just say I know when you need space. The others have been ready to tear down the door to your cottage for the last few days."

"I'd have killed them. They would cost a fortune to refurbish."

"I know." We both smile, but her smile fades. "Are they as bad?"

I shrug. "They're there. Not as bad as they were at the beginning of the week."

"I could have easily knocked out both Phil and Ali that night, Cass, I was so fucking mad. At Phil for not explaining dick. And Ali? I still haven't spoken to her since that night. Her apology better either be on her knees or the equivalent. And no, for the record, that is *not* what we think of you. You fucking know better than that." Damn, Jason must have been on a rampage when he went inside the farm after I walked home Monday night.

My face must reveal more than I thought. "Phil is on everyone's shit list, and competing for a close second is Ali. Corinna, Holly, and I are waiting to see how you want to handle this. We're yours to command, Captain." Em mock salutes me.

It makes me laugh a little sadly as I put my head on her shoulder. I can't remember the last time we'd had such a fracture in what I feel are some of the cornerstones of this family.

Respect. Trust. Honesty.

Em's head comes down next to mine. She repeats her question.

"What's your heart telling you, Cass?"

This time, I reply without hesitation. "He's gorgeous, arrogant, and used to getting his own way."

She chuckles. "Yep, I figured that one out in the few minutes I spent with him."

I slip my hand from hers and hook our elbows together. "He loves his brother as much as I love all of you. He apologized for what he did in the office." I think about what I'm about to say. "He doesn't want to sign the NDA. He wants me to trust him enough to tell him where I'm going to be so he can reach me."

Em just whistles long and low.

"And when he touches my hand, my fucking hand, Em, it's like my mind blanks."

"So what's the problem? He's hot as fuck, has excellent taste in women, and is basically a nice guy. Or am I missing a downside?"

"How about my schedule issue? You know, the reason I came to your office?"

"No. The reason you came down here is because you wanted reassurance you did the right thing. You already know how to fix the scheduling issue. And right now, those two people would do just about anything to make things up to you."

I sit back to get away from my sister, staring at her in wonder. "You mean..."

"I mean, you go to the extravaganza, have Caleb pick you up from the farm, and have Phil and Ali do all the end of event dirty work as part—not all—of making amends for the crap they dealt you."

Damn, this girl. She should have been a strategist, not an artist.

"Those girls rely on us, Cass, and we won't let them down. But I'm not going to let you let yourself down either."

I don't have words. I wrap my arms around her and hold on, not even realizing tears are sliding down my cheeks.

After a few moments, she pulls away, brushing at her own face. "Oh, I have something for you." She reaches for her sketchbook. Flipping to the last page, she turns it toward me. Caleb's face reflects back at me in artists chalks. It's so lifelike, I can almost smell the cologne I'm sure lingers in my office.

"Just what I thought," she murmurs with a smug smile. "You didn't answer me before."

I tilt my head to the side quizzically.

"What's in your heart?"

Letting out a long breath, I answer her honestly. "I don't have a clue."

"Good answer." Quickly spraying the paper so the chalk doesn't smudge, she hands the sketch to me.

After another long hug, I leave her office. I hold the picture of Caleb for a few moments before tucking it safely away in my desk. Soon, my fingers are flying, composing the memo to Phil and Ali about their assignments for the extravaganza.

I also begin mentally preparing myself for the phone call I'll likely receive from Caleb tonight.

Em's right. I'm about to let myself take a few risks and open my heart to a good guy for the first time ever.

No more hiding.

11

CALEB

After hanging up with Cassidy Wednesday night, I received a phone call from my number two at Hudson, Keene Marshall, ordering me on a plane down to Washington, DC that same night to provide information to the FBI regarding a corporate espionage case we helped break a month earlier.

It's now Thursday, and although we're both satisfied with the progress being made, our tempers are short because of the quick but necessary trip. After our last meeting, Keene and I loll around the corporate jet terminal at Dulles International Airport, waiting for our jet to fuel up to take us back to Teterboro.

Leaning against the wall, I check the time. It's only nine o'clock, not too late. Scrolling through my contacts, I find who I'm searching for. I connect the call and put the phone up to my ear.

"Cassidy Freeman." That voice. I can feel the smile break through the weariness across my face.

"Hello, Cassidy." Damn. Out of the corner of my eye, Keene glances up from his iPad in interest. Mentally wishing I was anywhere else but in the middle of a VIP lounge making this call, I turn my back on my best friend's knowing face.

"Mr. Lockwood," she replies in her typical cool voice, but this time, I detect a hint of humor in it. "Is there something I can help you with this evening?" I hear voices in the background, the sounds of glasses clinking, laughter, and male voices.

"Am I interrupting something?" My voice sharpens noticeably. Cassidy is sexy as fuck and I have no claim on her. Yet, I can't be the only man who notices her.

Her voice warms slightly when she replies, "No, you're not interrupting at all. The family was just sitting around reviewing our upcoming weekend. You've met everyone. I think you understand how rambunctious the group of us can be when we get together."

Remembering my unique introduction to the Freeman family, I let out a bark of laughter. "Yes, I certainly can. Who's taking on Phil?"

The laughter gets caught in my throat as I picture the slow curve of her lips and the spark in her blue-green eyes when she responds with a simple, "Me."

I clear my throat. Loudly. "Sorry, it's a bit dry where I am."

"Can you hold on just a moment?"

"Sure," I reply cautiously.

I hear her open a door and the sounds of the outdoors at night come through the line. "I apologize, but trying to have any sort of a conversation with my family listening is a challenge on a regular basis. Also, if I had to listen to Phil bitch and moan about having to pick up any more garbage, I was going to lose it." Her beautiful laugh mixes with the sounds of night.

I'd give just about anything to be there in person, watching her mass of glorious hair curl down her back, as well as the seductive curve of her lips as the sound trickles from them.

I don't care that the words she just spoke make absolutely no sense to me at this moment. I want to do everything I can to make her laugh like that again. "Tell me what I have to do to make Phil pick up garbage every day and I'll do it."

She laughs harder. "Stop, I can't breathe." I start laughing too.

Eventually, our mutual hilarity dies down and we're left with silence. Yet, it doesn't feel awkward. I'm grinning so hard. Talking to Cassidy is better than watching an episode of Shameless.

I flip around and come face to face with Keene. Crap. His eyebrow is raised as he pantomimes asking who I'm talking to. I flip him off and walk away, but he follows me. Fucker.

"I just wanted to make sure we were still on for tomorrow," I murmur quietly into the phone.

I hear her breathe. Shit. Is she backing out. "We are," she admits.

I breathe.

"But."

Fuck. This could go either way. "But..." I parrot.

"I need you to pick me up at the farm instead of at my place. And you need to know, it's going to be chaos here."

"Oh?" I ask, intrigued. "More so than usual?"

"Why, Mr. Lockwood, I do believe you are a bit of a smart-ass yourself."

"Just getting that memo?"

A muffled snicker comes through the line. "No, it came with the memo that announced you were autocratic and getting married."

"Not going to let me forget that one?"

"Probably not for a while, Caleb. Besides," she adds with definite humor, "we'll be out with your future husbands for our first date."

Caleb. The sound of my name on her lips fires a spark at the base of my spine. I snap to stand straight when I realize what she'd said. Damn, I hate not being right there. "You said first, Cassidy," I growl softly back at her.

"Pardon me?" she responds, confusion in her voice.

"You said first date, as in more than one. I'm holding you to that, you know."

She goes silent. Shit. I know I'm pushing too fast. I wait for her reaction. What does she do when she's backed into a corner? Does she walk away? None of this was in her file. It's seductive, finding out her true secrets.

"Let's get through Friday night, champ. Just because I said yes, doesn't guarantee a fuck. I mean dick. I mean shit." By this point, I'm laughing so hard, I'm bent over at the knees. Her cold voice would probably freeze my testicles if she was staring at me with those eyes.

"It doesn't guarantee you shit, Lockwood. Especially if you don't give me a clue on what to wear."

"Have you never been to Molly Darcy's, Cassidy?"

"I can't say I have."

"For an Irish bar, it's a nice one. Not super fancy. Something along the lines of what you were wearing Monday is more than fine."

"See how easy that was, Lockwood? Why couldn't you just say that last night?"

"Because then what excuse would I have had to call you?" I hear the announcement of my flight boarding. Finally. "Cassidy, I have to go. They're boarding my flight."

"I didn't realize you were traveling. This seriously could have waited until you had a chance to call tomorrow."

"I didn't want it to wait. I wanted to make sure we were still on."

"We are. Caleb?" Her voice is more hesitant than a moment ago.

"Yes?"

"Safe travels," she murmurs quietly before hanging up the phone.

I look down at my phone for a heartbeat, and two before getting my shit in gear. Shutting down my phone, I toss it into my bag and head to the gate.

Keene, standing at the end of the steps waiting for me, says nothing until we're on the jet, barreling down the runway. Gazing out the window across from me, he's casually sipping his drink and asks, "Cassidy? I don't remember you mentioning meeting a Cassidy when we had dinner a few weeks ago."

He uncrosses his legs and gets more comfortable in the leather seat as our plane jets across the night sky. He still hasn't looked at me. It's a technique I've used many times. Don't let your opposition think you want information so they relax a little, start chatting, letting details slip.

I don't bother saying anything. Keene's smart. Hell, he's fucking brilliant. In addition to also being a trained interrogator from his years of military service, Keene's background in criminal psychology makes him an expert at reading people while hiding his own emotions. It makes him an incredible employee and a pain in the ass friend. Fortunately for me, this is a quick hop back to New York. I can hold out that long.

I ignore him and take a sip of my drink. Staring out the window, I can feel his eyes on me, still waiting for me to respond. Instead of replying, I replay my conversation with Cassidy in my head. I wonder what she's doing tomorrow? If it were strictly business-related, it would be at the office. I'm mulling that over when a few seconds later, the pilot's voice comes over the intercom announcing, "Mr. Lockwood, Mr. Marshall, you are both free to use your electronic devices. Please relax and enjoy your flight to Teterboro."

Putting my glass down, I reach into my bag for my iPad. After I type in my password, iMessage pops up a message from Cassidy. My finger hovers over it a second before I press to open it.

Cassidy: I'm sure it will be hours before you get this, but I just wanted you to know I'm looking forward to tomorrow. We have an event at the farm I forgot about when I first accepted. I hope you landed safely. Talk soon.

I smile and begin to type back, oblivious to the sharp eyes across from me.

Caleb: What event do you have? And we'll forget about the part where I could tease the planner about forgetting an event...

I watch the little blue dots move as she types back.

Cassidy: Are you sitting on a runway somewhere? I thought you were boarding a plane?

Caleb: I'm actually in the air on the plane.

Cassidy: Are you trying to crash it? What the hell, Caleb?!?! Get off your phone!

Caleb: Relax, Pixie. I have my messages forwarded to my iPad. I'm not breaking any laws.

Cassidy: Oh. okay. Never tell Phil that. He'll demand we all do that and I'll never get any peace from him.

Caleb: I promise I won't tell, but it's not like he can't find it online.

I must make a sound resembling laughter. Keene is still patient and waiting. Bastard will wait for hours. I continue to ignore him and look back at my iPad when I hear another ding.

Cassidy: We try to keep him away from searching the web whenever possible. Can you imagine him with an open search engine? It's better to be at his beck and call for some things. Better for all our mental health, that is.

Now, I'm openly laughing. She's a sharp-witted delight.

Cassidy: So, what's with the nickname?

Caleb: ???

Cassidy: I'm fairly detail oriented, Caleb. You've called me Pixie a few times. Know so many Cassidys you have to differentiate me somehow? I'm the shortest, so I get the nickname to remind you I'm the short one?

I wait a few seconds for something to follow, but there's nothing. No dots moving, indicating she's still typing. Is she serious? She thinks she doesn't stand out?

Caleb: I hope you're joking right now.

Cassidy: About?

Caleb: Not standing out.

No dots moving. Holy shit. She has no idea how alluring she is with that hair, those curves and legs? And her eyes are mesmerizing. My frustration simmers and I begin to type furiously on my tablet, ignoring the intrigue from my seatmate across the table. And then I remember what I know from the file and I calm slightly. I backspace the infuriated remarks I had originally typed and replace them with:

Caleb: No, Cassidy. It's not because I can't remember who you are, or your height.

Cassidy: ?

Caleb: Look up Tree of Four Seasons, *Josephine Wall. I imagine if the fairy in the painting looked at me, her eyes would be yours.*

While I wait for Cassidy to search for the fairy artwork online, I look at Keene. "It's more than just getting laid. She's...different."

Keene checks at his watch. "You held out for 36 minutes. I'm impressed."

"Fuck you, brother. I wasn't going to say anything at all, but I need to talk this one through."

He sits up a little straighter. "Why? Thinking of bringing her home to Ry?"

"Ry's already met her," I inform him when I hear the ding.

Cassidy: That's a lot to take in before a first date, Caleb. But thank you.

Cassidy: Being likened to something that stunning is quite possibly one of the nicest compliments I've ever received.

Caleb: It's a striking piece of art with a lot of layers. A lot like the woman I'm talking to.

Needing to get this conversation back on lighter tones, I quickly type back to her.

Caleb: So, is this the point of the conversation where I ask what you're wearing? Or should I just ask for your address and drive over after my plane lands? ;)

Cassidy: LOL. Pig!

Caleb: You know, Pixie, you're making what would be an otherwise dull flight interesting. :)

"How did Ry meet her?" Keene asks.

Halfheartedly focusing on him, a smirk still lingering on my face caused by my back and forth with Cassidy, I make a distracted sound.

"How did Ryan meet her?" Keene enunciates each word deliberately. Clearly Keene doesn't respect the concept of ignoring someone. "Were you out to dinner or something?"

Distracted, I answer, "She's the answer to his prayers. She's his wedding planner." I look at my iPad, but not before I hear Keene's sharp intake of breath.

Cassidy: What am I going to do with you?

Caleb: Are you leaving that question to me? Because I have a few suggestions. But I really do need your address.

I fail to mention I already have it from the files I have on her family.

Cassidy: Scroll up a bit to farm animal reference...

Cassidy: I want to ask how your trip was and why you were out of town. I mean, you know what I do, but I don't know anything about you other than what's reported in the society pages.

At that moment, a hand reaches across my iPad, pushing it down. Before I can knock it away, Keene is leaning forward, in my face, with an incredulous and angry look on his. "Are you out of your fucking mind? Does she know you know everything about her going into this? She was a damn client of the company we bought, Caleb!"

Earlier in the week, I explained what happened when I pulled the background investigation on Ryan's wedding planners, Charlie coming to my office, and what I found out about my family. Because Keene has known me since I was a kid, he immediately understood how enraged I was, and how he's no longer the only one with a broken home.

Keene and I have a long background together. We went to school together from Kindergarten all the way through Harvard. We were together when Keene's sister was kidnapped when she was four years old. I helped him grieve through that loss and try to live a life after. I was there when his mother died, and his father checked out. Hell, I think we lost our virginity the same weekend at our senior prom.

We joined the Army together after Harvard. We've shed blood for each other, and shored each other up through the worst of times. And now he owns part of Hudson with me. Aside from Ry, there's no one in the world whose input I value, even if it often differs from my own.

Keene always proved to be an incredible asset; he sees things in black and white. In business, that's invaluable. He's able to cut through the crap to get to the most important issues.

The Freemans are clients or they're not. It wouldn't matter to him if they were clients of the former owners. And until Sunday, I never knew one of my own employees was still keeping tabs on them out of a sense of duty.

"I didn't own the firm when she was a paying client, Keene," I reply coldly. "And let me remind you, the family isn't an active account." I had already worked through his possible argument in my head about a hundred times before I showed up at her office.

"What you don't understand," my voice just slightly warmer than the Arctic, "is that her brother, Phillip, and her brother-in-law, Jason, do know what I do. They know we ran a background check on the company. As long as I'm honest with Cassidy about all of that and leave the choices up to her, they have no fucking problem with it."

"Well, that's just great. When do you plan on getting around to that? After you're done fucking someone who has been abused? We've seen how that shit plays out. You want to be another scar on her, keep this up. Just remember, they asked for someone who is now *us* to dig into their pasts to ensure no one could find out the things most people would consider debasing and degrading, Caleb. How do you think she's going to survive after you tell her what you know?"

Without thinking, I jump up and grab Keene by the throat. My iPad clatters to the floor unnoticed. "Do you think I give a fuck about what was done to her, you bastard?" I growl this into his face, which shows no expression. Asshole. "She's beautiful, brilliant, and strong. And by the end of the first meeting, she'll have you on your damn knees. So, fuck you and your assumptions about who and what she is based on a goddamned file of information you haven't even read. You and your black and white." I let him drop back into his seat and snatch up my iPad.

"I'll fucking figure it out myself." I hear the ping of my iPad

Cassidy: Is the topic of your job off-limits for now?

Cassidy: Is it because I won't answer the question about what I'm wearing?

I hope she's joking here. I scroll quickly past.

Cassidy: Seriously?

Cassidy: ???

I take a deep breath and begin to type. Her dots move at the same time.

Caleb: I'm sorry, Pixie. I was talking to my business partner. He's on board too.

Cassidy: Oh, sorry. I didn't realize.

Caleb: You have nothing to apologize for. The work conversation just got a bit intense.

If that isn't the understatement of the century.

Caleb: Right now, my firm is contracted to do some work for the government, so I can't talk about it much.

Truthfully, that's all I can tell her about the specific job I'm working on. In reality, that's all I'll tell her about what I do. At least until I can figure out if I need to open her barely scabbed-over wounds.

Ping.

Cassidy: Sounds like fun. Not. Just hope it doesn't involve you raising our taxes.

I shake my head, thinking of the massive fees we charge. Probably not a good idea to mention that.

I hear the captain announce, "Mr. Lockwood, Mr. Marshall, we are approaching Teterboro. It is time to prepare for our descent. Please stow all electronic devices. Your steward will be in the cabin to collect your drinks shortly."

Caleb: I have to shut it down, Pixie. We're landing.

Cassidy: See you tomorrow.

Putting my iPad away, I warn Keene, "You will treat her with the utmost respect tomorrow night, you ass."

By the tone of his voice, he assumes I've lost my mind. "You're bringing her to Mandy's party? Jesus, Caleb. Half the people there will report back to your—" I silence him with a glare. The only way he can make this conversation worse is to call that woman my mother. "You have to tell Cassidy sooner rather than later. Otherwise, you're setting yourself up for massive failure from the beginning."

I laugh at him. He seriously thinks to offer me relationship advice? To dictate how I tell the woman I'm more than a little captivated by that I know more about her life than maybe even her siblings do? Jesus, he's an arrogant motherfucker. It's moments like this I wonder how I've managed not to kill him over the years.

"Thank you, Dr. Marshall. Where should I send the bill for that bit of enlightenment?"

"I'm not kidding, Caleb." He leans forward. "As your partner, as Hudson's counsel, as your friend, you know I'm right."

I turn my head to the side and stare out at the land rushing up to meet us.

I hate when he's right.

"Let me handle this as I see fit. I don't want to spook her off the bat. What good does it do to mention all of this on the first date if nothing comes from it?" I say through gritted teeth. "Fair enough, buddy?"

"Oh, just fucking thrilled, buddy." He sits back, glaring at me.

As the plane touches down, we end the flight locked in a deadly stare down, neither of us giving an inch. Both of us pissed and worried.

As we make our way back into the city in silence, I can't help but wonder if I'm turning my back on fair advice.

But how do you tell someone you know everything about them and earn their trust?

12

CASSIDY

It's Friday. More accurately, it's Friday evening.

Caleb should be arriving soon.

I'll admit it, I'm a nervous wreck.

It's the first date I've ever agreed to according to my sisters, which isn't to say I haven't needed an escort on occasion. I normally took Phil before he married Jason. This is probably why I was goaded into a session of pre-date prep last night at the carriage house.

Seriously, did I need to have tweezers pluck hair there? On a first date? Ali must put out more often than that hot lawyer in the hotel room we shared the weekend Phil and Jason got married. For the love of God, that shit hurt!

Then came the clothes. Sweet Jesus, I swear I spent more time putting outfits back in their proper place after they left my house. I love my sisters, I truly do, but they're tornadoes in my calm space. But they do have an incredible sense of style.

It's how I ended up wearing a pair of tight-fitting, dark wash crop jeans, a black, long sleeve bell sleeve crepe shirt with lace inserts, and sky-high raspberry Louboutin's I got for an absolute steal online. I mean, who of the shoe obsessed wouldn't buy Christian Louboutin's for $148.00 from the man himself? I keep checking my credit card bill for an extra zero to appear at the end of the charge. My equally shoe obsessed sisters oohed and aahed appropriately. Lucky me, they're all so much taller than I am, they can't borrow my shoes. What they don't know is that I bought them each a pair for Christmas.

Mentally, I've barely permitted myself two minutes to think alone. I got up super early this morning and went to go see Matt. Sitting by myself in The Coffee Shop, Matt asked me a lot of the same questions Em did when I was in her office. He just dug deeper into some of the answers. Like, does the idea of being alone with Caleb trigger any sort of negative anxiety for me. I was surprised to realize I'd already been alone with him in my office. Matt, surprised by my answer, was even more taken aback when I told him the door was closed while Caleb and I were arguing.

Matt probed into my physical concerns. This has been a sensitive topic when I've thought about dating in the past. I was pleased to be able to talk about some of the sensations I was already experiencing, such as the anticipation of hearing Caleb's voice, the shivering warmth from his touch, knowing from my body's responses to his physical presence that my sexuality hadn't been mutilated before it should have been born, it was just dormant for the last twenty years.

I was pleased to be able to tell Matt that no, I wasn't afraid of Caleb physically with the caveat about coming up behind me when I'm unaware or sharp movements, like when he went to touch my face. I don't think I'll ever truly get past those reactions, even if they temper over time.

Matt and I talked for a long time about sex and that I shouldn't feel embarrassed about asking people I trusted about it. He said everyone who has been through a sexual trauma is different and only I will know what's right for my heart, mind, and body. He said that when I chose to make love with a man, it would be the most beautiful experience in the world.

I feel as if I've done all the preparation I can.

Even if this date turns out to be a complete bust, I thoroughly enjoyed most of the first date rituals my sisters took me through last night and earlier today—face masks, making sure I was wearing lip color that was the exact shade of my heels, shared giggling over the hot guy I was going out with. Because let's be honest, Caleb Lockwood is hot as hell.

I've been around my fair share of attractive men over the years. I'll even admit to being hit on by more than a few. Not even one tempted me to ever accept a date or anything else they may have directly or indirectly alluded to. Yet, with Caleb Lockwood, there's just something there. I remember the slice of disappointment I felt when I'd initially thought he was one of the grooms in the wedding.

If I ever thought of fantasizing about a man, I still don't think I would have imagined his muscled body, strong jaw, his dark, thick hair begging for a hand to run through it...

Jesus, who am I right now? I don't do daydreaming, at least not over a man. Especially one who should have me running for the hills. I dream of serenity. I dream of peace. I dream of laughter. I dream of family. I don't dream of hot guys who send tingles through my body when they touch my hand. I shiver in remembrance before I mentally chastise myself.

Get it under control, I warn myself. I still have the rest of this event to get through. And, he may be a good guy, but I don't know much about him.

I regroup by scanning the chaos of the Collyer Dress Extravaganza.

The dress extravaganza started out as a small way to help three girls, and it wasn't too long after we had opened the doors of Amaryllis Events. We helped them find a way to make extra money to buy their homecoming dresses. Over the years, it has morphed into us bringing in actual dresses by high-end designers. Amaryllis Events picks up the initial tab and those not purchased are donated to other local high schools. Tonight's event, the one I forgot when I made my date with Caleb, is dress selection night for Collyer's senior girls.

Over the cacophony of screeches and excited glee, there are gaggles of girls trying on homecoming dresses in the farm's main room. I lean against the wall in the back by the glass doors overlooking the lake, catching Phil's attention. He makes his way over to me and slips his arm around my waist.

"Great job." His eyes scan the room. "The girls are finding what they want."

"You can thank Em for that. I don't know how she manages to get the designers to give us the samples at cost each year. Dear God! Except that one. They probably gave us that one for free!" My eyes widen enormously at a sequined orange number with what appears to be a feather skirt. I elbow Phil, who quietly chokes on the inhale of his next breath. We glance at each other and quickly look away. We're breathing in hard to hold in the laughter.

A few minutes pass before we're again composed. Phil picks up our conversation as if the Baltimore Oriole mascot hadn't just come to life in our family room.

"I agree, Em does a lot, Cass, but you still run the program on top of everything else. It teaches these kids there are important things out there they can help with."

I smile. It always feels good to give back to the community we call home.

"Thanks. I love the first night of this. I can't believe I almost forgot it."

Phil turns me slightly. "Yeah. So, I heard about your date. By the way, you look great." His face shows his hurt briefly.

Shit. Phil may have been a clueless dick about the way he handled the whole Lockwood-Dalton wedding, and we've had our issues being the two most stubborn of our family, but he loves me.

I know down to my soul how much he loves me.

I reach up and touch his cheek. "I'm sorry, Phil. I never meant to not tell you. I assumed you'd heard, and then the girls were rushing me in all manners of things I will never tell you about. I guess a part of me was just trying to wrap my mind around the idea that I said yes."

He wraps his arm tighter around my waist without pulling me closer. I raise a perfectly plucked eyebrow when he smiles. "I don't want to mess you up before your date."

I snort.

"He's a good man, Cass," Phil says quietly, among the chaos in taffeta swirling around us. "He should be on his knees, thankful you said yes."

"You're making me freak out even more now, Phil," I say, half-joking, wringing my hands before wiping them down the front of my jeans.

"Don't be. It's your first date. If these girls can handle it, I know you can. You need to know dating isn't something you can plan or control. You need to be ready to jump, be ready to take chances, to be scared to death, to be hurt, and to laugh. And promise me you won't hold back the amazing woman I know you are." He kisses me on the temple. When he turns me to face him, his blue eyes lock with mine before he takes a deep breath and lets it out. "I've waited a long time to say this, Little Girl."

I am clearly confused. "Say what?"

He swallows hard. "You are strength, you are fire, and you are beauty, Cass. It's time to let others see it."

Tears begin to fill my eyes, making them brighter than normal.

"Ah, screw it," Phil says as he pulls me close. "I know living with me is like being on a spin cycle, but never doubt my love for you, Cassidy. Enjoy your first date, little one." He steps back, wiping under my eyes. Humor sets his eyes dancing before he says, "And if you choose to sleep with him, use protection."

"You ass!" I exclaim, then clamp my hand over my mouth as a few of the senior students pass by, snickering at our conversation. Our eyes meet and we both start laughing again.

"What? It's the same advice I gave to Ali, Holly, and Corinna when they went to UConn." As I fall away from his arm, laughing, he winks before looking past me. "Think I should go rescue him?"

"Who?" I ask, having lost all sense of self and time.

"Caleb. He just walked in."

I spin, my hair flying. As it settles, our eyes meet across the room. Cue the butterflies. "No," I tell Phil. "I've got this."

I'm so focused on Caleb, I barely hear Phil murmur, "I know you do, Little Girl."

I take a few deep breaths as I begin to make my way through the makeshift dressing rooms, occasionally hearing mothers and daughters arguing about dresses over the music being played through the sound system.

As I get closer, Caleb's eyes run from the top of my head to my shoes, and back up again. His eyes darken in what I think is appreciation.

"Hello, Pixie." His voice is dark and sexy as he holds out his hand.

"Hello, Caleb." I try to keep my voice under control, tentatively reaching out my hand. He grabs it and gently tugs me toward him. Despite the sky-high shoes, Caleb is topping me by around eight inches in height. Amazingly, I don't feel overwhelmed. I don't feel intimidated. I feel like curling my body against his. I'll have to think about that one later. When I can think, that is.

"So, what do we have here?" he murmurs next to my ear, sending shivers down my spine.

Jesus. He's only holding my hand. We're not touching anywhere else, and the feelings are stampeding through my body. It's startling. It's exciting. It's scary as fuck.

"Where, here?" I say stupidly, taking a step back and returning his perusal.

Caleb is wearing jeans, a black, button-down shirt that could be painted on his muscles with the sleeves rolled up. He's also wearing his customary boots. His eyes are the color of the deepest, darkest chocolate desert, ones I would love to indulge in. He smiles and waves his hand, encompassing the room, and it clicks.

"Oh, here!" I try to control my blush. I figure I've lost that battle when he starts to laugh.

I give him a brief explanation of the dress extravaganza, my hands moving as I gesture around the room. He's attentive, asking about how many people we have in the program, and the number of businesses from Collyer who participate, when I realize I've been talking for a while and I start blushing.

"I'm sorry. This is kind of my baby. I could go on for a while about it. Well, we should probably get going if we're meeting Ryan and Jared." Anything to get out the door without embarrassing myself further.

He nods. "Actually, we do need to head out. Do you have a coat? It's perfect out now, but it's going to get cool later."

I quirk my lips and make my way over to the closet where I grab my cashmere hooded poncho and purse.

"Ready?" he inquires while staring into my eyes.

Deep breaths, Cass. "Yes," I say softly on an exhale.

He smiles and reaches for my hand to guide me out of the chaos and into the unknown.

I'm on a date.

We reach his car—a dark gray Porsche. Caleb walks me around to the passenger side, reaches for the door handle, and holds my hand to allow me to slide gracefully into the low-slung seat. He trots around the car and I can't take my eyes off of him. My heart is beating wildly, but not from fear. I feel different around Caleb Lockwood than I do with other men.

I'm laughing at myself when he opens the door and slides in next to me. When his door closes, the air in the car is thick with an unknown emotion. We're staring at each other. I haven't even blinked my eyes until he speaks.

"Cassidy." Nothing else, just my name. He smiles, and I can't do anything but respond to it by smiling back. Did he hear me laughing and want to ask me about it?

"Yes?" I reply, waiting.

"Nothing. Just reminding you I know your name, Pixie." I narrow my eyes at him and he smiles, his eyes crinkling at the corners.

With a huff, I'm reaching for my seat belt when he grabs my hand. A slight flare of panic bursts through before I can control it. His eyes narrow, as if he can read my reaction.

One second passes, two. Slowly, he takes my wrist and brings it to his lips. "There's nothing to fear with me, Pixie. It's your pace the whole way."

How can he know I needed that reassurance? I nod slowly, relaxing. "Okay."

"Okay?"

"Okay, Mr. Lockwood. If you expect me to be so impressed with this date that you'll get a second, maybe we need to start the first?"

He grins and releases my hand before we both reach for our seat belts. Caleb brings the Porsche to life. After its initial purr to start, he puts it in gear and turns north toward Danbury.

Rosy Tomorrow's has been a popular Danbury restaurant for over thirty-five years. Between the fishnets gracing the ceiling and the unique memorabilia on the walls, it's hopping almost every night of the week. Having been here at least once a month since we moved to Collyer, I can honestly say they have some of the best French fries on the planet.

When Caleb and I walk in at 6:30, the restaurant is packed with easily an hour wait to be seated. Yes, the food is just that good. Normally when our family comes here, we order different dishes and pass them around the table.

As much as I'm nervous about this date thing, I kind of hope the Lockwoods and Jared have the same mentality about food. Otherwise, it might take me an hour to figure out what to eat. If I have to choose between buffalo calamari, lobster sliders, or the French dip, we might be here a while.

Caleb steps up to the hostess station to inquire where his brother is sitting when I get a text from Em telling me to have a great time. I quickly reply, thanking her for everything and asking about how the rest of the night went. She tells me not to worry and to have fun before Caleb makes his way back to me.

"Everything okay?" he asks, seeing my phone in my hand.

"Fine," I reply. "Em was just letting me know she saw us leave and to have a good time."

"Good. Let's go meet Ry and Jared," he says as we begin to make our way upstairs. "I have a lot of work to do to convince you to go out on a second date with me."

I turn on the stairs, laughing, intending to toss a smart-ass comeback at him, not realizing he's right behind me. With the stairs and my heels, our faces are almost perfectly aligned. Eye to eye, searching, probing for something, but what? A breath releases from my lips and I feel it reflect back on me from against his face. That's how close he is.

Caleb leans forward and lightly brushes his lips against mine, the barest of touches, his eyes locked on mine. Shivers course through my body which I know he can feel.

Holy crap. Did that just happen? My first, first date kiss? On a staircase at Rosy Tomorrow's?

I don't know whether to be thrilled it happened or annoyed it wasn't somewhere more memorable. I stand there blinking at Caleb at a loss for words.

"Keep walking, Pixie," he says gruffly. Unable to do anything more, I resume climbing the stairs.

Brett Eldredge is crooning about being drunk on someone's love when we reach the table. Ryan and Jared both stand. After the man-hug and back slapping that goes on between Caleb and both men, Ryan leans down and kisses my cheek.

"What on Earth made you accept a date with my brother, Cassidy?" He's smiling, but his expression is one of pure curiosity.

"I'm still not entirely sure, Ryan. I'll let you know at the end of the night. How about that?" I offer with a sideways look at Caleb. Caleb just shakes his head at me.

Maybe that's how I get through this date thing, keep thinking of it as a joke.

Except the smile Caleb gives me as he passes the menu has butterflies kicking up in my stomach again. Our date is no joke to him.

"It can't be because of his looks," Ryan laments.

Caleb turns to his brother and merely raises an eyebrow. "Yeah, if you keep saying shit like that to Cassidy, I get to say crap to Jared since we're practically twins, brother."

"Or his well-educated word choice," Ryan continues without missing a beat. "You would never know he went to Harvard, would you, Cassidy?"

"Really? Harvard? At least now I have a possible nickname for you," I say, giving Caleb a look.

He sits back in his chair, crosses his arms over his broad chest and laughs. "Call me that in public and I'll pull out your nickname. You seem to have more of an issue with yours than I would with mine."

Dammit, he's right. Now I openly glare at him until I hear Ryan and Jared laugh.

Jared controls himself enough to ask, "How did you get her to say yes again, Caleb?"

"Weak moment," I mutter, causing all three men chuckle.

I look at Caleb who's smiling broadly, and I feel the tension in my body release. I start to smile and get lost in Caleb's eyes. The two of us could be alone at the table. All I see is the intensity of his gaze focused on me.

Without breaking eye contact, I answer Ryan. "Actually, it might have been the way he apologized so nicely for hitting on me before his future husbands arrived at our meeting the other day."

Caleb groans loudly as I pat him on the cheek. Everyone bursts into laughter and I pull my burning hand away.

Wow. Holy sweet baby Jesus. Sixteen-year-old girls get through this? What are their mother's feeding them?

13

CASSIDY

About halfway through the meal, I begin to completely relax. I totally get why young girls can do this rite of passage and not have scars on their psyche.

A date. It's fun.

After thinking it over during our appetizer, even that quick kiss Caleb dropped on me before, was more like a brotherly peck than anything to get worked up about, right?

While laughing at some story Ryan feels the need to share about Jared, I decide to get out of my head and just go with the flow. My laughter comes more freely, and I start teasing these men like I do my own family.

Ryan and Caleb start trading embarrassing stories about one another that have Jared and I reaching for napkins to wipe the tears from our eyes. Ryan catching Caleb in the hot tub with some girl when he was sixteen; Caleb catching Ryan in the cabana with a girl when he was seventeen. The staff at the Lockwood mansion busting them for parties when their parents would go out of town. These two brothers are a hoot when you get them together. Beyond the mischief, you can feel the outpouring of love they have for each other.

Maybe our families aren't so different, even though one is through blood and one found their way to each other through chance.

I offer up a story about taking Ali, Corinna, and Holly college dress shopping, which has the three men groaning and offering their deepest empathy. Apparently, they can fully imagine losing Corinna to the cooking section of Macy's, fighting with Ali over the length of her dress, and trying to find Holly because she got bored with the whole thing and wandered off to Best Buy to look at cameras.

By the end of my lament, Caleb has a huge grin on his face and Jared has his hand over his mouth, trying not to spit out his drink. Ryan says while sputtering with laughter, "This is why we hired you. You managed to not commit justifiable homicide!"

I don't know if having a double date is a typical thing, but for me, I know having Ryan and Jared here with us has helped me enjoy it greatly. I'm sure there's a world record here somewhere.

I can visualize the headline now, "Soon-to-be thirty-year-old has first date! Scoop on page...!" I stare off into space with a small smile on my face and shake my head slowly, not realizing Caleb's eyes are on me.

He leans toward me. "Everything okay?" he murmurs close into my ear, inadvertently sending shivers down my back.

Great, all the tension missing from my body just came back in a rush. "I'm fine," I bluff, reaching for my glass of water. I want a clear head for the most part. Caleb is potent enough.

He shoots me a mild look and reaches for my hand under the table. Closing his strong hand over mine, he gives mine a quick squeeze.

My breath hitches.

I expect him to let go, but he doesn't. Instead, as he continues talking with Jared about a case, he starts to play with my fingers. His large, thick fingers curl between mine and drag them against each another, caressing them. He pulls my hand over to his thigh discreetly and begins to trace each digit with one of his.

I'm almost hyperventilating at this point. I have to escape.

Standing, I drop Caleb's hand. His eyebrows raise. "Pardon me, gentlemen. Before we leave, I need to take a private moment."

Grabbing my purse, I depart from the table and make my way to the restroom.

Slamming through the door, I race into the handicap stall. Locking the door, I whip out my cell phone as I slide to the floor with my back to the wall. Pulling up my messages, I text Em.

Cassidy: I don't know if I can do this.

Em: What happened?!?!?

Cassidy: It was going fine. Casual. And then he was holding my hand under the table. Is this normal, Em?

Em: Oh, sweetheart.

Cassidy: What?

Em: It's okay to be nervous, Cass. Holding your hand, even kissing you, isn't a big deal.

I think for a moment. I need to tell her.

Cassidy: He did that too.

Em: WHAT?!?!?

Cassidy: Really quick. On the stairs as we were walking to the table.

Em: Well, holy hell. How did you react?

Cassidy: I think I was in shock.

Em: Right? No shit!

Cassidy: I'm so afraid he's going to do something and I'm going to react, and then it's going to mess everything up, including the business.

Finally, Em's text comes through.

Em: First, I am so proud of you. I've been sitting here all night in tears. You have come so far, Cass. You're so beautiful and so damn strong that no man, including Caleb Lockwood, is good enough for you. The idea you even said yes? This is HUGE! Second, trust your gut, love. It may be untried as an adult, but you know it works. Third, this may sound way out there, but do you want to give him a heads-up so he doesn't push you too far? Maybe not everything, just that you're not as experienced as he might think you are?

I read her message a few times, and read it again. And then I realize I've been in the bathroom for a long time. Really long. I quickly type back.

Cassidy: I've been gone a while. I'll ping you later. Love you.

I make my way to my feet and stand at the sink. My face is pale. My eyes are wide. My chest is moving up and down with the force of my breaths as I contemplate Em's last message.

Do I need to let him know what happened to me? How could I seriously think I could do this? Phil's words about sixteen-year-olds being able to date come floating through my mind.

Bet they don't have to contemplate discussions like this.

I unlock the stall, wash my hands and walk out of the restroom. I turn the corner outside the door and walk right into Caleb. He's leaning one-shouldered against a wall. "Hey, Pixie. Everything okay? You were gone for a bit and I was starting to get worried." He reaches out and holds onto my shoulders. One hand smooths up to tip my chin so my eyes meet his.

Meeting his gaze, I make my decision. Go with my gut.

"Is there somewhere we can go to talk before we go out? Somewhere private?" I ask softly.

He suddenly looks concerned, maybe a little nervous. "What's wrong? Is something wrong with the family?"

Shaking my head, then nodding, I shake my head again. "There are things I need for you to know and understand."

He slides one of his hands down my arm, setting off those sparks, and captures my hand. "We settled the bill at the table. Let's head out to the car."

14

CALEB

I knew the moment Cassidy relaxed at the dinner table because her smile went brilliant when it happened. The rest of the meal was spent trading quips back and forth with my brother and his fiancé.

Never has so much hinged on a first date. If it went good, I had more time with Cassidy. But, at some point, I'd have to explain how I know everything I do about the Freeman family. I think I would rather be back in Afghanistan facing roadside bombers and gathering on-site intel than talking to Cassidy about the things I know about her. It would implode us before we had a chance to begin. I had only gained a modicum of trust with this woman, and soon I would have to shatter it if we're to move forward.

I rack my brain for where I can take her for this conversation she wants to have before we head to Molly Darcy's. That's assuming she wants to go after we talk.

We make our way into the parking lot with Ry and Jared ahead of us, holding hands. Cassidy stops with her hand on her heart.

"What is it, Pixie?" I murmur, needing to know her thoughts.

"Sometimes I work with people who don't have that special something. They go through the motions, but you know the marriage isn't going to last much longer than it takes to plan it. They have it," she says, nodding at Ry and Jared. My heart balloons in my chest. She's right. "It makes working with them a pleasure. It makes spending time with them more so."

"No one deserves it more than, Ry," I agree, knowing she understood from our talk on Monday.

She smiles with a touch of sadness in her eyes, but she masks it quickly. Idiot, I curse myself. She deserves it more than anyone I've ever met.

We meet the guys on the steps. "So, Molly Darcy's?" Ry rubs his hands together in anticipation.

"Actually, Cassidy and I have a stop to make first. We'll see you there in a bit." Ry raises an eyebrow and tilts his head while Cassidy flushes. Jared quickly whacks his fiancé upside the head and I nod my thanks to Jared as I open the door for Cassidy.

After we're settled inside my Porsche, Cassidy says, "So..." She plays with an imaginary piece of lint on her jeans, worked up by whatever it is she has to say.

"I figured we might check out the sights by the lake," I reply calmly, though my heart is starting to race while my eyes seek hers out in the dark confines of the car.

When they connect, she answers, "Okay." It's a long, drawn out word, her Southern accent seeping through. She places her hands on top of each other.

I turn on the radio. "Music preference?"

She waves one hand in the air, turning the choice over to me. As I drive to Kenosia Avenue, I realize I'm starting to feel something more than just an above average attraction for this incredible woman.

She's quiet on our way out to the lake. I reach over at one point and place one of my hands on hers, claiming her fingers. She turns to me and I glance over. Slowly, carefully, she returns the gesture and grips mine. I let out a sigh of relief.

"Why do I have a feeling I'm not the only one with something on their mind?" she says quietly.

I don't reply.

She sighs.

"At the lake, Pixie. We'll talk there."

TURNING OFF CHRISTOPHER COLUMBUS AVENUE, we arrive at a small twenty-five-acre state park. I get out of the car and take a deep breath of cold air. Reaching behind the driver's seat, I grab my leather jacket and shrug it on before walking around to open Cassidy's door. She's shivering.

"Where's your coat, Pixie?" Reaching down, she grabs it off the floor of the Porsche. I wait for her to pull the poncho over her head and hold out my hand to take hers as she steps from the car. The soft material brushes against my hand. "It's so soft," I murmur softly.

"Cashmere. A gift from the family for my birthday."

I turn her to face me and lift her hair out, then slide my hands down her arms until they reach her hands. "Can you walk in those?" I tip my chin at her shoes.

"If we stay on paths, yes."

"Come with me," I coax.

We start off down the path toward the water that will either lead to our destruction or the beginning of something great. Right now, I'm not sure which.

We reach a picnic table and bench. After making sure there are no animals around it or bird crap on top of it, I hop on top of it and hold her hand as she climbs carefully next to me. We have a gorgeous view of the lake. If I strain my eyes a bit, I can make out the birds on the banks huddling down for warmth in the night air.

Fuck, how the hell was I supposed to do this?

I want to kick my own ass. I feel like I've done everything wrong since we got to the restaurant, like the kiss on the stairs. I could feel her pulse hammering against her ribs where my hands were. The tension when I held her wrist. Then she relaxed so seamlessly with us at dinner, I'd thought she was ready for more.

All I did was hold her hand and she ran. Now, she wants to talk. I have no idea what to say.

I think back to the Thomas Paine quote Matt gave me that I have folded in my wallet, *"The real man smiles in trouble, gathers strength from distress, and grows brave by reflection."*

Having read Common Sense in college and knowing Paine meant the value of happiness didn't mean much without strife, I know Matt was trying to tell me I had to navigate this minefield with Cassidy before I would be able to fully experience joy with her.

Until then, it would always be between us.

I'm just about to start talking when Cassidy asks me, "Have you had a good time tonight?"

She's still facing the lake.

I turn slightly toward her. "Yes. Haven't you?"

Her profile reveals a wry smile. "Probably one of the best nights of my life. I imagine for a woman, the first date of your life would be."

I don't react. In fact, I think I'm frozen. Did she say what I think she said? "What?" I manage to croak out. I hope my voice holds surprise, when in reality, it's not a surprise at all.

Is she going there?

"Cassidy? Are you telling me that tonight is your first date? As in ever?" I hold my breath in anticipation of her answer.

"Yes," she answers quietly.

"Why?" There are so many things that why is for. Why are you telling me this right now? Did something happen where I tipped off what I know?

She's quiet, still focused on the lake, lost in thought.

"Pixie, why?" I whisper in the cold darkness.

"I didn't understand the first time it happened," I hear her say softly. "I didn't understand the pain. I was too young."

I feel like I've been slapped across the face. Holy sweet mother-fucking Jesus. She's talking.

She stands and steps away from the table, her delicate arms wrapping around herself. I stand and take a step closer to her. Her back is to me, but she must hear my feet in the fall leaves. She holds up her hand. "No, Caleb. I need to tell this my way. I need to do it on my own."

I keep my distance as she seems to pull her thoughts together. "I must have been four, maybe five? I don't know. I still technically don't know my age. I know I wasn't in school. There was no need to send the thing I was to school. To educate me to escape?" She laughs harshly.

I watch her from behind reach up and wipe her cheeks.

I want to be the one doing that for her. I stand where I am, my fists clenched at my sides, waiting for her to continue. Knowing what's coming and unable to stop it.

"I remember through the haze hearing that if I bled, that he would get more crack or Ecstasy, whatever he needed. So he let them hurt me more. Hardly ever my face, but my body was fair game." She takes a deep breath.

"Years later, we hired an investigative firm to make sure none of them could find us. The investigator asked me if I could describe any of them. I think by then, he wanted them as badly as we wanted to know if they were gone. There were so few I could describe because eventually, they would tether me, blindfolded, face down on the bed, spread eagle while they raped me."

I feel the rage burning through me as if I'm learning this for the first time rather than just hearing her soft voice say it aloud.

I want to go back in time and kill every one of the motherfuckers who hurt the baby, the girl, this beautiful woman standing before me who is ramrod straight, full of tormented pride and misplaced shame.

"I assume you got free? Did someone find out or did you escape?" I ask. It was in her file. I know Phil rescued her, but now I want her to tell me everything so I don't have to tell her I already know.

She makes a bitter sound of remembrance, her back still to me. "One night they didn't tether me down as much, or drug me as much, I guess. They were probably too whacked out on whatever they were on. I kicked the wall frantically and was screaming for my life." She takes deep breaths. "I figured no one would come, or would care."

Calming herself down, she takes eight breaths, the same technique I observed her using in her office. "Phil was in the apartment next door. His father had already used and forgotten about Phil after finding out about the new toy on the block. Phil told me later that until he'd heard me scream, he was practically catatonic in his own hellacious nightmare." Her voice begins to crack. "I'll never forget Phil coming in swinging his bat. He took out his father, two other men and my father, I guess? I don't know. God, years later, I can't fathom the adrenaline running through his veins. It was the only thing that stood between him and freedom and he used it to save me too. He could have just grabbed his shit and left, and instead he took on four grown men hopped up on drugs to get himself, a thirteen-year-old boy, and a nine-year-old girl out of hell."

She turns to face me, and there are tears on her face. I no sooner can stay away from her than I could stop breathing.

Stepping closer, I slowly wrap my arms around her. Using one hand, I start to wipe under her eyes. "What happened then, Pixie? How did you survive?"

She shakes her head, not wanting to say. "Tell me, Cassidy." I know, but she needs to get it out.

I watch her drowning in her memories. I grip her a bit tighter, trying to anchor her to me. "We ran. I was so hurt. I was bleeding so, so much. We couldn't, wouldn't, go to the police because we would have been taken into the foster care system. That's how Phil ended up with his so-called father and he refused to go back. He had been stealing small amounts from his father for a while and had hidden it. So, for a few days, we laid low in a shit hole of a motel. It was so bad. I can still hear the rats and bugs in the walls, but it was better than where we were because no one was trying to hurt us. Phil pushed every piece of furniture against the one door, barricading us in. I remember sleeping and eating chips. Eventually, we figured someone would suspect two kids, even in that hell hole and call the cops. So we left. Phil...oh God, I can't." She tries to pull out of my arms, but I hold her tighter.

"I think you have to. It's burning a hole inside of you," I encourage her softly.

My heart aches as this little warrior struggles to keep her family's secrets.

"Who the hell are you to know this? Who are you?" she screams at me. Tears are flowing down her cheeks. Her chest is heaving, her hands shaking as she tries to fight to get away from me. "You know too much already. Dammit, let me go!"

My arms open. "You've already let me in, Cassidy. You can trust me. Think about it. I deal with worse than this every day investigating the worst of people. Nothing you say is going to shock or repel me. I've seen what it takes to survive, and I know what people do in order to live. And if they do it for love..." It's not a lie, but it's not the full truth either.

The fear crumbles and I see her shattered heart reappear from underneath. She can barely get the words out, but I hear her.

"He prostituted himself to get us a ride out of Jacksonville. Before, his father had forced him to. It was the last time he ever did, and he did it for me. Oh God, he did it for me."

She pushes back into my arms and I pull her head to my chest, my breathing rough. My hand skims her neck and I touch the amaryllis tattoo I know is there from the file.

Strong, self-confident, pride. This family symbol is incredibly beautiful and fitting.

After letting her cry out her pain and fears while digging her nails into my chest, she calms down. Just when I'm about to suggest we move back to the car, she surprises me again by continuing.

"Phil has always been much more practical about what he did than me. To him it was the means to an end. To me it was—is—the ultimate sacrifice. What was so special about me for him to do that for?" she whispers so quietly that if the wind was blowing, I never would have heard her.

"We ended up in a little town in South Carolina. We met Em in the park we were sleeping in. Her parents had just been killed over a drug deal in front of her and they had the gun to her head when the cops busted in. She was placed with her great aunt in a trailer. Her Aunt Dee was trying to get her to talk when they came across us sleeping in the park. Phil wanted to run, but I was so tired. Dee convinced him to stay for a few days. With Dee, that was all it took. She gave us the only home we knew." Reaching up, Cassidy wipes her eyes.

"How long were you there?"

"Phil had graduated high school a few months earlier." Incredibly, she manages to smile softly through her tears. "Dee was so proud of him, of all of us. Then she was gone. We were there for about four and a half years. About halfway through it, Em started talking again. When Dee died in her sleep, we all grieved hard. Our family was shattered. The authorities wanted to take Em and I away, and Phil fought them with everything in him. Remember, this was the South. It was completely unseemly for an eighteen-year-old to watch over two fifteen-year old girls. He wasn't a kid, but he wasn't a man yet either. It didn't matter that he was a gay man. If anything, that made it worse. He was a bad influence. Phil worked two jobs and went to court to petition to be our legal guardian. We had social services breathing down our necks every month for a year. Once we turned sixteen, Em and I both petitioned the state to be emancipated. We got our GEDs online so we could get full-time jobs. We legally had to be able to support ourselves. It took a while, but we did it. Finally, we felt settled again." She goes quiet. "We met the rest of the girls later."

I hug her hard, rocking her small body back and forth. Giving her strength, comfort; whatever she needs. I feel her relax into me. I know from the file the rest of the story isn't easy to tell, but isn't as physically traumatic to her personally.

"With the three of us working, Phil got to cut back to one job. We had the trailer, and trust me, the upkeep on that wasn't a hell of a lot when you had three salaries coming in, even if you were paid piddly shit. But we all started to want something more. I started community college at night, got my Associates, and then went to the College of Charleston. It's a state school with a good business management and hospitality program. Em did the same, only her major was studio art. Phil got his AA. He found his calling working at a florist." She looks up at me, her eyes are wide and earnest. "It's what we were meant to do."

"I understand, Pixie," I murmur.

"I mean, we all can't go to Harvard." A bit of her sauciness returns as she draws out my alma mater's name in her Southern accent. I smile as she lays her head back on my chest.

The first thread of trust snaps between us.

She goes quiet in my arms and I rub my hands up and down her back, absorbing what she told me and reconciling it to what I had read in the file.

"How did you pick Connecticut?"

"Phil loved the pictures he saw in the library when we were thinking about moving. It also called to me for some reason. I have no idea why, but it felt like I was meant to be here. We all liked the proximity to New York for work, and we did some research on schools for the girls, found Collyer and made our home here." She goes quiet as she reaches under her hair and touches the back of her neck.

I don't interrupt our silence with questions or words. She hasn't told me about how they found the younger girls, how they chose their names, how they bought the farm or any of the other details I read in the report. The worst of the worst is out there between us. I know. She knows I know. And neither of us have gone anywhere. That's got to count for something, right?

"Why did you tell me, Cassidy?" She blinks up at me, looking uncertain. "Not that I don't feel honored you did, but why?"

Pushing out of my arms, she stomps away before spinning around. Throwing her arms out, she yells, "Because I'm not normal, Caleb! I'm twenty-nine years old and I agonized over what to wear tonight. A man holding my hand sends my pulse racing. You kissed me on the stairs as if it didn't mean anything to you, but it meant something to me. I can't have you not know when the little casual touches mean nothing to you, because they mean a hell of a lot to me. Every time you touch me, I feel something here." She hits her heart with her open hand.

Her breathing is ragged. I can hear her try to get it under control before she goes on.

"If you don't want to continue this"—she points between us— "because of my past or inexperience, that's fine. But I can't be casual." She stops and stares at me.

I stare back at her across the space of darkness.

During my tours in the Army, I thought I saw all kinds of bravery. I thought what Keene had done, stepping in front of a hail of bullets to save me had to be the bravest thing ever in this world or the next. Brother saving brother.

I was wrong.

The definition of valiant and brave were standing in front of me on a cold night, wrapped in a cashmere coat with the fall leaves swirling around her ankles.

"I think..." I say as I move closer. Her eyes widen—not from fear, just wariness. "You might be the most beautiful, courageous, strongest woman I've ever met." The disbelief creeps into her eyes. "No arguing, Cassidy. My opinion. And if it takes forever, you'll believe it too." Slowly, so not to scare her, I wrap my arm around her waist and pull her flush against my body. I lower my forehead to hers, just to hold her for a few moments.

When she looks up at me, her gaze holds a mix of hope, hesitancy, and amazingly, desire.

I can't resist.

Leaning down, I brush my lips once, twice against hers. I hear a soft expulsion of breath and settle my mouth on hers for a deeper kiss, hearing a delicate moan escape her.

I satisfy myself with this for a few minutes. I feel her arms tighten, pulling her body closer to mine. Without pushing, I gently run my tongue against her lips, seeking entrance. She parts hers and I slowly slip in between her luscious berry lips for what may be the softest, most sensual kiss of my life. Her taste is unlike anything I have ever known. It's this indescribable combination of cinnamon and sweet.

I have a hunger to know more than just her secrets. I want to devour her. I want to lay her back and kiss her all over, spending hours, days, months uncovering who this woman is. Layer by layer, reaching until I find the core of who she is. I need to feel her body against mine in as many ways as possible.

When we pull apart, her eyes blink open and look at me before her trembling hand touches her mouth.

I feel her body shake against me from a combination of the cold air around us and what I think might be fear of the unknown. And I realize quickly why.

Her first real date.

Her first real kiss.

If I have my way, I'll be her first everything.

Hell, I'll be her only.

15

CASSIDY

Caleb and I make our way back to his car, his arm holding me close to his side.

Between the conversation and my shoes, I feel a little wobbly. I must look a wreck.

I hope high-end sports cars come with mirrors. Otherwise, I'm going to resemble an extra in a horror film walking into Molly Darcy's. When I say as much to Caleb, he squeezes my shoulder. "You know we don't have to go if you don't feel like it," he offers.

What do I want?

I need a drink. I want to dance. I have to stop living in the past and feel alive.

"I think this conversation definitely put some negatives on the date point scale, Harvard."

When we reach the side of the Porsche, Caleb wraps me in his thick arms again. Dropping a kiss on the top of my head, he says, "Still keeping score, huh?" he teases lightly.

"I expect someone who looks like you would have some game. So far, all I've got is dinner and rehashing of my past which, for the record, makes me want to regurgitate said dinner."

"Let's not forget about our kiss, Cassidy," his dark voice says. I love how he claims it as ours. His eyes gleam at mine through the darkness at the lake. "I would think a kiss that sweet would definitely put me ahead for the night."

My heartbeat accelerates as I squirm a little, thinking of our kiss. My first kiss. Yeah, that definitely put him ahead.

He's so close to my body, he can feel my body shift and he laughs. Yeah, I don't think so. Reaching up, I see the surprise in his eyes a moment before I bring my lips to his.

This kiss is shorter, but ratchets up the adrenaline in my system. When I end it, his breathing is as uneven as mine. I turn around to open the car door. "Now we're even. Time to re-up your date game, Lockwood."

As the door closes behind me, I hear his low laugh. I quickly pull the visor down and thankfully find a mirror. I check out my makeup before reaching for my purse. It's not as horrible as I thought. I briefly wonder as Caleb slides into the driver's seat if my sisters put all the waterproof and sweat proof crap on me because they knew I was going to completely lose my shit, or because they figured it would get hot in the bar like they'd said. Either way, all I end up doing is touch up my gloss and dust my face with a touch of powder.

"Ready?" Caleb asks. After I buckle myself in, my eyes meet his and a small smile crosses my lips. After putting the car in gear, he reaches for my hand and we drive off into the cold, fall night.

As we make the quick trip from Lake Kenosia to Molly Darcy's, we listen to The Fray's "Over My Head." It's apt for my mood. I always wondered what it would feel like for someone outside of the family to know everything. Well, not everything, but to explain how I, Cassidy Freeman, came to be.

I think I'm still a bit heady with the idea that who I am, who I really am, was accepted. I know Jason accepted Phil, so there are people out there who aren't completely judgmental. But with women, there is a stigma, a humiliation that keeps us silent with fear. Because even if we are young when rape happens to us, somehow, we ask for it.

No one does.

Ever.

I was lucky to have the right people help me work through my issues so I didn't devolve into the animal I was bred to become. I cannot fathom what would have happened to my soul if Phil and I hadn't ended up with Em and her aunt.

I've worked with Matt. I've read the books. I know I have a healthy dose of PTSD, mixed with OCD and anxiety. Throw in my self-abhorrence and it's a Molotov cocktail waiting to explode within the confines of a relationship.

Over the last few years, I've realized part of me will always be that helpless girl, but I'll never be her again. I'm stronger than the people who brutalized me, making what happened to me something that doesn't dictate who I am day-to-day, that lives within me, but doesn't define my life. I can put on a smiling face to the world and hide my past hell. As scared as I am about certain areas of my life, when I open that door to my past, I expected men to go running.

I may have been a victim, but I'm no longer anybody's victim. I refuse to let myself be categorized, defined, or give up any more of my life by giving my past the power to control me.

Somehow, Caleb listened to what I had to say and saw that. He can't possibly understand it, but by not walking away, he made me stronger. He held my face in his hands and stared into my eyes. And there I saw my pain reflected, but there was no revulsion. No disgust.

And that kiss.

Holy mother of God, that kiss.

Right now, I think I feel like people do when they're told they've won the lottery; dizzy, out of sorts, and a bubble of happiness just ready to pop.

I'm a realist. Things may or may not work out with Caleb.

But forever, I will love him for this moment when I actually believe the words my family had been telling me for years about the woman I am.

Strong. Confident. Resilient. Beautiful.

As we park in Molly Darcy's overflow lot, Caleb turns off the car and turns his body to face me. "How are you doing, Pixie?" he asks quietly.

Despite the use of his somewhat annoying and somewhat cute nickname for me, I give him an honest answer. "I'm processing. It's not a story I tell, ever. I sure as hell never expected to tell it on my first date."

"Is there anything I can do?"

I sigh audibly. I brought all of my demons to the forefront of my mind. He knows this, and he knows I did it in part to brace him for what being with me would be like. What he doesn't realize yet is that they haven't ever really left that space. He can't shelter me from them, especially not when I sleep.

"Just don't lie to me, Caleb. If it gets to be too much, knowing about me and what I was, be honest with me. That's all I ask."

"Right now, I can't imagine a scenario where that would ever be a possibility." His response is immediate.

His phone beeps. Cursing, he reaches between us for it. "It's Ry. He said they have a booth toward the back near the dance floor. Are you ready?"

Am I ready?

Yes. Yes, I am.

I nod, and after a quick squeeze of my fingers, he says, "Wait here," and jumps out of the car. Jogging quickly around to my side, he swings the door open and reaches over the low-slung door for my hand. "Ready for part two, Ms. Freeman?"

"Part three, Mr. Lockwood," I say without thinking.

His eyes search mine, incredulously.

"Just because something is a difficult mess, doesn't mean you won't find something beautiful in it," I say softly, reaching up to touch his lips. "I like to remind myself of that. It gives me hope."

His eyes flare at my meaning. He reaches up with his hand, captures my fingers against his mouth while he kisses them hard.

"You're right, Pixie. Part three. Shall we?"

"Lead on."

WE WALK into Molly Darcy's and hear the blare of country music over the speakers.

I'm pretty certain the sound system is having a traumatic breakdown.

I remember Caleb saying something about this being a wedding reception. I raise up on my toes and he leans down. "Were we supposed to bring a gift?" I say loudly into his ear.

"No," he assures. "The couple asked for donations to Danbury's Pediatric Cancer Ward in lieu of gifts. Ry took care of the donation for all of us."

"I need to settle up with him then for my part."

He rolls his eyes at me.

"You do realize if I ask you out at some point, Caleb, I'm going to expect to pay."

"I'll just have to ask first then, won't I?"

I smile, pulling my poncho over my head. After draping it over my arm, Caleb's arm immediately circles my waist. I lean into his embrace, my head resting against his upper chest. His arm tightens. I find him smiling down at me, his eyes burning into mine. "Do you see your brother?"

After staring at me another moment, his eyes scan the room. His eyes catch on something and he starts cursing under his breath. "Yeah, I do."

At this point, I'm cursing my height as I bob and weave while Caleb keeps his hold on me. "What is it?"

"Keene is standing at our table too."

"Your best friend?" He nods, even as his eyes flash in displeasure. "You don't seem too thrilled."

"He's very black and white, Cassidy, where things are in the right or wrong column. With the life he's lived, things that have happened to him, I don't understand living that way, but I understand him being that way. What we have between us..." He trails off, while I mentally love the idea that he used the term us. "He just can't place it in the right column yet, so therefore it's wrong. I imagine he's going to be a dick."

I scoff. "Please. I deal with those daily. Remember why y'all hired me?"

Caleb turns me toward him and cups my face. "That's business. Just don't take anything he says to heart, Pixie. What matters is right here."

I tuck his words close to my heart as he leans down and brushes his nose against mine. "I'd kiss you, but those sounds you make when you do are for me alone to hear, Cassidy," he murmurs. At my sharp intake of breath, he smiles. I can feel his breath against my mouth and I lean in a little. "Uh-uh. Not here, sweet Pixie. Later."

Smiling, he grabs my hand and starts to weave through the bar area. A few moments later, we stop by the booths lining the dance floor. No sign of his friend Keene, only Ryan and Jared who are making all kinds of comments about where we've been for the last hour and a half.

Dismissing his brother by giving him the finger, Caleb manages to snag the waitress as she passes. Looking at me, he asks what I want to drink.

"Jameson, neat," I tell the harried woman. I'm certain she never expected her beloved Irish bar to turn into a country honky-tonk.

She turns to Caleb. "Bowmore." Ryan lifts an amber colored, half-filled tumbler to his lips with a twitch of amusement.

Of course. Men and their beloved whisky.

The harried waitress scurries away.

"So," Ryan starts. Jared shakes his head.

"Shut it," Caleb replies mildly. His arm goes around the back of the booth, his fingers quickly becoming tangled in my hair. Between our coats to my right, I'm pressed up tight next to Caleb's hard body. I can't complain about our proximity to one another.

I look up and find his eyes on me already. I subconsciously lick my lips and his eyes dart down to them. He smiles, I smile back, and I hear Ry and Jared thank the waitress for delivering our drinks in the background.

"Well, well, well," a dark voice booms, interrupting our moment.

"Keene," Caleb says on a sigh. Turning to face his best friend, he reaches for my hand under the lip of the table. I easily let him have it. When I look around Caleb, imagine my shock when I recognize the face.

"Going to introduce me, buddy?"

"Do I have to?" Caleb mutters under his breath. I squeeze his hand to let him know it's okay, and now it is. Caleb has no idea, but now I have an ace when it comes to dealing with his friend.

I slip on my business mask and reach for my drink. Jared catches my eye and nods approvingly, while Ryan winks surreptitiously. Reaching around Caleb, I introduce myself. "Cassidy Freeman." I hold out my hand.

"Keene Marshall. I work with Caleb at Hudson Investigative Services." He searches my face for some kind of reaction as he pumps my hand once, twice before allowing it to drop. Is that the name of Caleb's company? Interesting. I'll have to ask him about it later. Keene's dark green eyes are searching mine.

I hear, literally hear, Caleb's teeth click together as he clenches them against Keene's monochromatic thinking.

"That sounds like an interesting line of work, Keene. I imagine y'all have quite an interesting job."

"Really?"

"Yes." I reach for my drink, take a sip of the Jameson's from the crystal tumbler and set it back on the table, my eyes never leaving Keene's.

I wonder if Keene remembers me too when he asks, "Have we met before? There's something so familiar about you." As he leans his body against the back of the booth where Ryan and Jared are seated, he faces Caleb and I like we're his adversaries in a courtroom.

I merely raise a brow. It's not good to give away too much too soon.

"So, did Caleb mention he had our company run a search on yours before he asked you out?"

While Ryan and Jared gasp in shock and outrage, I keep my

expression in check and shrug, my shirt shifting silkily on my shoulder. While Caleb didn't specifically mention it, I'm not terribly surprised. Many of our higher end clients do. "No, he didn't. Was he supposed to? Did he have a to-do list from his work husband he had to mark off by telling me, Keene?" I hear Ryan choke on his drink.

He leans forward on the table, a complete power maneuver. "You don't think it's a morally ethical line you crossed, Ms. Freeman? Agreeing to go on a date with someone you're working for? Someone whose company investigated you?" His eyes are daring me to argue with him.

Ryan jumps in at this point. "Jesus, Keene. It was a business check. Cassidy has the right to make her own personal choices. Lay the fuck off."

Caleb is coiled like a snake right beside me, ready to strike at any second. Time to dispatch of the supercilious man before me in a way that's less bloody than what I think Caleb intends.

I reach for my drink. "Now that you bring up moral ethics, Keene, I can appreciate your point of view."

Keene starts to smile, while Caleb, Ryan and Jared's heads all turn toward me so fast, I think they may suffer from whiplash. I continue to look Keene directly in the eyes and lean forward over Caleb's legs. His hand automatically drops from my hair to my waist. My hand pats his leg, telling him I've got this.

"At least Caleb hasn't fucked someone he did a business background investigation on, has he?" Take that and choke on it, you sanctimonious shit.

"Neither have I, Ms. Freeman," Keene tosses back.

So arrogant. So cocky. Such an asshole. So completely wrong.

"Are you so sure?" I taunt. "By the way, has the tattoo on your thigh healed well?"

Keene's jaw opens slightly, and all the men are now staring at me. Finally breaking eye contact, I reach for my purse and pull out my cell phone, going to the photo app. When I start scrolling through the pictures, everyone at the table goes silent.

I pull up a picture of Ali and I from Phil and Jason's wedding last summer and slide my phone across the table. "Maybe you remember me from entertaining my sister Alison at the Plaza in the city over the summer? Or have you fucked enough women that one more is just like another?"

Keene reaches for the phone, and I dispassionately watch him look at the picture of me and my knockout sister and swallow. Hard. He places the phone carefully on the table and lets out a breath. "What you don't realize is that we were sharing a suite that weekend at the Plaza. Next time, you might want to have a care in how loud you are for the other occupants of the hotel." I pick up the phone and smile at my sister's image before placing it back in my purse.

I raise my eyes to meet Keene's shocked ones. I could not be more delighted with his reaction and I quietly think to myself, thank you Ali for keeping me up all night screaming with this asshole.

"When y'all were done and you left that morning—or would that be you snuck out—you didn't exactly have your pants on. I was in the sitting room and saw your tattoo on your thigh. By the redness of it, I could only assume it was new or infected. So again, has the tattoo healed well? Maybe you'd like to tell me more about who Riley is?" I lean forward with my chin on my hand. His eyes flash with some unreadable emotion.

Keene still hasn't said a word, his body frozen by what I've revealed. I feel Caleb's arm squeeze around me so tight, that if I wasn't taking shallow breaths to control my anger, I likely wouldn't be able to breathe. I deliver the kill shot.

"So, who had the moral fuck up first, Keene?"

Keene looks at me for another moment, then at Caleb before turning and walking into the crowd without turning back. Silence reigns around the table.

My eyes go to Jared first, his holding admiration. Ryan's eyes show that too, as well as shock. I turn my head to Caleb's and almost clock him, his face is so close. He leans down to my ear. "I have to know after our conversation earlier, how much you can take of me being blunt right now."

I tilt my head slightly, wanting to get the lay of the land. Is he pissed I just laid out his best friend like that?

I turn my face toward his and see heat, but not the angry kind.

"I think I can take it," I murmur back, taking a sip of my drink.

"I could not be more turned on right now than if you had spent the entire night whispering ways you wanted to take me to bed. That was so fucking hot," Caleb growls.

"I know he's your friend..."

Caleb shakes his head back and forth.

"No, Pixie. He has to work his shit out and either respect my decisions or stay the hell out of them." His voice is filled with admiration. "You knew who Keene was?"

"I didn't until I saw his face. Ali was seriously pissed he walked out on her without giving her his number." Well, she was pissed because she wasn't done with him yet, but I keep that to myself.

Caleb throws his head back and laughs. Once he's winding down, he reaches for his drink and holds it up. "A toast to you, Pixie. The strongest woman I've ever met." His eyes meet mine over his glass of scotch. They're warm and filled with heat.

I tip my glass back at him before throwing back the remainder of my tumbler of Jameson's.

Turning into him, I tip my jaw up at him. "You a little warm there, Harvard."

"Can you blame me?"

Shrugging, I turn back to Ryan and Jared who are staring at the two of us with stupid grins on their faces. "Anything else I can do to entertain you boys?"

Jared looks at Ryan, then over at me. "I think Ryan might have a bit of a crush on you now, just for the record."

Caleb glares at his brother. "For the record, brother, stick to your man."

Jared and I burst into laughter at the antics of the Lockwood brothers. Then a familiar chord starts playing and I start to smile. I turn to the man next to me. "Do you dance, Harvard?"

He finishes his Bowmore and slides out of the booth. "I've got some moves."

I wink at him and slide out. Shaking my body as I make my way to the center of the dance floor, I let Luke Bryan's "Move" flow through my body. I'm in my own world dancing when I feel Caleb pull me closer. My eyes fly up to his as his hips start swaying in rhythm with mine. Another first.

I'm suddenly dancing the way I've seen other people dancing in clubs. Caleb's leg is between mine, my hips pressed against his body, his arm banded low around my hips as our bodies move in sync to the sexy Southern beat.

My heart's thudding against my chest. Not from panic, but the full-body contact I have from chest to thigh. His sensuality is searing me through my clothes and into my skin, branding me. Here, in the middle of a crowd of people I don't know, Caleb makes me feel safe, uninhibited, protected, wild.

Free.

His head dips toward mine and I let out a small sound. He slowly shakes his head and mouths, "No."

My arms feel drugged when I try to lift them to circle his neck, but I only manage to reach his forearms.

I recognize this feeling as desire, having heard my sisters talk about it and reading as many romance novels as I do, but I never knew its potency. Its smooth touch is wrapping around me, freeing me from the chains of the prison I've held myself in for so long.

The scene around Caleb and I is out of focus, and the only clarity is the space which Caleb and I occupy. I feel warm from the Jameson's, warm from Caleb's body pressed against mine, warm from where he drops his head and grazes his teeth and lips against the side of my neck.

I imagine what I'm feeling is being reflected in his dark gaze. His nostrils flare slightly as he moves his body farther down mine so we're face-to-face. "Some moves," I manage to say.

A slow, sexy curve to his lips is my only response.

A slow song replaces Luke Bryan and we keep holding each other. "Do you have plans for later?" he asks.

"Later?" Confused, I lean back.

"Later, as in later Saturday. It's after midnight, Pixie."

"We have the Juniors coming in the afternoon; Sophomores in the early evening." I run through my planner out loud.

"I forgot what it looks like," he muses.

"What what looks like?" I parrot, confused. This man muddles my cohesive thought process.

"How incredibly hot you are when you go into professional mode. It was next to impossible for me to act with any decorum that first day in your office."

"You seemed to handle it well enough," I grumble. Despite how much of a debacle that ended up being for me and the problems it caused within the family, it led me to where I am.

With my resolution to not look back, I can't regret what happened. I can only be grateful it led me to right now.

My thoughts drift for a second to Keene. Right or wrong, black and white. Where would I be right now if those were the only choices I took along the path of my life?

"What are you thinking of, Pixie?" Caleb breaks into my thoughts.

"Keene," I reply honestly.

Caleb's face tightens.

"Not like that," I say, exasperated. I whack him in the chest.

"Explain, please."

"I was just thinking if the decisions I made were as black and white as his, we wouldn't be here right now. And what I would have missed out on."

"In some ways, that makes me more furious at him for the way he was behaving, but I understand what you're saying."

I nod and grab his hand, pulling it back around my waist. His face softens, and his smile is for me alone.

"So, back to my question. What are you doing later?"

"Is this a lead into asking me out, Caleb?"

"It is."

I take a deep breath. This next step is huge for me. "I honestly don't know what time we're going to finish, but if you want to come over for a late dinner..." There's a storm building in his eyes. For me. For this.

"I want."

16

CASSIDY

I'd just pulled the cheddar, bacon, and pecan pizza from the oven when my phone rang. Glancing at the name on the display, I answer it as I release a puff of air.

"Caleb."

"Cassidy." God, that voice. Low, warm, slightly husky, and a bit... echoy? Was he in the car already? I look at the clock and holy shit, it's almost eight. Leaving the pizza to cool, I quickly begin straightening up the kitchen and make my way into the adjoining living space. As I quickly glance around my typically immaculate living area, I hear him through what must be the Bluetooth in his car.

"I'm about fifteen minutes out. I hope that's not too soon? If you're still busy, I can drive around a bit." His voice is smooth, warm, anticipatory.

"No, no. That's fine. I'm just putting a few last-minute things together." Like me. Taking a deep breath, I slowly let it out so he can't hear me. "When you get through the farm's gates, take the road to the right before you hit the main building. It will lead you to the other side of the lake. I'm in the carriage house."

I hear the Porsche accelerate through the phone. "I'll be seeing you soon then, Cassidy. Give or take fifteen minutes." The phone disconnects in my ear.

I toss my cell on the couch and run up the stairs for my room, ripping my T-shirt over my head. Caleb is about fifteen minutes out. How did I completely manage to lose track of time? I know how. Up until a few minutes ago, I was too busy to even think about it. Now, with mild panic setting in, I'm asking myself what did one wear to have someone over for heavy conversation with the potential for...something?

Grabbing a pair of cranberry leggings and a black sweater that hits me mid-thigh, I quickly change as headlights pass outside the farm's entrance. A quick brush of my hair and some gloss on my lips, I look at my reflection. Am I ready for this?

As I watch the lights round the front of the main building, I grab an old pair of Chucks from the bottom of my closet. Taking one last look at myself in my vintage full-length mirror, I imagine I come across like a college student and someone who is overly comfortable with her company. Neither could be further from the truth, I think wryly as I bound down the stairs just in time to hear Caleb knock on the door. Taking a few deep breaths, I reach for the handle.

And take a step back in surprise.

He's bent down, fumbling with a bag that obviously holds a bottle of wine. I hear him cursing the frailty of dorky wine bottle bag handles as I stare at what he holds in his arms, which are dozens of sunflowers, ranging from bright yellow to almost a sunset orange, obscuring his face.

He's so busy retying the little knot on the inside of the wine bag without dropping the gorgeous blooms, he hasn't realized I'm standing here. I take a moment to lean against the doorjamb, studying him. Like me, Caleb opted for comfort and casual in worn jeans and a black sweater that molds against his body like it was painted on, showing off his broad shoulders and sculpted abs. I can feel my legs shift in anticipation of running my hands along it to touch him again. I sigh at the idea of being as close to him as I was on the dance floor at Molly Darcy's the night before.

I'm not sure whether the shift in the air from the door being open, or my sharp inhalation of air that makes him aware of me standing there. Suddenly, the wine and flowers seem insignificant as I catch a glimpse of those dark eyes.

Slowly standing to his full height, his chin has to dip for him to look at me. A lack of four-inch heels will do that to you. His eyes crinkle in the corners as he breaks into a full smile. Thank the Lord I decided not to wear my heels. I might have fallen off them by that smile alone. His eyes travel down my body, tracing every inch of it with his eyes. His eyes land on my well-worn Chucks and he tosses his head back and lets loose a deep-throated laugh.

"Now that's not something I never pictured you wearing."

I raise an eyebrow at him. "The whole outfit or the Chucks?"

"Pixie, I might have bet my car you even worked out in heels."

"Hate to break it to you, but I don't have a desire to visit our friendly orthopedic surgeon. I own my fair share of sneakers."

"Not sure I believe that. I might need proof."

I hold up my foot as if he's mildly dense.

"Uh-huh. One pair does not equal a fair share. Going to invite me in? Maybe I can see for myself?" he teases.

I feel the heat begin to travel up my cheeks as I realize we've been bantering with me on one side of the door, him on the other. "Please, come in."

He glances around as he steps over the threshold and into my home, my sanctuary. Seeing him look around is like watching a tennis match as he absorbs the essence of my home.

When we bought the farm and outbuildings, I immediately connected with the carriage house. Because of the number of bays to the original carriage house, the family figured there must have been a substantial master estate at some point absorbed by the land of one of the many subdivisions that surrounded our land in Collyer. My carriage house had five original bays which I converted to a two-car garage closest to the main entrance, with two enormous glass windows on either side. The fifth bay had been converted into a double French door entryway. On the soft cream-colored walls, matted and framed, are the architectural plans for the carriage house's renovation. I guide Caleb toward the back where the original tack and living quarters were. As we walk over random width pine plank floors covered with antique throw rugs, he would pause by the occasional frame to study it.

"You expanded the original building?"

"Yes."

"Why?" His gaze encompasses the room, absorbing the essence of the clean lines and expansive space.

I try to look at my home as he would. The floors continue into this space which opens up with raised ceilings and exposed rough-hewn beams. The original carriage house walls can be seen through floor to ceiling insulated windows which allow the historical value of my home to come through, while still insulating against the radical Connecticut weather.

"It was a fairly large space," I muse, not really answering Caleb's question. He moves closer to me, around the room with the large L-shaped sofa that faces the original fireplace, as well as a set of barn doors on the adjoining wall. Also visible is the kitchen and dining space. Set past the kitchen, my home office is visible, part of the expansion which the master suite is part of upstairs. "But certain things didn't work if I wanted to live in the home long-term. If I ever wanted a family, there was no room to expand and hardly any storage space."

"Do you?" he asks, still not looking at me.

"Want a family?"

He nods. I step in front of him, catching his eyes. "A little heavy conversation with your appetizer, Mr. Lockwood? Can I get you a drink with that?" I pretend to hold a waitress pad in front of me, as if I'm taking his order.

His eyes widen as he realizes what he was asking me. "Well, crap." Color darkens his cheeks. The edges of my lips twitch upward as he glances down, realizing he's still holding the flowers and bag he'd been fiddling with. "Shit."

I'm outright laughing at this point.

He shoves them in my direction. "Obviously, these are for you. Thank you for having me over, especially since you were working all day."

I take the flowers from him gently, lifting them up and burying my face in the outdoorsy scent. Carefree. That's what sunflowers remind me of.

I feel that when I'm with Caleb.

I want to kiss him to thank him for the flowers, but I'm not as certain about doing that now as I was last night.

My nose still buried in the flowers, I raise my lashes to catch Caleb's eyes. It's like he can read my mind. Placing the bag with the wine on the nearest table, he wraps his arms around me, pulling me close. With the flowers caught in between us, he lowers his head.

When his mouth touches mine, he lets out a small groan. Or is that me? Threading my fingers through his thick dark hair, I hold his head in place as his tongue traces the seam of my lips. Gasping in surprise, my mouth opens. Dipping in for a quick taste, our tongues dual for a brief moment before I break the kiss and step back. His reluctance to let me go is emphasized by the quick pull of my body back to his. His nose rubs against mine, keeping the contact between us.

I can feel my heart pounding against the stalks of the blooms he gave me. My hand that's wrapped around Caleb's neck can feel his as well. Its staccato beat and his harsh breathing tell me he isn't unaffected by that kiss.

We both know it wasn't an uncomplicated embrace. Our lives are so entwined already, that taking this further will just tighten the invisible threads binding us even tighter.

I step away, and he reluctantly opens his arms to let me retreat a few steps back. Our eye contact still hasn't broken from the moment he leaned down to take my lips. The current running between us hasn't dissipated. If anything, the invisible cord that stretches between us gets stronger.

With every second.

Shaking my head, I move through the living space into the kitchen with Caleb close behind me. With the island between us, I place the flowers on the island next to the sink. Moving around the kitchen for a vase and scissors, he eyes the spread on his side of the island with pure male appreciation, and a little awe. Yeah, there's no froufrou finger foods. I think the most delicate item might be the cheese plate. I've made the cheddar bacon and pecan pizza, mini chicken pot pie turnovers, warmed up leftover Philly Cheesesteak Dip from the event earlier with French bread, and a veggie and cheese plate.

Sue me. I get nervous, I cook and eat. I have a sister who's an athlete. She'll run it off me.

"Are we expecting anyone else?" he asks, not raising his eyes from the plates of food.

"No," I say, critically surveying the buffet before me. I suppose I did cook for a few, or twelve. "Too much?" I ask, raising my eyes to meet his.

"Are you one of those people who minds leftovers?"

"No."

"Then don't worry about it, unless you plan on pulling out a three-course Italian meal in addition to this. Then I might have to call you out for making too much food."

I pick up one of the pieces of French bread and throw it at his head.

He captures it and says, "Thank you," before dunking it right into the hot dip and shoving it into his mouth. "This is delicious, Cassidy. Where did you learn to cook?"

I laugh and hand him a bottle of water from the fridge. "Food Network. We're all addicted to it. Corinna can outbake all of us, but we're all great in the kitchen."

He moves around the island to stand next to me. His hand raises and I flinch inadvertently as he brings it to my face. His eyes soften and he hesitates before reaching to brush his hand gently down my cheek. "I think it's time to relax, drink a little wine, and eat a little food."

"Maybe more than a little?" I grasp at the conversation gambit. "I don't need that many leftovers."

"I'll take some home if it tastes as good as it looks," he promises. It's like he knows just what to say to put me at ease. He steps away, moves back around the counter and picks up a chicken pot pie turnover. Before taking a bite, he says, "Just show me where you want me?"

Grabbing two wine glasses and the wine key, I make my way over to the bottle he left on my end table and gesture toward the outside patio. I'm grateful my mouth didn't have an attack of verbal vomit and blurt out I wanted him upstairs.

In my bed.

It's like it was made for him.

Maybe when I was dreaming I did.

"I think you probably got the most choice view out of all of your siblings, Pixie," Caleb comments some time later.

We're ensconced on my double lounger overlooking the water on the property. There are two heat lamps keeping us mostly warm while we soak up each other's company in the cold evening. Most of the food, with the exception of the crock pot dip, migrated out with us. For someone who claimed I made enough for twelve, Caleb probably ate enough for ten. We're now nibbling on some fruit and cheese as the moonlight dances over the water. We've also managed to polish off one bottle of wine. Caleb has switched to water, whereas I'm still cradling the dredges of the first bottle. We're both full, mellow, and relaxed.

"I think more than the space, that's what called me to the carriage house," I admit.

"The water?" he asks, not looking at me.

"Yes. There's just something that calls me to it. When I'm upset. When I need to think. When I just need to breathe. And while we're not far from the ocean, I can't get there that easily."

"We'll have to take you out on the boat sometime," he declares.

I sit up so fast, I almost dump my wine. "You own a boat?" Seriously? When the hell did he have time to go out on it?

Laughing, he reaches out and grabs my shoulder to pull me back down next to him, closer than I was before. "Nah. We have a membership to a boating club where you can take boats out each weekend during the season. Neither Ry nor I want to put forth the effort to maintain the boat when the season is so short here."

"Ah, so you're lazy," I reply, cheekily. "I understand now."

"Lazy! Why you—" He rolls on top of me and starts to tickle me, relentlessly. And I can't fight back, as I'm holding a goblet of red wine over my head, giving Caleb easy access to my left rib cage.

Shrieking, I kick my legs out in modified self-defense. "I give! I give," I screech, laughing.

Dropping a kiss on my lips, he rolls off me. Taking the wine from my hand, he snags the blanket at the foot of the chaise and pulls it up over us as I settle back against him. Snuggling against his warmth, his arm tightens slightly over my shoulders as I lean my head against him.

"How is it I just feel so comfortable with you, Caleb?" I muse quietly. It's the truth. I've met a few men over the years as attractive as Caleb, but none who have set me at ease. Ever. I've never felt the urges I guess normal women do.

In the incredibly short time I've known him, I feel lighter, less burdened. Maybe it's because he knows the worst there is to know about me and doesn't care. He just sees me. Cassidy. Not the victim that was, but maybe the woman who has been hiding and waiting to break free.

I don't feel traumatized that he knows, I feel relieved. Like a cautious bird, I feel like I'm taking perch on a limb. I don't feel the need to flee. But there's something in me telling me Caleb will scare off the predators who will cause me to flee.

I feel his lips brush the top of my hair. "Maybe because we've both witnessed versions of Hell and come out the other side, Pixie. Maybe we recognize that in each other, and know the things we'll fight about and for are pretty much in line with one another." He goes quiet, getting lost in his thoughts.

I look up at his profile. I feel him absentmindedly stroking my hair, his attention over the water. His profile is tight in his memories? In mine? I reach up and touch his chin.

"Hey," I whisper. His eyes cut to me immediately. Even through the combined darkness and their dark pools, I can see something churning. "What is it?"

His eyes close as I continue to trace his strong jaw. "In many ways, Pixie, when I left the Army, I felt like I left one hell to walk straight into another."

Because of my conversation with Jason, I know exactly what Caleb is referring to, but I know he needs to get it out. "I've been told I'm a good listener." I say, quietly.

And just like that, Caleb starts talking, holding nothing back. He tells me everything from when Ryan came out to when he joined the military. He talks about what it was like being born into one of the wealthiest families in New England, and how growing up with a legacy of men who served, he was expected to join. He talks about how he never expected the camaraderie, and how he could shed the mantle of being a Lockwood and focus on serving our country. He tells me about Ryan's side of what happened, including the abuse he suffered at their mother's—or as Caleb calls her, the birth vessel—hands, just for realizing he was sexually attracted to men. Because it was a black mark against the purity of the Lockwood name. His anger at his mother doesn't scare me. If anything, it solidifies what I already knew about this man. He doesn't strike out for pleasure, but only in protection, and only when justified.

Caleb goes on to tell me about why he left the military. About how a Skype call with Ryan's drunk ramblings about his first broken relationship with Jason after years because he was falling for Jared. Ryan, now wary of love, didn't feel like he could trust in Jared. Caleb wanted to get on a plane to straighten out his brother immediately, but he couldn't. At the time, he was on a critical undercover operation where he was gathering preliminary intelligence on a hidden military target in Western Europe for an unnamed terrorist sect. He naturally leaves out any information about the group or the operation, but tells me about how he almost took a bullet because he was so distracted over Ryan's potential breakup with Jared. And about how Keene walked in, saving him, taking a bullet to the thigh meant for Caleb's forehead.

"When I left the military, I bought Hudson, and Keene came with me." He looks down at me. "You know, we don't just work there, we own the place. Keene and I needed the challenge and we knew working for someone else wouldn't work for us. Keene was about to be medically discharged from our unit, but not the Army due to the injury on his leg. He could have been riding a desk, worked as a lawyer or Intel, but he would've been riding a desk. If he was going to be behind that desk, he figured he would throw in with me and make money doing it." He sighs. "I need you to understand why I didn't just abandon him to his asshole ways. We've done everything together since we were kids. Prep school. College. The Army. And then there's Riley." Caleb let's out a deep, heartfelt sigh.

"Who's Riley?" I ask quietly, taking a sip of wine, remembering the tattoo on Keene's leg.

"She was Keene's sister. She was kidnapped when she was four from their family home. He's never given up hope she's alive, and it's been twenty-five years this past summer. That's why he got the tattoo with her name on it. He refuses to believe she's gone because no one's ever asked for ransom and they've never found her body." Caleb runs his hand through his hair, his pain evident.

"Did you know her?"

"We're about six years older so I do have some memories of her. She was a pretty little thing. Loved Keene—day to his night. After she was taken, his mother died soon after. Some think it was of a broken heart. He's never been the same since."

I feel a crushing pain for Keene. How does he live with that? My harsh words last night protecting my right to choose whether or not to start something with Caleb replay through my head. The food and wine I ate start churning in my stomach. I feel so ashamed over the way I used it to taunt him.

God, I was such a bitch.

"Don't, Pixie. I can feel where your mind's going. Keene has the right to make decisions for Keene, no one else. What you did last night," Caleb's hand firmly tugs my hair so I meet his eyes across the dark, "was something that may make Keene question his actions toward others and start to bring him back from the demons only he fully battles. They're locked inside him. I can't reach them, and trust me, I've tried. Don't ever question what you did last night. You stood up for your rights, and my rights. You stood up for the possibility of an us. Do you have any idea what that means to me?"

I shake my head no.

Caleb releases my hair and slides his hand up to the back of my neck where my amaryllis tattoo rests. His fingers absentmindedly trace the edges as his eyes remain locked on mine. "You made each other a promise to stand with each other. A vow?"

I don't remember telling him that, but then again, I told him so much last night I probably did. My head is in his hands so I know he can feel when I nod.

"I feel like last night you did the same thing for us. You fought for a chance, Pixie. We all have our demons and dark places we wake up from in the middle of the night. We know they never go away. It's in how we live the day-to-day that keeps them at bay."

Something that's been worrying me since the minute he asked me out comes spewing out of my mouth. "You don't think I'm tainted by what happened to me?" I hold my breath, scared of how he'll answer. As close as we are on the lounger, I literally feel his body lock. His immediate fury is almost palpable.

"What did you just say?" His voice is scary quiet in the dark of the night.

"I said..." I don't even get to finish. I'm flipped over onto my back so quickly, the breath whooshes out of my lungs. Caleb's face is mere inches from mine and he's breathing fire.

His arms are bent at the elbows, braced on either side of my head. The strength in his muscular frame pushes mine deeper into the lounger. I'm caged in, but I don't feel trapped. His fury over my question is evident in his harsh breath against my face and narrowed eyes, but I chance looking into his eyes and wait to see things I expect.

Disgust.

Revulsion.

Pity.

None of that is there. But it's his words take away the last concerns I have about that.

"Cassidy, you were a baby attacked by monsters. Monsters, for the love of fuck. For people who say they don't exist, they need to get their head surgically removed out of their asses and wake up to the real fucking world. You have no idea of what I fucking want to do to the people who hurt you. I pray they're all dead before I find them." I'm in shock over the depth of emotion I feel coming from him.

"I want your eyes to spark when I tease you. I want you to smile and laugh. I want to take you out and hold your hand. I want to get so buried inside your soul, the last thing you think about is kicking me out of it when you realize I'm no good for you, when I lay my own demons on you. What I don't ever want you thinking is that you're tainted by your past." He ends on a whisper, his eyes boring into mine in the dark.

Jesus, Mary and Joseph.

Is this normal?

To feel so much this quickly?

Because it doesn't feel like I'm the only one.

I see the swirl of my own emotions race across his face. Need, want, fear, hope. It's the hope that pulls me under.

I reach up and slowly drag my fingers over his face—tracing it, but not touching it.

The slow movement of his head as his face turns back to mine, eyes wide, would almost be comical under any other circumstances. "What?" he whispers.

"It's just something I do when I want to remember something important. When we didn't have money for a camera as kids, I used to do this to take a picture and put it in my permanent memory album."

Caleb's face contorts before he gets it under control. He bows his head to get it closer. Running my fingers through his hair, his head snaps up and I'm now cupping his chin. His lips brush the center of my palm, the tingle that courses through my system raising all the fine hairs on my skin. It's both the softest and warmest of caresses.

"You truly are the strongest person I've ever met, Cassidy Freeman. I want a chance. Just the chance," Caleb's voice rasps in the dark between us.

"A chance for what?" But I know. His dark eyes meet mine, not saying the words. Instead, his head lowers and our lips brush together with an unspoken promise made between us. To give this a chance. Breaking away, our eyes are locked on each other, our breathing ragged. The basest parts of each of us is out there on the table and neither of us are running.

I want this. I want the dreams I wished on the furthest stars, the fantasies I've only been able to imagine by reading what came from someone else's imagination. I want to spend the time getting to know this man, to lie in his arms. I eventually want to run my hands all over his body and taste him. His face reflects the same. And before I know it, the word I never expected to hear comes out of my mouth.

"Stay."

His face shows his hunger and his pain. I can see inside of him now. It's like I'm connected to him in a way I'm not even to my family. It's his greatest wish, his biggest fear. He wants nothing more, but doesn't want to move too fast. Fortunately, neither do I, so I quickly put him at ease. Who would have thought I would be the one putting him at ease?

"Not for that, Caleb." I roll my eyes at him. "I just don't want to let you go right now and it's getting too cold to stay out here. Stay and hold me tonight...maybe?" I take a deep breath, letting him in a little bit more. "Maybe if you're here, the dreams won't come tonight."

The tender smile that crosses his face before he pushes off of me is worth every butterfly dancing in my stomach. Pulling me up, he wraps me in his arms, rocking me back and forth slowly.

"Let put the food away and find out."

17

CASSIDY

"So, who was the little trollop with a Porsche parked outside her door all Saturday night and didn't get into the office until late Sunday?" Phil singsongs as he comes into the farm, swinging two bottles of wine on Wednesday. Jason comes in behind him and gives me a look of pity. Having just heard something similar from Corinna and Ali, I merely shake my head as I continue to chop lettuce for the salad.

There are times like these when the tradition of family dinner is a trial as well as a blessing.

It's not like they didn't try to subtly grill me when I showed up at the office at ten versus my typical seven the next morning. It's not like I missed a client. It's not like they didn't have a permanent smirk on their faces all day as I walked around with coffee, trying to generate some energy from a night of little sleep. It's not like their faces weren't over my shoulder when I read the card that merely said "Caleb" when the vase filled with a single perfect amaryllis arrived on Monday, or the basket of key lime cookies from Stew Leonard's on Tuesday. No, they were savoring this family dinner for all it was worth.

Based on the way they were already behaving, burgers were not the only thing about to be grilled.

Sighing, I move the second head of lettuce into the big serving bowl. Grabbing the chef's knife and bell peppers, I slice the tops off and begin slicing out the core of seeds while listening to my siblings make subtle taunting comments back and forth over me. Don't they realize by now that I'll talk only when I'm ready to? Chopping faster than I was before, I make quick work of the rest of the salad fixings. A shadow crosses in front of me and I quickly glance up, chef's knife appearing as if I'm ready to do battle. Jason just shakes his head and hands me a glass of wine, a smile on his handsome face. Not for the first time, I think to myself that Phil should spend more time on his knees thanking God for Jason. Raising the glass in a toast to Jason, I lean on my elbows before taking a long sip.

I wonder how much longer they'll give me before my privacy is stormed like the beaches of Normandy.

I don't have to wait long.

We're around the informal dining room table having just passed the salad around when Phil starts. "Well?" he demands, king to peasant.

Just to be a pain in his ass, I delay the inevitable. Seeing three identical faces on my younger sisters and sympathy on Em and Jason's, I deadpan, "A well is a hole dug in the ground in order to remove water, or maybe oil..."

Em spits her wine across the table into Phil's face before laughing hysterically.

Phil looks at her distastefully before reaching in his lap for a napkin to mop up the mess. The rest of the table breaks into gales of laughter. Phil says with utter disgust, "Seriously, you know she has no mouth control."

Swirling my wine around my glass, I glance at Em, whose eyes are sparkling with mirth before saying to Phil, "Is that why you like sitting across from her? You like having wet things randomly hitting you in the face? I didn't know you and Jason upped your kink level,

Whirlpool." The table erupts again. Dinner has now officially gone into the toilet.

Phil levels his gaze on me, knowing exactly what I'm doing— defer, evade, deflect. I've been doing a fine job of it since Monday. I really don't see a reason why it can't continue. But no, big brother, king of all he surveys, wants to know details. Details I still haven't fully processed myself yet.

Completely zoning out my family, I replay some of the things Caleb and I exposed about ourselves this weekend in my mind. Nothing. No sense of panic. I feel nothing but the essence of Caleb's strong arms wrapped around me when we woke up Sunday morning. We've seen or talked to each other every night since. One night, we had take-out dinner from Genoa in Ridgefield after he got done late at the office. Another was when we were at the caterer's tasting for the rehearsal dinner and yakked it up with Ryan and Jared. Last night, we were on the phone for hours.

Though we haven't spent the night together since, we've talked enough I feel the emotional bonds that grabbed me over the weekend perpetually wrapped around me.

The pull of something neither of us expected and both want.

Suddenly, the silence around the dinner table permeates through my haze. Shit. I lost the most important thing in a critical meeting. Control.

Phil is triumphant knowing I left myself open for a barrage of questions from my family. Corinna, Holly, and Ali all lean forward like a pack of lions, ready swoop in to take down their prey. Em opens her mouth, then shuts it, shrugs, and waits. I look down the table at Jason. He's the only one who appears pained by what I'm about to endure. He may be curious, but he's witnessed the date interrogation before. It's no picnic. Unlike me, Phil feels there are no boundaries to what he can and can't ask his sisters about their dates. From dinner, to whether there was desert after dinner, and did it have curvature to the left or to the right, Phil wants the details.

It's a damn shame he can't ask this level of detail about things like business. We might have taken over a small country with his inquisition skills by now.

"It's none of your damn business, Phillip," I snap, on the offensive. Will that buy me more time? Doubtful. There's a collective sputter of laughter around the table at the futile effort. My sisters have tried this and failed at his invasive tactics.

"Nothing is ever really my business, Cassidy. It's never stopped me from protecting those I love before," he fires back quickly, way more experienced at this game in our present roles than I. Oh, good play, Phil. The big brother card, trying to use my emotions to get me to spill my guts.

"What makes you think I need protecting?" The heads swirl from me to Phil. Wimbledon ain't got nothing on us when it comes to the speed of heads moving back and forth.

He leans back in his chair, knotting his fingers over his washboard abs. "Maybe because the last time you had a date it was with me for your senior prom, when I was still lying to myself that I wanted pussy as well as dick?" Looking over at his husband, he says, "I'm certain of which I want now."

"I'd hope so," Jason says mildly. Not helping, Jason, you damn traitor.

"Don't you want advice, Cass? From the people who know you best and that you trust the most?" Phil pushes.

The thought of trusting Caleb flies through my mind. I hold onto my silence stubbornly. Okay, so what if the last time I had a date was something like ten years ago? While that part is true, I don't need to share my entire dating experience to be dissected. Most of what Caleb and I shared was private, from the deepest parts of our souls. Doesn't he get it? When he was falling for Jason, there was so much he didn't want to share, so much he held back because...my thoughts slam into a wall.

Oh shit, I'm falling for Caleb Lockwood.

I literally feel the blood drain from my face. My mouth opens and a choking gasp comes out of my mouth. I vaguely hear Em telling my other sisters to shut the fuck up as they start demanding answers on top of each other. My hand, now shaking, reaches up to touch my mouth. My eyes don't leave my brother's.

Phil stands, comes next to my chair and pulls me up into his arms. "I got you, Little Girl," he croons softly into my ear. It's what he's always said since the day he met me and was trying to get me to hold it together. My arms tighten and I bury my face into his neck. For how my brother comes across now as a self-absorbed drama queen, he has always been my rock. "I should have known you were just waiting for Prince Charming to come riding in," he whispers in my ear, reminding me of the many nights he'd read me fairy tales, well into my teens, when I just couldn't keep the nightmares at bay any longer.

I giggle into his neck. Phil stands to his full height, leaving my feet dangling off the floor. I grip his shoulders tighter. Suddenly, I feel another set of arms wrap around me and the scent of rosemary mint. Em. A kiss on the top of my head and a whiff of Chanel, Ali, followed by kisses on each cheek from Holly and Corinna, before each of their arms surround me in a cocoon of familial love.

Suddenly, I feel a wet lick on the back of my thigh as Mugsy joins in the family circle, not wanting to be left out. I let out a squeal in Phil's ear, who immediately drops me.

"Dammit, Cass", he curses me. I stumble backward into Em, and we both tumble to the floor laughing. We continue to lie there as our sisters collapse on each other. Jason laughs into his wine and Phil glares at Mugsy, who tilts his head in confusion, tongue lolling to the side.

"The best thing you ever did was adopt that dog," I tell Em.

She's still clutching her stomach. "Oh my god, Cassidy. Here we are, about to have a full out sob fest and in comes Mugsy."

We both break into laughter again.

Phil, back to his normal self, is more aggravated that his rare emotional moment was ruined by a dog. "Well, I see what happens when I try to be supportive, so get off your ass Cassidy and start talking about the hotness that is Caleb Lockwood." At Jason's mild look, Phil retreats slightly. "What? He is hot for Cassidy."

Ali reaches down a hand for Em and I, pulling us to our feet. I search Ali's face questioningly, wondering what it was about Keene Marshall that attracted her to him.

She raises a perfectly arched eyebrow. "Something on your mind, Cass? Other than Caleb?" she smirks.

I open my mouth to ask her about Keene as we sit back down and resume dinner, but decide to save that for a later time. Really, it's none of my business, and besides, I do have something else I want to ask.

"What's sex like?"

A hushed silence falls across the table, with all eyes on me in some state of shock. Mentally, I note this topic for the next time we're having an argument at the office. It's an effective way to get them to shut up.

Em is the first to break the silence. "What do you mean, Cass? You've had sex since..."

I slowly shake my head from side to side.

"Cass, despite my earlier attempt at prodding you to talk about Caleb," Phil says, exchanging a glance with Jason to make sure he isn't being too invasive, "you've had what some who laughingly call "dates" since high school. You mean to tell us you haven't had sex?"

Leaning back in my chair, I pick up my wine and stare at the ruby liquid. "I needed it to mean something," I say into the depths of the glass. Realizing how that might sound to all my sexually active siblings, I continue. "I'm not judging the rest of you for living your lives so, please, don't think that. But it wasn't like I could stand to be alone in a room with a man. I still can't handle certain situations where I know I'm all alone. When I could function enough to be able to accept the occasional escort it was usually you, Phil. Otherwise, I was never interested." Swirling the wine around, I take a sip. "One thing I realized quickly during therapy is that for me, sex equates to trust, and being able to share everything about who I am. And essentially means it isn't just sex but making love." I look at the enraptured faces around the table. "I have to be in love." Taking a deep breath, I let it all out. "He knows everything about me, and I do mean everything. And he doesn't care. It's almost impossible to believe."

"And it's scary as hell," Phil murmurs, reaching for his husband's hand. Jason lifts his hand to his lips.

All the girls sigh, myself included.

"The idea of us makes his friends nuts, by the way," I continue, watching sappy faces turn into identical thunderclouds. "I'm not sure what it makes Ryan and Jared feel. It could cause a problem for the business if this doesn't work out."

"What do you mean his friends have a problem with it?" Holly demands.

"Screw the business," Corinna mutters simultaneously.

I recount what happened at Molly Darcy's. With a silent apology to Ali, I retell the part where I smacked down Keene. Her cobalt blue eyes flash in anger, but then an evil smile erupts on her face when she says, "Good for you, sister. I just wish I'd been there to do it myself."

Phil slams his fist on the table, making the plates jump. "Fuck his friends."

And that's all it takes for me to regain myself. "Didn't I just explain that Ali already has and I'm not into Keene? Keep up, Whirlpool." Em's wine ends up in Phil's face for the second time in one night.

"You did that on purpose," Phil accuses, letting go of Jason's hand to wipe his face.

My lips tip up as I shrug. It's a gift.

"Just for that, I refuse to show you how to grab a cock," Phil taunts. Jason puts his head in his hands, knowing this is going nowhere good, fast.

Ali snorts. "Please, Phil. She can get that down easy enough. It's not as if she has to go hunting for it each night like Jason has to for you. It's sucking cock that might get interesting." Ignoring Phil's indignant sputtering, she turns her laser stare on me. "I take it you have no idea yet how big he is so we can recommend items to practice with?"

Practice items? What in the hell?

Ali continues. "Same with nipple play. Cass has quite the rack, and she should practice feeling herself up so she doesn't jump through the top of that sexy Porsche if they decide to get down and dirty in there." There's a round of agreement at that statement. Suddenly, the table is filled with comments like "choking the chicken" and "two-finger tango," and a very disturbing discussion between Em and Jason about the best places to purchase sex toys.

I didn't need to know they agreed on that. Ever.

"Enough!" I finally yell to get my siblings attention again. "I'll figure it out."

Phil, never one to keep his mouth shut, leans over to say, "Sweetie, if you haven't done it, it's all going to be a shock to you. A man like Caleb has probably done it a lot."

While not wrong, I really didn't need that mental image. Sending a mental fuck you over to my brother, I also know Caleb would never place any expectations on me. "I appreciate the... insight you all have provided about your sex lives. There are things I will never be able to quite...forget. But seriously, I just wanted to know what sex was like. What does it feel like when it's good?"

"There's so much more than that, Cass," Em says patiently. "That's what we're, in a roundabout way, getting to."

I think quickly. "Okay, how about this. Give me something to do right now. I pass it, we stop this discussion."

They all burst into laughter.

"I'm serious! Give me something to. How did Corinna put it...deep throat? If I can do that, then let's assume that I'm not going to be completely inept and need *Sex for Dummies*, the deluxe edition delivered to my Kindle."

My sisters are leaning on each other in a heap of laughter, while Phil jumps up and runs for the kitchen. "You better not make it anything like a jalapeno or something, asshole," I call over to him.

"Noted," he calls over his shoulder, already at the fridge.

"This should be interesting," Jason muses. Phil comes back with an assortment of food that no one in their right mind would eat together. Mushrooms, Brussels sprouts, pepperoni, summer sausage, leftover bratwurst, cream, and a jar of pickles. Pushing aside his plate,

Phil begins to construct varying edible sculptures that when he's done, all remarkably resemble penises.

It's almost scary at how adept he is at this.

By the time he's done, food is everywhere and he moves them to be on display in the center of the dining room table. Holly has her phone out, snapping photos. Thank God. While I may want to block this memory from my mind for the immediate future, you never know when a good holiday present requires these images on a family T-shirt.

"No one expects you to be able to deep throat this one," Phil says, pointing to the pepperoni with the mushroom cap and Brussels sprout ball sac. "This is merely a display of what he could be packing in length, but it's highly unlikely. Most men lie about being this long." Dismissively, Phil moves to the summer sausage. "Now some men may have this kind of girth, but again, it's a rarity, so while a visual stop in our demonstration, it will not be what we practice on."

I look at the summer sausage and imagine that fitting down below. I think my vagina closes up tighter than it already is at the thought. The idea that Caleb might be packing something that thick actually worries me a little.

"Now, let's talk about what I suspect Mr. Lockwood might be packing in his pants." Jason, now not dissuading Phil, but fully participating, is staring at option three with interest.

Phil continues. "The brat is not only best for this because it has a soft but supple over skin, but it also curves. Something, Cass, most men will not admit their cocks do. The length is a little long because most people can't deep throat that amount, but then again, some can." Jason can't keep the smirk off his face.

Yeah, screw blacking out memories in my immediate future. Where's the zapper thingie to erase this entire evening?

Phil turns his Machiavellian gaze on me. "If you, sister dear, can remotely deep throat the brat, we"—he gestures broadly around the table—"will leave the functional topic of sex alone for the evening." Just as I'm about to agree to the challenge, Phil walks over to the bar and pulls out a shot glass. Filling it halfway with a concoction of cream and pickle juice, he then says, "And once you're done playing with your toy, you have to do a shot of this." He nods down at the glass.

I look at my sisters and they're all solemnly nodding. "Did he make you do this bullshit?" I demand.

Em raises her hand. "Melted vanilla ice cream with pickle juice."

Ali nods. "McDonalds vanilla milkshake while munching on the pickles. Which was really gross because they still had mustard and ketchup on them." She glares at Phil. He smiles back beatifically and gestures to Holly.

"Brandy Alexander and olive juice," she confirms to a round of "Ewws" from my other sisters. "What the hell, Phil?" Em exclaims.

Jason puts his head in his hands as he asks, "Were you trying to kill her?"

"We were at a bar. I had limited items to work with," he protests, affronted. We all shake our heads at him in disgust before turning to Corinna.

"I heard the stories from Ali and Holly. I decided to go for the real thing and then talk to him about it afterward. I figured I would rather spit it up on a guy the first time than gag with any concoction Phil could make up. He seemed to be getting worse as we all got older," she admits.

We all burst into laughter. Some of my stress dissipates realizing this wasn't some disgusting hazing ritual. In his own warped way, Phil really was trying to support his baby sisters.

"So, do you need a little mood music for your debut, Cass? Or are you going to just grab the wiener and give it a go?" Phil's eyes are sparkling with mirth, and some other unnamed emotion.

Just then, Luke Bryan's "Move" starts playing over the sound system. I remember the heat of Caleb's body pressed against mine as we were dancing. His arm was low and tight against my hips, pulling me against him, feeling the tight hard ridge of his cock pressed against me. I close my eyes. I feel no fear, just a hot burning want pulsing through me. A need to be able to be with this man.

To be whole.

Eyes fluttering to a slit, I stand and reach across the table for the brat. Briefly grateful Phil left the raw mushroom head off, I open my mouth slightly. The tip of the bratwurst slides between my lips. My mouth widens naturally as I start to feel the fleshy meat move toward the back of my throat. Pulling it out slightly, I lick around it, trying to get some of the meaty flavor away. In the distance of my mind, I can hear the demented sounds of my sisters whooping it up, cheering me on, and Phil saying "holy shit" over and over.

I must be doing it right.

I figure if someone was spying in on us, there would be no doubt about how obscene this is. We look like we're playing a crazy bachelorette party game we found on the Internet.

Tipping my head back slightly to open my throat a bit more, I manage to suck the brat down to where Phil has pinned in the Brussels sprouts. Holding it for a few seconds, I pull it gently out of my mouth and lay it on the table next to the shot. Right as I'm about to shoot it, Em yells, "In three or four parts to make it real."

Fine.

The first pull tastes like over-salted béchamel. Second, more of the same. By the time I hit the third and fourth parts of Phil's "cum shot," I'm not really tasting anything. I put the glass down and open my eyes fully to a round of applause. But the moment to top them all is when Jason turns to Phil and says, "I don't even think you did that well the first time with mine." That causes Phil to choke on his wine, echoed by the hysterical laughter from the women at the table, myself included.

When we all calm down, Jason turns to me and asks, "Now, what is it you want to know, Cass? What it feels like to realize you're in love, or what it feels like to have the physical connection with that person?"

Phil, serious now that fun time with food is over, reminds me gently, "Cass, technically you're not..."

"I know that I'm not technically a virgin, Phillip. But not since I was nine has anyone or anything ever been close to...you know. Besides, that has nothing to do with this."

"Cass, it has everything to do with this," Phil disagrees gently.

Sighing, I acknowledge his comment with a nod. "I understand your concern, but it doesn't fit here. Truly. I don't feel the same with Caleb. The fears are just silent."

"You've only known him such a short time, Cass," Ali argues.

"How long did it take Phil and Jason?" I counter. Standing, I pick up my wine and meander around the great room. "He knows everything already. There's no need to hide who I am and play games."

"But what about him?" Em asks. Holding up her hand, she declares, "I'm not arguing against this. I'm just wondering where his head is at."

"I'm not saying I'm going to jump his bones tomorrow, y'all." I'm exasperated. I lean my back against the bar. "If it makes you feel better, he let me in, and, no, I won't share what we talked about," I say before Phil can open his mouth to ask. "No amount of your badgering will make me tell you, Phil. That's between Caleb and me. But let me just say by doing so, I felt comfortable enough being alone with him, waking up with him in my bed with my back to him."

They all suck in a breath, knowing for me what that means. When I was a young girl, even school pictures were a traumatic experience knowing someone I didn't explicitly trust would be at my back. All my school pictures show me with a glistening of tears in my eyes.

I'm still not thrilled when I have a stranger at my back to this day, but I cope. But out-and-out trust, like I gave Caleb, is reserved for only those who hit the core of me.

I have no idea how he managed to navigate past my barriers so quickly.

"That's right. I. Trust. Him. Who knows? He may end up being an ass and doing something to break my heart."

Phil interrupts, growling, "I'll kill him if he does."

Waving his drama aside, I continue. "You told me, Phil. I couldn't plan for this. There's no way I could have. Hear me though. I feel unburdened and weightless when I'm with him. His arms give me strength and his smile gives me hope. Isn't that what I'm supposed to feel?"

My eyes scan around the table, where my sisters are reaching for each other's hands. Phil falls back in his seat, mouth agape. Jason's smile is both knowing and proud at how I'm taking my stand against my past, against my fear, and against my family.

I was tossing out plans, going on gut instinct and intuition, and diving headlong into whatever may come for my chance with Caleb and for love.

It was the right move.

Wasn't it?

18

CASSIDY

I can't remember the last time I consumed so much wine.

Snickering in remembrance, I think about how we were a bunch of drunk idiots, falling all over each other laughing. Each time one of us caught another's eye, we were all set off again. To someone peering in the window, we must have looked like a bunch of deranged hyenas.

Family fun with food night continued long after my little demonstration. Swallowing my cappuccino, I think my throat hurts from the hysterical shrieking as Phil would randomly pick up one of his pieces of food art and proceed to show us how the pros did it.

I, of course, made it my mission to get Corinna to drink shots of the nasty cream and pickle juice mixture. What? Just because she'd actually sucked a cock didn't get her out of Phil's life lessons on blow jobs. Phil offered up his husband to me for a live demo, which both Jason and I politely declined, and then proceeded to laugh at Phil's drunken audacity.

To call last night epic would be an understatement.

By the time Caleb started texting me, we had completely rewritten the description of food porn and killed about six bottles of wine. Ali and Em nabbed my phone out of my hands and started sending voice messages to Caleb over my phone. This escalated to dumping their drinks over their heads and a selfie of the three of us was sent. Quickly realizing how out of control we were, I told Caleb I would call him later. But shortly after Jason got me back to my place, I face-planted into my bed.

Nothing stops work though. We've got a small wedding out at Candlewood Lake on Saturday, an engagement brunch on Sunday, and a Lockwood-Dalton tasting Sunday evening for the main event. Perhaps more than one if Caleb and I manage to get together. A small smile plays on my lips. Yeah, my sisters said I showed the potential for mad oral skills last night.

Now, if the stars would just align so I could see Caleb.

I'm still sipping the cappuccino I picked up from my early morning trip to The Coffee Shop, where Ava and Matt continued to smirk over my continued revenge against Phil. I let out a little laugh as I hear him go on in his office to Ali and Em about the incredible taste of the new latte I've been bringing him lately, and how amazing it is that Ava and Matt figured out a way to take out the extra fat. Oh, Jason, you doll. While revenge is typically best served cold, this one is best served long-term—hot, with an extra dollop of whipped cream.

I'm comparing my daily schedules for the next few days, grateful for their lightness, when my phone pings.

Caleb: Do you have control over your phone again, or is it still in the custody of one of your sisters? ;)

I groan, remembering everything we sent to Caleb in a fit of drunkenness, and literally bang my head on the desk repeatedly. Has no one ever heard of a breathalyzer for a phone? Another ping.

Caleb: You're going to leave a bruise on your head if you keep doing that to your head, Pixie. Your skin's too delicate to put up with that kind of abuse.

I tense before my head snaps up, then my breath catches. My doorway is filled with Caleb, dressed in a navy blue, long sleeved polo, jeans, and boots, his windswept hair framing his rugged face. An amused smirk plays around his mouth as he continues to type on his phone. Finally raising his head, his smile broadens as the text reaches my phone and dings.

Caleb: Since I still don't have your work schedule, I took a chance you might be available today after a night like that. I went by your house and you continue to amaze me. Here you are.

I begin to type a reply.

Cassidy: You know, you would know my work schedule if you simply signed the NDA, which can be accomplished right now since you're here. Easy peasy.

I put my phone back on my desk and lean back in my chair with my hands folded over my stomach. A small smile plays on my lips at this game of push and pull we have going on. When his phone buzzes in his hand, he looks down and begins to type. My phone dings.

Caleb: I want you to trust me with the deepest parts of you—your heart and your soul, Cassidy. Wouldn't an NDA for work almost be superfluous?

I don't bother responding with a text. "You want in that deep?" I whisper. My heart is racing.

He immediately replies as he pushes his body away from the doorjamb, making his way toward me. "I thought I made that clear the other night. If I didn't, that was a gross negligence on my part."

The smile spreading across my face is enormous as I stand up, and I imagine it's unlike any other I've ever worn.

Caleb reaches me and slides a muscled arm around my waist, pulling me to him. No hesitation. My head tips back, my eyes glowing. His are like liquid chocolate as they narrow on mine, his smile fading as his lips come close. I sink my fingers into the thick strands of his hair the minute his lips meet mine. There's nothing tentative about this kiss. This kiss is about need, want, and desire. His for me, mine for him. I need his lips on mine to breathe under the tidal wave of emotion that's just swept over me.

When our kiss breaks, I lean my head forward on his chest. I continue to scrape my nails against his neck, his scalp—wherever I can reach. Caleb nuzzles his nose and lips against the side of my neck while murmuring, "I missed you. Those texts last night drove me nuts. All I could think about was jumping in my car and showing up to be where you were." He leans down and brushes his lips against mine again.

"After that kind of welcome, I'm kind of glad they did."

He squeezes me tight. "What's your day like?"

I lean back in his arms to focus on his face more clearly. "Actually, fairly light until Saturday morning. Why?"

"Come be with me, Cassidy." He takes a deep breath. "Your pace all the way. I just want to have as much time as I can with you." His eyes probe mine, worried he's pressuring me too hard, too fast.

I think back to the conversation I had last night with my siblings. We might have only been on a few official dates, but they certainly weren't the "So, you don't like wearing blue? Why?" kind of a date.

He's shown me his darkness, his laughter, and his light. We've spent hours upon hours talking about the most hidden parts of our souls, the areas we allow only those closest to us to access.

While I'm reminiscing, our eyes meet. A million words are said and yet not a word is spoken. I know if I go with him, I won't be coming back the same.

I reach up and brush my lips against his. "Yes."

Suddenly, I'm airborne and being swung in a tight circle against his body. Our faces are so close, our breath is being exchanged for one another's. It must be the reason I'm getting so heady, so dizzy.

"Seriously?" he whispers, disbelievingly.

"Do you want me to say no?" I tease.

Caleb puts me down and places his hands around my face, cupping my chin. "If you aren't ready, yes, I do. There's no rush. I'd wait as long as you need because I'm not going anywhere." He leans forward and kisses my forehead, the tip of my nose, and then my lips. His eyes probe mine, waiting.

God, did he just say that?

The bonds beginning to wrap around my heart start to tangle, making my chest feel tight. What I feel is messy, complicated, and scary as shit. It's a leap of faith the likes I haven't taken since I grabbed Phil's hand and he carried me through my own blood to escape hell into the streets of Jacksonville, to the dark unknown. It's causing my heart to beat faster, my cheeks to flush, and my body to mold into his. I reach up, covering his hands on my face. Sliding my hands down, over his forearms, I feel the sprinkle of hair covering the thickly veined muscles. My hands make their way to his biceps, running over the curve of his shoulder before cupping his face in return.

His eyes are burning into mine over such a simple touch. When I reach up, pulling his head toward me and return the same caress by brushing my lips against his forehead, his nose and his lips, he understands how moved I am without words.

Keeping his face close to mine, I whisper, "Pick me up in two hours at my house. I just need to throw a few things into a bag."

He nods a few times, our faces still touching, before slowly detangling us. It's as if he can't bear to let our bodies not touch. With a kiss on the tips of my fingers and an expression on his face that requires me to remind myself to breathe, he's out the door.

Two hours before my life changes.

19

CALEB

I can't believe she's here. On my rooftop deck, gazing out over Tribeca with joy, and a little bit of awe on her face.

Once again, I give a mental high five to my brother for his amazing job of fixing up our home in the historic Powell Building. Despite the high loft ceilings, white walls, and modern features in the kitchen and bath, Ry managed to soften the other surfaces with hardwood, Persian rugs, and artwork. As I was giving Cassidy a tour earlier, I gave Ry total credit, explaining that after living in tents for the better part of eight years, a mattress on the floor would probably have been perfect. When she pressed me on my favorite parts of the condo, I said it was easily the electronics system. God, it's total man porn. That got me a completely feminine eye roll. Oh, and the fact that we have the private rooftop deck where you can just sit back and watch all of Tribeca go by.

She completely understands the rooftop deck. In the middle of crazy New York City, it's the equivalent of her lake.

The condo is a showplace, but the view makes it a masterpiece. Particularly now that Cassidy Freeman is standing in the middle of it.

I sit back, slouching with my hands crossed behind my head in the lounger, as she snaps photo after photo on her cell phone and texts them to her sister Holly. I can't honestly think of a single place in the world I would want to be right now but here.

How did she come to mean so much to me so fast?

She's smart, dedicated, and quietly determined. She gives back to her community out of the goodness of her heart—not because it looks good on the society pages. She wears a tattoo as a badge of familial honor stronger than most people have for their blood families. Her caution isn't a coy game; it was beat into her, almost costing her life. She has no idea who she is, and instead of giving up, she transformed herself into a devastating force.

I'm falling in love with this amazing woman who has told me so much about herself. Because of an unfailing sense of right and wrong. Because of wanting to be fair to me.

Her strength brings me to my knees.

Her honor is like a sword to my gut, slowly bleeding me.

I never thought I would say Keene was right.

What started as an issue to be dealt with in time is quickly becoming a tidal wave of guilt. I know so much more about her than she thinks I do. I've seen everything from former investigator reports, to court documents, to trial records, to testimony of former inmates associated with the man presumed to be her father and his associates.

What would she say if she knew?

She shared the beginning of her deepest secrets with me and I pretended not to know to allow her the free will to tell me on her own.

Will she understand that? Will she give me a chance to explain? Or will she run?

I close my eyes, imagining the worst, and must make some kind of noise as I do.

Cassidy spins around and her cheeks flush as she glances down at her phone, misinterpreting my sound as one of protest.

As if I would begrudge her photos to her sister.

"Sorry, Caleb," she says softly, walking over to me and putting her phone in her back pocket. "Here we are, finally together with no interruptions, and I'm texting my family as if we have forever."

"Remember what I said, Pixie? We do." I offer her a slow smile, pushing aside my dark thoughts, which she returns. I hold out my hand and pull her half on me, half on the lounger. She's wrapped around me and I have my hands slowly stroking her back. Our bodies conform, as if they were made for one another. Her phone pings, but she ignores it. While I hate she misinterpreted me, I can't say I hate having her so close to me.

Drowning in swirls of blue and green, I tell her, "I don't mind, Pixie. Ignore my caveman tendencies to hog all of you and send everything you want to Holly."

"How did you know?" she asks, not without a bit of wonder.

"I can't imagine the rest of your family getting excited beyond one or two pictures. Holly, I imagine, is probably thinking of asking Ryan if she can set up a photo shoot," I respond wryly.

She reaches back and grabs her phone. Laughing, she turns it toward me.

When I read the message, I laugh along with her. I had practically quoted Holly without having seen the text.

Quickly tapping out a reply, she settles in next to me. My arm slides back around her and moves up and down. The anticipation levels start to arc between us. I feel her shiver a bit. "Cold?" I ask, pulling her tighter against my side.

"No," Is her quiet reply.

I tilt my head down and promptly get lost in her eyes. Her features are exotic between her dark curls, pale skin and sea-green eyes. Her lips are plump, and since I'm sure as fuck not a saint, I've spent several nights imaging them wrapped around my cock.

Her compact body is lush with curves, and she has long legs for such a petite woman. I've imagined how they would wrap around my neck while I tasted her, or maybe my hips as I push steadily into her. I can feel myself hardening behind the zipper of my jeans, my dick vibrating with awareness of what may happen. I run my hand down my face, turning my eyes to look over at the sinking sun when I feel it.

Her mouth.

Lightly.

On my neck.

Just a small taste—barely a graze of her teeth and a flicker of her tongue.

I jerk back.

Holy fuck. Did that just happen? Did she just taste me?

My dick is at full attention, even as she blushes furiously and starts to move away. My arms tighten as I start to roll over, trapping her with my body. She squirms in embarrassment as I stare down at her wide eyes.

It did happen.

I catch her flailing hands in mine by simply threading my fingers through hers. Not tightly. She could pull away at any time. Her head is turned to the side, her cheeks flushed as brightly as her lips. She's upset. Why?

Because I pulled back in shock?

Suddenly, it hits me, and I'm overwhelmed with tenderness and joy. She wants me, but isn't quite sure how to proceed. My instinctive reaction must have seemed like a rejection to her.

My heart starts a hard beat in my chest. My breath picks up in speed. "Cassidy." Her name comes out in a tender whisper.

She won't look at me. Because I'm watching her so closely, I see a tiny tear form at the corner of her eye. I lean down and capture it, then run a line of kisses down her chiseled cheekbone to behind her ear. Her breathing starts to increase. I know I have her attention, even as she refuses to meet my eyes.

I nip behind her earlobe and soothe it with my tongue.

I feel her body react as mine did. Beautiful Pixie. Didn't know what that would feel like, to me or herself. "I wasn't pulling away, Pixie. No chance in hell of that. Do you understand now?"

Her head turns and her gaze locks with mine as she nods slowly. I take a deep breath and am completely unmanned when she pulls her hand away and ghosts it over my face, her fingers grazing over my eyebrows, my nose, my lips. Just before her fingers move past my lips,

I gamble and suck one into my mouth for a brief instant. She gasps, and heat flares, turning her eyes into flames.

I am undone.

I slide her head into the crook of my elbow and fully rest my body on top of hers. She adjusts her legs and instinctively wraps one around my hip. I reach down and pull it higher. Pushing my hips into hers, I hear her audible sigh as her eyelashes flutter.

I leverage myself over her so I can find a better angle to reach her lips, not wanting to scare her, but by doing so, I push my hips deeper into hers.

She moans in pleasure.

I take her lips in a slow, drugging kiss. I was holding her leg against me but, suddenly, her other leg comes up to join it, locking behind my lower back. I'm thrown off balance and end up with both elbows framing her face. She reaches up and grabs my head and pulls it down to hers. Clashing tongues dual, snaking between each other's mouths. Hers darts in mine and I chase after it immediately. Our heads angle to find that perfect placement, all the while rocking our bodies against each other.

I might come in my jeans.

Ripping my mouth away, her eyes flutter open to lock with mine. Her breasts are heaving, her nipples straining the thin sweater she's wearing in the October chill. I want nothing more than to lean my head down to capture one of them between my teeth and suck on it, but I won't here.

Despite the relative privacy of the roof deck, there are still too many eyes in the city.

"Pixie, I won't take you up here." Just as hurt starts to encroach on her features, I use her own maneuver and glide my hand over her face, not quite touching. I brush her lips lightly before saying softly, "It's not like your house, Cassidy. There are people here who have telescopes, and have no qualms about spying on their neighbors." Her eyes clear and embarrassment paints her cheeks. "There's only so far I'm willing to let someone watch me go with my woman and we just hit it." I do a push up over her to get enough clearance to get off the lounger. "It's time to go downstairs." I hold out my hand.

I wait for her to take it. Willing for her to.

Heartbeats pass, but she places her hand in mine.

Pulling her up, I wrap my forearms around her luscious ass and pick her up. Quickly, I make my way downstairs, through the condo and into my room.

As the door closes, I realize I've waited my whole life for this moment, for this woman.

I only pray to God I don't fuck it up.

Any more than I already have.

20

CASSIDY

I know Caleb Lockwood is going to be my first lover. Whether he's aware of it or not, I've already handed him my heart and soul. My body is simply his to claim.

I shiver in anticipation, thinking of what happened on the rooftop. I never imagined it would feel so natural, so primal, so instinctive. It must be the combination of nurturing and trust he's shown me.

Let's not forget the man is sexy as hell.

I stand in the middle of his bedroom absorbing more of his essence simply by being in this space where he sleeps. Surprisingly, I'm not nervous. This strange calm has settled over me. With my hands clasped in front of me, I look around and glimpse a rich red armoire, his deep mahogany bed, and the midnight medallion velvet quilt over crisp white sheets before feeling strong arms slide around my waist from behind. They tighten and pull me close against his broad chest. I tip my head back as he leans down to nip and suck at the exposed skin between my neck and shoulder. I get a whiff of the rich cologne he's wearing.

Oh. My. God.

"You have to talk to me through this, Cassidy," Caleb murmurs against my neck. "I need to know where you're at."

"Here's good."

Chills run through my body as he soothes the area with his tongue.

"Good." I feel his smile against my neck.

My nipples, though they had softened slightly from before when they were rubbing up against his muscular chest, were tightening again. And they weren't even being touched.

I slide my hand to wrap around the back of his neck, tangling it in his thick hair. One hand slides down to my hips and he slowly begins to rock into me. The other travels north toward my cashmere-encased breasts. Slowly, he starts strumming his thumb against my rigid nipple while still working the tendon on the side of my neck.

I gasp at his movements before letting out a soft moan of desire that can't be misunderstood.

My hand drops from his neck and I reach around the back of him, reaching for him. He quickly moves the hand from my thigh and captures my hands before they can reach their target, his rock-hard body.

I turn my head farther and twist slightly. Our eyes meet. I'm panting. His gaze is banked in fire.

I want the blaze.

"Let me touch you," I whisper.

"I can't." His voice is jagged.

"Please." I'm almost begging.

"Cassidy," he breathes. "I want to make this as beautiful for you as I can. I don't want to lose control."

Wiggling around so I face him, I pull my hands free and place them on his biceps. His chest is moving up and down under his untucked polo. I can feel his tension under my fingers.

Instinctively, I reach for the hem of my sweater and pull it over my head. Once my hair clears, I toss it somewhere. Frankly, I could care less where it goes. I'm now standing in front of the man I love in a sheer black bra that leaves nothing to the imagination. His eyes fly to mine, incredulous I pulled such a move. I shrug.

"Lose the control, Caleb. I trust you."

I've never seen a myriad of expressions cross someone's face in such a short span of time. Hot, heavy desire, anticipation, and tenderness are all projected at me. "You trust me." It's a statement, not a question.

I nod, not quite sure how else to show him.

Reaching up, he pushes my hair back over my shoulder. His fingers trail down over my clavicle toward my breast, cupping my fullness, outlining my nipple through the sheer material. The bite of the material against my sensitive skin causes me to throw my head back and moan. My legs feel weak and they buckle, but he catches me.

"You trust me." He repeats again, his dark gaze capturing mine. He leans down so his eyes are the only things I can see before his lips crash against mine. His tongue thrusts into my mouth, his fingers still playing with my nipple, his hips rocking against mine. My fingers lock behind his neck, trailing into the collar of his shirt. I need the feel of his skin against mine. My body is begging for him.

Breaking away from the kiss, he holds me tight against him, cradling my head against his hard chest. I can feel his erection against my stomach. Caleb's heart is pounding as he rocks our bodies back and forth. "You trust me," he sighs.

He nuzzles the top of my hair, and his hands slide down to cup my ass, lifting me into a kiss so tender, a tear trickles down my cheek. He notices and brushes it away with his thumb.

Releasing me, he pulls off his polo. As his abs come into view, I try to take in a deep breath, but I can't fill my lungs. Oh my god. This is happening. With Caleb. Now.

As his head clears the shirt, he pulls his arms out and immediately reaches for me again. I hold up a hand and he immediately pauses, waiting to see if I'm okay. I just want to look at him. All right, I know I'm lying. I know I'm going to touch.

Pulling my lower lip between my teeth, I start at the waistband of his jeans. They're riding low, so the band of his black boxer briefs are visible. I reach out with my finger, tracing the line softly. His skin is like warm steel, and the little trail of hair tracking down toward his cock has me intrigued.

I'm so focused on that spot, I catch his cock twitch inside his jeans. The moment that happens, I feel him inhale so harshly, my eyes fly up.

His eyes are almost black with passion. His arms are at his sides, his hands fisted to keep from reaching for me while I explore his body. The veins in his arms are popping a little as he holds himself back from touching me.

I step closer, not the least bit afraid of this man. Both of my hands rest on his lower stomach. His harsh growl echoes through the room as my hands slowly rise up over each ripple of his abdomen to his chest.

I want to know if his nipples are as sensitive as mine are.

When I reach his pecs, I raise my gaze and meet his eyes. I wanted a blaze.

I think I just unleashed an inferno.

"Cassidy." Just my name, but a warning.

"Caleb?" Just his name, but a question.

"Baby, I know you trust me, but I'm hanging on by a thread. If you do what I think you're going to do, your sweet ass is going to be on top of my bed about two seconds after your lips hit my chest."

Lips? Huh, I hadn't thought of that.

Seeing the intrigue on my face, he groans, even as he moves his hands from his sides to my waist. "Go ahead, baby, but then, it's my turn to reciprocate. And Cassidy? I plan on spending a long time doing so."

I nod blindly. I feel like my eyes must be glazed over as they lock in on their target, his nipples. Nestled in a sprinkling of chest hair, they're tightly puckered, waiting for my mouth to suck, my teeth to nibble, my tongue to lash.

I don't disappoint.

Switching from the right to the left and back, I can't get enough of the taste of Caleb's hard body beneath my mouth. Tightening his grip on me, I don't stop. I'm ravenous for the taste of this man. I'm in such a haze of desire, I don't even realize I'm being lifted from the floor and being carried across the room until my back hits the velvet of the quilt and I'm separated from my newfound addiction.

Caleb slides his fingers up my arms to trap my hands. His chest is heaving, and a fine film of sweat is on his body. I realize, with a little amazement, I did that to him. Me. I stare up at him with wonderment and desire as I arch my body into his. He slowly rolls his hips into mine as he buries his head into my neck.

Thrust, retreat. Gasp, groan. I feel his thickness through his jeans, and he feels the heat beneath mine. He raises his head from my neck and looks down at me. It's a parody of what we're about to do.

There's nothing shameful here. My eyes brim over with tears. He releases my hands to use his thumbs to wipe them away. His fingertips trail down my face, my chest, brushing down the sides of my breasts. His weight presses into mine, stilling the wave of our movements.

Almost too slowly, his hands drag over the sheer material along the sides of my bra, reaching the clasp in the back. I feel his fingertips along my spine as each hook and eye are undone. It isn't until the last one is released that his eyes leave mine. They drop down to where his hands are pulling the material away from my breasts. When the material is bunched between us, obscuring his view, he taps my arms. "Lift."

My arms move away from my body one at a time, giving Caleb the leverage to peel the impeding material away. I bring my arms back down around his shoulders, framing him as he fully cups me. His hands smooth back and forth, inching their way closer to my dusky nipples. "Beautiful. And mine." He lowers his head.

As Caleb captures a nipple fully in the heated depths of his mouth, I gasp, my nails scraping through his hair, my legs shifting beneath his anxiously. He scrapes his teeth on the part closest to the areola. I shudder in reaction. He pushes the nipple to the upper roof of his mouth and begins flicking it back and forth with his tongue. I cry out. He looks up, and once he realizes it was a cry of pleasure, a sensual look crosses his face.

Caleb lets that nipple loose with a satisfied smile. After a soft, "The other one's lonely, Pixie," he begins the same torment. Only this time, I'm not a passive player.

I reach down as best I can and touch him wherever I can. I run my hands down his arms, scratching my fingers over his shoulders and nipples, earning a growl against my breast. Wow, what that does to me! I almost levitate off the bed.

By now, I can feel the wetness dripping between my legs, preparing me for when he takes me. My sheer panties are no match for how my body is preparing myself for him. I'm moaning, trying to figure out how to push up against Caleb to relieve myself of this aching feeling. My teeth scrape against his skin. I manage to roll him over partially without dislodging my breast, and in the process, I wrap my arms around his waist, my hands finding their way into the back of his jeans. Touching the band of his boxers, feeling braver than I've ever been in my life, I slip my hand inside to touch his amazing ass with my bare hands.

Suddenly, the voracious sucking stops.

"Cassidy." His tone is now guttural. "Baby, you have to stop." He starts to reach behind him to move my hands up, but before he can reach them, I start to move my right hand slowly around toward the front of his hip, over smooth, hairless skin toward my goal. He traps my hand inches from his cock.

We stare at each other a half a heartbeat before his lips are back on mine, like I'm the only water in the desert.

Caleb rips himself from my body and stands at the edge of the bed. Our bodies are visibly shaking from the force of our desire, or from the need to be touching one another, I'm not really sure which. Probably both.

He runs his hand over his face before saying, "I want everything to be perfect, Cassidy. You're making it difficult with all the touching, baby. For all intents and purposes, you're a virgin."

Raising myself on my elbows, unknowingly placing myself in a more provocative position, I ask disbelievingly, "Are you insane, Caleb? While I may not have your experience—"

"You have none." He drops his head, rubbing a hand along the back of it.

"Not my choice."

"Exactly. Which is why I'm trying to—"

"I choose you." He freezes at my declaration, stopping whatever he was about to say. "I choose you, Caleb. You're not going to hurt me. It's already been beautiful and perfect, so please, let me love you too." I hold out my hand.

He stares at it for a moment before taking a step back toward me. "Hold on a second."

I drop my hand and flop back onto the bed with a drawn-out groan. He chuckles. "You're the first woman I've ever brought here, Pixie."

My eyes shoot up to him as he makes his way over to the armoire, and I watch him grab a box of condoms. "Part of loving you is protecting you. I didn't want to reach for one of these and not find it in an inopportune moment."

"Let's go back to the first part of that statement," I say as Caleb puts the box on the bedside table.

He tosses the packet near the top of the bed and reaches for my legs. Pulling me by the ankles, I'm pulled to the edge of the bed. "What part? Oh, the part about you being the only woman I've brought here?"

I nod, hesitantly.

His hands smooth over my body as he reaches for the clasp of my jeans. "It's simple, really. It's our home. Only permanent people come here. Lift up, baby."

I think I stop breathing as I do as he asks. Caleb skims my jeans down my legs and tosses them over his shoulder. Watching my face, he raises his hands to the snap on his jeans.

"Wait." I scramble to my knees on the bed, crawling to the edge. He stops. "I want to do it," I whisper.

He swallows hard. Giving me a sharp nod, he reaches for my

hands as he steps closer. Placing them on the button of his jeans, he says hoarsely, "Just the jeans for now, baby."

I nod as I bury my head into his shoulder, my hands making quick work of the snap. I can feel him nibbling on my shoulder as I work on the zipper. I'm trying to figure out how to not get his cock caught when he reaches down and clasps my hand. "It's easier if you hold me back and undo the zipper with the other hand." His voice is husky. "Just remember, wherever you touch, I'm going to touch as well." After a quick nip at my ear, he holds still.

My breathing accelerates. He's going to let me touch him. Slowly, I slide my hand down. I hear Caleb's rough pants in my ear as my fingers slide over his cock. Sweet Jesus, it's both thick and fairly long. Maybe I should have practiced on something else last night. My eyes can't meet his. He raises a shaking hand to my cheek in between his short breaths. "It'll fit, baby. We're going to fit so you'll forget where you end and I begin."

Just him saying that has me so excited, I run my fingers up and down his shaft again, squeezing along the way. A long moan erupts next to my ear. "Cassidy. Jeans. Off. Now."

Oh, right. I use my other hand to reach for the tab while protecting him with my hand inside.

Once the zipper is down, he seems to explode from his pants even through his boxer briefs. He sighs in relief as I push the jeans off, over his taut ass, and they fall to the floor.

Caleb toes his socks off and suddenly, we're down to two scraps of material between us.

I hear a ripping sound, and realize my panties have been shredded. Caleb pulls the remains out from between my legs, unrepentant. "I could tell they were bothering you with how wet they were." His grin is almost feral at this point. My jaw unhinges slightly.

While I recover from that demonstration, he tackles me back onto the bed, his hands beginning to skim all over my curves. His fingers trace my breasts, but don't linger. He gives each one a quick suck as he starts to trail his hands and mouth down my body. "Baby, are you sure you want me to let go?"

I nod frantically. I'm about to explode from just the idea of what I think he wants to do.

He props himself up between my legs, drawing a single finger from between my breasts, down over my ribs, over my hips, around my clit until he taps my core, transfixed with where his finger is circling. I'm writhing on the bed, my body a quivering mess. "Caleb," I moan, fisting my hands in my hair.

"Yes or no, baby. Do you want my fingers to slide into you? To feel that slick heat? To taste it?"

I never knew words could turn me on more. Maybe it's not the words, maybe it's Caleb. I twist from side to side, unable to stop moving. Caleb places his hand on my lower abdomen to stabilize me, holding me still while I pant out, "Yes, to all of it. Do it, Caleb. I can't take it anymore!" I moan as his hand glides down and breaches me. My back comes off the bed, supported only by my shoulders.

There's a chuckle from down between my legs. "Yeah, baby, you're ready. You're so hot and wet. Do you want me to push a little?" It must be rhetorical because he begins to stroke my heat with two wicked fingers.

In, out, in, out. I feel them rasping against my overly sensitive tissues. My hips begin to follow Caleb's fingers in a pattern. I'm reaching for something, but I can't quite put my finger on what. "Need something more to get you over the top, baby? I think I know what it is," he says, his breath rasping over my wetness.

In between one heartbeat and the next, my clit is being treated to the same treatment my nipples were. It's being flicked, nibbled, rolled and sucked. Caleb's fingers are still thrusting in and out and it's too much.

All my senses blank before I feel everything clench and shudder. I moan his name as I convulse through my first ever orgasm. I reach down and clutch Caleb tightly to my body, unable to lose the connection, my legs wrapping tightly around his shoulders. Tears pour from my eyes as I stare unseeing at the coffered ceiling.

After my legs stop trembling, I slowly lift my head to find Caleb looking at me with pure pride and possession on his handsome face.

His mouth is wet with...me. He's in the process of cleaning up his fingers by slowly sucking on them one at a time. "How are you doing, baby?" he asks softly, reaching up to wipe away a stray tear.

I start to speak several times, realizing I can't, before I decide the easiest course of action is to just open my arms. He crawls in between my legs, snagging the condom along the way. I realize that somewhere during my comedown, Caleb lost his boxer briefs and is as naked as I am.

"Are you still sure, Cassidy?" His eyes search mine, serious and ready to call a stop if I say so.

This man is everything I saw couple after couple find in my line of work and never dared to expect for myself.

His heavy weight covering me doesn't scare me, it warms me. His body covering me doesn't cause me panic, it fills my soul.

As he slides his nose against mine, I realize that I've been hovering on the edge of falling in love. With him still willing to wait until I was ready, I toppled over the cliff.

"I'm so ready for this, Caleb." Sliding my hands up to his jaw, I capture his lips. "Make love to me. Please."

He bows his head. "Okay, baby."

Quickly sliding on the condom, he shifts us on the bed so I'm up higher. I wrap my legs around his waist as he lines himself up to my entrance. Pushing in slightly, he stops.

His hand flies into mine. "You and me, Cass."

"You and me, Caleb."

His face is solemn as he begins the push and pull to feed himself into me. I'm so wet from my first orgasm, it eases the way somewhat, but it takes a few times for him to ease past my tightness until he's fully seated. I can feel his balls grazing against my ass as he grinds against me.

"Is it uncomfortable in any way?" Caleb questions, holding his body taught. A bead of sweat runs from his hair down his jawline.

Quickly, I shake my head no. It feels amazing. I'm stretched and filled. It's not going to take much to send me over the edge again. I also suspect by the sweat coating Caleb's body, it won't take long for him either. I lift my hips tentatively and moan as I feel new sensations. He drops his head for a moment to catch his breath before raising his blazing eyes back to mine. "Ready, baby?"

I nod frantically.

He pulls back a little. Instinctively, I pull my hips back a little as well. When I feel his cock start to slide into me again, I thrust my hips forward. We both gasp. "Again!" he growls. We pull back and push forward, our hips colliding. "Again!" His voice is guttural. Again, our hips slap together. This time, he grinds and circles his hips. I gasp. Oh my god! What was that? "That's it, baby. Reach for it." Again. "Tell me what you need. Do you need my finger wet with your juices sliding up and down your clit as I grind into you? Whatever you need, I'll give it to you."

I don't know if it's the words or the imagery that pushes me over, but I feel myself tighten around his cock. Throbbing. Incessantly. I moan long as my hips move out of sync, faster and faster. "That's it, baby, come for me, come on me." His eyes are losing focus, going hazy. Suddenly, they snap open and his jaw sags. Through my own orgasm, I feel pulses. "Oh, Cassidy." Caleb leans down and kisses me ferociously at first, then softly, as the weight of his body pushes mine deeper into the mattress as we come down together.

As we cling to each other, he peppers my body with kisses. I stroke his shoulders with weak arms, my energy drained, and unlock my legs from around his back. My feet skim down his luscious ass and down the backs of his thighs as they come to rest on the mattress.

While my body has turned limp, my heart is still in overdrive. I'm shaken down to my core. Emotionally, I feel like I jumped out of a plane with no parachute. I thought I was prepared for this, but I didn't have a damn clue.

As if he can read my mind, Caleb pushes up and stares at me, searching my eyes, then rolls us over so I'm lying on top of him, keeping us connected. I drop my head to his chest, trying to keep some of what I'm experiencing to myself.

"Cassidy?"

I shake my head. I can't look at him yet. I know I'm too vulnerable, so I squeeze my arms around him instead.

"Baby, I need your face."

I shake my head again and he laughs. "Okay."

He quietly rubs my back, occasionally dropping kisses along my head.

"I don't think I've ever been given a gift as beautiful as the one you just gave me," he muses quietly.

I finally look up. "This?" I ask, waving my hand to encompass our bodies.

"No, baby, the gift of being your first choice." He kisses me. "I hope you always think you made the right one."

Kissing him back, I put my hand on his heart. "I know I will."

21

CALEB

Right now, as I watch Cassidy's chest rise and fall in slumber, I know the truth.

I'm not just falling for her. I'm already in love with her.

She's everything I've ever wanted.

Courageous. Brave. Loyal. Beautiful.

And right now, I'd give up everything else in my life if she would understand why I didn't tell her what I knew from the beginning.

Because I have no idea how to tell her now without the warm light in those glowing orbs flickering off when she presumes I betrayed her.

22

CALEB

The past two days with Cassidy have been the closest thing to perfect. Yesterday, when I would have been super lazy and called in for food, she gave me an appalled look when she saw the prices and immediately went into the kitchen to see if there was food worth cooking. I told her if it couldn't be cooked in a soup pot or the microwave, then she was risking her life asking me to help. She promptly put a knife in my hand and said that if I could throw it at someone, I could chop lettuce.

Is it any wonder why I'm in love with this woman?

We spent last night watching an old Mel Brooks movie, *Spaceballs*, on the big screen. When I paused it to explain to her that as an investigative firm, we cracked more people's accounts because they had the password one, two, three, four, she shrieked with laughter and almost wet herself. She actually had to race to the bathroom.

Fortunately for Ry and Jared's furniture, she made it in time.

She also found it funny that good ol' Mel gave the impression of men fighting with their dicks. When the movie was over, and I told her she was welcome to have a battle with mine, it led to an interesting discussion. I'd say I was the victor, as Cassidy ended up passed out, and I barely held in there long enough to pull the quilt over the two of us before cuddling next to her.

It's early on Saturday morning and she's dressed in just her panties and my flannel shirt from yesterday. She's such a petite thing. Even fully buttoned-up, the shirt still gapes almost down to her breasts. I have her perched on the kitchen counter while I do the one thing I feel confident doing in the kitchen—make coffee. Her long dark hair is twisted up with a clip and her amaryllis tattoo is on full display.

"What time do you have to be at the wedding today?" I ask her, walking over with her cappuccino.

She puts down the bowl of Cheerios she was eating and spreads her legs so I can stand between them. Giving me a quick kiss to thank me, she takes a sip before answering. "Two. But I have to be back at my place by noon to get all my stuff and change." Pointing at her outfit, she grins. "I don't think this is quite the wedding attire they're expecting."

My arms go behind her and pull her into me. "What do you wear to your events?" I ask, truly curious.

"It depends. For something like your brother's?" I nod. "Black tie, just like the guests. The idea is to try to blend in. I'll have a small earpiece in, but that's the only thing to distinguish me between a guest. In fact, we'll have a table in the back." I frown, not liking the idea of her in the back. She catches on pretty quickly and asks, "What part of that don't you like?"

"The part where you're not next to me."

"I am working, Caleb. It'd be like you taking me to your office for the day."

"So, come to my office for the day," I immediately counter.

She pulls back, surprised. "Seriously?"

I pull her back to me. "I want you with me, Cass. If it's a huge issue because of the flow of work, I'll understand."

She bites her lip, thinking. Damn, that little move is hot. I'm already semi hard again. "Let me see what I can do."

I smile like a gluttonous kid with a basket of Halloween candy.

She holds up her hand and says sternly, "I said, let me see. No promises."

I'm about to lean in to show my appreciation for her concession when the doorbell rings. "What the hell?" I grumble. It's eight in the morning on a Saturday.

Knowing it must be someone on the approved list to get past the doorman makes me more irritated. If I'm lucky, it's Ry and Jared and they forgot their keys.

I'm not that lucky.

Keene is standing on the other side of the door when I open it up, a secure envelope in his hand. "Hey, man. This will only take a minute." He walks past me and starts to make his way toward the kitchen.

Quickly following after him, I state, "That's good, because that's all I've got before Cassidy and I have to leave to get her back for a wedding."

His steps halt. "She's here? You never bring anyone here."

My anger rises. "She's not just anybody, Keene. Get used to it."

Cassidy chirps, "Keene, before you go into another rant on why you don't like me, would you like some coffee?"

Keene turns, ready to blast her, and freezes. His eyes widen and he's staring at her, checking her out from head to toe. I can't say I blame him. With her hair up and wearing my shirt, she's adorable. In the light of the condo, and with what she's not wearing, her birthmark just below the base of her collarbone in the shape of a heart is completely visible. She looks beautiful, and well-loved.

Mine.

What she doesn't look like is a doormat.

"Actually, Cassidy, I'll be happy to take a cup if it wouldn't be too much of a problem," Keene accepts, his voice soft.

What the fuck?

I smack the back of his head as I pass by him for good measure. It's great he's not being a roaring jackass, but don't hit on my woman.

Asshole.

"Not a problem at all. If you two have work issues to discuss, I'll have it waiting in the kitchen when you're done." She pivots and walks away. Keene can't take his eyes off her legs. He sees her tattoo in its full glory.

"What the hell, man?" I seethe when Cassidy's out of earshot. "You were practically eye-fucking my woman."

"Sorry. I just got lost in my own thoughts for a second. I promised myself I wasn't going to be an ass after the other night. I owe her an apology," he replies with a completely straight face.

Reasonable. "Okay. What do you need? I really do need to get Cassidy to her wedding today."

"It's about the Armstrong case. Apparently, they're refusing to sign our terms for a start on Monday. We already have ten guys in the air on their way to Portland." Keene taps the file against his opposite hand.

Crap. "Come on back to the study and let's wake some people up on the West Coast." I turn and head down the hall.

I see Keene give the kitchen a final penetrating stare from the corner of my eye.

23

CASSIDY

Caleb and Keene make their way into the kitchen after figuring out some work issue. I heard them go into the study about thirty minutes ago. Both of their voices were raised against whomever they were speaking with. Finally, I heard Keene lay down the law. It wasn't the words that resonated with me as much as the tone. I chuckle softly, thinking I would not want to be on the other end of that scolding. Big brother was apparently righteously infuriated. I imagine it would be the same when Ali got her panties in a wad over something. For someone so passionate, the way she can freeze out people with her body language or a word is impressive. It must be a lawyer thing.

Pulling out the cream and sugar, I place them at the end of the bar, along with the fresh cups of coffee and some croissants. I start humming a tune I've sang since I was a little girl. It's funny how these things come back to you. I remember nothing but the horror of my childhood, but at some point, someone must have sung "Au Clair De La Lune" to me and it stuck. For me, it's a song of peace and tranquility. After the last few days with Caleb, I'm certainly in such a place.

The men are still talking when they come back into the kitchen, so I don't disturb them. Moving around the island, I pick up my

Kindle to get the news. Caleb waits for Keene to finish his relatively mild rant over the "jackasses in Portland who can't tell what day of the week it is" before coming over to kiss me on the cheek. "Thanks, baby, for laying all this out."

Keene offers me a small smile. "Yes, thank you, Cassidy. I didn't mean to act like a dick this morning."

Well, knock me over with a feather. I narrow my eyes at Caleb and he shakes his head. He didn't say anything? Wow. "You're welcome, Keene. It wasn't any trouble. If someone here actually knew how to cook, I could have done something more. But I figure his brother and Jared knew any groceries would rot before they got home."

We all laugh at the complete honesty of that statement. Keene's eyes sparkle. Honestly, he's a handsome man when he let's go. I'm beginning to see how Ali got involved with him.

"Is everything all fixed? I know you can't talk much about your business," I say quickly. Both men nod, but surprisingly, it's Keene who speaks up.

"Does Alison run into this a lot with your contracts?" He holds up a hand before I can respond. "I understand confidentiality and know you can't tell me details. Some days it's just helpful to know I'm not the only one running around at the last minute with my head on fire."

I lower my eyebrows thoughtfully and take a sip of my fresh cappuccino before responding. "Without getting into names, I do remember one wedding where the bride forgot she was getting married. Seriously. She wasn't skipping out on the groom, she just forgot what the date was."

Both men gape at me.

"I know it seems ridiculous. I was pounding on her door for probably an hour before she woke up. Her bachelorette party was the night before and she had a massive hangover. She thought there were two nights between the party and the ceremony, then spent another thirty minutes arguing with me that I had the wrong date. As if." I mask my laughter by taking a sip of my drink.

"What happened?" Caleb asks, a huge grin on his face. Keene is astounded.

"Well, after she called three friends and her mother to verify the date and was screamed at by each, she tried to pass the blame onto me. When we got to the church, she was a stinking, hot mess. Literally stinking. I think Em wanted to hose her off. Instead, we managed to find the gym associated with the church open and got her in the shower. Since the stylist had walked out, we, as in Em and I, blew out and braided her hair, got her ass dressed and down the aisle, barely fifteen minutes late. After she got back from her honeymoon, she sued us."

Both men spit out their coffee at the same time. "Are you shitting me?" and "What the fuck?" are yelled at the same time. I feel a little more redeemed.

"Yep. Fortunately, Ali pulled all the emails from our servers where we send automated reminders. When we walked into the courtroom, we had no less than five countdown reminder emails going to both the bride and the groom the day before the ceremony. It also helps she showed up drunk for the rehearsal dinner, and the photos the witnesses provided were classic." I break out into gales of laughter.

Keene is looking at me with admiration. "Nice. Did you guys countersue?"

I shake my head no. "We were trying to build a reputation at the time. We were too new. If it had happened today, maybe Ali would have. She was happy with what we got as a settlement. It paid off the last of her student loans," I say with a smile on my face.

"Amazing." Keene shakes his head and turns back to Caleb. "I take it back, I want to keep my job. These people are practically normal."

Caleb laughs and tags the back of my neck and gives me a quick kiss. "What were you singing when I first came in, baby? You've been humming it since yesterday morning."

""Au Clair De La Lune." I don't remember where I ever heard it, and it took me forever to realize what it was I was singing, but it always made me smile as a child. Now, I tend to sing it when I'm particularly happy."

Caleb smiles and kisses me again, and when Keene clears his throat, I blush. "Sorry, Keene."

"That's okay," he says awkwardly. "Did your parents sing it to you? One of your siblings maybe?"

Caleb's face, which is still in front of mine, gets serious. Shit. With as much as I've shared with Caleb, I forget the people in his life he's closest to don't know. I'm going to have to have to tell them or let him.

This just got more complicated.

I hate feeling pity.

"I don't know," I reply quietly. "It's a tough subject for me." I'm somber when I reply to Keene who's singularly focused on my face. "I actually have no memories of my life before I was four, and what happened after isn't something I discuss. Ever."

Keene puts down his mug and mutters at the counter. "I'm sorry I brought it up."

I slide off my stool. "Not something you intended to cause harm over." I walk into Caleb's arms and he squeezes me tightly. His nose brushes against my ear. "I've got you."

I whisper back, "I know." I pull away with a smile and check the time.

"Oh crap, Caleb. It's already nine-thirty! I'm going to shower so we can head out soon. I won't have time back in Collyer. Keene, I'm sure I'll see you again." I race out of the room.

I have to admit, I probably had a half hour before I would have really had to freak out, but between the time and the way Keene was looking at me, I suddenly wanted to be anywhere other than in the kitchen under the admiring eyes of the man I love.

And the suddenly admiring eyes of his best friend.

24

CALEB

As the weeks pass, it's getting harder and harder to not tell her.

She trusts me, and I feel like I can conquer the world.

I feel like a king.

I feel like I'm deceiving her.

When we're together, we talk about everything.

Anything.

So much.

Not enough.

She knows so much about who I am, what I do, what I want to become.

A great brother.

A good friend.

And, someday, a beloved husband and father.

But the things I need to tell her, I can't bring myself to say.

It's bad enough I referenced her family pact that first night I stayed at her house. Thank God she never realized she'd never told me about it.

Since then, I've almost slipped any number of times when she's opened up about her past.

I've almost told her the man who she thinks is her father is still in prison.

I know the address of the building where she was once kept.

I know of all the Freemans. Emily is the only one who kept her real name.

How do I tell her I know all of this without shattering what we're building?

Every night, she curls into my arms and I keep her nightmares away.

What if I'm setting her up for new ones?

25

CASSIDY

I'm lying in bed, pressed up against Caleb's chest when Morpheus decides to pay me a visit instead of one of his wicked brothers.

I walk silently across the grass. My dress is white, with a delicate lace over it that skims past my knees. There's some invisible pull guiding me toward the gazebo in the distance when I hear voices and laughter, and when I turn to hear the sound, I stop in delight.

A red balloon appears and floats upward toward the bluest of blue skies. Chubby little hands grab for the balloon.

The determination of the little girl is evident. This time it won't get away. Her dark curls bounce around her head as she reaches and stretches.

I can't see her face.

A woman with long, dark hair is standing next to a man holding a camera. A man taking pictures of this adorable child. I've come across a family photo shoot. I pause, marveling at the child's blooming beauty.

The woman, sensing they're no longer alone, turns and smiles at me. It's brilliant, welcoming. Then, I watch as it fades into sadness.

I've can't place her, but she's so familiar. I just wish I could erase her sadness.

I smile back, content to just observe. I come back so often to this park and to this beautiful family, enjoying their happiness in each other.

The woman is talking to the photographer as she captures the balloon before it flies away. I watch as she ties it around the little girl's wrist, gives her a kiss on her face and strokes the side of her cheek before stepping away.

The love she holds in her heart for her child is undeniable. Visible. I can feel it, a mother's love.

I can't move. I'm watching the little girl with wonder as she bounces her balloon up and down a few times. She's laughing as it hits her in the face once.

She giggles. The sound echoes in my heart.

Small arms wrap around the little girl from behind. It's a little boy. I imagine he's promising to tell her stories of fairy tales of princes rescuing princesses when they get home.

I bask in the love emanating from the scene that has unfolded in front of me. It's like the warmest rays of the sun kissing along your skin after you step out from a damp room, heating any chill in your bones from within.

I can't help but envy the people in front of me.

The woman's face morphs and her expression changes to despair. Tears cascade down her cheeks. She turns away from the photographer and stares directly at me.

She walks up to me and I can't catch my breath. Suddenly, her hand lifts to my face, trying to brush away my tears.

I don't even realize I'm crying.

Suddenly, I hear my name.

Cassidy.

"Cassidy! Cassidy, baby, wake up. Are you all right?" Caleb is leaning over me, looking worried, wiping the tears away from my face.

"Yes. No. I'm not really sure," I answer honestly.

"A nightmare?"

I shake my head slowly. "I don't think so. I just don't know what it was. It's happened a few times, but not with this much clarity."

He rubs his thumb over the apple of my cheek. "Do you want to talk about it?"

I nod against his hand. "Later. We need more sleep. We both have a big day tomorrow."

"Come here, baby." Caleb tucks me against his chest and I wrap my arms around his heavily muscled torso, resting my head against his heartbeat. The sound drags me back under, into the realm of sleep.

"Don't let go," I murmur.

"Never," he vows, squeezing tighter.

26

CASSIDY

I t's the Saturday after Halloween and Collyer is a sunburst of fall colors. If I had time or inclination to look out my window, I'd likely witness the Collyer seniors scrubbing frantically to remove Halloween paint from our bay windows. Each year, Collyer businesses offer up their windows in a silent auction for parents to bid on as part of a fundraiser. Each year, the highest bid for each storefront is matched by that business. All the money went toward the senior class to offset the cost of their senior prom.

For the last few weeks, as I've been leaving the office, there's been no less than ten of Collyer's seniors on our porch, making our ancient Victorian eerily creepy. It's also screwing with our ability to concentrate on our jobs. Ali's said it's been fortunate we've had a run of high-end Halloween events. Otherwise, it might scare off the customers. She did this with a blinding smile, knowing I've been traumatized over some of the Halloween costumes. There are just things you can't unsee.

Caleb's been nothing but amazing. He's listened to me rant when I've gotten home to the farm, dished up dinner I've prepared in a crock pot (because his cooking skills still haven't improved much), and ran out to Baskin Robbins on the night I called him in shock because the costume optional wording on an invite meant if you weren't wearing one, then clothing was also optional.

As we get closer to the wedding, he ends up spending more and more nights with me, unless there are a couple of days together I can head into the city. It's just too much when I could have an event ending at ten one night and a meeting starting at nine the next morning. I told him to feel free to use my home office for whatever he needs so he isn't sacrificing his work hours, since I'm either on-site or at the office late.

I know intellectually that when his brother's wedding is over, my schedule is going to lighten somewhat, but if the boom Ali is predicting occurs, we're going to have to consider hiring some of our interns as full-time employees. Either that, or we're going to have to get a lot more selective about the jobs we take. That doesn't leave a pleasant taste in my mouth. We built this company by taking on the smaller jobs other people wouldn't. I need to figure out a way keep those clients and still let go of some of the control of micromanaging everything.

I'm tapping my pen against my planner, waiting for inspiration to strike when I hear a disgruntled voice in my doorway. "You don't look that busy. I don't see why you couldn't go get your own lunch, or send one of those kids loitering on the porch."

I turn my eyes away from the planner and spreadsheets I was reviewing and meet the cool green eyes of Keene Marshall. "Well, this is a surprise. No, a shock. What are you doing here, Keene?"

He walks in, carrying a familiar bag from Genoa. Raising it, he doesn't answer directly. "Where do you want this?"

My lips quirk at the idea of Caleb chose choosing to use Keene as his errand boy for lunch. "I'll take it to put in the kitchen. Thank you." I reach for the bag, but he holds it out of reach.

"I'm under orders to ensure you eat, Cassidy. So, if that occurs in the kitchen, then let's go," Keene advises before turning to step out of my office. The tantalizing smells of Genoa waif behind him.

Damn, I really don't have time for this. Sighing, I stand up and meet him in the hall.

As we're walking down the stairs, Keene mentions offhandedly, "I can understand why he's concerned."

"Hmm? What do you mean?"

"Caleb. You've lost weight since I last saw you, and you didn't have any to lose." Keene runs an assessing glance over me from top to bottom that draws my eyebrows down. I frown at him, uncomfortable, and continue to make my way to Corinna's domain, the kitchen.

When I walk in and find Holly, Phil, and Ali sitting around a couple of open boxes of pizza, I realize Caleb hadn't just been thinking about me. My heart warms and spasms at how much he takes care of me, even amid his own responsibilities. "So, we had a lunch delivery." I sidle up to the counter and gesture for Keene to take a seat.

Holly smiles. "Be sure to thank Caleb properly for us, Cass." A round of agreement goes up from my siblings.

Keene mutters, "I'm not sure I want to hear this."

I frown, and Phil and Ali narrow their eyes before ignoring him, and return to their lunch and banter, not in that order.

Taking a bite of my Chicken Russian, I decide to ignore Keene. "Will do. We should thank Keene too for carting it all out here."

"If Genoa delivered this far out, I'd have to run six miles each day," Ali moans as she reaches for another slice of pizza.

"You can run my miles for me, sister," Phil is quick to offer. "In fact, starting tonight. You know you want to."

We all laugh at the face Ali makes at Phil. Keene's lips even tip up, I note.

Corinna spins around with a gloriously decorated cake and says to Phil, "If you run your miles, you can have a slice of the leftovers of this. Otherwise, you have to wait until the night of the wedding."

Phil practically salivates. "That's the Lockwood-Dalton tasting cake. Sweet Jesus, Corinna, that is beautiful. What flavors did they end up choosing?"

Corinna waves her frosting spatula near his lips. "Dark chocolate with ganache filling, alternating with lemon and a lemon curd. Topped by a lovely white chocolate icing." She stands back and moves toward the sink. "But, since you don't want to run and just want pizza..." Her voice trails off.

Phil stands up and stalks toward the sink. "Give me that spatula."

Corinna, no one's fool, "Maybe I'll save it for Em. She ran this morning."

"Em is not the one who raised you from the time you were sixteen. Hand it over." Phil is a white chocolate addict.

Ali has her head thrown back, laughing. She's in a tight-fitting suit that sets off her eyes and long legs. I glance quickly to my left and see Keene's focus is entirely locked on her. Hmm. Something to think about later.

Holly, who normally remains so unobtrusive, says, "You know we only have a few more minutes for lunch, and I think I would like to eat and not take pictures of Phil's continued entertainment value or the rising tension in the room. Can we just finish eating so Cassidy can mother-hen us and we can all get back to work?" I catch Holly's eye as she winks. She hasn't missed a thing behind her camera's eye.

Keene's attention turns to me. "Mother-hen?" He sounds amused.

Corinna pipes in. "Oh, totally. Even if Phil was the one who tried to adopt us, Cassidy was the one who was our "Mommy" while they finished raising us."

I jump in with a gentle, "Corinna, I'm not sure Keene's interested in our complicated history. He just came by to drop off lunch."

Corinna waves me off; not a shy bone in that girl. "Listen, if Caleb's going to be around, Keene's going to know eventually, right?"

I open and close my mouth like a guppy, turning to Ali beseechingly for help. Her face serious, she glares at Keene for a few moments before shrugging.

"Then I get to tell it, Corinna." Phil wipes his mouth. Taking a drink of his soda, he leans against the counter. His eyes brook no argument and I relax. Corinna—for all her enthusiasm about life I wouldn't tamper for anything—believes the world is her best friend. Phil takes a deep breath and gives Keene a very edited version of our early years.

"I met Cassidy when I was thirteen and she was nine. Both of us in horrific living situations, we escaped them together. A few months later, we met Em and her aunt who were a gift from God. They took us in until I was eighteen, and Cass and Em weren't quite sixteen before she passed away. Instead of letting the girls go into foster care, Cass, Em, and I battled the lovely state of South Carolina for about a half a year until the girls' case could be heard to declare them as emancipated minors. When I was twenty, and Cass and Em were eighteen, we met Ali, Corinna, and Holly, who were all just about to turn sixteen. They'd been removed from their homes and had no desire to return. They also decided to go the emancipation route. All the girls and I moved to Connecticut to begin our lives free from the past." He takes a deep breath and I smile softly at him. A million memories pass between us in an instant. "So, that's how I ended up with five very annoying sisters, Keene. One of whom still won't give me the white chocolate spatula."

Corinna shakes her hair and hands him the coveted spatula. He pulls her close and kisses the top of her head. "Now, get that cake out of my face before you have to make a new one."

A burst of laughter comes out around the room. Keene shakes his head and attacks his salad.

Em strolls in and says, "What'd I miss? And it had better not be the pizza. I'm already ready to go out and hose off the Collyer senior class making Windex squeaking sounds every time I get into a sketch."

~

"We really do appreciate you bringing lunch by, Keene," I remark as we're climbing the stairs back to my office. I'm not quite sure why he's following me back up, but I can tell he has something on his mind.

"It wasn't any trouble, Cassidy. I had business in the area, and Caleb asked me for a favor," he replies easily. Stepping slightly past my door, he waits for me to precede him into the office. "Do you prefer this open or closed?"

"Open, thank you." I'm not comfortable enough with Keene to have a closed-door conversation. Despite the slight warming during lunch, he's still not one of my favorite people. I'm so grateful Phil stepped in to give our very edited family history because I can only imagine what Corinna would have shared. I drop into my chair behind my desk and contemplate the mounds of work ahead of me.

Keene sits down in one of my chairs and steeples his hands in front of his mouth. I can tell he's thinking, so I finally decide to break the silence to move him along.

"Don't you have somewhere you have to be, Keene? I actually hate to be rude, but I have quite a bit of work to get through today."

He leans forward, elbows resting on his knees. "What happened to you, Cassidy?"

That's what he wants to ask? The fucking audacity. "None of your damned business, Keene. Now get out." I stand, despite my knees shaking in anger. I only hope my voice isn't betraying me.

"What happened to take you away from your family? You have to have one. Don't you remember anything?" he asks, ignoring my anger.

"I want you to leave," I whisper. Now my shaking is transforming from anger to something different. Something buried and painful.

"You don't remember anything about how you got there? Did you ever want to find out?" He pushes harder.

"You need to go. Now." I try to make my voice stronger, more commanding.

"Did they ever try hypnosis techniques to get you past the block you have up from before you were four?" he persists.

"Yes! They did all of that, Keene!" I finally shout. "The working theory is what I left behind was either so bad I can't let my mind go back there, or it was so good I'm ashamed to. Is that what you want to know?" I'm breathing hard. Tears start to fall from my eyes and I turn away and sob. Heart-wrenching sobs. I'm so lost in my tears, I don't hear the angry voices behind me throwing Keene out my office.

I'm not sure how much time passes. The next thing I'm aware of are footsteps behind me and a hand laid on my shoulder. I tense, ready to scream when I hear in a heartbroken voice, "Baby."

I fly around and there's Caleb. I launch myself into his arms, mumbling, "He had no right..." into his chest.

I feel Caleb's arms tighten around me and he whispers, "I know, baby. I'll deal with it when we get home."

Bending down, he catches me under the knees and carries me out of the office. I vaguely hear him ask one of my siblings to get my phone and purse, and dropping it by the house later.

Right now, I was going home.

27

CALEB

I f Keene was standing in front of me right now, I probably would have ended a lifelong friendship, a business partnership, and shot him with his own gun.

Instead, I have him offering quiet apologies while I have my woman sitting outside, wrapped in a blanket, looking at the water.

"What were you possibly thinking, Keene? Isn't there a fucking law term for this shit? Asked and answered?" I rail at him relentlessly.

"You're right, Caleb. I was wrong to keep pushing. There's nothing to excuse what I did to Cassidy earlier." His calm voice makes me wish I could reach out and plant my fist in his face.

"You weren't just wrong to push. You were wrong to ask in the first place," I spit out.

"I was only trying to determine if she got the proper care, Caleb. Based on the life she had before, it was questionable whether mental health care would be included," he calmly tries to explain.

"You're not the one who'll have to listen to her damn nightmares tonight, asshole," I rasp out. I hear his sharp intake of breath. Yeah, put that in your perfect world of black and white and spit out some logical analysis. "For all our sakes, can we go back to what you should have learned in Kindergarten? If you can't find something nice to say to my woman, don't say anything at all? Better yet, just stay away from Cassidy until she's ready to see you. And if something comes up because of the wedding, we'll figure it out." I'm suddenly exhausted. Out the window, Cassidy pulls up her knees to her chest and wraps her arms around them. She's rocking herself.

I need to get out there.

"Gotta go." I abruptly hang up on Keene saying, "Caleb, tell her..."

I toss my cell on the counter and make my way outside to Cassidy. She doesn't even glance up when I walk out.

Shit.

I maneuver myself carefully between the glass of wine I poured her earlier, the arm of the lounger, and get behind her. She's stiff at first, but finally rests against me. I comb my fingers through her hair, trying to relax her, and eventually, her curves yield into the planes of mine. She shifts slightly, placing her head against my heart.

I pull the blanket up and tuck it tighter around her. "I'm so sorry, Pixie." There's not much else to say. I sent Keene there not only to bring her lunch, but to maybe see her in her element and thaw toward her a little bit.

Not bring devastation to one of her places of solace.

She sighs, tipping up her head to rest her chin on my chest. "You had no idea he would go there, Caleb. Even if you were trying to force Keene into playing nicer with others."

"Still, if it hadn't been for that, you never would have been in that position," I counter quietly.

I had come clean to her earlier about my reasons for sending Keene to her office. I wanted to push my lifelong best friend to see the woman I loved for everything she is.

Too bad I couldn't push myself to be as forthright about other things.

Moving aside her hair, I kiss the center of her amaryllis tattoo. "You've never told me about this."

Surprised, she half turns and says, "Haven't I?"

I shake my head. It's making me nauseous. I'm lying even as I'm trying to give her comfort. I know all about her beautiful tattoo.

She reaches up to touch it and smiles before tucking her head back down on my chest. I resume my grazing of the beautiful artwork on her neck with the tips of my fingers.

"Phil was researching flowers one day for his classwork and came across the Greek myth of Amaryllis. He fell in love with it. So did Em and I once we heard it." I feel her smile against my chest. "I assume, Harvard, you know the story," she teases. I squeeze the back of her neck. "Yes, but only because it popped up when I was looking up your company website."

Her laughter is soft, and I feel the tension leech from her. I'm suddenly glad I asked her this. "So, family ink? Since I can't see Phil's, I assume not everyone's is in the same spot?"

She shakes her head no. "We all chose somewhere that meant the most to us personally. For me, with my anxiety, I tend to rub my neck a lot. I want to be reminded of what the tattoo is supposed to represent when I feel stressed. I need to be reminded of what Phil told us our family is meant to represent; pride, determination, and beauty. No matter what happens, I have that. Some people over the years have refused to do business with us because they've seen the one on my neck, on Ali's foot, or on Phil or Holly's wrist. Em and Corinna's are the only ones not typically visible. We won't change who we are. We can't change our past. We'll always have that." She goes silent with those words.

I'm meanwhile seething on the inside, knowing some of those individuals are likely in the same social set of my birth vessel. I know she's awaiting some kind of reaction to what she just told me.

I lean down and kiss the center of the tattoo and she sighs. We sit in the quiet solace of the night for a few minutes before she says, "I've been having dreams."

I squeeze my eyes closed. I don't want to imagine what they're about, but I'll gladly bear this burden if she wants to talk about them. "Do you want to talk about them?"

She nods. "At least this one I do." Her voice is confused, hurt.

My arms tighten. "Go ahead"

"There's a little girl in them. She's so happy and giggling. And there's a woman there. I'm pretty sure it's her mother. At first, the mother's happy, really happy, then she gets so sad. I think..."

Knowing her ear is against it, I try to keep my heart regulated, but my mind is running a mile a minute. "What do you think, Pixie?"

"I think the little girl in the dream may be me," she whispers sadly. "I think it's a memory."

"So why are you so sad about it, baby? It sounds beautiful." I'm confused. Why isn't this in her file? Why hasn't she shared this? Shouldn't there be a sketch of the woman somewhere?

"Because of what Keene said today. Maybe I'm blocking what happened to me because maybe my family gave me away to those monsters like Ali, Corinna, and Holly's families did. Maybe it wasn't like Phil not knowing who his parents are or Em's parents dying. Maybe someone didn't want me and wanted that to happen to me." Tears start cascading down her cheeks. "What if it's the woman in my dream? For years, I've thought that dream only came because I was happy. Maybe it's some kind of subconscious warning? I don't know, Caleb. I just don't know." She's so frustrated, its palpable.

I tread carefully. "Do you want to talk to someone about it?"

She shakes her head emphatically. "No. At least, not now. I have too much going on to go there. I can't open myself up to that right now."

Nor could she handle the knowledge of what I've been holding back.

"Later then. Whenever you're ready."

She fidgets for a second before taking a deep breath. "Will you be there?"

I respond past the huge lump in my throat. "Always, if you'll let me."

That's nothing more than the simple truth.

28

KEENE

Her eyes.

    Her hair.

    Her heart-shaped birthmark.

No memory of her early childhood.

"Au Clair De La Lune."

It keeps cycling on repeat through my head on a loop. I've thought of nothing but Cassidy since that morning in Caleb's kitchen, and then after that catastrophe at her office.

Two weeks before Ryan and Jared's wedding, I decide. I pick up the phone.

"Hello," the grumpy voice on the other end of the line mutters.

"Charlie? It's Keene. I need you to come into work early tomorrow." Taking a deep breath and a huge gamble with the only family I have left in the world, I add, "I'm going to need the full Freeman file."

Silence.

"Charlie?"

"Why?" Suddenly, his voice is alert and suspicious. Good for you, old man. And this is why Caleb authorizes your huge-ass salary.

"Because..." I almost choke and swallow hard.

"Because..." he prompts, still suspicious.

"Because, there's a possibility Cassidy Freeman may be Riley."

I hear him suck in a huge breath. "Oh my god, Keene. Have you said anything? Are you sure?"

"No and no. That's why I need the file."

He swallows so hard, I can hear it over the line. "I'll meet you there at seven." He quickly hangs up.

I put the phone down, pick up my glass of Scotch and start humming "Au Clair De La Lune," the familiar tune coming back to me as if I had sung it yesterday instead of twenty-five years earlier.

29

CASSIDY

We're eight days from the Lockwood-Dalton wedding. It's crunch time. Not even one of us has a free day or evening from now until the wedding itself.

It's well after normal business hours at the office. Otherwise, I know we'd never have a client again after the way my siblings are bickering back and forth. When we pull late nights like this, they tend to forget we're not at the farm. I just hope this time they remembered to lock the door.

Phil is bitching about the lack of sex he and Jason are having. I hear Em yelling at him to shut up because it's been months for her, and when he's gone that long without, he can start talking about dick rot for all she cared.

It's a good thing I get to spend one night in the city with Caleb tomorrow because I have a late afternoon meeting with Ryan and Jared, which could go several hours. Caleb managed to swing his schedule so we could have lunch. I'll go to my meeting and I'll stay over with him before heading back to Collyer early the next morning.

Trust me, Phil has already managed to find a way to bemoan this fact when we were discussing this at the morning meeting. Ali nailed him with a muffin and told him not only did his husband come home and climb into the same bed every damn night, it wasn't my fault if Jason's rotation at the hospital was off so he could be in the wedding. And if Phil wanted to sit at the nice table with me, he needed to shut his trap.

Yep, that's right. Jason is in the wedding. When Caleb told me Jason was asked to be the other groomsman standing up for Ryan, tears of joy slid down my face. I was so overwhelmed Jason and Ryan had repaired their friendship. Caleb said Ryan was just as nervous about asking Jason as he was about asking Jared for his hand. He was kidding, but it was reflective of how much he wanted his other brother with him on his big day. Not only did my siblings all side with Caleb that I would sit with him during the reception, but so would Phil.

Phil was prancing around like a queen until he was told he needed to keep his earbud in for any emergencies. That squashed his Lifestyles of the Greenwich and Famous moment.

I chuckle as I quickly type an email with a pen between my teeth. The caterer wants confirmation on the final number of 528. I review my planner and find we still haven't received 20 RSVPs. I quickly pull the contract over, scanning for the section on final decisions within fourteen days of the wedding. Finding the section on catering, I confirm the language. I mutter out loud, "So long as the excess of outstanding invitations doesn't exceed ten percent of the guest list." Got it. I finish the email to the caterer, upping the final count to 548.

"Damn, you look so sexy right now."

I jump, startled and thrilled to hear his deep voice. Caleb's standing in the doorway in his Joseph Aboud custom-made suit. I bite my lip and remember the outfit I have on. I'm in leggings and a University of Charleston sweatshirt. He's in a Ermenegildo Zegna tie and shoes. I'm wearing another pair of Uggs. "Sexy, huh?" I sit back and grin at my man. "Now you? You look good."

He walks into my office and closes the door. Leaning against it, I hear the very definitive snick of the lock.

Hmm, interesting.

He smiles at me, his eyes radiating heat despite their humor. "Do you know your siblings are arguing about sex?" He pushes away from the door and prowls toward me.

"So I overheard." I move to untwist my legs from my chair, but he holds up a hand. I stay where I am and decide to play with my man a little. "Is there a last-minute problem with the wedding, Mr. Lockwood? Something you or one of the other grooms may have overlooked?"

He shakes his head at me, his eyes glittering with even more humor. "Never going to let me forget that, are you?"

"Nope. Gonna let me forget I threatened to chop off all of Phil's hair that day?"

"No, but that was just hot."

I laugh as he lowers himself closer for a kiss, and it's one hell of a kiss. By the end of it, my legs are wrapped around his hips, and his arms are boosting my ass into his erection. He lowers his forehead to mine. "I got off early today."

I roll my hips and smirk. "Doesn't feel like it."

He squeezes my ass in retaliation and I moan. I have a new appreciation for my brother's bitching—I've been too long without my man as well.

"As I was saying, I got out early today and figured I would come to you. I even convinced Keene to take most of my early morning meetings tomorrow, so if you can arrange your schedule tomorrow so we can leave for New York an hour earlier than you had originally planned, I can stay over tonight and drive us both in tomorrow."

I quickly think about what's due tomorrow, but I can no longer concentrate when I'm nestled up to Caleb. "Put me down for a second and let me check." I turn and bend over toward my computer.

Caleb groans behind me.

Looking over my shoulder, I find him staring right at my ass so I give it a shake. "Down boy. If you want an answer to your question—" I moan as I feel his strong hands slide up the insides of my legs. When they reach the apex, they slide back and forth in between, rubbing the seam of my leggings against my barely-there T-back panties. My breathing quickens as I hear him drop into my desk chair behind me. "Caleb." It's a long, drawn out sound.

"Cassidy," he murmurs. "Anything wrong with me doing this?"

I know he's checking to make sure he's not triggering any flashbacks, but I manage to get out, "No desk sex."

He pauses what he was doing, so I push my hips back. He didn't have to stop everything. "Why not?"

I've obviously wrecked his little fantasy.

"Because I have contracts and plans for your brother's wedding spread out. I really don't want to be here half the night putting everything back in order when I can be home in bed with you," I reply tartly.

"Great answer." He spins me around. "Really great answer. And because it was such a great answer, you get to choose. Wall or chair? We'll do desk another day."

I giggle at his good mood promptly restored. Then I study him sitting in my desk chair. How would that work, exactly? He sees the curiosity cross my face and says, "Chair it is!"

My giggle erupts into full-out laughter until he strips my leggings and panties down my legs. "Caleb!" I'm half laughing, half mortified. My blinds are open for Christ's sake.

"Sorry, but..."

"Not sorry?"

"Pretty much," he says cheerfully. He's already unbuckled his pants and is working on the zipper. By the time we get him unzipped and slide on a condom, we're both laughing hysterically.

"We have way more finesse than this, baby." I'm out and out laughing. It's true, we do, but I can't bring myself to care.

As if on cue, Big and Rich's "Save a Horse, Ride a Cowboy" drifts from my computer speakers, and I double over laughing. I can't help it. Caleb looks at me with complete disbelief. "You have this on your Spotify playlist?"

"I wouldn't be a good Southern girl without it." I can't help but sway back and forth to the bar theme music of the South. I self-consciously realize how utterly ridiculous look. I'm naked from the waist down and I'm shaking it in front of my office desk.

Caleb is strangely silent. His face is rigid with sexual tension and entirely focused on my swaying hips. His hands are clenched on the arms of my chair.

Whoa, Nelly. What just happened there?

I hesitate. "Cal—"

But before I can get his name out, his hand clasps me around the back of my neck and his mouth is clamped down on mine. His tongue is pushing hard and deep. "You have no idea...hot... lap dance —" before his mouth crushes onto mine again.

When he lets me back up a few minutes later, my lips are swollen and I know I've now left wet, damp marks on his pant leg. Somehow, I just don't care. Neither will he.

Standing up, I let the heat of his kiss flow through me and decide to make my man's night while trying not to look like a complete ass.

I push him back in my chair as I pull my sweatshirt over my head. The wheels allow the chair to move him about six inches back. I sway my hips back and forth as I slip my sweatshirt off slowly, letting it fall to the floor carelessly.

I'm caught in the stratosphere of the sexy song that's come on next and feeling like a complete idiot when I notice Caleb's face. My desk is about to be decimated unless I do something. Shucking my bralette, I saunter over to him. I'm still trying to figure out the logistics of chair sex when he quickly spins me around to sit on him, my back to his front.

His cock nudges against my dripping folds. With one swift push while rocking my chair forward, he's fully lodged.

"Ahhhhh," I moan, reaching back to stabilize myself against the sides of his legs. My chair rocks backward, creaking beneath our combined weight.

In the space between the reality of where my body and where my mind has gone, I hear our panting.

This is not sweet, tender lovemaking. My man is taking me.

And it feels amazing.

My head is tipped back over his shoulder, and because my legs are closed, the penetration is deep. So deep. At this angle, Caleb's girth is stretching me while the curve of his cock is nailing my G-spot, putting continuous pressure on it. When he bottoms out, he grunts. After a moment of letting us both adjust, Caleb uses the rocking motion of my chair to quickly get us moving.

He rocks the chair back and my inner walls try to clasp him as he partially retreats. He sits more forward, and I clamp down on him tighter. On one rotation, he slides his hands from my hips to my inner thighs, and quickly spreads my legs by pulling them on either side of his thighs. I have to lean forward to grab a hold of his knees for purchase.

I'm quite literally riding him in my desk chair.

I'm never getting rid of this chair.

Just as I have that thought, one hand slides up from my legs to my breast and tweaks my nipple, while the other slides over to my clit to do the same.

I'm panting, "Caleb!" as the final squeeze he gives my clit pushes me over the edge and into oblivion. My hands clench against his knees and my head tosses back, raising my breasts into his waiting hands.

Caleb is maybe a half a heartbeat behind me. Holding onto both of my breasts, he thrusts, once, twice, three times before grinding his hips tightly to mine and screwing in. I can feel his release jettison in short bursts.

He collapses his head against my spine.

I feel like I was just run over by a herd of stampeding horses and snicker to myself.

Caleb's hand slides from my breast to rest over my heart. "What's so funny, my love?"

And just like that, the atmosphere in the room changes. I sit up, still connected to him. "What did you say?" He sits up slightly as well.

"I just asked what was so funny," Caleb says mildly.

"Not that," I whisper. I'm desperately trying to reach for my phone, slapping my desk repeatedly. If he said what I think I just heard, I sure as shit don't want it to be remembered to country music, dammit. I manage to find the next song on the playlist, Sarah McLaughlin's "Train Wreck." Really freaking appropriate. "What did you call me?" I ask quietly.

"Oh, that." In my mind's eye, I can picture him preparing to tell me it's a term of endearment, like baby. I'm bracing myself when I hear it.

"I called you my love, Cassidy." I feel his hard chest directly against my back. "You are, you know. I love you so damned much. It keeps growing every day." He kisses the center of my tattoo.

The first tear slides out of my eye, landing somewhere on my collarbone, right over my funky-shaped birthmark.

Oh my God. He loves me.

Caleb Lockwood loves me.

How on Earth is this possible?

I raise my hands to my face and quietly sob while he begins stroking my back and my shoulders, dropping kisses here and there, trying to calm me down. "Cassidy, would it be possible for me to see your face?" he asks quietly.

I don't want to lose my connection to him, so I contort myself to the side and he leans forward. His arm comes up to cup my face. He runs his thumb under my eyes to capture the tears trickling down. "I love you, Cassidy Freeman. I think I started falling the first time I was in this office. I know I'm going to be in love with you forever." He brushes his lips across mine, like a vow.

I reach to touch his face, storing this moment into my memory bank as one I want to remember for eternity. "I never expected to fall in love with you, Caleb, and I never thought there was someone out there waiting for me. I never knew he would come walking through my door and would never leave my mind. I never expected he would find my heart because I wasn't sure there was one to give." I lean forward to kiss him. "It's yours now. Please be careful with it."

"I promise, my love. I will," he chokes out, his emotions making his voice crack on every word.

I stay wrapped in his arms, clothing everywhere on a freezing cold November night, basking in the warmth of his love.

Phil was right months ago.

You couldn't plan for love.

You sure as hell couldn't control it.

But I sure as hell was going to try to hold onto it with everything I had in me.

For the rest of my life if I could.

30

CALEB

My love.

My heart.

My soul.

She stirs slightly in my arms in her bed with a smile on her face. I wonder what she's dreaming of.

I lean down and brush a soft kiss on her upturned lips.

She settles deeper into my arms and stills.

Maybe it was selfish of me to tell her how I felt before she knows, but I couldn't hold it in any longer. My love for her has been ready to burst out of me for weeks.

She's the other half of me.

The dream I didn't know I was chasing.

The quiet to the storm in my soul.

Besides, I don't care about what's in that file.

She has to understand that I only care about what's in that file because I love her.

I only care because I know it will matter to her.

And I'm petrified she's going to walk away, no matter how much I love her.

31

CASSIDY

One week until the wedding.

As we approach Thanksgiving, I'm thankful for so many things. I figure if I start listing them now, I might be done by the time the wedding is over. I start ticking them off in my head while I'm in New York City the next day.

Caleb. My family. Caleb. Ryan and Jared. Caleb. Being on schedule for the wedding. Caleb. Not meeting Mildred Lockwood yet. Caleb.

I must admit, I'm a more than a little concerned about Mildred Lockwood. With everything I know about the woman's character, I keep expecting something to happen. The only time I'm sleeping well is when I have Caleb's arms tight around me. When we talked about it this morning, his face became grim when he said he was concerned about the same thing. Apparently, some part of Hudson was on Mildred watch. Either she was somehow aware and behaving, or she didn't care and was going to strike out anyway. Sadly, for Ryan and Jared, either was a very real possibility. A discussion about protecting the grooms was the meeting Caleb could not get out of this morning, and why I would be hanging out with Keene next door, so I didn't need to go through all the security protocols twice to get back onto the executive floor.

I was squirming internally over the hour I'm supposed to spend with Keene. After our last interaction, was it wrong I was kind of hoping he'd get a conference call and I'd have to wait with my planner in the lobby? I've been trying to convince myself that whatever happened in my office the last time I saw him were likely due to Keene relating my own circumstance to his missing sister. And it wasn't like we were real chummy before that.

I'm trying to give him the benefit of the doubt because both he and I are going to be in Caleb's lives for a long time.

Walking around Rockefeller Center to kill time, I stop at Dean & DeLuca to grab bagels, pastries, and coffee. I figure if Keene and I can't get along for more than a few minutes, I can shut him up by shoving something in his condescending mouth. Within a few minutes, my cherished morning cappuccino and ammunition were in my hands as I made my way over to the building holding Hudson Investigative Services.

Huh, funny. When Caleb told me where his office was, I had never put two and two together. I realized it was the same location of our former investigator, Thomas Laskey. Checking the address, I get a little chill. Same office too. I suppose it makes sense. The setup would be ideal to just buy and not require a lot of modification. I tense for a moment, wondering if Laskey's client list transferred, but then relax. Truthfully, it's not like there's anything left to hide. I told Caleb the worst there was about me on our first freaking date, for Christ's sake. He stuck around. What hasn't been told is details which can be shared over time.

Lost in my thoughts, I don't notice the man who steps on the elevator with me until he speaks in a familiar growl. "Well, beautiful. You've always been a sight for these sore eyes."

My head flies up. "Charlie! Oh my god! I was so caught up in my own thoughts. How are you?" I swiftly push past two disgruntled people to stand next to Charlie Henderson, my former investigator when we used Thomas Laskey to investigate our backgrounds.

When we decided to change over our identities, we didn't want anyone from the past to find us. Charlie quickly became an advocate for our decision and soon became someone we openly trusted.

"I work here, beautiful." He taps the discrete brass plaque displaying merely the name Hudson on it. "New boss picked me up as I was getting ready to chuck a paperweight at the old one on the way out the door. Even had my shit packed up and everything. I'd already written a big ol' fuck you resignation letter to Laskey. Wanted to shit on his desk on the way out, but figured the old Missus woulda frowned on that."

I let loose with an ear-splitting grin, taking note of the "old Missus" comment. He hasn't changed one bit. Tolerating Charlie takes a special kind of gift. He's freaking brilliant, but it takes a certain kind of person to call him a friend. Or an employee. Or longevity in marriage, apparently.

"I can see that. So, how did the new boss make it worth your while to stay?"

"Took me into a conference room and let me point out everything wrong with Laskey's place. He didn't necessarily agree with me on some things, but on the stuff he did, he had my back one-hundred percent." His hair, snow white and sporting a style popular with early 80s by a news anchor, keeps flopping over his glasses. "Offered me a promotion to head a new division—Missing Persons and Protective Services."

I shake my head, a huge smile still on my face. It's so like Caleb to recognize talent within cantankerous personalities. First Keene, then Charlie. I lean forward, press a kiss to his weathered cheek and say, "Couldn't have been a more perfect job created for you. You do so much good for people, Charlie."

His pale cheeks get all rosy as we land on the Hudson executive floor. Both of us step out, and Caleb's waiting in the main executive area with Keene. Both stiffen upon seeing me with Charlie, then relax when they realize we're arm in arm.

Charlie leans down to not so quietly ask, "Which one of these bozos are you here for, beautiful? Mind you, neither one is good enough for the likes of you."

I laugh boldly at the outrage on both Caleb and Keene's faces. Both send withering stares Charlie's way.

"I'm visiting for a short while with Keene while Caleb's in a meeting. Then Caleb and I are meeting Ryan and Jared for a final scheduled walk-through for the wedding for the rest of the afternoon." I pinch Charlie's arm. "I saw a Mr. and Mrs. Charles Henderson on the guest list. Does that mean you'll be all dapper in a tux?" I tease.

He sighs, beleaguered. I lift my arm holding the Dean & DeLuca bag to my mouth to stifle my laughter. "Yes, and let me tell you, the wife is going all out. Hair, nails, the works. This shindig is costing me a fortune." He turns his bright blue gaze on his bosses. "Don't I have to see you two people enough? Now I have to share Thanksgiving weekend with you? I don't suppose there'll be a room with football on?"

I'm outright laughing at this point. This conversation is pure Charlie. I lean up to whisper in his ear, "No, but if you behave, I'll put you at a table near my family and put a bottle of Dewar's underneath it for you as a gift." Dewar's is Charlie's favorite Scotch Whisky, and while it wasn't going to be on the bar menu, it would make him a happy man.

"Oh!" He straightens up and pats my hand. "You're a good girl, Cassidy Freeman. Remember what I told you, even if they brew up, storms don't last forever." Kissing my cheek, he turns to Caleb. "Are we meeting?"

Caleb jerks his head toward the open conference room door. "I'll be just a moment. I want to greet my woman properly."

Keene lets out a loud sigh. "Here we go." He turns his back and I debate pulling out a croissant to shove in his sanctimonious mouth.

Caleb gives him the finger as he reaches for me, and I hear Charlie chortle as he makes his way to the conference room.

Caleb pushes my hair off my face. "Hello, my love. You made it back relatively unscathed, and you managed to go shopping." The humor in his voice isn't hidden.

I give him a quick kiss and open the top box to show him the contents. "Oh, these are for you, Keene, and anyone else who wants some. Nothing big, just bagels, pastries and whatnot. I figured you had coffee here."

"And yet, you needed to buy your own," Caleb comments dryly.

"Shut it, love. I was dragging this morning." He smiles broadly at that, knowing exactly why I was.

"Keene, do you want to peruse these boxes before I take them in? You know once I do, they're gone."

"Is it safe?" Keene comments with his back still to us. Unthinking, I reach into the bag, grab a small muffin and toss it at Keene's head with unerring accuracy. He stills, turns, and shoots me an incredulous look.

"Yes, I just did that. If we could keep the snarky comments to a minimum for the next hour, we might survive, okay?" I snip at him.

"Wow, you really are on fire today, Cassidy." Keene moves closer to peer inside the boxes Caleb had taken from me and opened on the counter. Grabbing a few tissues from the reception area, he chooses a chocolate croissant and a cinnamon roll. "Ready?"

I turn to Caleb. "Let me know if anything needs to be altered due to security measures. I don't care how much of a hit we take on the profit. Safety is much more important than anything else." He stares deeply into my eyes before giving me a thorough kiss.

"I think I need bleach," Keene mutters.

"I think you need to shut the hell up," Caleb retorts when he lets me go. "Keep my woman relaxed for the next hour." As he turns and walks away, I watch blatantly because the back side in one of his custom-made suits is just as gorgeous as the front.

When the boardroom door closes, I turn to Keene. "Where to?" Keene doesn't say anything, merely gives me one of those penetrating stares and gestures to the open door behind me.

I turn and walk in, and immediately stop in my tracks, sucking in a deep breath. He doesn't say anything as he makes his way around the desk as I silently walk over to the windows and stare out over to the Manhattan skyline. "I don't know how you get any work done in this office. This is breathtaking."

And for the first time, I'm on the receiving end of a full Keene Marshall smile. I smile in return before turning my gaze back to the city below. We're silent for a few minutes, lost in the cityscape.

"It was tough for the first month," he admits, turning his chair to face the view. He doesn't move closer, which I appreciate. "We were waiting for additional security protocols to be installed so we could take on the kind of work we wanted to." I glance over at him and he answers generically, "The government stuff."

I nod.

"And we would stand in our offices and get lost in the view because the desert is nothing like this." He's silent for a few moments. "Needless to say, it took us a long time to adjust." He swivels his chair around, trying to end the conversation.

Not quite yet.

"Caleb told me you got shot saving him," I say quietly. "That your tattoo I was so facetious about the first night we met covers it." Keene stills. I turn to face him, leaning a shoulder against the windows. "I'm sorry for that. I was trying to protect myself and I didn't understand why you wouldn't give someone a chance. I struck out unfairly. I hope we can move past that." I pause, taking a deep breath before admitting, "I love him, Keene. I hope to be in his life a long time."

Keene unconsciously rubs his leg. "He's actually saved my life more times than he knows, just by being there. I should have given you a chance."

I nod, knowing this is the closest thing I'll receive to an actual apology.

"But Cassidy, there are things he hasn't told you yet. Things you need to know."

I face Keene head-on. "Will they change how I feel about him?"

He shrugs. "I don't know."

"Do you think these things will come out over time? Are they critical for me to know right now? Like, was he already married? Is he dying?" My heart cracks open a bit, praying the answers are no.

His frustration is palpable. "No, nothing like that. But it's important."

I settle a bit. "Then let us figure it out, Keene. Sometimes, blasting information in someone's face isn't the best way to handle something. After all, I just learned that with you, didn't I?"

Keene growls and grabs the cinnamon roll, taking a bite. With a mouthful of food, he gestures to a couch along the wall. "You might as well get comfortable. We have a few."

I start to walk to the couch when I gasp. "Oh! I didn't know it was an actual piece of art." I drift over to the art hanging over the couch.

I hear Keene swallow. "Art?"

"It's going to seem silly, but I must have seen this painting before and I can't remember where. I've dreamt about it for years though. Only in my dream, it comes to life with a beautiful woman with long dark hair tying the balloon to the girl's wrist. Silly, isn't it?" I turn to face Keene, but his face is still, no emotion. Crap. I must have offended him by not knowing a famous piece of art. Personally, I'm just grateful I can tell Caleb it wasn't a memory at all. "Never mind. Let me just sit here and review the information I need for my lunch meeting. They should be wrapping up next door soon enough."

Sitting under the picture from my dreams, the one I described to Caleb, I pull out my cell phone and planner so I can review the lists, never missing the glances I keep receiving from across the room.

32

KEENE

When Caleb comes to get Cassidy from my office, I stand in front of the painting. Moving it on its hinge away from the wall, I tap in the code on the safe behind it. Pulling out the thick file inside, I close the safe as well as the painting hiding it. The tab reads RILEY.

Rifling through the pages, I find the photo I had the painting commissioned from.

I close my eyes and remember the day as if it were yesterday.

Keene, sit here and hold your sister! All Mommy wants this year for Mother's Day is a nice photo of you and Riley for her bedside table.

But Mommy, Riley won't sit still!

Hmm...well, maybe if we give her something to hold onto?

How about this, Mrs. Marshall? The photo man hands Mommy a red balloon. Riley gets excited and starts crying MINE! MINE! MINE!

Mommy's long, dark hair falls over Riley's face as she ties the balloon to her wrist. It smells good. Just like the wildflowers in the back of the house.

Is that better, baby girl?

Riley's face lights up. Mommy laughs and so do I. Even though having a little sister is a pain, she sure is cute. Maybe next time Mommy and Daddy would have a boy.

The photo man takes the shot.

I'm jerked from my memories of the day the picture was taken and look at the painting. The one Cassidy thought was a famous piece of art she happened to remember.

The one I am now almost one hundred percent certain my sister just sat under.

I set the photo on the desk and sit down.

My hands are shaking.

What am I supposed to do?

Should I tell Caleb what I'm almost certain of now?

I put my head in my hands and grip the back of my neck. After the wedding. That's soon enough.

33

CASSIDY

I t's finally here, the day of the Lockwood-Dalton wedding.

I didn't get much rest last night, despite Caleb's best attempts at loving me to sleep. My mind wouldn't shut down. It felt like a teleprompter perpetually scrolling, running through the lists of things we needed to do. I was up well before my 6:30 alarm and slapping away my love's hands as he tried to pull me back down into my bed.

Standing in the shower, I feel grateful that Em had convinced me we should have a stylist do our hair for this wedding. We would have very limited time to do it ourselves with the schedule we were having to keep. There were other things I needed my team focused on other than worrying about fitting in stylistically with the Greenwich elite.

Lost in my own musings, I don't hear the shower door open. I give a little bit of a shriek when I feel Caleb's arms slide around my wet body before I start giggling.

"You don't have to be up for hours!" I laugh at him.

"Hmm. This is much better than sleeping. Besides, I want to go with you today."

"Seriously? You know I'm going to be in complete work mode,

right? I'll be able to spend, like, maybe twenty-minutes total with you before the ceremony starts."

He nips my neck. "And you know how you in work mode turns me on."

Oh, well, there is that.

"Besides, I know the estate like the back of my hand. Consider me a living map."

And a living guard? The thought creeps into my mind as I turn in his arms. "Are you worried about Mildred?"

"Yes." No lies. No hesitation.

I frame his face with both my hands and lean up to kiss him. "Okay then. I can always use a living map and an extra set of hands."

Relief flickers across his face before humor sets in. "So, what's the deal? Not washing your hair?"

"Nope. Em has someone coming in to style it later. All the Freeman women are being given the special treatment today since the grooms are so low-maintenance," I snicker. This wedding is anything but low-maintenance.

"Oh, well, if your hair is the only thing I can't get wet..." He lowers his mouth to the crease between my neck and my shoulder.

"Ohh, Caleb. Dammit, I didn't plan on the time for this. Mmm."

"You woke up early and I'll be quick." His eyes are hot but steady. "I need you, my love. Today is going to be intense."

I give myself a little boost and wrap my legs around his hips. "Well, as long as your quick includes full service."

He laughs as he presses me up against the shower wall and lowers his mouth.

Six hours later and I'm wishing we were back in the shower with a Brillo pad and a gallon of soap to scrape off the feelings I have from being on the grounds of the Lockwood estate. With its grand stone exterior, imposing turrets, and well-manicured lawns, the mansion should be a wedding planner's dream.

In reality, this place gives me the creeps.

As mild as the day has been for November, I've had a perpetual chill since I walked in with my family, the high-end furniture rental delivery, and the VIP restrooms delivery service at 8:00 a.m. sharp.

Fortunately, I've been able to spend a great deal of time outside behind the house in the courtyard where the ceremony and reception will actually be taking place.

For the last two months, I've been a little put-off by the fact Mildred Lockwood has passive-aggressively refused to let us on-site to take measurements by already having daily events at the estate. I know it's infuriated the grooms and Caleb to no end. Ryan's come close to having his mother thrown off his own property on several occasions. It's taken all of us to calm him down and to not let her be the focus of the wedding. Instead we've had to rely on pulling county surveys and aerial photos for our wedding plans. Now, I'm appreciative.

There's no way I would've wanted to spend a minute more than I have to here.

I'm just grateful Caleb has no desire to spend time in the future at the old family stomping grounds either, or I might be spending more time dealing with my PTSD issues.

I pause. Where the hell did that thought come from? Why would a house trigger my PTSD?

I look around. It's just a house, albeit an enormous one at over 12,000 square feet on five and a half acres of land. It has a lovely gazebo by the lake, which we'll be incorporating for the vows. The chairs are being setup in two sections; the back section divided into three pie shape pieces with two aisles to allow both grooms to approach, then the front section has the traditional two with one center aisle.

Phil has outdone himself with the gorgeous primroses incorporated with lush fall colors, making sure that Ryan and Jason's vision is artfully captured. I glance over to the courtyard which easily holds ten people at the fifty-five tables, room for the orchestra and dance floor. Corinna and her culinary interns carefully move each layer of the six-tiered cake into place. The caterer and head chef walk around checking linens, silverware, glassware, and chargers, making sure that for the elite of the elite, everything is perfect.

Around the side of the house, the VIP washrooms have been setup with the property waterlines, with attendants already being briefed on their responsibilities. In fact, as I glance around, tuxedoed staff members are already moving toward their final briefings. Glancing through the cathedral-size windows at the front of the house, I can see from my vantage point the valet has already setup, and all the delivery vans have started to move out or have been directed to the large tents at the edge of the property, offering a covered place to hide the aesthetically offending vehicles which adds an additional method of privacy.

I look down at my watch. It's 1:45 and the wedding starts at 3:00. I have fifteen minutes before I need to head inside to get myself ready. I pull out my lists and check off items. I'm a little shocked when I see we're actually ahead of schedule by fifteen minutes. I'll take it.

My phone beeps. It's Em.

"You almost ready to come in? We're early in here if you can believe it." Her voice holds the same shock and awe I'm feeling.

I laugh. "Don't jinx us. I was just thinking the same thing out here. I'm making my way in right now."

"Wait, you mean it's on schedule out there too?" Now she's laughing as well.

"Right? I just saw Corinna set the cake up, so she should be heading to the house soon too."

Em lets out a long, low whistle. "Damn, Cass. Final briefings?"

I jog up the three steps of the stone patio, which wraps around the back of the house before turning around for a final sweep. "Already in progress. Vans have been moved under the tents. Valet is setup. I expect guests to arrive in"—I pause— "thirty minutes. And the chief steward and concierge staff we hired are waiting in black tie to escort everyone from the front door through the foyer, into the back." As I walk into the house, again, an inexplicable chill hits my bones. Wrapping my arms around myself, I ask, "What room are you guys in?"

Before Em can respond, I hear a nasally voice behind me. "Against my wishes, your associates were set up in the secondary library. I expect you should be able to find it."

I mutter into the phone, "No more than ten," before hanging up and turning to face who I know will be Mildred Lockwood.

I am not wrong.

Mildred Lockwood is the epitome of elegance in her classically cut thousand-dollar St. John suit. This is the kind of woman who demands to be catered to and doesn't care who she has to run over to get it. Things go her way or she gets them out of her way.

Aesthetically speaking, she's an exceptionally attractive woman for her age with formerly dark hair, now well-mixed with salt and pepper and light eyes.

Too bad her eyes have no soul.

Even wearing a business suit and heels, I'm several inches shorter than she is. She leans over me, trying to intimidate me with her height, her wealth, her dismissive manner.

I remain silent, knowing this will antagonize her further and get her to show her cards faster. My heart is beating rapidly in my chest, much in the same manner it used to when I would be locked in the room with the men who hurt me as a child.

This woman is nothing but evil.

"I can't believe you'd dare to show up here." She sneers as she moves even farther into my space. Her emphasis on the you in her sentence takes me aback, and I see the chief steward looking over with some concern. The last thing we need is the mother of the groom causing a scene in the foyer thirty minutes before guests are expected to arrive.

I'm about to quietly demand she be escorted to get ready or get out when I hear a very welcoming voice behind me.

"Be very careful, Mildred. Ryan and I are trying to uphold appearances for your sake, not ours." Caleb stands next to me, not touching me in this crucial moment. Knowing that I have to stand strong, I hold my ground.

Her eyes, silent but deadly, cut from mine to her oldest son's. She's about to speak when Caleb cuts her off.

"Cassidy, if you'd like, I will escort you up to the secondary library. I believe your family is waiting for you." Caleb cuts his mother's sputtering off with a simple raise of his hand. "You have two options. You can get dressed and shut your mouth for the next six hours, or you can get the hell out and deal with the fallout. Either way, you will behave today." His eyes are stone cold, and he's coiled like a cobra ready to strike.

Her eyes drift to mine. "I'll be quiet. For now." With a final glare of contempt, she drifts off toward the grand staircase to the master suite. Out of the corner of my eye, the chief steward lets out a relieved breath.

Once she's out of sight, Caleb turns me into his arms. "Are you okay? What the hell am I saying? Of course, you're not."

Still shaking, I wrap my arms around his waist and squeeze tightly. "After today, we're not coming back here, right?"

"Never. I swear," Caleb vows.

"Great, because this place gives me the creeps," I mutter.

Caleb puts his arm over my shoulder and tucks me into his side as we walk down the short hallway to the second library. He mutters into my ear, "You're not the only one."

34

CASSIDY

T-minus ten minutes.

I'm the last to finish getting ready. I check out my reflection in the mirror one last time while attaching the earbud that will remain in until the last guest leaves.

The deceptively loose chignon the stylist threw in has been pinned up using faux pearl hair pins. I have larger faux pearls in my ear to help disguise the bud, a half strand of inch-sized pearls tied by a blue satin ribbon around my throat, and a triple band elastic cuff of matching creamy pearls covering my earbud's receiver on my right wrist.

Overall, I went for a simple, understated elegance with my short sleeve, mock turtleneck gown. Turning sideways, you can see the opening that exposes my back from the top of my shoulders to the top of my waist. Thank you, Nieman Marcus sale event.

As I gather up my clutch, I take eight deep breaths. I have the rest of the evening committed to memory. Yes, my small clutch is in my hand with my cell phone inside as a backup, but I'd prefer not to pull it out. I'm now Caleb's guest, not coordinating the largest wedding in our small company's history.

I either need to do something or throw up from being in this house alone.

I make my way back into the main foyer where guest after guest is being escorted through. Excellent. I catch the chief steward's eye and he moves forward to escort me down. I can easily merge in with a group so I don't interrupt the guests who need to be escorted.

Trailing in with a group of four, I spot my family, already strategically placed around the amphitheater like seating. Caleb and Jason are waiting toward the audience's right, so I want to sit on the left. I spot the back section of chairs where a Freeman isn't already sitting.

"Planning on making an escape?" Keene's voice comes from my left.

I let out a puff of air. "No, we're trying to scatter ourselves so we can make sure if any problems arise, one of us can be in place quickly."

He surveys the milling people and sees that in all the external sections, at least one Freeman is sitting, with the exception of Holly, who I happen to catch making her way from Ryan's groom's room, down toward the gazebo for the procession.

"Nice." He leans down and mumbles quietly, "Is this like us making sure Charlie sits next to Mildred for the ceremony until there can be tighter control?"

I lift my hand to my stifle my laugh. "Well played."

"Caleb mentioned you had your first interaction with her before." I nod. "I'm sorry. We would have spared you that." While his words are about Mildred Lockwood, his face tells me he's not just apologizing about that. Masking any discomfort I may feel, I nod slowly, accepting his apology for more than just my interaction with Caleb's mother. I don't know why I'm giving it, I just feel like I need to.

His face relaxes marginally.

Keeping on topic, I shrug. "I was expecting it to be unpleasant, but..."

"But...?" he prompts.

I wrap my arms around my waist. I'm about to let him in a bit and share when I hear the opening music.

"We're about to start. Better find your seat, Keene. We'll talk later."

He waits a heartbeat before moving and makes his way down a few rows to take his seat.

A string quartet from the orchestra begins the hauntingly lovely strains of Pachelbel's Canon in D. The audience of more than 500 stands. Ryan and Jared make their way from the open doors of the pool house and the rec room respectively, each holding a small hand carved wooden box. They meet in the center, clasp hands and walk together, straight toward the gazebo where Caleb, Jason, and Jared's two brothers are waiting for them. You can barely make out Holly in her black, formfitting gown, snapping pictures.

There's something about the flash throwing me off. Rubbing my head, I make a mental note to talk discreetly with Holly about it later. The last thing we need is for the photos to be overexposed.

Suddenly, my breathing accelerates, and my vision begins to go black around the edges.

"I don't understand, Aunt Millie. Why do we have to leave?"

Aunt Millie looks down at me with a big smile, saying, "We just do, baby girl."

"But I was having so much fun watching the boys," I complain.

"I know, baby, but we have somewhere important to be. I think your Grandpa is going to try to meet us tonight. It's a surprise for your mommy. Don't you want to be a part of it?"

"Grandpa! Yay! I love Grandpa!" I shriek.

"I know you do, baby girl. So, this is the big surprise. Grandpa is coming in on a boat on the lake! Then you can bring him to Mommy at the house. She'll be so proud of her princess."

Aunt Millie starts walking faster. And faster. Pretty soon we pass the gazebo, but I don't see Grandpa in the boat. It's a bunch of strangers.

I remember what Mommy told me—stranger, danger!

And I start to scream.

I'm shaken from whatever the hell that was to now by my hearing my brother say in my earpiece, "I hope Holly got that shot of Ryan and Caleb. It's a keeper."

The justice of the peace begins to wrap up the ceremony. "May the love you have demonstrated today continue to grow and be enriched each day. May you continue to lean on each other and face any new challenges with courage.

"Ryan and Jared, we've heard your promise to share your lives in marriage. We recognize and respect the covenant you have just entered into here today with each of us as witnesses. Therefore, in the honesty and sincerity of what you have said and done here today, and by the power vested in me by the State of Connecticut, it is my honor and privilege to declare you married.

"You may kiss your groom!" There's quite a bit of loud applause, and even a few whistles, encouraging the two grooms.

"Ladies and gentlemen, may I be the first to present, Mr. Jared Dalton and his husband, Mr. Ryan Lockwood!"

As cheers go up, an orchestral version of Christina Perri's "A Thousand Years" plays softly as the grooms walk up the aisle. My sister races along the perimeter, capturing every ounce of joy on their faces. Following them are Caleb, Jason, and Jared's brothers.

I give it a minute, glancing toward the stage. The chief steward has made his way up next to the justice of the peace. "Ladies and Gentlemen. If you would kindly make your way to the courtyard. Hors d'oeuvres and cocktails will be served while we wait for the Misters. The first course will be served soon after."

I hear the murmurs on what a beautiful ceremony it was. I only wish I remember seeing it. Blinking back tears, I know I need to get it together.

Looking down at my watch, I see it's exactly 3:45. We're on schedule.

Focus on that, Cassidy.

You'll figure the rest out later.

35

CASSIDY

It's 7:00 p.m. The announcement of the newly married Ryan and Jared, the first dance to a beautiful arrangement of Lady Antebellum's "I Run to You," and the first two courses are all completed on time. My family is murmuring quietly in my ear about the toasts and cake cutting being up next. Phil, who's sitting next to Jason at the Lockwood family table with me, gives me a brief look.

So far, so calm.

That was about the best we could hope for with Mildred Lockwood knocking back martinis like they're water. By my last count, I'd seen her down eight. Caleb muttered in my ear that he thought it was more because she had a bar in the master suite. Lovely. We could only hope she would pass out and we could escape this night relatively unscathed.

Caleb leans over and presses a kiss behind my ear. "Game time." He stands and heads toward the orchestra leader. As a consensus, all the groomsmen had decided to let Caleb speak on behalf of both sides, citing since he lived with both grooms, he would obviously do the best job.

During the rehearsal dinner the night before, Caleb joked they just wanted to throw him under the bus, and that there had better be a reward for doing this. After he saw me standing in the crowd smirking, he promptly agreed he had already been given his reward.

We left shortly thereafter for him to claim his reward.

After the song wrapped up, Caleb conferred with the band leader before being handed the microphone.

"Good evening, everyone. Once again, on behalf of Ryan and Jared, we are so thankful you chose to spend your holiday weekend celebrating their marriage." He pauses to let the applause die down. "I was unanimously nominated to speak on behalf of both groom parties, so Ryan, Jared, if you don't like this toast, blame your other brothers."

The crowd starts laughing uproariously. My man is good at this. I lean on my hand and smile at him.

He catches my eye and winks. "Some of you may not know I've been very involved with helping to plan the wedding. In fact, at one point, I was making so many decisions I was mistaken for actually being one of the grooms."

Oh. My. God. I'm going to kill him.

My mouth gapes open, even as my eyes narrow. I hear Phil choke behind me, Jason whack him on the back, and even Keene let out a mild snicker. Not to mention the hilarity of my sisters proceeding to tell Charlie and his wife the story that I could hear through my ear piece.

"But once that small misunderstanding was resolved, I realized my ability to make these decisions for my brother and Jared showed me just how much I knew them, inside and out. I found out when you plan a wedding, you will undoubtedly learn a lot about people. When I did, I was more impressed with not only the men they were, but the love they have for each other." Caleb smiles broadly, looks out at the nodding crowd and continues.

"Jared, since the day I met you, I saw what an amazing match you were for Ryan. You balance him and provide his heart with the home it's been searching for. I'm so glad to finally be able to call you brother."

I look over at Jared, who is discreetly wiping his eyes with the back of his hand.

"Ryan..." Caleb pauses, taking a deep breath. His voice cracks slightly. "Before he died, Dad and I used to talk about the man you would meet one day, since we know what men can be like." He waits for the small laugh he was hoping for. "All we could hope for was that he cherished you like we did, like I still do. I'm so glad you found that with Jared." Caleb smiles at his brother, who has picked up his dinner napkin to wipe his own eyes.

"So, on this momentous occasion, I ask you to raise your glasses. Ryan and Jared, in the words of Shakespeare, 'I wish you all the joy you can wish.' Cheers!"

As the crowd echoes his toast around the courtyard, both grooms walk up to Caleb to embrace him. When Ryan and Caleb hug, they whisper quietly to each other before both break away.

I turn back to the table, dabbing at my eyes with a napkin to find the hate-filled eyes of Mildred Lockwood on me. Phil, not being completely obtuse, casually leans forward on his hand and whispers into his mike, "I think we may have a problem."

I think we do too.

I just have no idea what to do about it.

36

CASSIDY

It's 10:00. Finally, there's no one left on the estate but the family and a few close friends. Mildred has retired to her room to recover from this debacle, as she put it.

Caleb has called it. The wedding is officially over for tonight.

Tomorrow, vendors who had more structural setups will come back to break down, but for tonight, Amaryllis Events is off duty.

My siblings have already changed. Caleb is trying to convince me to go home in my dress, and that we can be there in thirty minutes, but I convinced him it will just take a moment. I want something comfortable to sit down in. Besides, I also don't want to leave a single thing in this house if I don't have to.

I head down the short hallway, entering the doorway to the secondary library to find my bag with my comfortable clothing. I'm distracted, already in the process of removing my necklace as I walk in when I hear the door slam behind me. I jump.

Mildred Lockwood is standing there, pointing a small gun at me. "You couldn't stay gone, could you, you little snot-nosed brat," she hisses as she moves toward me.

Holy shit. I step back, hoping against all hope one of my siblings is still listening through the earpiece. "Excuse me? Gone from where? The house?"

"You always were, you know. Even as a baby," she continues, and advances on me. The look in her eyes is maniacal. This woman is more than drunk, and she isn't just crazy. She's so far past crazy, I don't even know if there's a word for it.

"I don't know what you mean, Mrs. Lockwood. Perhaps we can sit down and you can tell me." I hold her eyes, but gesture to the two couches in front of the cold fireplace.

"It's all your fault. It always has been." She's waving the gun around. "If I had just killed you the first time instead of sending you to Jacksonville, I wouldn't have lost my Jack. And then, much later, when my husband found out about my affair, thereby breaking our prenuptial agreement, the fortune that should have been mine was split between my two worthless sons and I was given an allowance to live on. He said I should be grateful. Fuck gratitude." Her voice is demented and churlish, accusatory and bitter.

My face freezes. "Jacksonville?" I manage to choke out in a whisper of the only word that's made any kind of sense to me. The word that terrifies me.

How can she know about Jacksonville?

"Yes, you stupid, pathetic piece of trash, Cassidy Freeman. Or should I call you by your real name, Riley, since you were sitting so close to your brother Keene tonight?" I can feel the blood drain from my face. "Ahh, so neither one of my know-it-all sons or his pathetic best friend decided to clue you in? You know? You look just like your mother, Riley, with your father's eyes. But I knew who you were months ago." She walks up close to me and slaps me across the face.

I only feel a slight burn, I'm in such shock.

"How?" It's all I can manage right now. Deep breaths, Cassidy. Nothing she's saying makes sense. It's not even remotely possible. If it was, Caleb or Keene would have told me. Right?

She makes a sound that must be what the devil calls a laugh. "I have spies everywhere, little girl. The tech department at Hudson is very informative, and so is Caleb's assistant. I know everything inside the file Charlie Henderson keeps up-to-date about you because I own his wife. Oh, yes." My face contorts at her next words. "Even Charlie's imbecile of a wife isn't beyond corruption. She loves money. And as much as my son pays her husband, it isn't enough to keep the men she's fucking on the side happy.

"Did you know how huge the file is on the Freemans? By the way, how stupid was that name choice? You've never been free. Not since I knew where you were the whole time and could have had you taken. Again. Oh, I was content to let you live so long as you didn't bother my life." She pauses and caresses the gun. The next thing I know, it's pressed against my forehead. I suck in a breath and begin to pray as tears stream down my face.

Caleb, where are you?

"Why the fuck couldn't you just stay in South Carolina like the rest of the white trash? Nothing bad happened to you there, huh? Why the hell did you need to move back here?" Mildred screams in my face, tapping the gun against my forehead. I feel its cold brutal weight against the center of my forehead.

It sends me into full body convulsions.

"Now I have to decide what to do with you. Do I just kill you like I did your mother, or do I send you off again? A pity about the way those men had to take it with a bat. They'll no longer be useful for this type of work, though they are eager for revenge. Do you remember them, Riley? I'm surprised, after being here all day. They're related to most of our staff here, cousins and whatnot with a taste for the forbidden." Her smile is nothing short of demonic.

"You killed my mother?" I whisper in anguish, unable to process the rest. The mother I never knew.

In the recesses of my memory, I remember Caleb telling me about Keene, "There are things he's lost personally that made him who he is."

A mother? A sister?

Me?

"Tell me," I demand in a whisper at the cretin in front of me. "I want to know why. I deserve to know why."

"You deserve nothing more than what I give to you, you stupid bitch. But as a last wish, I'll indulge you. There's nowhere for you to go." She holds the gun on me as she walks over to the side table of liquor. Not taking her eyes off of me, she removes a stopper and takes a long swig of something clear directly from the decanter. Vodka, I presume.

Putting down the decanter, she wipes her mouth with the back of her hand. Moving forward again, I can't help but despair at how steady she's still holding the gun.

Caleb! I'm screaming inside. I'm never this late. Come find me!

"I was having an affair with Jack Marshall, Keene's father. He was leaving your pathetic mother to be with me. I was walking out on this crappy life and those two brats. We were going to be together. What Jack failed to mention was that to not throw his wife off track, he was still sleeping with her." She slides the gun over my cheekbone seconds before pistol-whipping me with it. I can feel blood flowing down my cheek.

"And along came pretty baby Riley. Jack was so fascinated by how fucking cute you were, he decided not to leave his wife! It's all your fucking fault!" Mildred laughs again. "But you're not so pretty now are you, Riley?" She smirks, indicating with pleasure her handiwork with the gun.

"How?" I swallow hard. It hurts to move my face. "How do you know I'm her? I don't remember anything about that."

I refuse to think about what must have been a flashback at the wedding, what my Aunt Millie did to me.

Oh. My. God. Caleb's mother sent me away? To be brutalized and raped?

The horror of it starts to slam into my mind.

This. This is what Keene was alluding to in his office. Caleb knew more of my history than I had told him. But if Keene knew, why didn't he tell me either? I inwardly groan. Because I essentially told him not to.

In my mind, I can hear myself saying to him, "Then let us figure it out, Keene. Sometimes, blasting information in someone's face isn't the best way to handle something."

The man I love and my...fuck, the bile starts to rise...my brother. And neither of them knew I was about to die unless someone was listening through the receiver still in my ear. And it was dead silent.

I swallow hard. I might die.

"Because, Riley, you bear the same birthmark." She drags the gun down the front of my gown to just below my collarbone with unerring accuracy. "Right. Here." She taps it with the gun. "In the same fucking spot both your mother and brother do. You look like that bitch—same shaped eyes, same shaped mouth. And speaking of that mouth..." Crack!

Her other hand comes up and slaps me across the face again. I feel another trickle of blood and reach up. She lifts her hand to show me how she turned her diamond inward, her face in a twisted facsimile of a grin. "Besides that, you have memories of her. Keene's a smart man and has been piecing it together. He realized when you started humming your lullaby. When you recognized the picture in his office. When he saw the birthmark after you fucked my son!" She screams the last at me as she cocks the gun.

"I didn't know they were memories, Mrs. Lockwood." My voice is flat and lifeless. I've lost all hope. All chance.

"I don't care." That much was obvious. She pushes me back and I stumble, but I manage to stay on my feet. Barely.

She takes aim.

"Please don't." I'm begging, but not for myself. I'm begging for my family. For Phillip. For Em. For Ali. For Corinna. For Holly. For Jason. None of them deserve this.

I'm even begging for Caleb and Keene. Neither of them need this to end this way.

"I like you begging, Riley. It reminds me of when your mother did it. Goodbye, Riley Marshall and Cassidy Freeman. I'll be happy to never see your face again."

As the loud reverberation of a gun being fired hits my ears, I feel the fiery hot slice against the side of my neck. I stumble backward and fall into something.

And then there's nothing.

Only darkness.

37

CALEB

I wonder what's taking Cassidy so long to change. I glance at my watch—it's 10:15. She said it would take her ten minutes tops to gather up her stuff and change so we could get the hell out this place.

I'm standing in the foyer with Keene, Charlie, Phil, and Jason. Thankfully, my mother had already retired before the end of the wedding festivities or I would be a lot more antsy than I am right now, despite being given the third degree by the men around me about my relationship with Cassidy.

"So," Phil drawled. "Do I need to ask your intentions toward my sister?" Jason buries his laughter in Phil's shoulder. I also notice Charlie and Keene's stances change as they wait for the answer. Huh. So, my love has a few protectors on her side.

"Endlessly honorable. I love her, Phil," I respond without hesitation.

"Then when are you going to tell her you bought out Laskey's company?" Phil shoots back. "Even if she's told you the worst, she still deserves to know."

My face goes blank. The air in the room stills. "How did you know?" I ask quietly. I'm not upset. I'm trying to gauge his reaction.

"Ryan mentioned it one night over dinner," Jason offers, moving from behind Phil to stand next to him. Their hands lock. "He wanted to let us know about the initial background investigation and why you did it. That led to Phil asking questions." No shock there. "And the rest came out."

"I've been waiting for her to tell us about it, Caleb. It was our right to know." Phil's tone is both angry and hurt.

He deserves to be both.

I drop my head and run my hand across the back of it. There's no good reason and there's no good answer. "I have no answer, Phil. None that will satisfy anyone, least of all Cassidy. I thought I would tell her pretty quickly on in our relationship, but she surprised me by telling me the worst of it first. The rest of the details didn't seem to matter. I didn't go looking for the information." Charlie confirms what I'm saying to be true by nodding. "I ran a check on the company for the wedding and it triggered warning flags Charlie had put in place to protect you all."

Phil nods. "I can understand that, but I'm not in love with you. This is going to hurt her. She may not understand why you didn't tell her, especially after all this time."

The acid which has been burning when I think about the secrets at the foundation of what I built between Cassidy and I starts up. "I know. I just can't figure out how to say what I need to."

Phil, ever the smart-ass, taps his chin. "Yeah, I don't think there's a way to say it with flowers either."

Everyone, but me, bursts out laughing as intended. I check my watch. Another five minutes have passed. "Phil, do you still have your earpiece in?"

"Yes, I turned the transmitter off though. Why?"

"Can you turn it on and see what's keeping Cassidy? I want to get out of here."

"Sure, give me a second." He reaches into his pocket, grabs the small black box and flicks a switch. When he does, he stays quiet for a few moments and his face goes chalk white. "Oh God, Caleb. You have to get to her. Your mother...oh my god!"

"Give it to me. Give it to me now!" I bellow. He fumbles the bud out of his ear and hands it to me. What I hear almost immobilizes me.

My eyes flash up to Keene's. In his face, I finally see what I hadn't before. I'm stunned for half a second before I ask, "Are you armed?"

He pulls back his jacket as he nods.

"Charlie?" A second nod.

"Both of you outside the library window ready to take out my mother the first chance you can without hurting Cassidy. Jason." I swallow hard. He's an ER doctor. "We might need you after."

"Phil, I need you to call 911 and tell them to come in silent. The code for the front gate is 7-6-1-3. Can you do that?" He's frozen to the spot, about to go into shock. "Can you do that?" I yell at him. I have this awful feeling every second is going to count.

"Yes," he whispers.

"Go. Now."

We all run.

I break through the library door heartbeats after my mother has shot the love of my life. Her body falls back as I scream.

I can't get to her fast enough.

The animalistic shrieks of "I'm glad the bitch is finally dead!" are ringing in my ears as I run through Cassidy's blood to find out if she still has a pulse.

Somehow, she does.

"JASON!" I scream. He comes running in, his tuxedo jacket off, ready to use it to apply pressure.

Phil's standing at the doorway, screaming. "Oh God. Oh, Cassidy. Little Girl! What the fuck happened?"

"Gunshot wound to the neck. I can't tell where the blood is coming from though. There's no other obvious signs of a bullet." I'm frantically running my hands over her body.

"Caleb, put pressure on her neck. It grazed her. Let me do my fucking job!" Jason yells at me. Slowly, carefully, he reaches behind her head and I see it. The blood. "Fuck, she must have tripped when she fell. Fold your coat up and give it to me."

Vaguely I'm aware of someone shooting, and from the voices, I know my mother's hand was hit by a shot from outside the window, and the gun she was holding is halfway across the room.

As Keene and Charlie enter the room, Keene lets out a sound of wounded desperation as Charlie moves to cover Mildred. I hear the sirens in the distance. After what I heard in the headset, Keene's reaction makes complete sense.

How did I miss it? Her mother's hair? Her father's eyes? Her brother's smile?

I look from the woman I love to the brother of my heart, and then to Jason.

"How much blood is she losing?"

Jason replies grimly. "Too much. They're going to want to transfuse, and with her blood type being so damn rare..."

I make a snap decision.

"Keene, you're in the ambulance with her."

He's stunned. "Wha—what?"

"There's no time. I heard what Mildred said to her in the headpiece. I know why this happened. I'm going to have to stay and talk to the police." I give him a hard stare. "But I heard her tell Cassidy she's your Riley. Your sister."

Hearing it confirmed brings Keene to his knees next to me.

I grab his shirt. "Just one thing. Don't you dare let her fucking die on me. I'll be there as soon as I can." I release him. "We'll get into why you didn't tell me later, but there's no fucking time now. I know you two share the same blood type and she's going to need a transfusion."

He nods. Almost hesitantly, Keene reaches for his sister's hand for the first time in over twenty-five years. Phil can he heard sobbing quietly in the background.

The entire atmosphere in the room changes. The sounds from Mildred turn into animalistic howls as the police storm the house. Jason starts tossing out orders like he's in the middle of an ER.

And me, I begin begging God for a chance to make all of this right.

Hoping I have a chance to atone for not explaining everything in the beginning.

38

KEENE

A s I sit in the back of the ambulance on the way to Greenwich Hospital, I break down. Completely break down.

After twenty-five years of promises to find her, Riley's here. I hope she knows I never stopped loving her.

After seventeen years of my actively searching, Riley's here. I hope she knows I never gave up on her.

After knowing her for two months, I hope she can forgive me for being such an asshole. God, I was such an asshole.

As I listen to the blips and bleeps, my heart starts to go into over-drive. They need to move faster! What if I lose my sister before I ever truly get her back?

"Will someone drive this fucking ambulance faster? My sister is dying back here!" I scream, tears rolling down my face.

And then I feel it. A miniscule squeeze of my hand. She's not done fighting yet.

Riley...Cassidy, isn't going anywhere.

39

CALEB

It's been three days since Cassidy was brought to the trauma unit.

After dealing with the police at the house, and a second ambulance to take Mildred to the hospital under police guard, I made it there just in time to watch Cassidy be wheeled in for surgery to close her neck and her head. She did, in fact, require a blood transfusion. In one sense, Mildred being as drunk as she was saved Cassidy's life. She was actually aiming for the center of her chest.

I shudder to even imagine it.

The biggest issue is the head trauma. When Cassidy fell and the bullet hit her, she tripped on the edge of the carpet as she instinctively tried to move from it, and ended up knocking her head on the edge of the stone desktop in the library. That, more than the neck wound, was concerning the doctors. They had to shave a six-inch band of her hair above her tattoo in order to close up the gash with about fifty stitches. There was also a small drainage tube placed to pull blood away from her head so it didn't build up against her brain.

The first time I heard that, I think I met Phil and Keene in the bathroom as all three of us vomited.

She still hasn't woken up.

Between Cassidy's family, Keene, Charlie and I, we've taken over the trauma care waiting room at Greenwich Hospital. I've personally taken up residence in her room. Just let someone try to kick me out.

I have to figure out a way to beg for her forgiveness.

I have to explain what I've actually known since before we met. Because right now, it's probably so twisted with Mildred's lunacy, I imagine she's thinking the worst.

I still have no idea how.

My head bows to rest on the bed while I think about what's happened since Cassidy was settled into this room.

The only time I've left Cassidy in the last three days was for Keene and I to contact the Attorney General due to the complete compromise of Hudson. When I had Phil hand me his earpiece, I heard every word my mother had said about Hudson and after. With the Greenwich Police present, we explained the information I heard in my statement. After listening carefully, he said he needed to absorb the information with how it pertained to the open cases and call us back, but not before letting us know he would do everything possible to make certain my mother was convicted of every possible crime she could be.

After, we set a trap to bring down the traitors within Hudson. Fourteen people, including my executive assistant and Charlie's wife, all walked into it. Within hours, they were arrested and are now facing criminal charges.

Charlie, while heartsick, was not only a pragmatist, he apparently loved the Freemans more than his wife. "I can always find another wife. I can't find more kids to love."

And people wonder why I keep his ass around?

So here I sit, praying over the only woman I've ever loved. Apologizing over and over about everything that's happened. Holding her hand, kissing it, hoping for a sign of life. Maybe she'll open those gem-colored eyes and blink at me. Maybe she'll smile. Maybe she'll...

"Go..." comes a raspy voice from the depths of the bed.

Oh my god, she's awake. What did she say?

"Cassidy, love?" I ask cautiously.

"Need you to go," Cassidy says with dull eyes. She repeats the word, causing my heart to begin to bleed. "Go."

I reach for the nurse's button as I stand, but she stays my hand. "Go." Her eyes are open, looking directly at me.

They're not blazing, they're dull. They're in pain but they're alive. They're beautiful. Her face is so pale, the skin is almost translucent. If I were to glance away from her perfect features, I imagine the bag with the drainage behind the bed would be visible.

I wouldn't care if she didn't have a single lock of hair on her head or a million stitches. She would still be the most beautiful thing in the world.

Even if she just told me to go.

"Baby..." I start to say, but I manage to hold it in. Barely. Because I feel like all of this is my fault. "I'm so fucking sorry," I choke out.

"Need you to go," she says again.

My heart stops. She means it. She wants me gone. She can't forgive me.

"I need..." She pauses, closes her eyes and swallows. "I need you to go, Caleb."

Even as my heart stops beating inside my chest, I think back to the words written on the piece of paper in my wallet that Matt gave me so many months ago.

I let the tears flow over. I reach up and brush a wayward curl away from her cheek and whisper, "I will always love you, Cassidy Freeman."

I see her eyes flare as I bend down to brush my lips against hers. The tears from my face drop onto hers, and I carefully brush them off before kissing her forehead.

It may be the last time I get to touch my love. My heart. My soul.

I stand up and start to draw my hand away when I feel a small movement that causes me to look down.

I feel her fingers gripping at the sheet as she tries to inch her hand with the IV closer to mine.

Tentatively, I move my hand closer. Her fingers curl slightly over it and she sighs. Her eyelids lower, and her lips have a small smile on them.

"Go," she whispers. "Need you to go get the others."

Need you to go. Not go.

My heart aches as the blood slowly starts pumping through it again.

"You're not telling me to go?" I choke out in disbelief.

"No." Her eyes crack open. "I reserve the right for angry later. Should have tried to tell me."

I half-laugh, half sob as I gently lay my lips on hers. "I know, and you're right. You can reserve the right for whatever you need later, my love."

"Love you, Caleb. Always. Understand why. Talk with Keene. Told him. Office. He'll understand. Painting." Her lips are against mine the whole time she says what she did, so I'm not sure I got it right.

But I understood the most important thing.

"I love you too, baby."

"Go get the others. Come back."

"Always," I vow, my lips still on hers.

She smiles. "Okay." Then her eyes close again.

As I push the button for the nurse to come in, I thank God for miracles. It's going to be okay.

Eventually.

40

CASSIDY

I'm back at the carriage house after having been checked out by what seems like every doctor at Greenwich Hospital. It was a long eight-day stay.

The final damage? A required haircut as a result of the stitches in the back of my head. A scar along the crease of my neck which will be barely noticeable after it fades. Bruises galore from the hits Mildred inflicted to my face that get worse every day. Fortunately, even pistol-whipping me with her gun, she didn't manage to break my zygomatic bone. Instead, it left a hell of a bruise and a gash which was taped up by the time the EMTs got me in the ambulance.

I was discharged today. Caleb is thoroughly pissed because he couldn't be there with me. The Attorney General has flown up to New York to discuss the impact of what Mildred did to the AG's overall case. Even though we were both busy—me being discharged and him with the AG—I was getting increasingly concerned pings from Caleb.

Missing you.

Is everything okay?

Can you just ping me to let me know you're okay?

And then, finally.

We're done. Keene and I are on our way. I'll be there soon to hold you.

Tears welled up in my eyes when I got that one. I sent him a quick *"Good. Going to rest now"* before I put my phone down and relaxed back in my bed.

I could hear my family moving around downstairs, their voices a comforting background noise, but I was missing something.

Caleb.

I really wanted his arms around me and the sound of his heart under my ear.

Moving slowly, as the adrenaline has sucked out more energy than Ali on a five-mile trail run, I swing my legs over the side of my bed and start to walk to my bathroom.

"Busted," an amused male voice, not the one I'm waiting for, but a beloved one nonetheless says.

Turning, I find Phil lounging in my doorway with what appears to be one of my serving bowls filled with ice cream on a tray.

"Is that Baskin Robbins Chocolate-Peanut Butter?" I ask, my glands salivating at my favorite ice cream flavor.

"Is there another kind?" He smirks as he strolls into my room.

"There shouldn't be. Hey, what the hell are you doing?" I ask as he starts to lift the spoon to his mouth.

"Oh, I figured if you were out of bed, then you must be fine and this was up for grabs," he remarks innocently. But I can see the dark edge in his eyes, daring me to argue with him.

Sighing, my shoulders droop. "Phil, I'm still in gross hospital clothes. All I really want to do is pee, wipe the hospital smell off me and change into something soft and comfortable. Is that too much?" I'm almost in tears with the effort it's taking me to have the discussion.

Immediately, the edge is gone. "No, Little Girl, it's not. Why don't you head to the bathroom and start with the cleanup? Tell me what you want and I'll hand it in."

"My old College of Charleston hoodie and a pair of sleep shorts. Bottom drawer dresser. I don't care if they match."

A few minutes later—gross clothes handed to Phil that I don't care if he burns—I'm sitting back in bed with the ginormous bowl of ice cream cradled next to me. They must have dumped the full quart in here, with about a pint of fresh whipped cream.

Taking another blissful bite, I'm so not complaining. I'm eating this until A, I get sick. B, it melts. Or C, I fall asleep. I gently shove another spoonful into my mouth and sigh. All I need is...

The door opens.

Caleb walking in and making me forget about the ice cream.

His eyes meet mine across the room and I start to sit up.

"No, baby, don't move," he protests. He drops his bags near the entrance of the room and crosses it in a few quick movements. Placing his knee on the bed, he moves my dark hair away from the left side of my face and hisses.

Misunderstanding, I babble, "It just looks worse than yesterday. The doctor said since there's no longer an open cut, I could put something on it to hide the bruising. Em has this makeup that should work."

He puts his finger in the center of my lips to hush me. Leaning over me, he touches his lips gently on the bruise, kissing it better. My heart melts faster than the ice cream. He gently traces around my face and lips with his finger. "I want to kiss you to reassure myself you're okay. I don't want to hurt you though."

"Be gentle, Caleb. It should be fine." I reach for his jaw to angle his face toward me.

His lips meet mine, and I feel only a slight twinge where the cut is next to the corner of my lip. The kiss is slow, soft, and filled with so much emotion.

I feel Caleb's pain, his regret, his fury, his desire, his promise. In this one kiss, he's cherishing me. He's worshiping me.

We break apart and our eyes lock in a bubble of desire before his sharpen and change to perplexed. Glancing down, his face changes to one of utter disgust. When I see why, I start to giggle. Maybe I should have added a final option for when I would stop eating my ice cream.

D, when Caleb's hand ended up in the center of it while kissing me.

Lifting his hand from the puddle of chocolate and mashed peanut butter, he holds his hand carefully over the bowl. "Well, I can't say this has ever happened before."

My giggle turns into a full-blown laugh. I groan and reach up to my cheek to hold it, but can't stop the snorting sounds that erupt.

His face tries to look stern, but his eyes are filled with humor he hasn't shown for far too long. His deep laugh collides with mine and pretty soon, we're both doubled over—me with my hand holding my bruised face, him holding his ice cream-covered hand over the bowl so as not to get it on my bed.

Finally, after our hilarity calms down, I wipe my eyes. "Let me get you a towel."

"You are not leaving that bed for the next several days, my love." His voice is firm with no room for argument. "I was already briefed downstairs. I know the doctor said to rest."

"Rest, Caleb. Not be a prisoner of my bed." I pout. The full one requires too much cheek movement.

"But that could be so much fun," he returns with a wink.

My jaw unhinges. Ow. Wince.

"Okay. Maybe in a day or so, that could be more fun," he amends.

"I...you. What. Seriously?" I stammer.

"Want to try that again?" he asks, amused.

Taking a deep breath, again, and again. Huh. Only three needed. "You want me looking like this?"

"Cassidy, I honestly can't think of a time or a place I wouldn't want you. Even if it was your hand stuck in the bowl of chocolate ice cream."

Shit, the ice cream.

"Yell for Phil," I tell him.

"But I don't want Phil," he counters in a sexy rasp.

"Yell for Phil to come up here if you're not going to let me out of bed to help you with the ice cream, you dork." I roll my eyes, the only part of my face not hurting.

Smirking at me, he gives me no warning before he yells, "Whirlpool!" at the top of his lungs. "You know," he says conversationally, as we hear my brother stomp up the stairs, "You're going to have to share why you call him that."

As I laugh under my breath, I agree while we wait for Phil to throw open the door in his normal style. "You bellowed, bratwurst?" Phil drawls as he strolls into my room.

Oh. Hell. No. He. Did. Not.

"Are you kidding me right now, Phillip? Did you just go there? You better send your husband up for everything, and I mean everything. I might get out of this bed and get stabby real soon. Ow!" I forgot my head and cheek temporarily in my hissy fit at my brother.

"Tsk, Tsk, Cass. You need to be careful. What do you need, Caleb?" As he walks farther into the room, he sees Caleb's hand suspended over the bowl of formerly chocolate-peanut butter ice cream and begins to laugh. "Okay, so first, a towel and wash cloth. Then some more ice cream, perhaps?" Smirking, Phil goes into and reemerges from my bathroom with some older towels. "You know, Cassidy, if you're going to get into this food play stuff more, you really need to get darker colored sheets and towels."

I grab the bowl of melted ice cream. As I start to hoist it in the air, Phil snags it from me before dashing for the door, laughing. "Calm down, Little Girl. You need some more food before you take your next dose of pain meds. Caleb, I was just about to come get you anyway. Cassidy, Keene's here too, sweetie. Oh, by the way, I totally get why Ali banged him. The daggers are about to fly downstairs." He pauses, and then says gleefully, "I don't want to miss a thing!"

I suddenly realize I haven't talked with Keene. Not only did he help save my life, but he's my brother. I can't avoid this forever. "Why don't you send Keene up with it?" I say to Phil, but I'm talking to Caleb.

"Are you sure, baby?" he murmurs. "This is your sanctuary."

"Our sanctuary," I correct, and I'm rewarded with a smile and a kiss. I think for a minute before I speak. "I'm not quite sure how this goes, Caleb. I don't really remember having a brother or a mother, but he does. I need to get to know him. I have to try to figure this out." I see Phil smiling at me with love and pride. "For all of us."

Caleb places a kiss on my forehead "You're amazing." He turns to Phil. "Put Keene to use. Send him up with everything."

With a quick smile and a thumbs-up, Phil departs to go wreak havoc on the rest of my house. Caleb pulls me back against him and ah, there it is. His heartbeat.

I start to relax until I hear, "Bratwurst?" said with great humor over my head. I groan.

"No, not happening. Not now. Let's talk with Keene. Let me relax." And maybe after I kill my brother. Maybe. I peek up at Caleb beneath my lashes, mentally chanting please don't push it. Please don't push it.

Smirking, he kisses my head again as I snuggle back against his chest. Caleb's long fingers are moving through my hair when we hear a quick knock on the door and Keene steps into my room, carrying a tray with another vat of ice cream, pain meds, and an ice pack.

With his familiar arrogant air, he glances down at the tray, announcing, "I have what appears to be a diabetic coma with a chaser of frostbite to be eased by..." He looks up and the words die on his lips as he gets his first view of me unbandaged since the hospital.

At first, I'm not sure if it's because I'm wrapped in Caleb's arms, but when his eyes move away from my face, I can see the pain and vengeful fury on his. For me. Thinking back to the early days when we first met, I wonder who would have thought it?

"She's okay, man," Caleb reminds him quietly. They exchange a meaningful look between them that I can't even begin to interpret.

Keene nods slowly and walks toward the bed, depositing the tray on the bedside table. "Right. So, as I was saying, Phil put everything on here you needed, Cassidy." He's cautious. "He mentioned you asked to speak with me?"

I tap Caleb's arm and he lets me up, out of his embrace. Sliding off the bed, I walk to where Keene is. I'm at least a good foot shorter than him, so I can't imagine why he's holding his breath when I come closer. I touch his arm and simply say, "Thank you."

Keene continues to hold his breath.

"Thank you for never giving up hope. Thank you for being smart enough to find the clues. Thank you for listening to me that day in your office. Thank you for keeping Caleb sane. Thank you for keeping him safe so I could find him." I look over my shoulder at the man I love, whose eyes are shining back at me. I take a deep breath and continue. "Thank you for letting me figure out how to deal with this in my own time. For dealing with the police, and for what I know you're doing to keep us safe—*me* safe. Just...thank you," I end on a whisper. I squeeze his arm and walk back to the bed, and this time, I crawl beneath the covers, resting my head on my pillow as I feel my eyelids start fluttering closed.

Keene opens his mouth and closes it a few times before gruffly saying, "It was my pleasure".

Keene and Caleb talk briefly about Mildred and how she'll remain a permanent guest of the State of Connecticut since she was a flight risk. Good. I bet the bitch looks awful in orange. There's more talk about security at the farm, and some back and forth about background checks on the new tech team. I make a mental note to ask about that later.

Just as my eyes are about to remain closed, I hear Keene say, "Cassidy," softly. Not Riley.

I hurt for him.

I open my eyes and focus on my biological brother. Keene is standing in the doorway, his arm braced above his head. He stares out the window while saying. "I wish more women, more people for that matter, had your strength, honor, and will to fight." He nods at Caleb before leaving us in the comfort of my room.

I make a snap decision. "Keene!" He pops his head back in.

"Caleb can't cook for shit and I'm under doctor's orders to not leave my bed for a while, but..." I look into his eyes, my brother's eyes, and they spark with what's been missing.

Hope.

"But?"

"We'd love to have you over for dinner. We have a lot to catch up on."

Keene swallows once, twice, then gives me a quick nod and a

smile before walking away. As I hear his footsteps down the hallway, I hear him call out, "I'll bring takeout!"

I start to smile. Our lives will end up okay. We'll work to make it that way.

Caleb, out of the blue, says, "You know, you really designed this room for complete decadence."

I grab the new ice cream bowl from the tray. Plowing in another mouthful of ice cream, I nod. I did.

"You know the only thing you're missing in here?" Caleb asks casually as he reads the medicine bottle before shaking out one of the 800 mg ibuprofen. Handing me that and a glass of water, I take the pill, hoping it kicks in quickly to alleviate the pain in my cheek.

Swallowing, I ask, "No. What?"

"Someone to share it with." His eyes are intent on mine. Waiting. Patient.

My heart thuds in my chest.

My mouth opens and closes.

For just a moment, the fear of my past tries to reach out its feelers and grab hold of me to drag me back. I fight back the shadows. No more. It's time to face the future standing in front of me with my heart open instead.

"No, Caleb, I'm not missing that. I already found it."

Leaning back, I pull back the blanket to welcome him into my bed, my arms, my heart. With no secrets left between us.

His eyes wildly dilate before he climbs into his place.

Right next to me.

EPILOGUE

CASSIDY

It's Memorial Day weekend, and there are plans to celebrate by the lake on the farm.

From my bedroom window, I see casual beauty. There's about forty of us who will be here today, so we went for four large, round tables covered in white. Casual elegance. That's the effect I wanted. Low flower centerpieces in red, white, and blue make it easy for what we know will be lots of easy conversation and laughter going long into the night. In front of each place setting is a Mason jar which holds a red, white, or blue candle to be lit as the sun goes down. Each jar has a tri-colored ribbon glued carefully on top. Even the cake Corinna made is red, white, and blue.

Jared and Ryan spent most of yesterday wiring the speakers from the farm to face outward. Jared volunteered to play DJ for most of the day from his Spotify app. Ryan said of course, because Jared just wanted to play with all the tech porn toys. Jared shrugged before we all broke out into laughter.

I look up at the beautiful blue sky with a smile on my face. Weather was expected to be mid-70s with a low of 50. Perfect. Then again, it was going to be perfect anyway.

I was getting married today.

To say it wasn't an easy road after Millicent Lockwood shot me, finding out Keene was my biological brother, redefining family dynamics, and learning so much about my life was based on the greed and jealousy of the woman who was the mother of the man I love would be the understatement of the century.

Shortly after I was released from bedrest, Caleb and I began counseling with a wonderful team Matt referred us to.

There were nights where one or both of us were up pacing the floor, our demons too much for us to deal with in the dream state. We fought with each other and for each other. There were tears, pain, and grief, but through it all, I kept two very important things in my mind.

That bitch wasn't going to win, and I loved this man far too much to give up.

After the first few months, the difference became noticeable. Our nightmares eased. Our smiles outweighed our grief. We started sleeping through the night more, clinging to each other rather than pushing each other away. Caleb eventually stopped trying to handle it on his own and started talking to me about the things causing him the most pain—the betrayals perpetrated by his mother that led to my kidnapping, my mother's death, my attempted murder, his brother's pain. His own guilt.

Then we talked about all the blessings. I remember a little over two months ago when I taunted him by saying had this never happened the way it had, he never would have been able to resist me as a teenager and I would have ended up knocked up. We would have had a whole different set of problems then.

He stood there, shirt off, and gawked at me. It was priceless. I fell back on the sofa in hysterics for a good twenty minutes of which Caleb was a statue, with only a jaw that kept trying to move up and down.

When he was finally able to move, he fell to his knees next to me and pulled up my skirt and said, "Now's a good time to practice," before lowering his mouth between my legs, and my laughs quickly turned to moans.

Neither of us moved for quite a while after that.

I smile slowly at the memory.

We'll never forget that night because right after we finished practicing, Caleb found his jeans and pulled from his pocket the black opal surrounded by diamonds that's resided on the third finger of my left hand until just a few short moments ago.

Kneeling down next to me, he told me I was right, that we were meant to be together. I had tears streaming down my face as he promised he would love me forever, and how even then that wasn't long enough. And would I please expand the love I have for my family to include him?

After furiously nodding my head yes, because I couldn't get the words out, we made love so tenderly. A long, long time afterward, we talked about what we wanted for our day of celebration. And here we are, a little less than two months later with me waiting to be with my closest family and friends, ready to become Caleb's wife.

Then there was Keene. Slowly, my brother and I are building a foundation not on past guilt and pain, but upon the respect and friendship we're finding for each other as adults.

It's by no means easy. I mean, come on, it's Keene. He can be difficult on a good day. I reach up and touch the ruby earrings in my ears and recall our conversation from last night.

"Hey, brat." I roll my eyes. Keene glories in calling me by a teenager's nickname.

"Yes, brother dearest?" My intonation equates this to Mommy Dearest.

"Come with me for a second?" I pause and size him up. He's nervous. He hasn't been nervous in a while around me, so I squeeze Caleb's hand and walk over to my brother. Keene opens the door that leads from the farm, out to the back by the lake.

I smile. In less than twenty-four hours, I'm going to be Mrs. Caleb Lockwood somewhere near this very spot. I stand still for a moment with a huge smile on my face, and feel Keene's arm slide over my shoulders. I loop mine around his waist. After a few moments, he gives mine a quick squeeze as I give him a smile. "Sorry, Keene. I'll give you three guesses what I was daydreaming about, but you should only need one."

He barks out a quick laugh. I tighten my arm a bit.

"What's up?" I ask curiously. It's not like him to call me out when we've got a room full of people. We've gotten close, but he's still very private.

Keene clears his throat and pulls out a small worn-down velvet covered box and holds it out to me. When I reach for it, he doesn't let go. "I managed to save these in case I ever found you. They were Mom's favorite. If you didn't have something to wear tomorrow, I thought they might be appropriate."

Tears clog my eyes. I try to speak, but I can't. Removing my arm from his waist, I take hold of the box he's held onto for me for almost twenty-six years now. I open up the box—it has slightly rusted hinges.

Inside are a perfect pair of emerald-cut ruby earrings.

The tears start falling, even as I move into Keene's arms. "She would have loved to have been here, Cassidy."

"Cassidy Riley," I mumble into his shirt. He moves me back and grabs both my shoulders, his face pale.

I wipe my eyes. I want to see his face as I give him this gift back. I close the box and kiss the top. "I am so wearing these tomorrow. They're my something old and something new." I take a deep breath. "You know I don't legally have a middle name, right?" He nods. "Tuesday, when you file the papers, I will legally become Cassidy Riley-Freeman Lockwood. Even though I've been a Freeman longer than I knew I was a Marshall and I'll become a Lockwood when I marry Caleb, I always want you to know I am so proud to be your sister, Keene. I love you."

"Are you sure?" He reaches out to touch my face.

I feel his hands shake against my skin.

I nod. "Absolutely sure. I talked this over with Caleb. We're both so happy to have you as our brother."

He yanks me into his arms, but not before the sun bounces off his glistening eyes.

I'm jerked back from my memory as the door to my room opens. Phil stands there in a light blue silk shirt, Navy slacks and dress shoes. His oh-so-blue eyes are glowing.

"You look beautiful, Little Girl," he whispers.

I move away from the window and directly into his arms. He

rocks me back and forth like he has since I was nine-years-old. I'm about to start crying when I hear, "I've just about decided he's good enough for you."

I laugh lightly at the broken tension. He always knows what to say. I lean back in his arms and cup his face. "Thank you, Phillip, for being the first man to protect me, the first man I loved, the first family I ever had, and the first brother I ever had. So many firsts you've been to me." The tears fill my eyes anyway. "Thank you for putting together my wedding exactly the way I wanted it."

Tears run unchecked down his handsome face. "Thank you, Cassidy, for all the same reasons and so many more." He pulls me back in his arms for a final hug before we make our way downstairs. "Are you ready?"

After dabbing my eyes, I ask him, "How do I look?"

He runs his eyes over me over me from head to toe, giving me a huge smile. "Perfect."

Holding out an arm, I loop mine through his. As we walk down the stairs, I hear the quiet click of Holly's camera shutter behind us.

It's two minutes to the farm from the carriage house. Normally, I would have walked it.

Everyone balked at that idea last night, especially my sisters. They said even if I didn't want to be treated like a princess on my wedding day, my shoes sure as hell would be. Checking out my Christian Louboutin lace pumps, a lovely gift from my husband to be, I have to agree. Instead, we're taking the half mile ride in Caleb's Porsche.

He's already at the farm, waiting.

Phil's driving like a granny so he doesn't mess up my hair and so that he doesn't lose Holly, who is perched precariously on the back of the car, getting photos around the lake. We're making jokes, but I'm almost too tranquil to participate in our usual banter.

As we pull up to the front door of the farm, Phil helps Holly off the car and gives me a stern look. "Stay right where you are."

Serenely, I wait for him to come around. He opens my door and offers me his hand. Holly is clicking away. During the ceremony, her interns will take up the slack, but I know her camera won't be far away for the rest of the night. The three of us walk in and hush comes over the room.

"Oh, Cassy," Em says in awe. She's in a light blue, curve-hugging dress. Ali steps up next to her in a Navy-blue, silk wrap dress. Her killer smile is on display, as are her tears. She's about to wipe at them when Em yells, "Dammit, I said dab! Don't fuck up your makeup yet!"

I start laughing. There's no help for it.

Holly hands her camera to Corinna, who starts taking pictures as Holly quickly undoes her French braid. Strand after strand of sunset colored waves comes down around her shoulders. She too is in a blue dress, though hers is a sweetheart neckline with spaghetti straps in a royal blue that goes to the floor. Quickly flipping her hair upside down, Em spritzes it before she flips back up.

"How does it look? I was hoping that putting it in a braid wouldn't do too much damage. Oh, good," she says as she makes her way to the mirror.

I just shake my head. Phil's arm wraps around my waist. He's shaking with suppressed laughter. Four down, one to go.

"What about me?" Corinna's sultry voice demands. Her cold-shoulder dress skims her lush figure tightly under the breasts before flaring out in a soft baby blue. As my flower girl, she demanded her heavy locks have an appropriate flower girl crown.

Typical Corinna.

I look at my brother and my sisters, and my eyes well up. "You're all so beautiful. So beautiful. I can't believe you did this in two months."

"Well, hon, it's not like you wanted anything complicated. You wanted Caleb and family. Everything else was negotiable," Em points out realistically.

"But this is everything I ever wanted," I argue.

Ali comes up and wraps her arm on the other side of me. She tips her head to rest on mine. "No, sweetheart. He is. The rest of it is just stuff."

I squeeze her waist at that very true comment.

"Are you ready?" Holly asks. She's over by the door wiping at her eyes. She shoots a guilty look at Em, who is giving her a fulminating glare at not dabbing. She's just tossed a single amaryllis out the door at Jared. The agreed upon high sign.

Am I ready?

The words that come out of my mouth have never been truer.

"I was born ready."

~

I WATCH from behind the sheer screens we erected so Caleb can't peek into the farm's main room.

Corinna begins the processional to Sara Bareilles' "I Choose You." Fortunately, she doesn't have to throw any flowers as Phil already scattered so many red, white, and blue blooms, we'd be lucky if we all didn't take a header in our heels. Instead, she holds a stained-glass box I had in my room with an amaryllis on it.

Next went Holly, carrying a single amaryllis, her face serene and slightly tipped as if she knew where her photography interns were hiding. I bet the photos of her would be gorgeous.

Then Ali, her stride as strong as her smile. Her head sways from left to right, blessing everyone with it. It falters for a moment when she reaches the front and her eyes meet Keene's. Oh boy. I hope someone got that on camera. I'm thoughtful as I look at my sister. And my brother.

Em lookst at me over her shoulder. "Saw that, did ya?"

"Oh yeah," I couldn't miss it.

"I hope that's not going to bother you, 'cause I don't think they're done yet." Not giving me a chance to react, Em pauses a second before she takes her first step. "By the way, Caleb looks hot." And she makes her way down the aisle.

Seriously, did she just say that to me on my wedding day? I stamp my foot. Phil is in hysterics next to me, wiping his eyes.

"What the hell, Phil? I didn't pull that crap on you! Though Jason did look hot," I admit.

"She didn't do that for you, Little Girl. She did that for me so I don't cry walking you down the aisle."

Oh. Ohhh. I reach for my brother as the music changes to "Marry Me" by Train. It's our cue. He gives me a quick kiss on the cheek before pulling my thin shoulder length veil over my face. We step out into the sun.

As soon as I'm visible, I hear Caleb's gasp. Like our wedding, my dress is fairly casual. A tea-length informal gown in lush satin covered in lace, with a lace and jewel neckline. It still shows off my curves. My hair, which grew back from being shaved, is twisted up in an updo so you can see my mother's ruby earrings. I have Em's delicate gold bracelet around my right wrist.

My something blue is for Caleb alone.

I carry a bouquet of amaryllis in front of me as I walk at a steady pace to Caleb who is standing in front of an arbor made of red balloons. His eyes are wet and he isn't trying to hide it. Behind him stands Ryan, Keene, and Jason. Phil will take his place there after he walks me to Caleb, who is nothing short of delicious in a dark red shirt and navy dress slacks. The rest of the groomsmen are all wearing some variation of blue on blue, like Phil.

"You're beautiful," he whispers as we approach. He shakes Phil's hand, gets pulled into a hearty embrace, listens to what Phil says and nods. "I promise," he says to my brother.

Taking my arm, he turns us to face Charlie.

That's right, Charlie. He's performing the ceremony for us today, but we're going to the justice of the peace tomorrow to make it legal. In our hearts, this is the ceremony that counts and the day we'll celebrate with our family going forward.

"I've had the honor and privilege of knowing both Caleb and Cassidy for years. Knew 'em both individually long before their paths finally crossed. Seeing what I've had the pleasure of seeing, I have to admit, I might've thought about putting these two together sooner. Took too damn long if you ask me." Behind us, the small crowd laughs uproariously. Caleb and I grin at each other. This is exactly what we'd wanted.

"Now, I'm not a mushy kinda guy, but this woman up here, the first time I met her, she grabbed hold of my heart and never let go. Same with her brother and sisters. If I'm damn lucky, maybe I'll be asked to officiate at the other girls' weddings soon." Now I'm the one hooting at my sisters who all have the exact same expressions of horror on their faces.

That'll teach you to give crap to the bride.

"But back to Caleb and Cassidy." We all turn back to Charlie. "I used to tell Cassidy that storms don't last forever, but today, I want you both to know true love does. You'll be able to lean on each other through the storms you might experience in the future." This is something we're well aware of already. Caleb squeezes my arm tightly.

"The vows you are about to make are going to last forever. Only the gravest of sins, the wrongest of doin's should be cause to break them. So, before entering into them, do either of you or anyone object to this marriage?"

No one speaks up, but we didn't expect them to.

"Now, I expect you've heard enough outta me for a while. Caleb and Cassidy have written their own vows. Caleb, why don't you start us off. Wait!" We all wait for his next direction. "Cassidy, first give Emily that buncha flowers so you can hold your man's hand." The snickering is almost out of control from our family and close friends.

I turn to Em and hand her my bouquet. She smirks and blows me a kiss before I turn back to Caleb and take both of his hands.

"All right, Caleb. Go on ahead." Charlie takes a step back and I look into Caleb's eyes. The chocolate depths are swimming with laughter, joy, and love. My favorite combination.

He brings my hand to his mouth and kisses it. "Cassidy, my love, I think the first time you calmly called your brother Phillip in such a calm voice after he dropped a ticking time bomb in your lap, I knew I was in trouble." The audience, especially my family, roars. "You had steel and strength in your eyes, kissable lips, and a stubborn tilt to your chin that dared anyone to cross your path in that moment. I was completely hooked." More laughter.

"You'll be thrilled to know that as a male, I felt it was my sworn duty to try to add an additional roadblock in our courtship by being a smart-ass in your office that first day. I mean, it's not like we needed any more help in that area in the upcoming months. Our courtship was so dull after all." I smile and laugh at that. To hear Caleb joking around about everything that led us here is such a relief. But then, his eyes get serious.

"It wasn't too long ago I listened to you thank someone for everything they did for you. Now, it's my turn to do the same." He pauses and takes a deep breath.

"Thank you for loving me."

"Thank you for giving yourself to me."

"Thank you for sharing your family and mine."

"Thank you for not letting me give in to the dark."

"Thank you for always giving me your light."

"Thank you for your smile in the morning."

"Thank you for your arms at night."

"Thank you for your strength when I need it."

"Thank you for your courage."

"Thank you for your heart every minute of every day. I promise to cherish it for the rest of our lives."

By the time Caleb finishes, I can't see his face any longer. I'm a wreck. I reach under my veil to wipe my eyes when I hear Em hiss again, "Dab!" as she shoves a tissue over my shoulder. I try to recover some of my makeup as I dab it with the tissue. I want to memorize the expression on Caleb's face. His eyes are shiny from his unshed tears and full of love, but his lips are quirked up in a cocky grin, questioning me on how he did.

I know I can beat it.

Charlie's voice booms out next to us. "Sweet Jesus, boy. You had me tearing up. Cassidy, you able to talk yet, girl?" I nod. "You ready?" I take a deep breath and look into Caleb's loving eyes.

I'm so ready.

I bring his hand to my mouth and kiss it through the veil. "Caleb, when you walked into my office, I was disappointed for the first time ever in a client. I didn't want you to be the groom." Everyone laughs. "There was a spark between us, but after the stunt you pulled that first day, I'd be damned if I'd admit to it. By the way, does this mean I'm technically marrying Ryan and Jared too?" The screaming laughter from everyone stops the ceremony for a few minutes.

Caleb just shakes his head, laughing. When everyone calms down, Caleb says to me, "You ready to continue?" I grin at him and nod.

"It wasn't easy falling in love with you because we had to fight so many demons along the way." He squeezes my hands and I squeeze back. "I always knew we'd come out on top because after a while, I wasn't worried. I had faith in us." I take a deep breath. "And if it's a girl, I think that's what her name should be."

I can hear wave after wave of gasps across our small group.

I hadn't told anyone what I suspected.

Caleb visibly staggers. Ryan puts his arms out to catch his brother in the event he falls. "What? You're...we're...?" He can't even form a coherent sentence.

I nod frantically and quickly rush out with, "I know we didn't plan for this, but..."

His mouth hanging open, and then I see it.

The joy in his eyes.

Right before he drops to his knees and wraps his arms around my waist. His head lands in the region of my stomach and I hold him tight.

I look blindly past Ryan's face, which has a huge grin on it, into that of Keene's. My brother by blood. His eyes are wet as well, his hand in a fist over his heart. I smile.

Behind him stands Jason, and while he's smiling, I can see he's scanning me like the doctor he is.

My eyes lock with Phil's. The boy who turned into a man between one heartbeat and the next. The brother of my heart who saved mine. His hand is over his mouth and the tears are flowing over it.

Suddenly, I'm airborne as Caleb is swinging me around in his arms. "Oh God, I love you."

He starts to make his way down the aisle. I swat at him. "Caleb!"

"What?" His face is alight with joy. I know he's ready to give me the world.

All I want is the rest of my wedding.

"How about we let Charlie finish? Then you can carry me down the aisle?" I demand.

He bellows out a laugh before turning and putting me back down at the altar. "Charlie! Let's wrap this up! We have a lot to celebrate!"

"Apparently so," Charlie drawls, coming up to us again. Before he says anything else to finish the ceremony, he leans forward and kisses me on the cheek. "Congratulations, beautiful. You'll make a great Mommy. You've already had a lot of practice." He nods toward my sisters.

My eyes fill up. His words mean so much. I lean over and kiss his cheek quickly. He clears his throat and continues.

"As a symbol of marriage, your wedding ring will represent your commitment to each other for life. It's a symbol of your love for one another. Corinna, can you bring up the rings?" My sister quickly steps forward with the box. Charlie opens up the glass box and removes two rings, handing my ring to Caleb and his to me.

"Caleb, take Cassidy's ring. Place it on the third finger of her left hand and repeat after me. I, Caleb."

"I, Caleb..."

"Give you, Cassidy..."

"Give you, Cassidy..."

"This ring as a symbol of my eternal love and commitment to you."

"This ring as a symbol of my eternal love and commitment to you."

Once the ring is slid on, Caleb lifts my hand and kisses it, his eyes never leaving mine.

Charlie clears his throat. "Cassidy, it's your turn, honey. Take Caleb's left hand. Place his ring on the third finger of his left hand and repeat after me. I, Cassidy."

I look at Caleb with every bit of love in my heart. "I, Cassidy..."

"Give you, Caleb..."

"Give you, Caleb..."

"This ring as a symbol of my eternal love and commitment to you."

"This ring as a symbol of my eternal love and commitment to you."

I capture his hand next to my cheek and nuzzle it through the veil. I am so ready for this thing to be off.

Charlie adds, "I could go on about these two."

Caleb interrupts. "Please don't."

Charlie, as if Caleb hadn't spoken, says, "But I think there's been enough happening today and we all want to celebrate. All I'll say is this. Beauty may fade, money may be won or lost, but the love you feel right now will grow stronger with every day that passes. Hold onto that, and you'll live a life that most people will envy."

I smile up at Caleb. Truer words...by the poet Charlie Henderson.

"And since the State of Connecticut is such sticks in the mud that a real justice of the peace has to redo all this again tomorrow, by the power invested in me by nobody but the love of the two people in front of me, I am proud to present to you Mr. And Mrs. Caleb Lockwood...and baby!"

Caleb lifts my veil before laying one a hell of a kiss on me as he dips me back.

It ends up being my favorite wedding photo, because everyone I love in the world, including my husband, our child, and our family is framed perfectly in it with a hovering red balloon that manages to escape the others, trying to make its way toward the heavens.

THE END

WHERE TO GET HELP

Child abuse victims are often too scared or too ashamed to tell anyone of the trauma they endured. Even more tragically, they may encounter skepticism when they do muster up the courage; particularly if the abuser is someone who is considered "trusted" (such as a family member, a friend, or a respected authority figure). The best way to stop child abuse is to report it to local authorities, who will conduct an investigation and potentially prosecute the abuser.

In the United States, the U.S. Department of Health & Human Services (HHS) provides support through its Child Welfare Information Gateway (https://www.childwelfare.gov), which promotes the Childhelp National Child Abuse Hotline (https://www.childhelp.org/child-abuse/). The hotline provides anonymous crisis assistance, counseling, and referral services 24 hours a day, 7 days a week at 1-800-422-4453.

COMING SOON

There are sparks between them. Will they act on them or will they run?
In Fall 2018, find out what happens between Ali and Keene.
To be notified of the release of Free to Run, sign up here:
smarturl.it/FTR_Release
Add it to Goodreads here: smarturl.it/FTRun_GR

ACKNOWLEDGMENTS

I don't know where to begin other than to say, if I miss someone please know you are in the most important place – my heart.

First, to my husband. There are not enough words to say what needs to be said. You've travelled along this path with me every step of the way. From the moment I took over our kitchen table, to supporting the ungodly hours I kept, and with your unwavering belief in me, you've always stood by me. You've always been there. I know you always will be. Without your constant love there is no way I could have had the courage to be me. Just remember you kissed me first.

To my amazing son. There are so many reasons I could use to sum up how much I love you but maybe this will do – I just love listening to your heartbeat. I am so proud of who you are and what you do every day. Follow your dreams, baby, wherever they take you.

To my mother, who literally could not look at the teasers for this book so there is absolutely no expectation of her reading it. Thank you for every advantage you gave me as a child I had to become an adult to appreciate. You've evolved into more than just my mother but a trusted friend. I am so blessed. To my father – I miss you every single day you're not here with us.

Jen, what do I say to you? There aren't enough words to express my love, my joy, my gratitude for your love and friendship. From the first day we met, we've climbed mountains together. This one just happened to be a mountain of words. You stood by me as I agonized writing some of the scenes in this book. You pulled me from the doldrums when I didn't think I could go on. You and I both know the biggest push you ever gave me. Thank you *again* for hanging up on me that night. You are still the best gift I have ever been given. I love you beyond bearing.

To my Meows; Jen, Tara, Alissa, Greg, and Kristina. We finally have our compound! Just like we always dreamed of. Next stop, making the virtual a reality. Thank you for the constant encouragement in this and in every area of my life. When's our next trip?

My Betas, particularly Spoon and Toasty. Thank you for dropping what you were doing to read what may have been screen shots as I was re-writing on the fly. For the phone calls, the kicks in the pants, the refusal to let me give in, and for doing something which is really hard – giving honest feedback.

Ash, I could fill a page with my appreciation for your love and support. If it wasn't for you, I would have tossed this aside a long time ago. From that first moment in Charlotte, we clicked. We dove into this together and we'll have each other through it. Even when we hit the "crossroads" we'll still "dream" together. Love you, babe.

Alessandra Torre, my mentor and friend. Without your openness, willingness to answer questions, and desire to give back to the community you love, I *know* I would still be struggling with many aspects of this craziness. Just remember when I tackle hug you, it's all of my pent-up emotions bubbling to the surface.

Corinne Michaels, thank you for making sure I was doing this for the right reasons and some fantastic music along the way.

Jenna Jacob, from the moment we met we just clicked. I love you so much, woman! Thank you for your kicking my ass when I needed it the most.

To my editing team, Trifecta Editing Services. Wow! Amy, Lyndsey, and Dana – you challenged me on my decisions and pushed me farther all while having fun in the process. You made me, Caleb and Cassidy shine. I solemnly swear, I'll try to check myself on as many "eyes and looks" in the future!

To Holly Malgeri from Holly's Red Hot Reviews. Thank you for pushing me to be better on my first release and activating that wonder twin power and sending jars of cupcakes to carry me through.

My cover and brand designer, Amy Queue of QDesigns, I'm still not sure how you managed to sync our minds to make it perfect, but I am not complaining. Thank you for getting to know me and my characters. You are so gifted it blows me away.

To the team at Foreward PR and especially Linda Russell – you are absolutely unbelievable! Our "quick" introduction meeting (cough...2 hours...) will live in my heart forever.

To Nazarea Andrews and Inkslinger, thank you for taking a chance on this unknown author and promoting Free to Dream.

To any bloggers who took a chance on this new author's book, please accept my heartfelt gratitude. From large blogs to small ones, your thoughts matter. So many readers depend on you for insight and guidance. Just the idea you took the time to read Free to Dream is an honor I will never forget. Thank you from the bottom of my heart.

To my readers, I don't know how to express what you have given to me. You are the heart and soul of this industry. What you have done by picking up this book to read is completely surreal. Whatever led you to this story, I am humbled. I am overwhelmed with gratitude. The words thank you aren't enough for taking a chance bur for now they will have to do.

And finally, my thanks to the words of Thomas Paine for sparking inspiration long after he penned them.

ABOUT THE AUTHOR

Tracey Jerald knew she was meant to be a writer when she would re-write the ending of books in her head on her bike when she was a young girl growing up in southern Connecticut. It wasn't long before she was typing alternate endings and extended epilogues "just for fun".

After college in Florida, where she obtained a degree in Criminal Justice swearing she saw things she'll never quite believe and never quite forget, Tracey traded the world of law and order for IT. Her work for a world-wide internet startup transferred her to Northern Virginia where she met her husband in what many call their own happily ever after. They have one son.

When she's not busy with her family or writing, Tracey can be found in her home in north Florida drinking coffee, reading, training for a runDisney event, or feeding her addiction to HGTV.

To follow Tracey, go to her website at http://www.traceyjerald.com. While you're there, be sure to sign up for her newsletter for up to date release information!

54493927R00176

Made in the USA
Columbia, SC
02 April 2019